WAISTED

Center Point
Large Print

Also by Randy Susan Meyers and available from Center Point Large Print:

Accidents of Marriage
The Widow of Wall Street

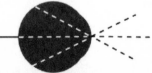

**This Large Print Book carries the
Seal of Approval of N.A.V.H.**

WAISTED

Randy Susan Meyers

CENTER POINT LARGE PRINT
THORNDIKE, MAINE

This Center Point Large Print edition
is published in the year 2019 by arrangement with
Atria Books, a division of Simon & Schuster, Inc.

The text of this Large Print edition is unabridged.
In other aspects, this book may vary
from the original edition.
Printed in the United States of America
on permanent paper.
Set in 16-point Times New Roman type.

ISBN: 978-1-64358-352-5

The Library of Congress has cataloged this record under
Library of Congress Control Number: 2019944723

To Jeff, who makes my dreams
come true every day

If I didn't define myself for myself,
I would be crunched into other
people's fantasies and eaten alive.
—AUDRE LORDE

CHAPTER I

Everyone hated a fat woman, but none more than she hated herself.

Alice knew this to be true. Today's proof? She, along with six other substantial women, stood in the parking lot avoiding each other, as though their abundance of flesh might transfer from body to body, despite all waiting to board the bus for the same reason: "the unique opportunity to spend an entire month exploring ways to bring yourself into balance."

Balance, as written in the *Waisted* brochure, implied weighing less. The virtually memorized pamphlet tucked in Alice's jeans pocket promised a new life. The women scuffled in the leaves in the parking lot of a designated Dunkin' Donuts—a meeting place Alice suspected, for no good reason, had been chosen with deliberate irony. She pushed away thoughts of mean-spirited motivation, chalking up her suspicion to nerves and rising hints of buyer's remorse.

The thick smell of donuts blew around with the scent of fall leaves. As Alice shuffled from her right to left foot, pulling her suede jacket tight against the wind, a redheaded white woman approached with an outstretched hand.

"I'm Daphne." Being much shorter, she had to look up at Alice. "And nervous as hell."

Before Alice could do more than shake Daphne's hand, a uniformed woman came into view, self-importance emanating from her stiff shoulders to the black pen she clicked on and off.

"No talking, ladies. Line up, tell me who you are, and then march on board." She checked names against a paper fastened to a red clipboard. One at a time, the women climbed the steps of a repurposed school bus. After the last participant dragged her crazy-wide thighs up the stairs as though this ascension were an Olympian event, the woman in charge marched aboard.

"Listen up. I'm the driver. Here are your rules." Though she wore no cap, an invisible one seemed perched on her head. "You will have five minutes for any last texts or emails that you wish to send. After that, you will give me your cell phones and wallets. Tell your loved ones you'll speak to them in four weeks. Until that time—"

Daphne, her voice breaking, raised her hand. "What if—"

The stern woman held up a hand. "No exceptions will be made. Every one of you signed agreements containing this information. You will be allowed to write letters. This is not meant as punishment; it's your first step in freedom from your past. From this moment on, you concentrate on yourselves and no one else."

Alice stared at her phone, pulled up the keyboard, and then closed the screen. She repeated the exercise three times until shutting off the device. She'd already sent all the explanations to her husband that she could muster. To her parents as well. Additional messages wouldn't help justify her actions.

The driver walked down the aisle, hand out. When receiving each phone, she peeled off a sticker—a small name tag, it turned out—and placed it on the back of the device. "To ensure you get the right phone back," she explained.

After handing over her phone, Alice unfolded the creased and much-read brochure.

"Waisted: Where You Discover You Can," the luminous cover announced.

A photo of a sprawling mansion, rays of sun shining through clouds and dappling the windows with sparkling promise, covered the front. Adirondack chairs dotted the green lawn. Giant sunflowers waved from a garden in the distance. Muscular women with strong-looking legs lay on straw mats.

An avalanche of fancy words for slimming down drew her in, once again, like a magic potion. Idealized photos revealed attractive, plump women in yoga positions, diving into a pool, and sitting cross-legged in circles. Alice read again the quote she'd highlighted in yellow.

" 'If there is no struggle, there is no progress.'—
Frederick Douglass."

She pushed away thoughts about the brief
paragraph regarding filming for educational
purposes.

None of the women sat far from the front of the
bus, though nobody shared any of the bench seats.
They only darted covert glances at one another.
As though imitating the brochure, they formed a
virtual UNICEF poster of heavy women: white,
black, Hispanic, Korean, and Indian. And then
there was Alice, representing mixed race, though
who knew into which category they'd slotted her.

Alice tried to ignore her period cramps and the
nausea brought on by exhaust fumes. Perhaps
the first test of fortitude "as you embark upon a
journey of inner exploration to reevaluate your
lives and learn how the mind-body connection
affects your body," was this bumpy ride to the
Northeast Kingdom of Vermont. After traveling
for hours, Alice wanted to separate from both
her outer and inner explorers. Sleep threatened to
overtake her, the day having begun with an early
train ride from Boston to Springfield.

Alice needed food, water, and ibuprofen.

The women surrounding her were dressed as
though they were headed to a brunch attended by
friends they wanted to impress. Without phones,
zoning out with headphones and a playlist was
impossible. A dark-skinned woman with red

glasses clutched an unread paperback, but most of them simply gazed out the window.

After three hours, they left the highway and turned onto a two-lane state road. Neither homes nor businesses appeared on either side. The area seemed deserted.

The driver made a sharp left, though no identifying marker beckoned from anywhere, and steered the bus up a narrow paved road. After driving up as though on the ascent of a roller coaster, the ride evened out as the road gave way to tamped-down dirt. They slowed to a crawl along a single-lane road bordered by a low rock wall until reaching an open area fenced in by barbed wire. Here the bus entered a road bisecting a magnificent field strewn with fiery maple leaves until resuming its journey to the top of a long circular driveway.

Alice put a hand to her heart as the vehicle shuddered to a stop. From this vantage point, high up a mountain, she beheld the breathtaking view: multiple valleys colored by a riot of October colors.

"You've arrived." The driver's sardonic grin unnerved Alice. "Enjoy."

Across two football fields' worth of grass loomed a yellow mansion, topped with a copper-topped cupolaed roof. A vast white porch curved around the building.

The women exited the bus and walked the long

brick path leading to a set of broad perfectly painted brown stairs.

Hanging from a porch beam swung a cryptic wooden sign.

Welcome to Privation

CHAPTER 2

ALICE

Seven Years Previously

When Alice Regina Thompson arrived at her parents' home in Boston, she could only be described as emaciated by love. Broken love. Although she was twenty-eight, and although she'd lived in New York City since college, the rambling Victorian still epitomized home to her.

Her jutting clavicles and razored cheekbones panicked her parents. Despite having been early enrollees in the war against sugar, Alice's mother and father raced to the kitchen and prepared butter-soaked, syrup-drenched stacks of pancakes.

Alice wanted to please them, but she couldn't take a single bite. She apologized, left the table, and climbed the stairs to her still-intact girlish bedroom. Tears fell as she tortured herself with images of the man from whom she had wrenched herself; the man who had lied to her for four straight years. Still, hope trickled even as she wept, thrilled that she could feel her hip bones poking through her jeans, excited by the newly concave bowl of her stomach.

The crazy white boy her parents called him—which made more sense coming from her black father than from her white mother. Patrick had reeled her in with a patchwork of menace and musical genius, with his buzz-cut hair, his scruffy leather jacket, his boyish-tough ways. Dope dealing (minor, she assured herself) and gun carrying (just for show) had excited her at twenty-four—Alice being the child of her parents' straight-laced love, spiked with politics and doing the right thing. Her parents' goodness somehow brought on her bad-boy habit.

Perhaps having sensed that Alice was wising up, Patrick gave her an engagement ring—an oversized marble of emerald that flashed each time she moved her hand. A coke-deal-fueled piece of bling, a ring even a girl as unschooled in jewels as Alice would know to be worth multiple thousands of dollars.

And then Alice found out about the not-exciting wife back in Louisiana. Soon that gumball of a ring was financing her return to Boston.

Whispered parental conferences culminated in convincing her that a regular job, a well-paying job, a do-gooder job, using that public policy degree for which they were still paying New York University, would cure her of Patrick.

The underused Cobb Community Center needed a manager, a perfect position for Alice. There she stumbled into a long-won neighborhood war, played out through basketball games so intense the multihued crowds of spectators resembled *West Side Story.* Alice, born and raised in the Mission Hill section of Boston where the Cobb was situated, understood this cast implicitly. The community was mixed enough to fight Boston's past as a racist city—and mixed enough to confront the reality of the present.

Alice inherited two staff members: a dedicated custodian and an apathetic athletic director, Dave, who earned his check by reading the *Boston Herald,* flirting with the neighborhood girls, and inflating the balls piled in his office. Neither a slower reader nor a less successful flirt had ever existed.

By her second day at the Cobb, Alice noticed the sad girls halfheartedly jumping rope in a corner and boys throwing deflated volleyballs short distances, appearing hopeless about the chances of escaping the room's perimeter.

"Give the little kids some time," she told Dave. "Tell the guys to take a break."

"You're kidding, right?" he asked. Then he chuckled, unaware how laughing marked his possible future collecting unemployment.

Alice marched from his office into the cavernous gym, forcing her way through the crowd of sweaty bodies.

"Give me a moment! " she yelled at full volume. The young men running on the court continued

17

passing and throwing balls as she stood on the parquet flooring. The smell of rubber assaulted her as the basketballs whizzed by.

The young men on the court that day were black. Dave was white. Alice appeared both or neither, depending on the eyes of the beholder. Being overlooked by any culture came as no shock to her.

Patient and expressionless, she waited. The boys continued running around her as though she were a prop.

The ball flew over her head. When they ran by, their skin brushed hers.

Alice had learned endurance from her father, along with sports, manners, and the gift of analyzing situations. Her mother had passed on the gene for righteousness. Both parents taught her the benefits of determination.

Alice, who stood five foot ten and change, darted out and up and caught the ball while Dave, slack-jawed, stared from the entrance.

"Give me your whistle," she said.

Dave ignored her, though whether from disrespect or disbelief, Alice didn't know. He gaped as he took in the scene, turning his head from her to the guys as though weighing odds and betting on the boys.

She threw him the kind of stare that her father would have thrown. Zeke had been one of the first black basketball players from his hometown of

Madison, a small city outside Atlanta, to receive a college scholarship. Her father took no shit, whether as a tenacious point guard or during his tenure coaching basketball and teaching history at Boston's venerable English High School.

Dave lifted the lanyard from his neck. Alice put it on. She wiped the mouthpiece, blew once, twice, and then, when she realized she needed to blow it a third time, she continued until every one of them stopped running around screaming at her to hand over the ball.

"Out. Under your own power, please. Calling the cops is the last thing I want to do today." Alice had learned the art of talking tough without a bit of screech from her mother, who barely topped five feet. Bebe, a delicately pretty girl who had no interest in sleeping with the local hoods, needed backbone growing up in Red Hook, Brooklyn.

The young men shuffled out with sneers and narrowed eyes, sucking their teeth and muttering. The little kids, wide-eyed at seeing their heroes/ bullies vanquished, tiptoed out after them.

"Lock it up, Dave," Alice instructed.

He shook his head and cocked an eyebrow, maybe wondering why God sent this stupid woman to mess up his perfect setup. Then he locked the doors.

"They're gonna be real mad." Clearly, Dave believed the toughs would win the war.

Ten minutes later, Alice taped up an oversized rectangle of cardboard. Scrawled in thick black Magic Marker was the following:

**Gym Closed Due to Lack of Respect.
Will Reopen in One Week.
Rules and Schedules Will Be Posted
at That Time.**

When the gym reopened, the problems disappeared. There was an understanding now: the guys needed the basketball court; Alice required policies. They called her Miss Alice. She treated them well, helping them find jobs, get back in school, and advising them on how to fill out tax forms and open bank accounts. Memories of Patrick-the-crazy-white-boy-married-musician faded as she worked on changing this one corner of the world.

Soon she met Clancy Rivera. The tall column of confidence, a filmmaker as shiningly groomed as the musician had been deliberately ragged, captured Alice's heart. He appeared outlined in truth.

Once again she began to eat.

Seven years later, the Cobb boasted a preschool program, senior exercise classes, an after-school center, a ceramic workshop, and adult education ranging from graphic design to online literacy.

Alice and her board of directors hunted for funds weekly. Today, for example, she was laboring on a small grant for a new stage curtain, which she hoped to install before winter.

As Alice leaned toward her computer, her skirt band dug into her ever-expanding waist. Rather than working through lunch, she should have been downstairs lifting weights. Jumping rope. Walking the treadmill. Instead, Alice slipped a handful of orange Goldfish from the box she supposedly kept for the kids who ran in and out of her office.

Calm reigned at the Cobb at two o'clock, before the onslaught that occurred when school let out. The library, art room, and dance studio waited, empty. A few lonesome old-timers walked in circles around the gym, relaxed in their no-name sneakers. During these sacred hours, they stretched or threw a ball without fear of the neighborhood hotshots—who were sleeping off the previous night's high—or school kids hogging all the space.

By three, the place would fill up as though Alice were giving away candy. For now, though, she enjoyed silence as the staff prepared for the day, or, more likely, hid from her to gossip, flirt, or text unseen. They hated her "no cell phones turned on while working" rule, always trying to circumvent it by swearing to sick children, about-to-die fathers, and at-death's-door grandmothers.

Each time, she reminded them that the Cobb had a phone and someone who answered it.

The front door opened with a screech, a warning sound she appreciated. Too often she was alone in her office, and over the years, there'd been incidents. Addicts shot up in the bathroom on a regular basis—as did women in business suits who worked at the nearby insurance company. Hidden caches of stolen computers and phones would be sold in the basement unless Alice remained vigilant.

Footsteps sounded. "Hello? Anyone here?" a woman called.

Alice recognized the voice. Her assistant director's ex-wife. She rose and pulled at the constricting waistband of her skirt rolled into a bent circle of sweaty agony. She shrugged on the light cotton cardigan to cover her sleeveless top, stuffed her feet back into her low-heeled pumps, and walked to the lobby.

"Evie," Alice said. "Long time."

"Yup. Pretty long. Ken here?" Evie's sour expression didn't presage a friendly visit. Before Ken and Evie's bitter split, she visited often, kidding around with Alice. Now, with Alice on Ken's side, their interactions were frosty. Ken had cheated on Evie and lied, but he had also been Alice's second in command from year one. It killed Alice, but she counted on Ken too much to carry Evie's water, so she remained on Team Ken.

"Where is he?" Evie asked. "The boys are outside. He's missed the last two visits."

Alice tried to think of a proper walk-the-line response that was sisterly to Evie while also loyal to Ken. "How are they?"

"How are who?"

"The twins. JD and Bennie. I'd love to see them."

"Well, that makes one of you who works here." Evie tipped her head to the side. "He owes me September child support. It was due on the first." She peered down her glasses and nodded, in total agreement with herself. "So, where is he?"

"He's not coming in for another two hours."

Evie stayed silent, as though sweating information out of Alice.

"Tonight he'll work late. There's a game. Ken has to lock up." The quiet became uncomfortable. "Looking good, by the way. Great."

"I lost weight." Evie swept her eyes up and down Alice. "Meanwhile, you went and got even fatter. You pregnant again?"

"And what? Carrying the baby in my thighs?" Alice laughed as she considered using one of the confiscated knives locked in her desk to cut out Evie's tongue.

"You better watch it. You can't carry it all that well, you know. You got more gut than butt. Doesn't work for you. Be careful and keep an eye on your handsome husband."

Alice crossed her arms over her breasts. She swelled, her stomach lurched into a Mount Vesuvius and bubbled over, spilling down to make an apron of flesh.

Alice's mom had taught her many things, but not how to be an outright bitch. Still, by thirty-five, Alice had learned her methods.

"I doubt I'll see Ken. You should write him a note and put it in his box. You got paper?"

"Just give him my message when he comes. Not like he's rushing to give me what's mine."

"Write what you need him to know." Alice handed her a notebook and pen from the table under the bulletin board, squared her shoulders, and walked back to her office.

Alice never trusted where she stood with anyone. Black folk assumed she was mixed—they had sharper eyes than any white person for the telltale signs. Then they gave off signals that they considered themselves deeper than her, or they presumed Alice thought she was better than them.

Liberal whites were too damn eager to show how much they loved her right from the get-go, scarcely able to control their eagerness to adopt her as their very best new friend. *"Black lives matter!!" "Oh, do you want me to call you African American? Black? Half? What are you, anyway?"* Said with a smile, because they admired all cultures! Which, of course, allowed them license to pry at will.

"What are you?"

Color shaded most every interaction in her life. Both her cultures could irritate her, especially their similarities. Jews, like her mother; Southern-backgrounded black folk, like her father—both sides always ready with opinions, blunt, bold, not giving a damn what they said. If a thought came into their brains, they shouted it out.

Sometimes she thought it would be worth a million dollars to live her life with people who kept their goddamn opinions to themselves.

She reached into her bottom desk drawer and got out the family-sized bag of M&M's she regularly stashed under a pile of unused files and stuffed them into her mouth by the handfuls. Overly sweet chocolate pasted her tongue, while the gritty bits of shell wedged like shrapnel between her teeth. Machinelike, she scooped out the candy, shoved in the pieces, masticated, and began again, hardly waiting to swallow as her full hand stood ready like an eager soldier, prepared to send the next wave of reinforcements to their deaths.

CHAPTER 3

ALICE

Experience had taught Alice that M&M's lodged first in her belly and then attached themselves to her thighs. She needed to shove her fingers down her throat and expel them before they rooted, but moments after eating the last piece of candy, the phone rang, kids piled in, and her office opened to a revolving door of complaining staff:

"My budget doesn't account for the holiday crepe paper that I buy every year."

"My check was wrong."

"Everyone gets more of everything than you give me!"

They crowded around her, clutching for help and off-loading their frustrations.

"I'll put in for an increase for the supply line," she promised, and then sent the athletic assistant out for a burger and fries.

"I'll call Central Office, but they won't be able to issue an immediate check." She smiled and offered the child care teacher a handful of Cheetos from the box behind her.

Eating her way through anxiety—her childhood

habit—returned more each year. As a girl, she pushed away name-calling by either side of the racial aisle—acting all "sticks and stones" as her parents instructed, and then stuffing down the fury.

During Alice's childhood, her mother got hurt and teary whenever Alice yelled, *"You'll never understand my life!"* Inevitably, the discussion turned to how hard Bebe continually tried to know her struggle, followed by a one-sided conversation about the Holocaust, as it had touched distant relatives, or in which civil rights demonstrations family members of theirs had marched.

Fearful of upsetting her mother any further, something that always ended badly, Alice had used her allowance to buy potato chips. Playing in the Mission Hill Little League, competing on the after-school swim team, and taking dance lessons with Miss Margie kept her muscled, but now, where she'd always been a powerfully built girl—thin for occasional stretches, sometimes chunky, but always athletic—Alice had worked her way up to postpregnancy, full-fledged fat. Six years postpregnancy.

And, of course, there was Clancy's condemnation of her increasing dress size. His disapproval led to secret lunches and dinners with S.J., aka Sharon Jane. S.J. had been her best friend since thirteen, sneaking everything from wine coolers, to forbidden concerts, to McDonald's binges, to throwing up the Big Macs they had just inhaled. They never stuck their fingers down their throats more than once or twice a month. They weren't crazy girls. Now Alice monitored her purging with the same sense of responsibility as she did her menstrual cycle.

She picked up the phone after chasing the last whining employee from her office, needing the connection you got only from best friends. "I gave in again, S.J."

"What happened?"

"Evie, that bitch, Ken's ex, called me fat."

"So you ate."

"So I ate. And I wanted to get rid of it, but the teeming hordes took over my office. And then, just when I thought it was safe, Keely came in."

Sharon Jane already knew the child was Alice's favorite kid from the after-school program. The opinionated eight-year-old exuded energy. When Sharon Jane first met her, she saw the girl's love for Alice in seconds. The child worshipped everything from Alice's wild waves to the sharply modern jewelry she wore.

"Uh-huh. How long?"

"Since eating?"

"Since last time throwing up." Sharon Jane shuffled papers loud enough for Alice to hear. Her sign of *I'm at work; time to hang up.* Who could argue with a school nurse?

28

"Couple of weeks. But yesterday was a truly awful eating day." She ticked the list off on her fingers. "First, my regular breakfast at home."

"With Clancy and Libby?"

"Uh-huh."

"So, peanut butter on whole wheat." Best friends remembered each other's dietary habits.

"Right. But then, when no one was looking, I had a midmorning bagel. With cream cheese. And then, as though he has a secret camera on my office, Clancy called, asking 'How are you doing?' using that tone I know all too well. I'm sure he's all worried about how I'll look at the awards dinner. I never should have told him I was dieting. And the dinner, by the way, is only two weeks away, so I damn well better purge. Anyway, that led to mac and cheese, to pie, to M&M's, to burgers—I can't even . . ."

"What time was the last of it?" Sharon Jane was no doubt thinking the same supposed facts as Alice:

Food travels down the esophagus at a rate of approximately one to two inches per second— the entire process takes about five to six seconds. In the stomach, food tends to hang around for a little longer; this depends on a variety of factors, including the amount of food you have consumed, how much fat it contains, and the acidity of the stomach. However, all food should leave the stomach within two to four hours.

There was still time to get it out. "I better run. My mom's home with Libby."

Fifteen minutes later, Alice opened her apartment door, ready to rush through with a frantic "I need the bathroom!" but she was stopped by the sight of her girl cradled in her grandfather's well-muscled arms like a doll held by a friendly giant. Libby's soft curls appeared transparently bouncy measured against her grandfather's deep-brown skin.

"Momma!" Libby used her hands as leverage to bounce from her grandfather's lap to throw herself at Alice.

"Sweetness." Alice leaned over and buried her face in the scent of her girl's day: playground sweat, Grandma's molasses whole wheat cookies, and Grandpa's lime cologne. Plus, something else recognizable, but not everyday familiar.

"Macon's here?" A trace of her brother's clean-laundry smell lingered in Libby's hair.

Maternal love and the requirement to purge roiled.

"He met us at the park." Her mother's smile reflected the joy she derived with every breath Macon took. "He's using the facilities."

Damn apartment had only one bathroom.

"I'm home, and I want the bathroom!" Alice yelled down the hall. "You better not be using it as a library."

"Don't yell at him," her mother said. "People get all tied up from that sort of thing."

"By 'tied up,' you mean *constipated,* Bebe?" Her father shook his head. " 'Facilities.' 'Tied up.' Stop being the queen of protection, sweetheart; our delicate ears will survive the proper terms. Macon's intestines can handle Alice."

Bebe turned her attention to Libby. "People shouldn't be shouting, honey."

Alice rolled her eyes and shouted at the bathroom door again. "I mean it! Put down the magazine!" No more stocking the bathroom with all those juicy weeklies and monthlies. It only encouraged folks to stay.

"Can you see through walls?" Her mother stacked up dirty bowls and cups littering the coffee table. "Leave him be."

Alice placed Libby on her mother's lap before her mother could stand up. "Snuggle," she demanded. She went into the kitchen area, aggravated by the open layout, which allowed no privacy from her always-watching family, and grabbed a sleeve of saltines from the cabinet.

"Eat something nutritious, honey. White flour will kill you—"

"I don't want Mommy to be killed!" Libby's alarm stopped Bebe short.

"Of course not, baby girl. I didn't mean that. Let me explain hyperbole."

With her mother's attention monopolized

briefly by trying to untraumatize Libby, Alice shoved in as many crackers as her mouth could hold, following them with a glass of lukewarm water. In Bebe's world, if processed flour was *trayf*—poison—hurting a child was pure evil. Her mother would love nothing more than wrapping her family in down, flannel, and vitamins. Macon's kitchen shelves, lined with dried lentil and bulgur, must have brought Mom to ecstasy.

Alice believed that her mother loved her children the same, but she also believed that Bebe loved Macon with less disappointment. Her brother had lived up to his name from the start. Her parents had searched for strong names, though Bebe was the adamant one; Alice's father would have been happy with any name his wife found euphonious. Proving how African American he was wasn't something that Zeke Thompson felt the need to establish.

Meanwhile, Bebe combined her strangling love with a determination to provide her children with rock-solid foundations, including their names. *Macon* honored Macon Bolling Allen, the first African American man licensed to practice law in the United States, and Alice bore the name of Alice Allison Dunnigan, a civil rights activist and the first black journalist to accompany a president, Harry Truman, on a campaign trip.

Their middle names held what Bebe considered to be the best of their Jewish heritage: *Regina,* for the first female rabbi, Regina Jonas, a German woman, who was murdered in the Holocaust; *Ossie,* for a Jewish basketball player from the 1940s, Ossie Schectman of the New York Knicks—though most thought it was for actor Ossie Davis.

"Heavy hangs the head holding these names," her brother teased their mother, and yet, look at him: working his way up the ladder of Boston's legal community. Bebe probably had a secret Macon Ossie Townsend for President fund. (Despite her joy at Barack Obama's election in 2008, Bebe was a bit miffed that he had taken away Macon's shot at being the first African American president of the United States.)

The solid sound of Macon's footsteps sent Alice racing for the bathroom. After locking the door, she ran the water full force, letting it crash into the porcelain. She fell to her knees, feeling the familiar cushioning of the thick, gray bathmat that blended with the stone floor.

Soggy saltines came up colored with M&M's and mixed with French fries and hamburger. Partially digested ketchup-tinged bread resembled bloodied tissue.

Well-being overtook Alice—the welcome calm that followed her induced storms. Valium of her own making. She promised herself she wouldn't end up like this again. At least not for two weeks. Or a month.

After washing her face and gathering her long hair into a ponytail, Alice sprayed an orange cloud of air freshener. She dabbed lavender on her wrists and temples and rinsed her mouth with Listerine.

Again, she vowed this to be her last time.

Sponging the countertop and swiping around the toilet brought the bathroom back to pristine. Clancy would stand for no less. They had bought the condo when she was pregnant—leaving his loft in East Boston, where they lived together for a short time before marrying—sharing the space with an overwhelming amount of film equipment. Tripods, video cameras—from the smallest to his Red Epic, lighting equipment, and microphones—the list unwound forever. Filmmakers traveled heavy.

The loft's cement floors would have shredded baby knees. Here, at the converted brewery, glossy oak caressed their feet. Granite tiles in the kitchen and bathroom warmed the floors with heated coils. Located at the seam where the Mission Hill and Jamaica Plain neighborhoods met, Alice's residence was simultaneously spitting distance from her childhood home and a million psychic miles away from the society of her upbringing.

"To what do I owe the pleasure of the entire family visiting?" she asked as she entered the living room. "Did Mom sound a call to order?"

Bebe picked up Libby from school three times a week; her work offered flexibility. After years using her hard-won MSW—writing papers and studying while Zeke, Alice, and Macon slept—working for the Massachusetts Department of Children and Families, she now had a private practice. Of course, as Zeke mentioned almost weekly, her clients were more pro bono than profitable, smiling as he, once again, deemed her born to be a social worker.

"I needed a Libby fix." Alice's father stood, stretching until he appeared taller than his six foot four. "And now I could use a gallon of Bengay."

"I keep telling you that you better exercise some." Bebe shook her head in exasperation. "If playing with a five-year-old puts your back out, shame on you. Maybe you should leave that desk and get a little exercise." Alice's mother put her arms out. "Come on, baby. Give Grandma some sugar before we go."

Macon and Alice raised their eyebrows and grinned. Alice raised her hand to her mouth to hide her rising laugh. Depending on their moods, they smiled or squirmed when Bebe peppered her speech with Southern expressions or Zeke called them *tatelah* or used some other Yiddish word. But when Zeke adopted the Yiddish *Zayde* as his grandpa name, they had to admit, despite themselves, that they cherished his doing so.

"You're not staying for dinner?" Alice asked.

"We didn't want to impose. Macon's taking us out tonight."

"Macon." Alice bowed her head and genuflected. "Most holy Thompson light."

"Don't say that in front of Libby," Bebe said. "You know we have no favorites."

Libby wiggled from her grandmother and ran to Alice. "What did you say wrong?"

"Mommy's naughty, honey." Macon made a scary face. "So bad!"

"Stop that." Bebe glared and shook a finger at her son.

"Everyone's just teasing, Libs." Macon pointed back at his mother. "Except Grandma. She has no sense of humor."

"Don't say that. You'll confuse the child. And I'm terrifically funny, mister."

"You're turning her into a little therapist, Mom," Alice said. "It's settled. We'll all have dinner here. I'll call Clancy to pick something up."

"He'll be exhausted; don't make him stop on the way home."

"He works in a studio, not a coal mine. Stopping won't kill him."

"It's no problem for me to run down the street." Zeke threw Alice a conciliatory smile. "He's fighting rush hour. Now, what should we have? What do you think, Libala?"

Once together, her parents merged into a new culture. They should have coined a name for Afro-American-Yiddish lingo, an equivalent of Spanglish. Perhaps Bliddish.

"How about Indian food?" Bebe said. "Clancy loves it."

"And you thought *I* was the favorite?" Macon asked Alice. "Your husband knocked me off that pedestal the day he knocked you up."

When Zeke laughed, Bebe punched him in the arm, which resembled a tern pecking at a lion. "Don't encourage them." He ruffled Bebe's thick white hair, cut in her signature straight-angled bob.

Her parents appeared opposite in every possible way physically: short to tall, fine-boned to sturdy, light to dark. Alice loved the sight of them, always in love. She wanted Clancy and her to be like that in thirty years. She wished her marriage could be like theirs now.

"How about something healthier?" Alice shifted. "I got a reminder today that I need more salad and less rice."

"You are a beautiful woman, baby," Bebe said. "Why are you starting on that again?"

"Ken's ex-wife, she came in and told me that— Libby, go find your drawings from last week to show Uncle Macon." Alice waited for Libby to leave the room and then continued.

"Evie said I . . . bulked up."

"She's a bitch, that one. Always was."

"Mom, how would you know?"

"I heard the stories from your work. Listen to me: you're brilliant. Gorgeous and curvy. You're a strong black woman. Don't pay attention to her bull."

"Mom, I passed curvy long ago. I'm now officially fat."

"You're perfect. Built just like your father. Be proud."

"If I wanted to be an athlete, then I would be proud. And I'm built more like your mother than my father."

Her mother ignored Alice's reference to Grandma Sophie. "I'm staring at you, Alice. You're lovely."

"Mom, you see me with a mother's eyes, and I appreciate it. But you are a tiny white woman telling me that I can be a fat black woman—"

"I didn't say that! I said you're a strong black woman—"

Zeke stood and put his arms out. "Stop. Both of you."

"This has got to be the stupidest fight I've heard from the two of you," Macon said. "Let's order dinner. Salad, samosas, and anything else anyone wants."

Bebe and Alice glanced at each other. They knew. They both knew what Zeke and Macon never would—the disdain with which the world treated fat women—but they fought the battle with far different weapons.

The scariest thing of all for Alice was this: wondering if her mother believed that black women didn't have to worry about being fat, or shouldn't worry, as though the fear and health issues of weight gain didn't matter for her, as though she were less than. In her backbends to embrace the experience of a black woman, did even her mother view Alice as some sort of damn black mammy?

CHAPTER 4

ALICE

D o you want Daddy and me to put you to
sleep? Or Grandma?" Alice touched her lips
to the top of her daughter's head. Faced with
attending the New England Film Awards, Alice
could happily clean the oven. She'd kept to her
pledge not to purge in the past two weeks. She'd
also gained three pounds.

"I want to go to Daddy's party." Libby treated
the ceremony with awe, desperate to see Clancy
accept his Mobie—the glass Möbius of filmstrip
used for trophies.

"Sorry, sweetheart, but Daddy's party is adults
only." Clancy wiggled Libby's toes.

Libby climbed out of bed, fell to her knees,
and clasped her hands in prayer. "I want to see.
Please, please, please."

Alice knelt beside her. "How about praying to
end hunger?"

Libby shook her head. "We'll add that. Maimeó
said God hears as much as we want to tell him if
our heart is in the right grace."

"Do you mean *right place,* honey?" Maybe,
maybe not. *Maimeó*—Irish for *grandmother*—

appreciated the lingo better than heathen Alice.

Libby threw her head back. "Mom, God's grace is thorough and full."

Maimeó's words spoken in her daughter's voice unnerved Alice, who hoped the panoply of cultures contained in Libby simmered to a reduction of love and not confusion. Clancy's parents—his Irish mother and Puerto Rican father—advocated constant quiet prayers. Antique reliquaries shone in the Beacon Hill brownstone where they had raised Clancy. His home was quite the opposite of Bebe and Zeke's home in Mission Hill, Alice's childhood home, where ragged John Coltrane posters still hung on the walls. Political rallies replaced church, and voting scored over prayers with Bebe and Zeke.

Alice-the-kid delighted in *Free to Be . . . You and Me* and toughening up for marches. Alice-the-teen wanted nothing so much as being thin and beautiful.

Clusters of crucifixes from Maimeó tangled like best friends in Libby's musical jewelry box. A crystal ballerina twirled protectively each time Libby opened the pink glass box, also a gift from Maimeó. Alice's mother offered up a handcrafted wooden box of Etsy provenance upon seeing the girly object, but Libby preferred the feminine fragility and tinkle of Chopin to a chunky box painted with peace symbols.

In truth, her mother-in-law's choice surprised

Alice. She hadn't expected the music, the spinning dancer. Clancy's parents, the upright Kathryn and Sebastian Rivera, lived stern. As could Clancy.

The very same qualities with which Alice and Clancy fell in love, could now irritate them. She'd come to Clancy unraveled and melancholy, a pliant Modigliani. He possessed enough laser focus for both. Her pulse ran hotter, and he needed that. Bebe and Zeke swaddled Clancy in their *gemütlichkeit*. Clancy, being raised where politeness and scripture reigned over unrestrained admiration, became thrilled by the overinvolved parenting.

Now Clancy thought Alice's parents were neurotically entangled in their children's lives, while Alice feared the part of Clancy that appeared to be spit out of his mother as though born of an ice maker. His father, so polished that emotions slid off before they could make any impression, belied any stereotype one might pluck out for a Puerto Rican.

Until he smiled, Clancy could resemble a mannequin deserving of a fantastically well-cut tuxedo. His composure unnerved some, including, at times, Alice. When he beamed, he looked like someone who didn't know he was more handsome than a husband should be— smiling Clancy still bowled her over. When they met, five-foot-ten Alice weighed 117 pounds.

Lovesickness followed by glittery lust had cut her into a babe. Clancy circled her waist and ran his hands from ribs to hips. He thought Alice luscious; almost threatening in her beauty.

They married before the glitter fluttered away, with her three months pregnant. She hadn't known how much Clancy liked his women slender and tall. He didn't realize that Alice had never been that thin before and never would be again.

Now he acted like Alice had fooled him. When they entered an event such as the award ceremony, she caught his shame and the room's thoughts. *Why is that handsome man with such a fat woman?*

The awards room appeared smoky, not from forbidden cigarettes, but through well-chosen lighting and décor, as though the Boston Filmmakers had searched for a noir venue. Everywhere Alice turned, a woman wore an elastic-tight, coal-colored dress slashed to the lowest allowable point on her bony chest. Men paired black trousers with granite shirts.

Clancy, a fluid line of black, his glossy brown hair razored into an actor's cut, smoldered. Alice's Spanx, though torturous, at least provided a firm playing field for her Tadashi Shoji dress. The fabric had dazzled swinging from the hanger, even with the massive amount of material required for a size 18. Now she worried about providing a field of too-big sparkling Alice. That Clancy had brought home a dress in the correct size killed her. Black washed her out, he said, so he'd bought a dress in bronzed copper. She reminded herself that he framed shots and worked with color and balance all the time.

Of course, a filmmaker was aware of wardrobe.

She said all this to herself while imagining him leafing through her magazines, going on sites like Dress Beautiful, where the full-sized fashion plates shopped. He didn't trust Alice to not embarrass him.

Since her post-Evie binge, Alice kept from purging—sticking to protein and vegetables in preparation for dressing up. But a few weeks did not a thin Alice make.

"That's just plain ridiculous," S.J. had insisted when Alice put forth her theory that Clancy feared she'd embarrass him. "Your husband is a perfectionist. This is his night. Naturally he wants to control every detail, including framing his wife's beauty."

Sharon Jane afforded Clancy every benefit of the doubt—never forgetting how during the musician-boyfriend years, mopping Alice's tears had become S.J.'s second job.

Now, watching wraiths in black swan around the room, Alice believed her theory on Clancy's dress buying. She couldn't compete, so he tried to make her into Nefertiti.

"How do I look?" She tugged at the shuttered crepe swathing her hips.

Clancy took her hand. "You stun the eyes."

"Too much?" She gestured down with her chin toward her cleavage. The square neckline met the top of the three-quarter-length sleeves in a sharp right angle, allowing a pillowing effect.

"Oprah wears Tadashi," he answered.

Before she could examine the non sequitur, he placed a hand behind her back and gently pushed her toward the nominee tables. "Sit straight and tall. That dress brings out your regal side. Now, please, go buoy up the troops."

Clamped in chrome on table 3, a glossy card read Prior Productions, Clancy's company. Alice knew everyone there, just as Clancy did her coworkers. Some jobs conspire to make a family of everyone, and they both worked in those environments: film debuts, fund-raising events, holiday parties, and potluck dinners. Gossiping and complaining about work made for conjugal glue.

The audio engineer sat beside Alice's place card, a smile stretching from jug ear to jug ear as he rose to hug her. Rufus revered Clancy and transferred his worship to Alice. Across the table, the husband-wife writing team, Marisol and Gus, held hands. To the left of Clancy's seat, Harper perched. Jealousy rose in Alice upon seeing the director of photography, who doubled as Clancy's work wife. Harper's cheeks were dimpled as though she could barely stand her own cuteness. Since when had scrawny become such a gift, even if matched by streaky gold waves and beauty queen skin? Harper, a Georgia peach, was always intent on convincing Alice how *open* she was. How much she *adored* being in a multi-cultural environment such as Prior Productions.

Harper grinned too much, and her damn dimples could be used to sharpen pencils. Alice worried how cute Clancy found Harper. She reminded herself of the previous night's lovemaking. Of late, she found herself counting. Twice a week signified fidelity, right? The problem was using the concept in reverse: if they missed a week, did that prove faithlessness?

He cheats on me; he cheats on me not. All she needed was a giant daisy from which she could pluck petals.

"Sugar!" Harper slipped over one seat to claim Clancy's. She air kissed European style. "That dress is to die for! Tadashi?"

Alice nodded. Harper, raised no doubt on *Vogue* and *W* while Alice was flipping through *Mother Jones* and *Ebony*, recognized the designer. Bebe had never allowed fashion magazines to grace their home. Eventually, when Alice hit the teen-age years, Bebe permitted *Essence*. Though it covered the same articles as every other women's magazine, Bebe bowed to Alice's need to learn the art of womanhood from sources other than her white mother. All Alice had to do was whisper the word *hair,* and her mother bought any product *Essence* suggested. When Alice wanted a subscription to *Allure,* she accused Bebe of cutting her off culturally.

"Need a drink?" Harper asked.

"Clancy's on it."

"Of course." Another dimple display exploded. "Try some of these appetizers. I grabbed a plate for the table."

Harper took a stick of *rumaki* and slipped the entire piece off the small skewer with her teeth, keeping her lips spread, protecting her bright red lipstick from the oil slick of bacon and chicken liver grease. She rolled her eyes in mock ecstasy. "Take one," she mumbled around the food.

Alice watched, fascinated, in a car accident sort of way. Alice's mother would kill her if she spoke with food in her mouth like that. Bebe insisted on strict adherence to the rules of proper eating, as inherited from Grandma Sophie. In restaurants, ninety-year-old Grandma still hissed at them to watch out for what the goyim might think of them. From Zeke's family, Bebe picked up the constant admonitions about not giving *them* anything bad to say about you.

Alice reached for a boiled shrimp and then pulled back. She couldn't pull off opening wide

Harper-style, and she couldn't afford to mess up her five-layer perfect lipstick job. Plus, there was her Spanx-punished stomach. Ice-cooled water was her limit tonight, and then only if the bar had straws.

Harper turned as though she carried a divining rod. "The food is coming out! I better gather the troops."

Alice almost knocked over her water glass as she stood. "I'll get Clancy."

"Keep Rufus company." Harper twitched her nose, a move she must have thought cute, but she reminded Alice of an underweight rabbit. "Don't want to be alone, do you, Ruf?"

Alice's paranoia grew. What secret message did Harper have for Clancy? She stood and blocked Harper. "You stay. Shop talk is more fun than small talk."

Rufus held up his hands as though stopping traffic. "Whoa! You know I can hear you, right? Don't fight over who gets to leave me. You can both have the pleasure of not being in my company. Plenty of not-me to go around."

Alice's manners kicked in. Harper made a beeline toward Clancy.

"Sorry," Rufus said.

"About what?"

He picked up a napkin, wiped invisible moisture from his mouth, and placed it back over his lap. "How weird Harper can be."

"Weird how?"

Rufus shrugged. "She's gotta win everything, whether it be tonight's trophy or getting the boss to the table. Goddamn maniac. All Harper, all the time."

Before Alice could respond, Clancy placed a tall gin and tonic before her. With a straw. His slow smile said, *Hey, girl, I got your back.* He slipped into the chair next to her.

"Nervous?" she whispered. Poor Clancy had been up for the major Mobie three times and never won.

Clancy clasped her hand with his icy ones. "Make it or break it time."

"That's not true. You know everyone venerates your work."

"Venerated. Yes. But we need commercial success. Show us the money, eh?" He shook his head, as though to come back to earth, squeezed her hand, and then lifted a glass. *"Salud, y, amor y tiempo para disfrutarlo!"*

A microsecond before Alice could translate for the table—a bit of married shtick—Harper stood and held her glass toward Clancy, all showoff work wife. *"Health and love and time to enjoy it!* Yes. And here's looking at you, kid."

Big deal. Harper spoke Spanish. Harper knew *Casablanca* was Clancy's favorite movie. The poster hung in his office.

"We're gonna win!" Rufus lifted his glass high.

"Don't put a *kinehora* on it," Alice said.

Harper laughed. "She means 'Don't put a curse on it.' Yiddish. Alice is our Jewish mother in residence. Nobody would guess, huh? What's the word for *eat,* Alice?"

Did Clancy shoot Harper a glare, or was that her imagination? Perhaps it was an innocent mistake—or maybe the woman was a flaming bitch trying to embarrass her in front of her husband and his colleagues. Alice erred on the side of caution and assumed the worst about this Southern Barbie doll.

"So how do you say it?"

Alice tipped her head. "I'm blanking out—the only word I can remember is *rachmones.* My grandma Sophie's favorite."

"What does it mean?" Marisol asked.

"*Compassion.* Grandma always said if you had *rachmones*, you had your place here and in the next world. Grandpa's favorite was *kurveh.* Yiddish for *whore.*"

Harper gave a tight smile. "Such a colorful language." She cut the meat on her plate into bite-sized pieces. "I love steak. I can't believe they served it. I figured this bunch of Eastern cruncholas for vegan."

Clancy laughed as though Amy Schumer were sitting beside him.

Harper winked. "You know what I mean. How many times have we been at those things where the choices were grilled tofu or some sort of stewed concoction?"

"Alice's mother is big on soup. Thick concoctions of every vegetable left over from the previous three weeks combined with grains of unknown heritage." Clancy cut into his steak and winked. When and in what world did Clancy start winking? "Ah. *Carne Argentina.*"

"Saying it in Spanish doesn't make it any less artery clogging." Alice smiled as though she, too, could be Schumer, though really she sounded like a priss.

And how dare he joke about Bebe, who picked up Libby from school and made dinner so many nights? But his hands shook as he reached for the salt, and she remembered his clammy skin and forgave him his stupid mother-in-law jokes. "But change is good, yes? Let's enjoy."

"Pass the biscuits," Harper said.

Marisol held out the wicker basket. "Where does it go? You're an eating machine."

"I exercise my ass off. Up at five every day. At the gym by five fifteen."

"Exercise alone can't do it." Alice regretted opening her mouth the moment the words escaped.

Harper gave a wicked little smirk. "You're right. I inherited serious metabolism luck. Most people need to work *so* much harder than me. Poor things. Makes me wanna cry as I finish another pint from my boyfriend's Ben and Jerry's." Harper offered the plate of biscuits to Alice. "Take some before I go wild. I could eat them until up is down."

"No thanks." Alice could scrape Harper's cutesy expression right off the woman's tongue.

"You sure?"

"She already said no, Harper." Clancy bit off the words in a clipped manner that replicated the cadence his father used when ending an unwanted exchanged. Like Sebastian Rivera, Clancy brooked no nonsense. And though Alice hated when her husband used the methodology on her, watching Harper bear the brunt thrilled her.

CHAPTER 5

ALICE

Harper looked down, seemingly embarrassed. "I become an animal around good food. Sorry." She reached across Clancy and squeezed Alice's forearm. "You're such a doll."

She was a doll? For what? Lending out her husband? Alice sucked Beefeater through a straw and then hacked the salmon on her plate into an edible jigsaw puzzle, nibbling a forkful of wild rice. When dessert arrived, she pushed the cake far away. For once, neither sugar nor chocolate appealed to her. Lord. Alice might as well be sixteen, seeking reassurance that her boyfriend wanted her and not the skinny cheerleader.

A man dressed in a slick suit walked onstage, stood behind the podium, and adjusted the microphone. Programs rustled. Glasses were taken off. Glasses were put on. Women surreptitiously applied lipstick in prayerful anticipation.

"My category is last," Clancy murmured.

Alice kept her fingers tightly laced with her husband's. Elastic edges of Spanx cut into her thighs. When he finally let go and reached for his coffee cup, she pulled the circulation-cutting material away from her flesh for a moment's relief. Her spurned cake screamed, *Why not? If not now, when?*

Harper gestured toward the plate as though reading Alice's thoughts. "Do you mind?"

Rufus rolled his eyes and then drained his beer. Marisol crossed her arms across her chest.

"Take it," Alice said. She placed a proprietary hand on Clancy's as Harper hoovered up Alice's dessert. Either the woman was a true bulimic or had a Faustian bargain in place.

Technical excellence came first. Prior Productions was nominated in every category and won for audio. Alice clapped for Rufus until her hands hurt.

Prior lost the editing award to its nemesis, Acrobat Films, underwritten by real estate magnate Finn Stockwell, leaving Acrobat free to dabble anywhere.

Marisol and Gus leapt up when their names rang out for best writing. Clancy rose, clapping, beaming with fatherly pride.

At long last, they reached the award for best feature. The audience shuffled. Men and women cleared their throats as the zenith of the night approached.

The local actor presenting nodded for the solemn moment. "First up, *Harvested at Night* from Outline Films. Five farmers work toward providing more than food, bringing food to market at night, beginning a collaboration with farmers and factory workers in India, that has thrived for twenty years.

"*Tattoo City* explores a small town in Bosnia and Herzegovina where tattooing grew from a cottage industry serving the local teens and bikers, to an art center that honors how people have marked their bodies since the dawn of time. Produced by Shorted Sight Films."

The actor read three more descriptions until reaching Clancy's entry. "From Prior Productions, *De Facto*, a film showing how history rolled in on a yellow bus, disrupting years of separate and unequal schools in Boston, long considered a study in cognitive dissonance, as the city known as a hub for culture crashed into a de facto segregated city school system.

"Last, *Waisted*, from Acrobat Films, the first of a triad of cinematic studies on women's relationship with weight, examining how an onslaught of easily accessed food and the upsurge of obesity crosses with the rise of self-hatred."

"Acrobat is pulling such bullshit," Clancy whispered to Alice. "After producing two reality shows—total trash—they suddenly decided to be documentary filmmakers."

"I didn't know that. What kind of reality shows?"

Harper leaned in as though she were part of the conversation. "They called it a docu-series, but it was a reality show with an upscale label. *Cured.* About families who searched for ways to cure a family member's cancer."

Alice nodded, not voicing her thoughts—the show sounded gripping.

"And the award goes to . . ."

Everyone straightened. Clancy reached for Alice's hand.

"*Waisted*! Accepting the award—"

"Son of a bitch," Rufus muttered.

"They probably paid the judges off." Harper drained her wineglass in one long gulp.

"Come on, guys." Clancy's protest sounded thin.

"You know how political this is," Marisol said. They all smiled and clapped for the Acrobat team climbing the stairs.

"A weight loss movie. Jesus." Clancy locked eyes with Alice, acknowledging that he knew she wanted to comfort him. He put her off with a slight shake of his head. She understood. Consolation might undermine his hard-clutched dignity.

"Women sequestering themselves to be told not to stuff their face? Who calls that art?" Harper scraped up crumbs of the dessert left on her plate. "Insanity."

Alice lay back against the pillow, watching as Clancy put away his clothes, commiserating about his loss until he asked her to stop. His way of coping meant locking away the feelings, which never worked for her.

"Do you like Harper's simpering girly-girl bit?" she asked.

"Do I like it?" Clancy, like most people, had a "tell" for when he was lying. Repeating Alice's question told Alice all she needed to know. He liked it.

"She obviously wants to sleep with you. Are you tempted? Flattered?"

Clancy stood with a perplexed expression, his trousers still in his hands. He opened his mouth, closed it, and finally shook his head, as though not believing his wife could say such a stupid thing.

"Well?" Alice grabbed a pillow and held it over her stomach. Speechless was never his style unless he chose it. Alice saw through his forehead, wheels turning as he figured his game plan, weighing options. He thought he was opaque, opening and closing the curtains to his core, but she saw him.

Women read their men. The opposite was, of course, less true; husbands rarely studied their wives. In the hierarchy of life, those on the bottom always learned the habits of the upper levels. Survival demanded this education. She crushed the pillow tighter. "You're not writing a narrative. *Yes* or *no*."

He tipped his head, taking on his professorial demeanor, as though she were a student in his documentary seminar. "Why are you asking such a question?"

"Why are you not answering?" she shot back.

"I am not sleeping with Harper." He raised his hands. "How did this become about you? Christ. I'm in despair about losing to that ridiculous film. Women whining. Eating."

"Did you watch the movie?"

"We vote; we see everything. *Waisted*? Absurd. Women desperate for someone to take them to a promised land." He looked at the pillow Alice clutched. "As though closing one's mouth and saying no to candy didn't enter their minds."

Alice stood, letting the pillow drop to the floor. "How can you have so much empathy for some and not others?" She let *empathy* drip from her mouth as though swearing. "You make a film that equivocates the pain of black children suffering the screams of frothing white adults to white kids afraid to leave their blocks. Empathic to a ridiculous degree. Yet where's your compassion for women who have hate slammed on them every time they leave home? And let's not forget *at* home."

"That hurt can be prevented with a variety of methods."

Clever Clancy, leading her to intellectual

discussion. Where he always won. Men played to win. Women played to be fair.

"Okay. Fine. You didn't sleep with her. But did she offer? Are you tempted?"

"Why must you bring up these things?" Clancy asked.

Given half a reason, Alice would transmogrify the deep desire to believe him into the category of truth. That knowledge frightened her. "Wanting shimmers between you two. The knowing looks. Your sparks smacked me all night."

"Her sparks. Not mine. Your imagination is wasted at that gym."

"I don't work at a gym!" She pressed her fingers into her temples. "The Cobb is a community center. The lack of respect you have for me is astounding."

Clancy marched over. He placed a hand on each of her shoulders. "The lack of respect you have for yourself is astounding. How dare you lecture me?" He spun her around, forcing her to face the mirror. "I'm a filmmaker. Never think I don't see you." He ran a finger over a photo on their nightstand from their honeymoon on Carlisle Bay in Antigua, a sun-kissed and love-drunk couple. Light reflected from the droplets of water in the nimbus of hair haloed around Alice's happy face.

Alice recognized the glow of pregnancy—at that moment a shared secret between her and Clancy.

"You were spectacular," Clancy said.

Hot tears slid down Alice's cheeks. "And now?"

"And now you need to stop eating. When you do, I'll stop looking at women like Harper. Though I only look." He tipped up her face and kissed her. "I never lied about finding you gorgeous. Did I pretend it didn't mean anything?"

"Was it everything?" She dug her nails hard into her palms.

Seven years ago, mutual attraction clicked them together like magnets, shocking her when love followed so soon after Patrick. They had found each other at a party, one to which Sharon Jane dragged her, a fund-raiser for Rosie's Place—the first women's homeless shelter in the country—hosted by the New England Film Association. Their meeting was like a movie scene too clichéd for Clancy to include in any of his movies. They spotted each other across a crowded room. A column of rose silk drifted over her newly angular body. Clancy's crisp white shirt tucked into slim black wool trousers perfected him— his flat gold watch stood out in an army of men wearing clumsy, thick timepieces.

Myths were true. Arrows struck. Bolts of sexual heat flew between them. For weeks, Alice and Clancy separated only for work. Clancy's name, his face, his voice, made up the constant, the only, playlist in Alice's head. Being in the early stages of heated love granted her romantic gold.

"You were pregnant when we made our vows," Clancy said. "Our love included the image of us becoming a family." The scrupulous rectitude and precise honesty on which Clancy prided himself became cruelty when directed at her.

"What does that mean?" Asking the question and wanting the answer were oppositional.

"It means I answered you fairly and truthfully. Your beauty and desirability were matched by your intellect. We held the same morals. And the baby to come. We fell in love. And so, of course, we married. But we met like a minute before. You know that."

"I was beautiful? Now what am I?"

"You are still gorgeous, if no longer stunning. Padding on your face blurs the line. Your body is lost under fleshiness. You are still spectacularly smart and good. And we have Libby. A life. I love you. You are my family. But my attraction to you fades when you are like this. I cannot lie."

Alice wanted to shake Clancy. Of course, he could have lied, would have lied. If he cared.

God, how Alice wished he'd lied.

When they'd married, his honest straight-forwardness thrilled her. Years of Patrick-the-crazy-white-boy-married-musician's dissembling had set her up to worship at the altar of fidelity to the truth. Now she appreciated the worth of a fiction borne of kindness.

My attraction to you fades when you are like this. Such candor forever squashed one's spirit. How on God's earth could she manage that knowledge?

CHAPTER 6

DAPHNE

M irrors, ubiquitous and omnipresent, reflected
Daphne's every angle, guaranteeing that
while painting wounds on actor Terrance Fields's
arms—he of woman-hating fame, he of race-
baiting renown, he of three-Oscar celebrity—
she'd see her ample behind with terrifying
frequency.

The scent of Fields's unwashed flesh rose as
Daphne bent over his shoulder and cleaned a
generous area of skin. His only bearable-to-touch
or smell areas were those she'd swiped with
lemon-scented wipes.

"I banged her, ya know." Fields pointed to the
People magazine on his lap. "What a whore."

Daphne kept silent as she traced a growing
jagged wound with another layer of liquid latex.

"Did you hear me?" Without waiting for affirmation, Fields jabbed a finger at the glamorous
full-page photo of the latest indie film star to hop
on a fame upswing. The flawless starlet stood
in a line of other fresh actresses clad in spring
green. The thought of him on her induced images
of garbage strewn on a field of daisies.

"Little miss ingénue, huh? Couldn't get enough. Wanted me to screw her—"

"Stay still." Daphne interrupted him before he moved into the details. She began disguising the latex with foundation, biting her lip as she worked toward the exact hue.

"But I can move my mouth, eh?" He gave his trademark ironic grin. "I'll tell ya, that one standing next to her? Emma Billington? Lips that could empty a steam pipe."

It was a truth universally acknowledged that a woman in need of working in Hollywood did not stab famous actors with latex carving tools.

"I'll tell ya something about these young actresses. Voracious. Little animals. They get someone like Terrance Fields . . ."

The worst players referenced themselves in third person.

". . . in front of them, and they're ready to drop to their knees upon sight."

Daphne tuned out Fields's verbal garbage. She'd ridden in this rodeo before. Humming helped, overlaying his words with aural fog until they became a fountain of Australian-accented syllables and consonants. She applied torn bits of stockings soaked in stage blood mixed with K-Y jelly—thick and gloppy—over the foundation, and covered it with sheer lip gloss, as this one needed to be a fresh wound, adding bruising power to the edges to provide a blistered appearance. She couldn't wait to attack his boxer's face bruises and cuts, forcing him to shut the hell up.

"I have an unusually high sex drive, ya know."

"So you've mentioned, Terry."

He hated being called Terry.

"I could do a few of these dollies before breakfast and still give you a poke for lunch." He snaked his free arm around and grabbed a handful of her behind.

She jabbed the fleshiest part of his meaty fist with the pointed end of a thin brush. "Next time I'll use the scissors."

"Don't fuck with me, dolly. Ya can't bruise the talent." He brayed his donkey laugh.

"You're playing a boxer. Maybe I'll pluck out your eye. Your rep for doing anything for art precedes you."

"That's why I like working with ya. You're a tough broad. I'd love banging that plump ass. You'd be a relief after jumping those bones with hanks of hair. A nice, fat, soft ride. Why do you think I always ask for you? 'Cause one of these days you'll say yes."

Daphne imagined carving her initials in his sweaty skin with her palette knife. The stupidity of leaving her kids and husband for weeks on end for a job that encompassed having to accept the abuse of people like Fields overwhelmed her.

And so, at that moment, Daphne decided to give up bruising people, to stop concocting edges of bones jutting out from wrists and creating wrinkled Martians. For every decent man like Tom Hanks, two dozen pigs like Terrance Fields waited. Time for a change. Daphne went home and opened Alchemy.

Seven years later, Alchemy Studio, located on Boston's pricey Newbury Street, attracted the wealthiest, along with the most scarred. Nobody grabbed her ass, her clients arrived showered, and she was home with the kids and her husband every night.

Instead of creating bruises and burns, Daphne masked and disguised them, helping heal women and men, however temporarily, of psychic and physical trauma. Not that she could wrap herself in the cloth of sainthood. Her clients were just as likely to be a patient of her sister Bianca's dermatology practice, needful of covering the temporary discoloration from Restalyne injectable fillers, as a homeless burn victim wearing keloid scars.

Ivy, a clothing expert, shared Alchemy's studio. Daphne painted them. Ivy draped them. She was a genius at the art of disguise by clothing, yet here Daphne was, in Saks Fifth Avenue, on Boston's Boylston Street, hunting for a sister-of-the-bride dress without help.

Some moments you didn't want witnessed by a friend.

Now, standing in the overlit fitting room, held captive by a twig of a saleswoman intent on drowning her in sacks of formless cloth, Daphne's choice to exclude Ivy seemed utterly senseless. Stupid. She wanted only to look attractive—perhaps classic—at her sister's wedding, as she told the young woman, but the twig treated her as impossible to prettify. She carried only disguises to Daphne.

No shock, that. The only surprise was how Daphne could forget the lesson learned at her mother's knee: fat women repulsed the world.

Daphne stooped to use the word *slimming* when describing the dress that she wanted, which perhaps the woman heard as "Bring me a swath of camouflage." Why else would the twig—young, exquisite, and bored, wrapped in a bandage—give a pseudosmile and hold up that gruesome mauve mother-of-the-bride outfit?

Anyone, and most particularly someone calling herself a "trained occasion associate," knew that you never put redheads in mauve. As a side dish to the insult of mauve, a color heralding ten years to assisted living, there was the outfit's shapeless cut.

Hadn't she noticed Daphne's coloring? Red hair—the wiry kind that jangled your eyes, not the flowing angel type—paired with skin so pale that without makeup it appeared flat and called for anything but this confused fabric with no idea whether it was pink, red, or violet.

Had she not heard Daphne's plea to be comely?

Sales twigs hated dealing with anyone over size 8. The disgusted twitches of their mouths before they forced their lips to form dead sales-smiles and how they gazed over her head gave them away.

Was this twig too young to understand? At Alchemy, Daphne offered women transformation as a blessing for the giver and the taker. Plain, plump, or scarred, she draped them in flattering cloth—jewel shades of teal, emerald, and indigo—to illustrate the magic of color and taught them the art of painting pretty, using her Hollywood tricks.

Maybe you had to cross thirty's threshold to learn how easy it was to show kindness.

"Go to Saks," her mother had insisted. "They carry what you'll need."

Daphne needed a dress that wouldn't force her sisters to pity her, her mother to be embarrassed, or her daughter to pretend Daphne's body didn't exist. Her son, nineteen and filled with his own life, would only notice her clothes if she wore none.

Daphne's father always said something generous.

Her husband's compliments came whether she

wore a tent or sparkling gown—which essentially meant nothing he said mattered.

"This will work well." Twig held a flocked hanger a bit higher and cocked her head to the side, seeming to compare her customer's curves to the width of the dress. Daphne pushed away the outfit, even as she kept hold of the impossibly tight, never-gonna-fit, unzipped black number hanging off her shoulders.

"Honestly, mauve's not a good color for me."

"Just try it." Twig eked out a dim smile. "This cut will work. Trust me."

Each clutched the mauve fabric many beats past social comfort. They fought for disownership of the dress, pushing and pulling until the twig released her hold, and—*poof!*—just like that, Daphne lost the fitting room battle.

"I'll be back to check on you."

Daphne imitated a woman with confidence. "I'll let you know if I need help."

"Of course." The woman dipped her head, thrown back to the world where class differences ruled. Daphne, shamed at pulling rank on someone who spent her day schlepping clothes to women with thick wallets, gave a genuine smile.

"Thank you for finding this." She held up the ugly dress as a peace offering. "I sincerely appreciate your help."

"No problem. Trust me. It's suitable for the occasion."

Daphne's chest constricted at meriting no more than "suitable for the occasion" in the stratum of fashion hierarchy. Not "gorgeous," or "sharp," or "exciting." Not even goddamn "pretty." At her sister's painfully elegant wedding, Daphne would wear something "appropriate," like something the Queen of England might wear.

"Breathtaking" would be left for others. "Suitably clad and wearing a stunning shade of lipstick" was Daphne's fate. She placed the hangered dress on a hook—a cherry Life Saver among the black caviar for which Daphne lusted. On the corner chair, she piled her street clothes: black cotton pants with an elastic waist and the black tunic top that she pretended she wore for the lovely lines and not because it skimmed over her body without stopping.

A closer examination of the outfit revealed three pieces, beginning with a slip intended to glide over the holy horror that foundation garments made of one's fleshy mounds. Then there was the actual dress: a study in upholstery for wide hips and big asses, holding only the grace of a decent bias cut. A long, shapeless jacket, designed for the sole purpose of coverage, finished the unholy trinity, the three whispering a woeful haiku:

No part can be seen
Fabric with no joy no hate
Simply sensible

A costume aimed at an old woman who gave up the fight years ago. "I'm only forty-three!" she wanted to scream.

Daphne caressed her chosen collection of urbane black dresses, low-hanging fruit plucked from impeccably aligned racks. Sane choices, with forgiving flowing fabrics. Crepe. Rich materials with enough weight to fall properly, but not so thick that they didn't drape sadder parts.

Nothing zipped. Daphne refused to try anything larger than an 18; not that she had a clue what size she should wear, always choosing new clothes by shape.

Quietly, careful not to make a crackling sound, she pried a peanut butter cracker from the snack pack in her purse and crammed it into her mouth. Chewing the orange Ritz to a fast pulp so she could swallow before the twig returned, she let the rush of mashed carbs and salty, nutty fat soothe her.

> **TIP:** Chew your food
> 40 times.
> To lose weight!
>
> *—High school wisdom*
> **OUTCOME:** 1 month masticating,
> 15 pounds lost.

Diet advice floated through her head as blood flowed through her veins. A year ago, when

71

Marissa, the third and youngest sister in the family, announced her wedding, Daphne vowed to lose many dress sizes before the nuptials.

She didn't.

With nothing left to try, she ripped the twig's disaster from the hanger, threw the jacket onto the chair, and held up the square sheath, a baggie for a body. Close inspection revealed swirls of deep mauve on deeper mauve—matte on satin, insult on insult—a veritable carnival of wretched pinked-purpled-red.

After casing herself in the slip, Daphne wiggled the dress over her head, but it refused to stretch over her breasts. She lifted it off and stepped into it feet first, facing away from the mirror as she slid her arms into the cap sleeves. Cap sleeves? What were they but yarmulkes for the fat on the top of one's shoulders, undersized half circles emphasizing the wiggles underneath?

She tugged the mercifully lined fabric up over her hips.

A quick tap on the fitting room entrance and then, without waiting, scorched-red lacquered nails snaked around the door and inched it open.

"Need any help?"

"I'm fine." Daphne resisted slamming the door, but when the woman kept pushing, the constancy of politeness won over Daphne's dignity, and she relented.

"Let me zip that up for you." Bony fingers

twirled Daphne in a magical salesperson move that forced the customer to face the mirror. Daphne focused on only the lovely Chanel Pink Explosion blooming on her cheeks.

Twig tugged at the zipper, sending Daphne further into a state of mortification so overwhelming that her cheeks might remain red forever. After what must have been a year, the zipper passed the impossible zone of what her mother had long ago named Daphne's "Namath back," an expression Daphne thought a Jewish saying, until Bianca, her athletic sister, explained their mother was comparing Daphne's build to that of a long-retired football player.

"There you go!" Twig patted her shoulder as though they'd fought a battle together.

There was Daphne. Not in a dramatic black something that highlighted her cleavage. No. There was Daphne in matte and satin, a bursting mauve frankfurter, her stomach screaming for a corset, her double-D breasts straining the material.

"Here." Twig sounded sorrowful as she held out the jacket, a blessed covering into which Daphne's arms slipped as though offered a reprieve.

Daphne's breadth of joy at how the ugly sack covered her Namath back grieved her. But the dress zipped. The jacket buttoned.

Flattering, classic, edgy—none of it mattered.

Surely her sister would serve enough wedding champagne to drown out this monstrosity. Daphne needed coverage. And she needed to get out of Saks.

Both dress and jacket fit, yes?

Daphne nodded at Twig. "I'll take it."

CHAPTER 7

DAPHNE

By six o'clock, Daphne had convinced herself the dress worked fine. With the right jewelry and makeup, her hair waving down her back, the outfit would fade away. Pink streaks—just a few—in her hair would edge it up.

She placed a few pieces of soft butterhead lettuce around the chicken arranged on an oval platter.

But mauve . . .

Daphne hip checked the swinging door connecting the kitchen and dining room, regretting having invited her parents to dinner. Tonight, simply being with the kids and Sam exhausted her.

"So, how'd you do shopping? Any problems?" Sunny's questions assaulted Daphne the moment she reentered the dining room.

Daphne placed the chicken breasts next to a bowl of steamed spring vegetables. This was food meant to suppress her mother's needling. "Everything was fine."

"Was I right about Saks or what? Everything they sell fits a size smaller than you'll find anywhere else."

"You sound just plain crazy, Mom."

"Can I see it on you after dinner?"

Daphne's middle school identity emerged. Sunny would pull the fabric away from her daughter's neck to see what size Omar the Tent-maker had provided.

In seventh grade, Daphne lived in fear of his shop. Sunny, home from a day of shopping for back-to-school clothes with her twelve-year-old daughter, would throw a Bloomingdale's bag on the brocade chair, forever in the foyer of their lavish house in the Boston suburb of Chestnut Hill, and exhale as though having escaped a day in the trenches.

"Do you realize how long it took to find skirts that fit you?" Her mother invariably shook her head in disgust. "Keep this up, and next time we'll be visiting Omar's."

Later, when Daphne recognized Omar's as a mythical place, and was armed with college awareness, she called out Sunny for the cultural insult and never shopped with her mother again. Why had Sunny led chunky Daphne into the boutique areas catering to teens camera ready for *Seventeen* magazine? Racks of clothes suitable for her sisters, Bianca and Marissa, mocked Daphne with their refusal to contain her. Sunny dragged multiple outfits to Daphne, who huddled in the fitting room wearing one of her father's discarded white business shirts—wrapping and rewrapping herself in the age-softened cotton each time her mother left.

"But you could be so lovely," her mother said when Daphne complained. "Let me make magic!" That was Sunny. Determined to carve all she loved into her vision of perfection.

"Any rolls in the kitchen?" her father asked.

"You don't need rolls," her mother addressed the question aimed at Daphne.

"I didn't say I needed them, Sun." He squeezed her arm with affection.

Daphne couldn't decipher her father's behavior, apparently unaware of the emotional issues churning around his wife and daughter. Sunny had fretted about what she considered her daughter's deficits since Daphne could remember. Her oldest sister, Bianca, suffered from acne. Every eruption meant being dragged to the dermatologist. Even with medical attention, Bianca experienced scars and humiliation—including those from their mother.

Surprising nobody, Bianca became a dermatologist. And married a surgeon.

None of them escaped Sunny's scrutiny and management. Scales for Daphne, the slathering of products for Bianca, and for Marissa, a push toward every acceptable boy Sunny found. She wanted neither a blemished, fat, or lesbian daughter.

Daphne guessed her mother semisucceeded

with Bianca, who managed her skin as though it were a Fortune 500 company always in danger of failing. And Marissa might be marrying a woman, but both brides would be wearing lipstick and gowns.

Now Sunny had only Daphne left to sculpt into her image.

Daphne's father surely crafted his unnoticing persona to live his life in relative serenity.

"I have challah in the freezer," Daphne said. "I'll pop it in the microwave."

"The microwave destroys bread. Don't bother." Her mother transferred the smallest chicken breast from the platter to her plate. "He doesn't need it."

"You know dinner without bread depresses me."

"It *depresses* you, Gordon? What, are you recovering from your years in a concentration camp?" Sunny poured ice water into her glass.

"I find it empty. What can I say? My mother spoiled me."

"Ah, the ultimate emptiness of a breadless meal. Didn't Kafka address that heartrending issue, Grandpa?" Audrey made a contrived face of suffering.

Daphne's mother rolled her eyes. Sunny and sixteen-year-old Audrey often acted as though they were the same age. "That your mother always stuffed everyone with mounds of bread doesn't mean Daphne should do the same. You should applaud, not chide her."

"How did I chide her?" Gordon asked, exasperated. "I just said I wanted a roll."

And off they went. Two people deeply in love arguing over the same issue for more than forty years of marriage. Her mother could monitor her father's gut within a millimeter of expansion.

Sam left the table. Moments later, the sound of the microwave whirred.

"See what you did, Gordy?" Sunny turned to Daphne. "What's he doing?"

"Tuning in Mars." Audrey's sarcasm brought raised eyebrows from Sunny.

"No comments on what we serve are allowed tonight, Mom." Daphne tried to sound light-hearted.

"What did I do?" Sunny directed a faux-puzzled expression at her husband.

Her father ignored his wife and held out his plate for chicken. Sunny rested tongs on first one piece and then another, settling on the second biggest breast. She placed the largest on Sam's plate.

"We have butter on the table?" Sam walked in carrying a basket of the steaming challah. Daphne imagined the bread, hot and eggy, breaking apart on her tongue.

"What this family needs is a live-in shrink." Audrey flipped her hair, a deep red wedge of angles, darker than Daphne's but thick and straight, whereas Daphne's sprang out in a mix of waves, curls, and frizz. Still, it was in the red family, proving kinship along with their full lips. "Maybe one who could help Mom notice that food alone does not a family make."

"For goodness sake, Audrey. Between you and your grandmother, it's amazing I get to have any food on the table. Last week the two of you treated the steak as though I were presenting a corpse. Now bread's the enemy." Daphne regretted the words the moment they escaped.

"You're never wrong, are you?" Audrey looked as though tears might spill any moment.

"I'm sorry, baby. I shouldn't take my frustrations out on you."

Audrey shrugged and stabbed a spear of asparagus.

"Promise me we won't be like this when I bring Rosie to dinner." Gabe speared a chicken leg. "This is what I came home for? We're like a bad episode of *Curb Your Enthusiasm*."

"The sphinx speaks." Audrey tapped her brother on the shoulder. "Thank you for once again representing the warmth of our family constellation."

"Are you marrying this girl?" Daphne's father coated a piece of bread. "One year in college and you're bringing potential wives home?"

"We'll be fine with Rosie, honey." Daphne tore

off the golden end of the warm challah, pointedly ignoring Sunny, and crammed it in her mouth, the sweet doughy warmth coating her tongue and wrapping her in safety.

"Why would we ever act like ourselves in front of company?" Sunny asked. "If we did, how could Grandpa and I have married off any of our daughters?"

> **TIP:** Sometimes the strongest cravings for food happen when you're at your weakest point emotionally. You may turn to food for comfort, consciously or unconsciously, when you're facing a difficult problem, stress, or just looking to keep yourself occupied.
>
> —*Mayo Clinic*
>
> **WISDOM VIA:** The weight loss therapist Sunny forced on her.
>
> **WEIGHT GAINED:** 8 pounds.

Sunny called Marissa after dinner, granting Daphne breathing space. Her mother rat-a-tatted as she paced the hall in her heels, clicking on the hardwood, every sound invading the kitchen where Daphne was cleaning up the dinner detritus. "Nobody wants wedding cupcakes! I don't care what Lili says. The cake is plenty. Does she think we need to gild the lily? What's so funny?"

Her mother waited a beat, probably lifting her brows to the invisible audience—a signature Sunny bit. "Please, Marissa, have something classic. Petits fours."

Daphne scraped uneaten bits of chicken and salad into the sink. After running the disposal, she reached for the leftover bread, about to throw it down, and then stopped. She considered giving it an overnight egg bath, letting it swell to twice its size. Come morning, the French toast would call Julia Child's ghost to earth. Toasted challah was also sublime with butter melting into every tiny crevice of the bread. Sam did prefer scrambled eggs and toast over sweets in the morning.

Butter never tasted better than at room temperature. Bread never appealed as much as when it was about to be tucked away, when it was calling for you to pluck off just a little more. Daphne tore off a corner of the challah and touched it with a whisper of butter. Just the tiniest amount.

She could tear the bread in pieces for freezing, ready for a tiny pan of stuffing to surprise everyone. She mentally composed a recipe as she nibbled.

Challah stuffing? Bits of butter dotting the top. Eggs thickening it. Carrots and celery sautéed with onions providing texture and surprise. The bread softened with warm milk. Would the onion overpower the challah? Would sweet bread even work for stuffing? Perhaps bread pudding was a better bet.

She took one more piece, just a shred.

Her mother walked in carrying the Saks shopping bag. "You're still eating?"

Daphne tossed the bread into the trash. "What are you doing with that?" She nodded at the bag.

"I saw it while I talked to your sister. What, it's a state secret?"

Her mother sat at the table and crossed her legs, the very picture of preservation in action: gym-toned and portion-controlled to a constant 108 pounds, and injected with age stoppers, courtesy of Bianca. Sunny bragged ad nauseum about the benefits of having a dermatologist for a daughter. She seemed to think that Sam's work as a cardiovascular researcher who could find a cure for the diseases plaguing half of her father's extended family could never compare with Bianca's skill injecting Botox.

Sunny pulled the outfit from the shopping bag as though the dress and jacket weighed fifty pounds. She held the clothes up and away with both hands. "Pink, Daph?"

"Mauve."

Sunny held out her hands in an imploring gesture. "Sweetheart, mauve is pink for old ladies. And with your hair? You'll be a cartoon. I told you to let me help you."

"I really like that dress."

Sunny snorted. "Nobody could like that dress. Darling, you know that you can do better. There are tons of lovely dresses in . . ." She stopped and peered at the tag in the neck of the dress—as though she hadn't already checked the number. "Eighteen? A size eighteen! And this fabric! What in the world?"

"It's silk Dupioni."

"Which means unforgiving, unless it's very expensive." Sunny bunched it up tight and released it. "Which this isn't. See the wrinkles? Imagine how creased it will get at the wedding. I would have led you to Tadashi. Or . . ." Her mother pursed her lips, probably trying to think of one other designer willing to cut its dresses like Omar the Tentmaker.

Daphne used so many tricks against crying. *Dig your nails hard into your forearm. Stretch your calves up and down till they scream. Imagine punching a hole through the wall.*

"How did you let this happen, Daph?" Sunny held the mauve disaster higher. The outfit swelled each time it swung into Daphne's vision until reaching proportions able to cover the circus fat lady. Hair streaks? Edgy jewelry? The only way to wear a dress like that was with a mask.

Sunny placed the fabric next to Daphne's face. "On top of everything else, it has a beaded neckline? My God. What a nightmare."

CHAPTER 8

DAPHNE

Daphne; sisters Marissa and Bianca; her sister-in-law-to-be, Lili; her mother; and Veronica—Daphne's assistant from Alchemy—were crammed inside the one-bedroom hotel suite designated for wedding makeup central.

The air-conditioning wheezed as Daphne further lowered it. An unseasonable late-September eighty degrees outside combined with the women's rising body heat threatened to create a humid brew that could threaten their carefully blow-dried hair.

Delicate lingerie floated over everybody except Daphne and Veronica, who wore Alchemy smocks. Thin white cashmere robes, gifts from Lili and Marissa, remained discarded, flung on the couch as increasing humidity tried to curl everyone's hair despite the cranked-up AC.

"Will she be doing your face?" Sunny asked Daphne. She nodded toward Veronica, who hovered over Bianca with a mascara wand.

"Don't move." Daphne took a step back and examined her mother's skin. Thick serum, rich moisturizer, a primer for aging skin, and a layer of foundation filled with the magic of mica crystals masked her mother's fine lines and wrinkles, making her appear five years younger than her sixty-nine years.

"Veronica took off ten years," Daphne said. "And in answer to your question, I always do my own makeup."

"I want you to be as kind to yourself as you are to us. You're a magician." Sunny took Daphne's hand and kissed it. "Such talent you possess. And such goodness."

Daphne blinked a few times, having never mastered a formula for warding off Sunny's kindness. "Lift." She tipped up her own chin to illustrate.

After warming it on her forearm, making it easier to spread, Daphne dabbed extra concealer on Sunny's age spots. Obvious traces could be dusted away with finishing powder. Most typically, artists began with the eyes, but Daphne sculpted the face first. *Allure* had called it her trademark when naming her a "Best of Boston" makeup artist some years ago. Before challenging a woman's eyes with shades unknown in nature, she used subtle coloring on the face, deepening and camouflaging, bringing out a woman's natural beauty.

Bianca preened, judging first her right side and then her left, practicing the mysterious Mona Lisa look she favored. Only her sisters knew that such an affectation hid the fact that she hated her gummy smile. Just as they knew she worried about her skin as though it might turn on her at any second.

"Thanks, Veronica." She turned to Daphne. "Hey, sis, why didn't you let me give you a free tweak like everyone else did?"

"I'm still fond of the way my face is arranged."

Bianca came close and squinted. "If it were me, I'd get rid of the elevens before they rooted like permanent horrors."

Daphne pulled back as her sister pressed on the offensive lines between her brows.

"Stop fooling around." Sunny waved away Bianca. "Let your sister concentrate."

After gazing at the array of blushes, Daphne swept a dusky rose on her mother's cheeks. Fair-skinned brunettes, sharing fine hair, slashes of dark, dense eyebrows, and small bones—her mother and sisters all possessed the raw material that could be transformed from ordinary-pretty to smoldering. Everyone but Daphne reached into closets secure in knowing whether choosing sumptuous Armani suits or jeans and white tees, they'd appear coolly finished.

Bianca, Marissa, and Sunny were tight and spare, while her body resembled silly putty grafted onto a lump of clay.

Her mother's sighing statements, the ever-present "Namath back" sobriquet, and the piles of baby carrots Sunny pushed should have doomed Daphne to a world of soccer games and tangled hair, but instead, she had become addicted to pilfering her mother's makeup and living in a world of make-believe, while model-lovely Marissa became the lesbian. Sunny still suspected God had made a genetic stockroom error.

Years before, at the age of eight, when expanding from teddy-bear cute to blocky, she had attended Wheelock Family Theatre classes—Boston's best children's drama program. Sunny hoped pushing her daughter onstage might encourage starvation.

At Wheelock, Daphne owned the parts of the shopkeeper, the mother, and the headmistress. Onstage, she inhabited her entire body. She learned cosmetic techniques that morphed her face into something approaching lovely.

Daphne didn't easily earn the insult flung at fat girls: "But you have such a pretty face!" Her appearance, including her eyes, the color of sea glass, presented a boring, blank canvas when unlined and without mascara. Daphne had to work for the offense of "such a pretty face," but work she did. By high school she glowed, glazing her face with tinted moisturizer, highlighting it with touches of copper, and topping the trans-formation with daubs of bronze-pink blush. She lived her life above her shoulders, dreaming of overcoming her broad back just as Barbra

Streisand overcame and even glorified her nose.

Daphne entered Boston's Emerson College intent on turning her body into a theater tool. But by her third year of studying theater, not looking forward to a lifetime of playing "woman drinking coffee," she learned to be an expert at stage makeup. Daphne became the artist everyone wanted.

The modern sculpture strewn around the DeCordova Sculpture Park and Museum appeared to be toys of the gods. An eagle woven into the grass via leaves of different shades was visible from the patio as the guests relished drinks and appetizers. Waiters wearing tight silver tee shirts and painted-on black pants complemented metal statues.

Indian summer's brilliant sun rested comfortably on women in sleeveless dresses, spun linen shawls glancing their bony shoulders. Daphne roasted along with the men in their suits.

Moisture gathered. Under her arms. Her forehead. The back of her neck. Wearing her hair down in a thick mat of waves had been idiocy. Waves begot curls that birthed frizz, as perspiration crept ever higher on her head, bonding with too much product, solidifying into a carpet of impenetrable sweaty kink.

Dabbing at her forehead with blotting sheets offered a few moments' relief until a new layer of dampness formed.

Sam tipped his head with concern. "Take off your jacket. You look like a cooked beet."

"Nice." Daphne imagined three shades of red battling for the horror of being her: shiny, vegetable-colored face; dampening mauve fabric; and dense, sweaty carrot curls.

"Isn't this place gorgeous?" Audrey wobbled toward them in strappy too-high heels. "I love, love, love it, and I love my dress. And I love you and Daddy." She threw her arms around Sam and squeezed him, and then fell on Daphne for a double cheek kiss, the strong scent of sangria explaining her burst of filial love.

"How much wine have you had?" Daphne asked.

"How long till I'll be in college? One year," Audrey answered her own question. "Better start letting go, huh?"

Daphne gathered her words of motherly warning and then swallowed before they took flight. "You are simply beautiful, sweetness. But you don't want to get sick."

As though by magic eraser, Daphne's admonition wiped the love from Audrey's face. "I'll limit the champagne if you hold off on the appetizers."

The treat in Daphne's hand grew heavier, as though the peppered grits in the martini glass had morphed into mini kettlebells.

"Watch yourself," Sam said. "You appear exquisite—now act beautiful to match."

"Sorry, Mom." She made an apology pout, looking six, and teetered off.

"What did I do to deserve you?" Daphne leaned her head against Sam.

"I don't want her growing up to be your mother. I want her to be like you."

"Chunky?"

"Kind. Here. Drink some of that expensive wine Lili chose." He held a delicate glass to her lips, letting her sip the earthy Pinot Noir, while she kept hold of her food. Her balding, crane-like husband's appearance hid a secret sensualist who wished she could appreciate his appreciation of her.

She sipped again. Alcohol and perimenopause combined in a flash of suffocating heat. Sam shook his head in understanding and coaxed off her jacket. The rush of air and relief in removing the sticky fabric brought ecstasy.

Thank you, she mouthed.

"Open up." He winked and popped in a tiny chocolate ball filled with bourbon.

> **TIP:** People who suffer from depression are especially vulnerable to sugar's evil power.
>
> —*Psych Central*

Sugar Busters! Diet.
WEIGHT LOST: 19 pounds.
WEIGHT REGAINED: 25 pounds.

Bliss suffused Daphne. Lili's family, a constellation of earthen to golden tones and Marissa's, from olive to the palest chalk, along with their friends of every shade, mingled as though posing for an ad for upscale peace. Joy to the world flowed. Audrey flirted with a young Indian man, a potent diamond stud flashing in his ear. Gabe with his Colombian girlfriend, Rosie, completed the frieze of their new century family.

Lili's oldest sister clapped. "Time to gather for the ceremony." She pointed downward from the patio toward gold and purple balloons lining a path.

Strung lights guided guests down a path leading to giant bronze hearts in the distance. They passed the brides, their final moments of singleness captured as they posed in a granite water garden—a miniature Stonehenge, water alight with golden flashes interrupted by purple bubbles of electrical magic.

A willowy column of inky black billowed around Marissa's pale legs. White beaded fabric shimmered against Lili's brown skin. They'd declared to hell with being hip and dressed in ebony and ivory. Fire red lipstick covered Lili's lips; smoke and grape lined Marissa's eyes. Their beauty blazed.

Daphne swelled with heat, tenderness, and sadness about the ugliness of her heart. Upon learning that Marissa had fallen in love with a black woman, her selfish reaction had every-thing to do with herself and nothing to do with Marissa's joy. Daphne prayed that her sister had chosen an ample black woman, a plus-sized lesbian embodying every possible trope of a big gay woman. Because Daphne, more than any-thing, wanted a large sister-in-law to join her in the family.

Lili turned out to be pin thin and reserved in every way but her bubbling laugh. Daphne, it turned out, had proven to be racially and cultur-ally stupid.

Rows of chairs tied with purple and gold curled ribbons faced the towering heart statues. Quiet fell as the Unitarian minister gestured for them to stand.

Lili and Marissa walked themselves down the aisle. Daphne's heart broke open upon seeing her tense baby sister so loose and happy.

They smiled and recited their simple loving vows. Lili's father's recitation of Audre Lorde's "For Each of You" hushed the already quiet night. Sunny, possessed of an amazing contralto, sang "Sunrise, Sunset," bringing tears to both families. Lili and Marissa each stomped on a glass wrapped in a napkin.

"Amen!"

"L'chaim!"

Audrey sat on one side of Sam; Gabriel on the other, hands linked.

A breeze caressed Daphne's bare arms, blowing away hot envy and leaving cooling love.

With dusk settling, they walked toward the celebration tent. Daphne loved dancing with her husband, leaning against Sam's chest, feeling his hands run up and down her back. She tingled in anticipation of champagne bubbles, fellowship, and family. The warmth of joining cultures enveloped the crowd, which headed toward the party in an undulating bracelet of mingled skin tones, crisp suits, and jewel-toned dresses.

Her parents approached holding hands. Her mother, lovely; her father, sturdy—she should appreciate the miracle of them.

Sunny separated from Gordon and walked to her.

"Congratulations, Mommy. Now all your girls are wed."

Sunny kissed her. Daphne recognized a danger sign in the tight smile. Her mother took Daphne's arm, pulled her close, and then turned to Sam. "Walk with Gordon. I need Daph for a teensy bit."

"Are you all right?" Daphne peered at her mother and saw no obvious cosmetic failure. "Do you need something?" She chastised herself for not remembering, not honoring, her parents' fallibility. Soon her mother would be seventy. Someday Daphne would take on the role of caretaker.

"You're aware there will be another round of pictures, right?" Her mother's pointed expression indicated that Daphne should understand what she implied.

"Do you want me to touch you up?"

"Daphne. Sweetheart. Look at you!"

Daphne glanced down, expecting wine stains, dribbles of grits, body fluids leaking, but all she saw was mauve. "What?"

"Your jacket! Where did you put it?"

"At the . . ." Daphne blanked, not knowing where Sam had left it after easing it from her shoulders. "Sam must have left it somewhere."

Sunny grabbed Daphne's upper arm. "Cover these," she whispered. "The photographer is everywhere."

Daphne couldn't talk and hold back her tears simultaneously.

"Don't cry." Her mother blew out a hot sigh. "You'll thank me when you see the pictures."

Cool and clean, Daphne walked into the bedroom. Scalding water and hot tears had washed away the wedding. Wrapped safely in a voluminous tee shirt and oversized pajama pants, Daphne settled next to Sam, who'd fallen asleep with a book on his chest.

Sam fell asleep faster than anyone Daphne knew. Most people assumed Sam's specialty, cardiac research, meant less time on call—which was true—but they dismissed the interminable hours spent reading journals, studying, and communicating with those whose time zones kept him from reaching them during the day.

Indeed, when people noted how incredibly decent Sam was—and he was—they missed the side that existed on a different plane from others. When they first lived together, when Daphne found him on the couch, gazing off with little expression, unmoving, no book in hand, no television playing, no computer whirring, she'd worried about depression. After some months, she asked him what was wrong.

"Nothing. Why should anything be wrong?"

It took her the longest time to understand why her husband sat, seemingly doing nothing. He turned ideas over in his head, needing no more than air to breathe.

Daphne took the book from his chest and took off his glasses. He opened his eyes, reached out, and touched a wet strand, gently pulling it out and letting it spring back.

"You erased your fancy style."

"I don't think I'm meant to be a fancy girl."

"Fancy enough for me."

She leaned against Sam's shoulder. "What a horror she is."

He gave a familiar whoosh of disappointment. "Your mother will never change. We simply need to keep her out of the bedroom."

"I know. You're right. It's just—"

"We should have been dancing tonight, not letting her ruin your night." He kissed her neck; the only bare skin available to his lips. He pushed up her tee shirt. "Let's make love. It's been so long."

"I 'let her' ruin my night? My mother grabbed my flesh and waggled it in front of the world."

"First, nobody saw." Sam laced his fingers behind his head. "Second, time to pull away. You're forty-three. Why can't you stop renting her space in your head?"

Daphne pressed her lips, refusing to enter this soundtrack of their marriage. He loved her. Body and soul. He'd give anything for that to be sufficient. Yada, yada, yada. She became so tired of defending her judgment that she wanted to tell him to take his love for her and shove it. Which proved her stupidity evermore.

"If I had the answer to that, I'd be a hundred ten pounds."

"You're doing it again. How many times must I prove I find you sexy before you stop worrying about Sunny's view of you? Do we have to wait until she dies?"

"God, Sam. She's my mother." As she said the words, she thought how much her mother's death would release her. "What a horrible thing to say."

"You know what else is horrible? Your mother ruling my sex life."

Daphne opened her mouth to answer him, but not a single response seemed equal to the cruelty of his words—that this was a rare misstep for Sam made the moment hurt no less—nor did the meanness make his words less true.

CHAPTER 9

DAPHNE

The following evening, with Gabe and Rosie back at Tufts University, and Sam holed up in his study, Daphne hungered for quality time with her daughter. She followed the television chatter emanating from the family room, determined to connect with Audrey. Seeing her daughter at the wedding, so nearly adult, Daphne wanted to pull in those last moments they might have before college.

Audrey curled on the large brocade couch, facing the enormous television hanging on the wall. On the coffee table, a minuscule pottery bowl held about a dozen peanuts.

"What are you watching?"

"*Pounded*." Audrey drew her legs in to allow room for Daphne. "Don't you recognize it?"

"Guess not. Sorry."

"Jeez, Mom. I record it every week."

Daphne turned her attention to the screen, where an enormous woman wearing a workout bra and Lycra bike shorts stood on a massive scale. Her arms looked like they were twice the size of Audrey's thighs. Rolls of fat showed both under and over the stretched fabric.

The number *278* flashed on the screen above her.

"What is this?" Daphne reached for a peanut. Honey roasted. Salty sweet grit.

Audrey answered without moving her head. "I told you: *Pounded.*"

"Yes. But what is it?"

"A reality show." Audrey glanced at her with disbelief. "You never heard of it?"

"You watch this?"

"Everyone watches it."

Another woman stepped on the oversized scale, her bra top twinned by a second set of breasts formed by fat hanging down below the stretched fabric. Bright red numbers blinked *341, 347, 351.*

Daphne, caught between fear, disgust, and overwhelming curiosity, peered at the television, wanting to freeze and study it but unwilling to reveal her fascination.

Looking away was impossible. Fat people, fatter than her, far, far, fatter, displayed like pinned bugs, letting America—maybe the entire world; maybe the secret obese of France also sat glued to their sets—see them in all their flesh.

"How long has this been on?"

"This is week three of season four."

Her daughter, the television genius. How proud she and Sam should be.

A starting weight of *356* flashed in bright red numbers. Below, in green, the woman's current weight of *339*. The number *17* settled and blinked. Seventeen pounds lost. She flashed a large smile as she stood with her arms to the side, fat forcing them away from her body. She resembled a grade-school drawing.

"How can they go on television like that?"

"They're helping themselves, Mom. You should admire them." Audrey tucked her feet under her butt, compressing herself until she resembled a pipe cleaner bent into modern sculpture.

Daphne worried. First, that she had no idea Audrey watched this show, and more so— keeping on top of everything a teenage girl watched was impossible—she'd have sworn that if Audrey followed a show such as *Pounded*, it would be with irony, texting barbs with her friends. But her daughter thought this display showed courage, which begged a million questions: Did Audrey think Daphne lacked the courage shown by these *Pounded* women? Did her girl think Daphne fat shamed and laughed at women like this?

Or perhaps she wished that Daphne could display the same courage as these women on the screen.

Her fingers twitched toward the peanuts left in the bowl. She balled her hands into fists.

TIP: Make a fist. Squeeze your fist to resist overeating or choosing wrongly.

In a recent study, squeezing muscles at the moment of your purposeful decision to help resist a bad choice seems to help people make healthier food choices.

—*Wiki How: Tricks to Increase*
Willpower & Eat Less

WEIGHT LOST: No idea.

They called Paul to the oversized scale. His mountain-like body was sloped, a triangle of a torso atop large thighs.

"You're right. They're courageous." Daphne smiled at her lovely, empathic girl. Audrey had always been tenderhearted—not counting her recent teenage snarky habits.

"I wish I could be that brave," Audrey said.

"Honey, that's crazy. You're such a wisp I worry about you."

"I'm a wisp?"

"You're tiny. There are times I want to force-feed you ice cream."

Audrey peered at her, seeming confused. "You worry about me?"

Daphne laughed. "Why do you keep repeating what I say?"

Audrey crossed her legs on the couch. "You never say a word to me about my weight. You don't worry about that. Or talk about it. I feel as though my body's invisible. When it comes to bodies, all you do is worry about what Grandma will say about yours. You never say a word about me. How I look."

"Because all I ever wanted was for you to feel good. I know you love Grandma, and she's wonderful to you, but it was . . . difficult having her as a mother. And I never want to do to you what she did to me."

"All I've ever wanted was for you to tell me I was doing a good job with my weight," Audrey said. "That I was thin enough."

"Baby, you do a phenomenal job with everything in your life."

"Sure, sure. I'm smart and good. You tell me those things endlessly. But you never tell me that I'm beautiful. Or thin." Tears started to stream down Audrey's cheeks. "And what do you do all day? You make people pretty."

Daphne froze. Everything she believed about her mothering tipped as though shown in a funhouse mirror. The tenets formed of how to lead Audrey toward becoming a strong woman now seemed a cyclone of ignorant mistakes.

Daphne woke on Monday knowing she'd failed her daughter. She'd probably have bombed with Gabe also, but his tender spots didn't match Daphne's motherhood deficits as laser perfectly as they did with Audrey.

Or maybe she had done just as awful a job with her son and simply didn't know.

All that wasted energy Daphne had pulled up, preventing herself from letting a compliment slip out when Audrey skipped around as a sparkly princess, not wanting Audrey to think Daphne loved her for being cute or small. She wanted to raise a rugged and free daughter, but Audrey chose red velvet over overalls every time.

At five, Audrey ran to Daphne, breathless, beautiful. "Don't I look pretty, Mama?"

"You're always pretty, honey. But more important, you're smart and sweet."

She had declared Audrey brilliant and caring. A genius. A good girl. Daphne believed herself on the path to raising a strong woman; instead, she gave Audrey the message that she, in fact, wasn't truly a pretty girl. Fighting the world's values hadn't worked. What the hell was a mother supposed to do?

Not only had she been blind, she'd blithely patted her own back for being caring and wise, even as she screwed up. How could she not be surprised at Audrey's wounds? Audrey had grown up with a mother changing people through cosmetics, one aunt molding and medicating faces into acceptability, and another who designed jewelry to drape around their necks. Her grandparents owned the exclusive Illuminate jewelry stores.

And Daphne expected her daughter to be satisfied that she was a good girl? A smart girl?

The white digital scale leered from under the double sink. Sam insisted on having one, but he kept it out of sight. He weighed himself with the constancy of a jockey staying in his class, but after each weigh-in kicked the offensive object back into hiding, vigilant, knowing Daphne's history with the machines.

Her mother's thinning campaign had hit hysterical heights during Daphne's adolescence, demonstrated when Sunny placed a wafer-thin bronze scale—it matched the dramatic back-splash behind the sink—square in the entry to the kitchen.

The family faced two choices: be weighed or leap over it.

Daphne and her father leaped. She soared, she flew, and she bounded—but she never stepped on the bronze monster.

Now Daphne contemplated Sam's scale. Her last weigh-in had come via psychological force. After that battle, she had refused all attempts to get her back on it, generating arguments, frustration, and causing more than one medical assistant to mutter, "Who gives a damn?" as they prepared Daphne for the doctor's entrance.

"My body; my decision," she'd say each time she visited the gynecologist, knowing she sounded ridiculous—as though she were fighting a guerrilla war with her doctor—and yet continuing to draw the line in the medical sand.

"Not knowing something doesn't make it not true," Dr. McLeod would say each time she visited. "What is, is."

And Daphne, each time, thanked Dr. McLeod for her Zen master wisdom, counting the minutes until the woman shut her mouth and stuck in the speculum.

Daphne worked hard for her ignorance, winning all battles against nearing a scale until five years ago when having her tubes tied. She'd been at Beth Israel Deaconess Medical Center's outpatient surgery center, in her paper gown, feet in skid-free socks, face-to-face with the giant iron medical monster.

"Step on." The nurse's bunny-covered scrub top straining against her breasts.

"No, that's fine. I'm antiscale." Daphne gave what she hoped was a sisterhood-is-strong smile, without hinting that Nurse Bunny was also overweight.

The nurse kept her flat expression. Daphne had expected more sympathy from a bunny-wearing member of the medical world. "No scale, no surgery."

"I'm just getting my tubes tied. Under local."

"No matter. We need it for titration factoring." Nurse Bunny gestured toward the weighing platform.

Daphne got on the scale backward. "Don't tell me what it says."

Amazingly, the nurse obeyed.

The last time Daphne had heard and faced a number had been six weeks postpartum, after Audrey, when she hit 212. Burned into her skull were her hateful (now-former) doctor's stinging words. The wretchedly thin man had studied the number on her chart with the eyes of a general in the war on fat.

"You're five foot four, Daphne. Even with the largest frame"—he measured her wrist with his fingers—"which you don't have, the heaviest you should be, again, if you *were* large framed would be a hundred thirty-four to one fifty-one."

"One thirty-eight is the very most you should weigh," he continued. "So, take a hundred thirty-eight as your outer figure and aim toward a hundred twenty-four. Got it? Next time I see you, you'd best be well on your way to losing fifty pounds. More. No more nipping at leftovers."

Daphne was sitting on the edge of the examining table, her paper gown rustling when she crossed her arms. She nodded like a marionette.

"Now be a good girl, scoot down, and put your bottom at the end of the table."

Sixteen years later, tile ground into Daphne's knees as she nudged the scale from under the sink in her bathroom. She stood. She pressed hard on the towel wrapping her hair, sopping up as much water as possible, calculating the remaining wetness as a half-pound.

Which she knew was bullshit.

She tapped the cold metal with her toe. Numbers tumbled like a slot machine.

192.08.

She moved the scale to a flatter surface.

192.08.

Only twenty pounds less than her heaviest recorded weight—and that was immediately following childbirth. And though she wanted to call it 192, she could round off numbers—actually, it was 193. So really, nineteen pounds less.

She kicked away the scale. Then she reached for some expensive hair goop and applied it. Her energy and money always slid in that direction. Always. Pricey hair products. Makeup made to order for Alchemy. Stunning jewelry, of course. Daughter of Illuminate, her jewelry box contained a tangle of rubies to match her lips and emeralds to complement her hair. Aquamarines for her eyes. Diamonds sparkled at her neck. Gold and silver wrapped around her neck and wrists, accompanied by the black made-to-hide fabric draping her body. Or, as her mother called her work wardrobe, "those black rags you wear."

Daphne's body ruined relationships. She hated people she should love, ignored people she did love, and, for the life of her, she didn't know how to stop eating.

Daphne hurried up the stairs to the Alchemy studios. She was late for her Monday morning meeting. "Sorry," she said to Ivy, her business partner, sitting in their shared office and turning the pages of *Vogue*. "Had to work out something for Sam's mother. She needs a root canal and gets terrified at the thought. No matter how much pain she's in she won't make an appointment."

"No problem. Single women never have anything to do but wait for their married sisters."

Ivy's constant jokes about marriage could lead one to imagine her desperate for male company, when in fact, she was so drop-dead gorgeous it could be called a disability. Daphne wondered if Ivy thought it made her feel better, leveling the field by pretending she panted for a wedding ring.

Ivy's hair was butterscotch, her eyes spearmint, and her skin crème fraîche—her friend was three confections men wanted to eat with or without a spoon.

They both attended Emerson as theater majors. Ivy's beauty had won her small parts in soap operas, but the slice of industry willing to accept her based solely on her gorgeousness bored her. Her killer ambition turned to fashion and image consulting with Alchemy.

"We don't have long. I have a nine o'clock with someone important enough to make you hate me."

"I have a page of reasons to hate you already, so don't bother telling me who it is." Daphne sorted through the mail without looking up. "Who is it?"

"You'll have to wait and see. I want you to die when he walks in."

"How soon before you sleep with him?" Sleeping with her famous male clients made Ivy more comfortable with them.

"He's awfully famous." Ivy looked at her watch. "I suppose by eight tonight?"

"Makes sense." Daphne opened the folder Ivy left for her. "How do the numbers seem?"

"Less pro bono would make them lots better."

"If we have a problem, we'll take it from my side."

Ivy peered at Daphne over her reading glasses. "Repetitive conversation 101? Just saying we should decide together how many billable hours we devote to—"

"To burn victims?"

Ivy's blind spot rose each time she examined the receipts. Ivy was correct: free services made up a quarter of Daphne's clientele, but she could afford it. Between Sam's salary and her stakeholding share in Illuminate, supporting herself had never been a problem. Her parents had blessed her with that lack of worry since birth, so she offered to remunerate Alchemy every month. Blood and love made up the pact between Daphne and Bianca; they understood bowing under judgment. Folks might help poor and homeless families with housing and food, but nobody thought about kids walking around wearing their poverty on their faces: eruptions and craters of acne visible to the world and ruining their lives, burns bisecting their faces.

"Ah, forget it," Ivy said, as always. "Both of us will enter heaven through the good works you perform in the name of Alchemy."

"I weighed myself today." Daphne kept her eyes on her chipped fingernails.

Ivy put down her pen. "What brought that on?"

"*Pounded.* Watching it with Audrey."

"Why? Why, of everything . . . ?"

Ivy ripped bits from her breakfast bagel as Daphne ran through the weekend from the wedding to that morning.

"I'm in shock at the number." Daphne refused to state the actual number. "Shock without any baseline of knowledge. I don't know what I *should* weigh. Last night, watching those men and women being weighed like heifers at market, I wanted to cry. And yet I was jealous."

"Jealous of their humiliation?"

"Jealous of them getting unstuck. See this?" Daphne circled her arms around her body. "I'm so sick of me. I want something other than the size of my stomach to be my first thought in the morning."

"You know you're a crazy woman, right? Your mother made you into a lunatic. You look fine."

"*Fine? Fine* is my zenith?"

"What do you want me to say, Daphne? That you're Angelina Jolie? You *are* fine. You're fine, and you're smart and good. You have a great husband and wonderful kids. Maybe your family bent you like a pretzel, but Jesus, be grateful for what you have."

"How much do you weigh?"

"What?"

"It's a simple question to which I'm certain you have an answer. How many times have you gone on and on to your clients about how important it is to weigh yourself *every day, same time, no exception?* I hear you."

"Important for me, not for you. My brand of crazy comes out in my overwhelming need to zip up a size two. That doesn't make it right or even—"

"Stop talking like a sanctimonious prig. What if I want that brand? Who said you get to own it? Weight and height, please."

"I'm five feet five inches—maybe a scooch more. I weigh a hundred and six."

Daphne came from around her desk, stood, and pointed at herself. "Me? Per Sam's no doubt very accurate scale, 192.08. I'm five foot four. No scooch. I'm one inch shorter than you and weigh eighty-seven pounds more."

"Who cares, Daph?"

"My daughter. My mother. Both my sisters. *Me.* Do you know what 86.08 pounds adds up to? The average weight of a twelve-year-old. I'm carrying a twelve-year-old more than you. Picture that. Spreading that all over you."

"I didn't realize how consuming this is for you."

"How are you supposed to understand?" Forbidden words started to escape her mouth: "That I think about my body every minute? That I worry about my thighs more than about the state of the world? That my sex life sucks because I can't stand baring myself to Sam?"

Despite her decades-long friendship with Ivy, to whom she revealed everything from motherhood worries to the results of her mammogram, this—this, she never talked about.

"I gotta do something," Daphne said. "I think about every bite I put in my mouth. If there are cookies hidden in the deepest recesses of the freezer, they scream until I eat them. Something must change. Whatever it takes. I can't stand feeling guilty for being me. Not anymore."

CHAPTER 10

ALICE

After climbing the wide white stairs to the porch surrounding the mansion, Alice ducked under the sign, WELCOME TO PRIVATION, despite its hanging well above her head. An expressionless housekeeper, her uniform starched sharp, held open the oversized door. Alice and the others filed in as the housekeeper nodded at each of them, pointing to where they should stand in the oversized entry hall.

"Find yourselves," she said after the last woman entered.

Paper signs with their names written in thick black marker, first name and last initial, lined one wall. Alice found her way to "Alice T." The redhead who'd introduced herself before the enforced silence stood to her left. Alice topped the woman by many inches. Being short made carrying weight harder—not that being tall helped Alice much. Here she was.

Daphne S. and Alice, side by side, were last in a line of seven women on the spectrum of synonyms: fat, stout, full figured, corpulent, fleshy, plump, portly, chubby, rotund, paunchy, potbellied, flabby, well upholstered, broad in the beam—though none was in the category of grossly or morbidly obese. Alice wondered if the seven had been chosen by the Acrobat Film staff for landing in the middle of the fat bell curve.

Being inducted into an assemblage willing to bare their pain for a documentary, in exchange for learning control, induced in them all an overwhelming desire to bolt. After all, nobody would label Alice a sharing kind of woman. Even in college, when girls tripped over themselves joining groups where they could stick together their experiences like Velcro—from film appreciation to being mixed race—Alice avoided easy ramps to instant friendship.

Everyone was frowning, faces tense. Nobody acted as though she wanted to be there. Including Alice. Who wanted to fit into a group of misfits bound by a desire to be thin?

The housekeeper walked down the line and placed either a purple or red cardboard sign around their necks. The paper, hanging from yellow yarn, shouted their height and weight.

Seung A., a Korean woman wearing an oversized sweatshirt and yoga pants, looked the youngest and most athletic. Magenta-dyed hair bounced in a top-of-the-head ponytail. Purple card: 5'3", 201 lbs.

Susannah C., white, gaunt faced, with a semi-medium build from her waist up, bloomed out to enormous hips and a mammoth-sized bottom. Purple card: 5'11", 280 lbs. She appeared to be in her late forties.

Jennifer F., black, probably in her early forties or late thirties, crossed her arms over her massive breasts. An oversized hourglass shape and large orange glasses contrasted with her grim expression. Purple card: 5'6", 225 lbs.

Lauretta J., a Hispanic woman, somewhere in her early thirties, smiled painfully—a grin broad enough to neutralize the frightened and angry faces in the room. Everything about her proclaimed a hunt for perfection: the spiraling curls spilling down her back, sharp-pressed clothes, and the glossy pink nails touching the edge of her sign. Purple card: 5'1", 178 lbs.

Hania M. possessed the sort of beauty that made other women uncomfortable, if not downright jealous, as they compared themselves to her exquisiteness, embodying not only "What a pretty face!" but also "What lovely hair!" "What soulful eyes!" Her rosy gold skin, waterfall of black hair, and rush of gold bracelets circling her forearm all called out South Asian, perhaps Indian. Alice placed her in the category of "most likely to finish happy and thin." Red card: 5'3", 170 lbs.

Daphne S., white, her plainness broken by a fizz of reddish-gold hair, had made herself memorable by lining her eyes expertly in shades of teal and brown. Red card: 5'4", 192 lbs.

And finally, Alice herself. Red card: 5'10", 220 lbs.

A massive man entered; he would have been right at home participating in a tractor-pulling contest. Even Alice and Susannah had to crook their necks to fully take him in. The shortest would need a stepstool to reach the top of his head. Few of their hands could span the solid girth of his arms.

"I'm Jeremiah Collins. Group commander. Let's begin."

Everyone appeared either terrified of or half in lust with this giant. Alice's antipathy was replicated by Daphne's furious expression.

Two decidedly not-fat women, twinned by frightening expressions and steel-cable forearms, entered and flanked Jeremiah. One was slight and innocuous, until you saw that each muscle appeared outlined with black chalk on her dark-brown skin. The other, her dirty-blonde hair skinned back so tight it lifted her brows, seemed ready to eat everyone for breakfast.

"Welcome to salvation, ladies," Jeremiah said, "where we'll teach you the path out from your anguish. I know you're in pain. Why else would you be here? You had to have a damn good reason to leave your loved ones, your jobs, your homes—even your children, right?"

A noticeable relaxation went around the room.

Yes. No doubt every woman wondered what the heck she was doing here. Alice would have happily boarded a bus home right now.

"Welcome to being the chosen ones. Why you?" He crossed his arms and let his eyes travel slowly from ponytailed Seung A. to Alice T. "You, among all women, showed that you have what it takes. You're tenacious." This he said to Jennifer F., who was staring out from her bright orange glasses.

Now he pointed to Lauretta J. and Hania M. "Inside you are magnificent women." He turned his gaze to Alice and Daphne S. "You possess love. You only need to turn it on yourselves. This we will teach you. You will each become your own team of one."

Despite having no idea what that meant, Alice was drawn in by his words. "Welcome to hell, ladies, where we recognize that life is unfair, and you pay the price for every action you take." Jeremiah ran a hand over his thick buzz cut. "You've eaten your way through pain, through loss, through happiness, and just for the plain pleasure of crunching calories between your teeth. Not one of you knows how to live with privation. So you landed here. The last stop."

He ran his eyes over the seven women lined up in front of him.

"What do you think?" Daphne S. said from the

side of her mouth. "Are we being indoctrinated into a secret army of the thin?"

The woman's uncanny ability to whisper without moving her lips impressed Alice, while her capacity to ignore the rules reminded Alice of her mother. Open flouting was a trait easier for white women to pull off without punishment.

Alice clamped her mouth shut and pretended she hadn't heard the woman speak. She needed to be the absolute best student in the room, just like her father had always taught her. "Don't be good, Al. Don't be very good. Be tops. Always. Twice as good as every white kid."

"Anytime you want to leave, just say the word, and we'll return your phone, your wallet, and call a cab to take you to the bus station—it's only a bit over an hour away. It's your prerogative. Here, you will get thin. Leave, you will remain fat."

"What's with his *An Officer and a Gentleman* routine?" the woman continued.

Alice turned her head the slightest amount, just enough to raise her eyebrows and message, *Be quiet; I'm not playing* with her expression.

Daphne, apparently immune to chiding, continued as though Alice had nodded with encouragement. "We're paying to be scared straight? You think that's the plan?"

"Eyes front." Jeremiah drew himself up, broadening his shoulder muscles.

The blondish trainer marched over. "Any more talking and you get a shot."

"What's a shot?" Daphne asked.

"You'll find out. Although you don't want to. And since you talked when I said not to, now you have one."

"You're probably wondering what you got yourselves into right about now." Jeremiah's face warmed with a toothy smile. "Listen up. I'm gonna give you the first five rules to get you to skinny. First, you'll learn your room assignments. When you go there, you'll change into your uniform. And then we'll tell you the next step.

"Remember: you're here to learn discipline, not dieting tricks. Not the damn calorie counts of an apple. If you're here, you already possess a PhD in everything from calories to carbs."

The women nodded like churchgoers finally hearing the right sermon.

He paused, obviously appreciative in advance of his next line. "Doctorates of dieting are bullshit. With me, you're going to get whittled into shape, mind, and body. Coleen and Valentina— your trainers—your gods, your mother, your father for the next four weeks—plan to carve you out from the lakes of fat you're lying in."

Hania M. cleared her throat and spoke. "Who is that?" Her voice broke with a nervous catch as she pointed to the short Paul Bunyan type holding what Alice recognized as a DSLR video camera. Alice gave her kudos for opening her mouth.

"He's invisible," Jeremiah said. "You don't see him."

"Actually," Hania said with great dignity, "I do."

The taller trainer—god, mother, father—stepped up. "No. You don't. You shouldn't need us to remind you of the documents you signed before you came. Disciplined women do not require reminding. Do not embarrass yourself."

Alice figured she was ahead. She was disciplined. She remembered the inclusions about filming in the pages-long document she'd signed. A strong sense of "Screw you, Clancy," had imbued her as she wrote "Alice Townsend" under the lengthy paragraphs that added up to "We're filming you. You give up rights to your image, which will be utilized for instructive purposes."

"Any more questions?" the blonde trainer asked.

Nobody spoke.

"I'm Valentina. Shortly, I will know you better than anyone, including your BFF." She used the colloquialism with the clipped measure of someone who did not want you to know that English wasn't her first language.

"Rule one: no speaking when you are lined up. Rule two: a shot will be given for each time a rule is broken. Rule three: no outside contact.

Rule four: three shots results in discipline as we determine. Rule five: arguments about regulations will result in dismissal from the mansion.

"Coleen will now give room assignments. You will follow us to the rooms. Your bags will be there. When the bell rings, leave your rooms and wait for instructions." She turned to the small, dark-skinned woman standing in a military position. "Coleen?"

Coleen gave a curt nod. Everything about her was severe, from her sharp shoulder blades to her defined thigh muscles. Her short hair, close on the sides with a low pile on top, appeared immobile, as did her pressed lips, outlined in a fuchsia lipstick, which stood in contrast with her somber expression and dead-serious eyes.

"Step forward when I call your name." Coleen scanned the room. "Susannah C."

The tall woman shuffled forward. Enormous thighs rubbed against each other. Her discordant body appeared grafted.

"State your stats." Coleen stood with her legs apart, hands gripped behind her military style.

Susannah reached for the red card hanging around her neck like a noose. Coleen smacked her hand away. "You know your height and weight. Don't read. Speak."

Alice understood Susannah's reluctance to state the facts. Reading allowed a sense of removal. Alice wanted to expunge her statistics forever.

Once she lost this weight, she planned to erase the knowledge of that, too.

"Five foot eleven," Suzanne said. "Two hundred and ninety."

"Two hundred and ninety what?"

"Two hundred and ninety pounds." Susannah's eyes appeared deliberate in their lack of focus.

"Do you have any idea what I weigh?" Coleen asked.

Susannah shook her head with the smallest motion.

"Take a guess. Come on: if you are here, like Jeremiah said, you're some sort of expert. Look at yourself. You could be a postdoctorate in fat. I bet you can do it with one glance."

"I'm really not good at this." Susannah's voice trembled.

"Sure you are!" Coleen's voice brimmed with false friendship. "Take a guess. It won't cost you anything."

Susannah raised her shoulders and pressed her lips together, her movements a clear indication of just how much this interaction cost her.

Jeremiah pushed in front of Coleen and put a hand on Susannah's shoulder. "Just try, hon. Like she told you."

"I don't know," Susannah whispered.

Coleen smirked as Jeremiah comforted Susannah.

Whatever program Alice thought she had signed

up for, this scene didn't match it. Perhaps she should have watched the *Waisted* documentary, but that would have meant asking Clancy for his screening copy. Instead, she'd registered in secrecy and simply slipped off, telling only her parents, who agreed to be on total Libby caretaking. She'd spoken to her daughter only at the very last moment, assuring her repeatedly that the time until Mommy returned would fly by.

Clancy, she notified by email. She left Boston based only on the knowledge that the film had been the first in a series on weight and women and that it had won the Mobie. She couldn't stand Clancy judging her one more moment.

Her decision horrified Bebe and Zeke, but family was family. Steel bound them. Clancy's role as their son-in-law never prevailed over a daughter's primacy.

Coleen pointed at Jennifer F., who cocked her head, her expression blank, her bright glasses contrasting with her dark skin. The woman glared with a force field of minus sixty degrees.

"You seem like a smart girl, Jennifer. How much do you think I weigh?"

Jennifer crossed her arms, reminding Alice of the girls she worked with who developed too soon, the ones hunched over in oversized sweatshirts. "I can't say, but I think you're mighty proud of the number."

"Are you in want of a shot?" Valentina marched to Jennifer and stuck her face close.

"You said no talking unless spoken to," Jennifer said. "She spoke."

Valentina jabbed her finger toward Jennifer's chest. "Coleen asked what she weighed, not your opinion."

"Sorry, ma'am. The parameters confused me." Jennifer nodded with a slow smile and ran her gaze over Coleen. "I'd say you're five foot two. Small as all shit, but I'm gonna say you weigh a hundred twenty-three pounds naked. Muscle is heavy, and you're covered with it."

Underground laughs slithered through the room.

Jeremiah left Susannah's side. The rising triumph of mirth receded. Jennifer F. remained cross armed and kept the expression that managed to stay mildly disrespectful while still blank.

"Coleen is five feet three inches tall. She weighs one hundred five pounds." He paced the line, stopping in front of Daphne. "Height and weight?"

Daphne appeared ready to punch Jeremiah. "Five feet four inches. One hundred ninety-seven pounds."

"So let's see. You weigh how many more pounds than Coleen?"

"Ninety-two."

"A math whiz! Nighty-two pounds ahead and only two inches shorter. Imagine losing an entire

Coleen. Would you become a freak? Hideous?"

Daphne stood silent, absorbing the humiliation.

"Let's put it another way: if you lose eighty-eight pounds, you'll be one hundred nine pounds. Is this a dangerous weight for you, do you think?"

Before Daphne could answer, he swung his attention to Susannah C. "You weigh two hundred ninety pounds. Most of it is hanging below your waist, right?" He shifted his gaze to the rest of the room. "Would you all agree?"

The room stayed silent.

"Ladies!" Coleen clapped her hands sharp and short. "Jeremiah asked a question. What we have here is an emergency room. Imagine he's the head physician, and you're the trauma team."

Valentina walked to Seung and put out her hand, gesturing for the woman to approach. "Come. I do not bite."

Seung seemed doubtful.

"Look at you all dressed for a workout." Valentina swept her hand over Seung's bright lemon sweatshirt and black leggings and tweaked Seung's ponytail as though they were all pals together. "I love the purple hair!"

Seung, trapped, moved her head up and down as Valentina tugged. When the trainer freed the ponytail, she held out her hand, Seung took it, and then, wordless, let herself be led to stand in front of Susannah.

"Where are most of her pounds?"

Seung circled a hand ambiguously around Susannah's lower half. Alice's stomach roiled.

Coleen released a movie-sized sigh and walked to where the two women stood. She took a handful of Susannah's meaty thighs. "Imagine this on a scale, ladies. Here we have her virtually carrying the equivalent of me—if I were soft, wiggly suet wrapped around her."

Coleen released Susannah and walked up to Alice. She outlined Alice's body with her hands as though drawing a pinup.

"I'm all over you. Do you feel me? Am I heavy enough?" Coleen reached up and put a hand on each of Alice's shoulders and spun her around. "How's your back, Alice?"

"My back?" Anger and humiliation competed for first place.

"Slipped discs?" Coleen asked. "Sciatica?" The trainer knew the answer. Medical forms had been required.

"I'm fine."

Coleen reached up and pressed Alice's shoulders. "Excellent. You're first. Squat down."

Alice obeyed, stymied by what gymnastic feat might be expected.

"Brace yourself."

Alice tightened her muscles.

Coleen leapt on her back. "Get up. Walk."

Alice, stumbling under Coleen's weight, tried to stand. Finally, after tensing her stomach muscles to protect herself, she rose and then took a halting step.

"Giddyap!" Coleen yelled straight and loud into her ear. She dug her hands into Alice's shoulders and wrapped her legs around her waist. "Around the room, please."

All the women held themselves in some way. They hugged their upper arms, laced their fingers, pressed their lips, and unintentionally moved closer to one another.

Alice circled the room, blinking away tears of pain and rage as Valentina narrated. "This is it, ladies. You are nothing but packhorses carrying hideous pounds of flesh, tying fat around your middle, your thighs, and your hips. You chew up every morsel of flavor and then let it lay on your body. A succubus, dragging you into the ground. A succubus you invited into the precious home you call your body."

CHAPTER 11

ALICE

When Alice finished her lap around the room, Valentina forced the rest of the women to carry Coleen on their back. Lauretta, the shortest, appeared destined to end as a deflated balloon on the ground. She struggled one short step at a time as her fellow *Waisted* enrollees took prayerful positions.

"Go," Hania whispered. "You can do it!"

Emboldened by Hania, the women joined in, quietly urging Lauretta forward until Valentina silenced them, moving down the line with her pad. "Shot. Shot. Shot," she said, continuing until Lauretta dragged Coleen in silence.

"Sorry, ladies, but you got fat alone," Jeremiah said. "You gotta learn to become thin alone."

Alice's cramps increased. She could tell that her tampon was soaked and that blood now leaked to her pad. She tried to catch Valentina's eye, needing the bathroom, ready to seek permission. How quickly they had broken them down.

Spasms went through Alice's lower half. "Valentina?"

The woman turned, anger coloring her face.

Alice rushed out the words. "I need the restroom."

"You'll wait."

What would Bebe do?

"I'm not asking for permission. I'm asking where it is."

"And I'm telling you to wait."

"This isn't a wait situation." Alice turned left to right, trying to guess which way to walk.

Daphne stepped forward and stood beside her. "Me, too. I must go. *Now.* It's a medical emergency."

"You are grown women. Act like it," Valentina said.

Jeremiah, meanwhile, was smiling as he marched around the perimeter of the room, which almost made Alice's head pop off with rage. She headed toward him.

Valentina hurried after her, followed by Daphne. "What do you think you are doing?" She reached out to grab Alice's arm.

Jennifer stepped forward. "Let. Her. Go."

Alice tried not to chuckle when the blonde woman jumped back. She hadn't done it much, Jennifer's version of "Boo!" But it always remained in her arsenal. The ease of scaring a white woman made her want to laugh. Or cry.

Valentina sent them filthy glares. "You," she said to Daphne. "Wait here."

Daphne stepped back with a smile.

"Go that way." Valentina tipped her head toward the door in the back of the room. "And hurry."

Alice raced down a well-appointed hallway, past a grand staircase, distantly aware of the colonial portraits hung. Her first moments of gratitude since arriving came when spotting sanitary products in the Puritan-simple bathroom. The need to rush fought with desires to never go back; to duck under the mysterious sign and escape.

No wonder they took phones and wallets. Otherwise, mass exodus was certain. She reminded herself of the Mobie. How these folks produced excellence enough to win awards. There must be a method to this madness.

When Alice returned, the women were grouped by twos: Seung and Susannah, Jennifer and Lauretta, and Hania and Daphne.

Valentina nodded toward the last duo. "There's your place. With your buddy and the cute one."

And boom: Alice and Valentina had become enemies.

"How did we end up three to a room? Do you think because we spoke up the most? How am I going to fit this all in one drawer?" Enough underwear covered Hania's bed to satisfy a small country of plump women. She stroked the one outfit they had let her keep: the "going home" clothes they'd been told to bring, meant to spur them on in anticipation of being sent home at least forty-plus pounds lighter. Which sounded insane. Ten pounds a week or more?

"More likely, they set up the pairings before-hand." Alice didn't believe her words but wanted to comfort the younger woman. Documentary makers witnessed, never forced, drama, but they stacked the cards in favor of the spectacle.

"They must have washing machines." Daphne pointed to her own small pile of all-black under-wear and bras.

"What if the machines break?" Hania squinted as though foraging for disastrous possibilities. "What if we have to wait turns?"

"We'll wash a few pieces in the sink." Alice tried to hide her dismay at sharing a room with two strangers, trying to convince herself that the gathering nightmare storms would recede and soon this place would match the words in the *Waisted* brochure:

Those joining us in the green hills of Vermont will be afforded the unique opportunity to spend an entire month exploring ways to bring them-selves into balance.

Mindfulness. Forthrightness. Honesty. We believe by bringing these values to the forefront, women will have the opportunity to choose exactly who they want to be.

"The sink? With three of us in here sharing

one bathroom?" Hania threw herself back on the bed, splaying across her rainbow of silken underthings. Seen in XXL, red silk lingerie appeared sadder more than appealing. Alice struck the thought from her brain. Why shouldn't Hania parade around like a model for Victoria's Secret? If the girl couldn't do it now, in her twenties, when would she?

The convent-like room measured perhaps twenty by thirty. Three twin beds covered with white quilts decorated with sprays of cornflowers, made a U. Each was allotted a nightstand with one drawer, a shelf above her bed, and a white milk-glass reading lamp.

Daphne picked up the pillow and gave a connoisseur's squeeze.

"Down or foam?" Hania asked. "I can't believe they didn't let us bring pillows."

"Foam. Hard as a rock," Daphne answered. "Maybe they thought we'd secretly stash popcorn inside ones we brought. The commander wants us to be uncomfortable. Build us up. 'Commander'! Sounds like he's trying to build a tin-pot army." Daphne grinned at Alice. *I'm funny! I want to be your friend!*

White girls wanted credit and acknowledgment for acting the way any decent human should behave. That Boston remained such a hub of racism—some hidden, some as obvious as the weather—didn't register with them. Alice had no intention to be grateful for *normal.* White girls aching to be her friend ripped out her kishkes, as her mother would say. Connecting just shouldn't require gymnastics.

She suspected Daphne was Jewish. One Jew usually recognized another. Her mother loved to talk about the special connection between black and Jew, but each time Alice thought of this, arch conservatives like Sheldon Adelson came to mind. When she said this to Bebe, her mother waved away the words with "Every group has idiots."

Jewish and mixed-race folk were linked in their desire to claim those who belonged to their tribe. Even now, she and Sharon Jane alerted each other upon spotting a newly discovered member. Recently S.J. texted her *did u know Pete Wentz has a black Jamaican grandfather?*

They were no different than Bebe lifting her chin, pointing to a picture of Scarlett Johansson, and saying "Jew." Alice's father, another player in the game, would reply, "half-Jew, to be accurate."

Finding Jewish-black celebrities was her parents' idea of a Google jackpot. Rashida Jones! Lisa Bonet! Tracee Ellis Ross! They'd read names aloud to Macon and Alice. Who but mixed-race and Jewish people had so many sites devoted to listing members of the tribe?

Now Alice smiled at Daphne, feeling her

father's encouragement at the generosity of turning up her lips. Even if the woman's bravery in helping her get to the bathroom had been eagerness to demonstrate her liberalism, her willingness to take a hit for Alice did show courage.

Hania groaned. "I can't sleep on foam."

"Call housekeeping. Call Valentina," Alice said. "She's sure to help you."

"That woman has it out for you," Daphne said.

"For us." Alice opened the drawer to put away her underthings and pulled her hands away as though spiders lay in wait. "What the hell?" She picked up the slithery material and shook out an article of clothing made of mottled orange-yellow stretchy fabric that would not have been out of place on a rocket ship to Mars.

Daphne reached into her dresser and withdrew a matching one, using her fingers as pincers. "What on God's earth is this fabric? And who in their right mind wears that color?"

"I think they chose it with intent." Alice rummaged further and came up with a shapeless, slightly sheer nightshirt. Also a shade of rotting pumpkin. "What's our theme here?"

"Halloween?" Hania asked.

"Harvest? Vegetable death?" Daphne moved to one of the three chairs arranged in a circle on the round rag rug, the jumpsuit still in her hand. "The brochure called the place austere. Designed to help us find the inner strength we need to rely on our own resources for change."

"Through shame and torture?" Alice asked. She sat opposite Daphne as Hania folded her silky things, aware Hania might be the left-out point of their triangle.

Alice and Daphne could bond over missing their children. Where Hania had put up a picture of her boyfriend as her single allowed personal item of a nonhygienic or skin care nature—the exact words of the emailed instructions—the others displayed family pictures.

Daphne had teenagers: an attractive, if pouty, daughter, so thin she appeared breakable. Alice wondered if the girl's fragility came naturally or if she starved herself. The son, with his Clark Kent spectacles, matched the geeky-hip affect favored by boys these days. Daphne's husband's uncomfortable smile said he preferred holding the camera to being photographed.

And Daphne? She held the same pose universally used by fat women. The same position Alice, and likely Hania, if she became a mother, would hold before the camera. Hiding behind her children, angled so that only her face and spill of hair showed. In Alice's shot, Libby sat in her lap and Clancy stood over her, giving her the ability to cut off her thighs with cropping magic.

Daphne shook out the hideous jumpsuit. "Why would they pick something so obviously unflattering? A tee shirt and sweats would work fine. Yoga pants. A sweatshirt. Shit, even a sports bra would look better."

Hania, frowning, joined them in the circle. "Everything about this is mean. Do they actually believe this will help us lose weight?"

"Do they care?" Alice asked.

Clancy had never trusted the principals from Acrobat Films. He said their supposed genius masked misogynist visions. Their cold documentaries bordered on vicious, whatever the topic. In his opinion, Acrobat Films were a nest of nihilists.

"We'll go through this together," Daphne said.

"What's their end game, I wonder?" While planning this trip, Alice flew on wide wings of rage, never questioning why the film company underwrote the entire operation, including covering the salary each of them was surely losing by participating. At the time, she saw only the online clip included in the web application, which showed five women around a table discussing their body image in ways that brought Alice to tears.

They hadn't been wearing jumpsuits.

"Did you notice how they stressed *alone?*" Daphne asked. "That we gained *alone* and will only lose *alone?* Do you think that philosophy works?"

That Alice's best friend, Sharon Jane, provided

her with solidarity was a given. Friendship sustained women's fortitude.

"No," Alice said. "But I believe their goal had us walking out looking good. To make their point about their philosophy. There must be an argument for what they're pushing. I can take whatever crap they hand us if I can walk out of here a new person."

"So you think it will work?" Hania asked, as though Alice were an oracle.

"I do believe that." She held her hand out and helped Hania to a standing position.

"Let's put on the hideous motherfuckers," Daphne said. "We'll be the sisterhood of the traveling bulges."

CHAPTER 12

DAPHNE

Daphne felt both better and worse than she'd imagined. She wondered why any of them was there. These were the women she met at Weight Watchers, so this could simply be a spa where they learned to eat well and got massages.

Except it wasn't. And that's what made her feel worse. What neuroses connected this disparate group?

A bell sounded. Daphne jumped off the chair at the sound and then laughed. "What the hell are we doing here?"

Alice nodded. "As the kids at my community center say, I feel you."

Gratitude washed over Daphne. She'd always felt a need for female camaraderie. Here, she recognized, it might save them. "Time to face the pumpkin suits."

The three of them turned from each other for privacy, pulled on their jumpsuits, and prepared to leave the room.

"Have we landed smack in the middle of *The Handmaid's Tale*? Should we worry?" Daphne tugged at the clingy fabric sticking like a layer of unwanted skin.

"*The Handmaid's Tale*?" Hania asked.

Daphne withheld judgment. Reading wasn't everyone's source of comfort and joy. "*The Handmaid's Tale* is a story of women held—"

"Oh, wait, wait . . . with Elisabeth Moss. And Samira Wiley. I saw the show but didn't read the book. I'm not a big reader," Hania said. "I'm a geek. I build code. You know."

Daphne *didn't* know. Coding meant no more than a computer-related word to her. Who should be judgmental now?

Hania swiveled from Daphne to Alice and back. "Don't you find this place a bit too intense? Are we in danger?"

"Of course not." Daphne wished she felt more certain. She raised her eyebrows at Alice. "Right?"

"My husband sort of works with the guys running this show. Well, they're colleagues. Both filmmakers. These guys might be rough, but they want what we want. I think they're what I need."

Daphne exhaled. "Okay. Tough I can take." She stiffened her shoulders, took a deep breath, and led the way out.

Women were emerging from the other bedrooms. The seven, including Daphne—bulges and curves in the usual and most unusual places, stuffed in their iridescent stretch suits—walked the plush burgundy carpet lining the hallway floor. Daphne wanted to shake off her uneasiness and declare the end of hating herself. When she returned home, Sam and she would talk about everything openly; they'd build a transparent life.

Still. This place.

A cavernous gym to which they were led swallowed up the women. Daphne tapped Alice with a surreptitious finger. "What do you think this room was before?"

"A staging area to sell slaves."

"And now they use it for sex trafficking," Daphne said. "They're getting us in shape for the buyers."

Hania widened her eyes. "Quiet! Valentina is watching. Do you want a shot?"

What would shots bring? Carrying Coleen on her back, if it was meant to break her, had begun the job well. The muscles and tendons in her back felt as though she'd been stretched on a medieval rack.

Valentina and Coleen prowled like cats as Jeremiah consulted with the photographer. Perhaps instructing them to get crotch shots. Possibly the entire operation was a cover to make porn for fat freaks, with Acrobat bankrolling films to make money from a subset of men addicted to seeing fat women strain as they exercised. Why not? Weirder perversions existed. Indeed, only porn could explain these bizarre semi-sheer outfits. Daphne turned to Alice, ready to run the theory by her, but Alice's slight head shake warned her to keep quiet.

Leather and steel devices loomed everywhere. Old-fashioned medicine balls were stacked in piles. A track circled the room. A tall wooden laddered frame climbed the far wall.

An iron box held hand grippers and some odd contraption of wood, springs, and a pulley. A pyramid of Russian kettlebells lurked in a corner.

A colossal platform scale dominated the room.

Daphne shifted from foot to foot, watching Seung pull on her ponytail, raveling and unraveling her coil of purple hair. Lauretta examined her bright nails as though meditating on the meaning of life. Waiting was hell. Daphne tried to estimate the size of the gym. The room rivaled the enormous entry by at least a factor of five. The rubber floor, a dusty black, felt gritty even through her sneakers—but that had to be her imagination, right?

The air smelled of cracked leather and acrid metal. Missing Sam and the kids doubled her over. How much did she hate herself to leave them and volunteer for this?

Jeremiah stepped forward and held out his hands as though bestowing a benediction. "Welcome to your new home, ladies, where everything is up to you. How hard you work, how much or little you eat—everything is in your control, your decision-making. Each of you will be stripped to your essence, uncovering who you are and if you have the strength to become a normal size. You all know the most obvious thing about being fat. Nothing hides it. Walk around fat, walk around announcing your weakness."

With those words, Coleen, across from them, pushed a chrome button. The walls turned from dark to a reflective surface. Mirrors engulfed them, mirrors sharper and brighter than Daphne imagined existed; mirrors that made her think of Sylvia Plath's words: *I am silver and exact. I have no preconceptions. / Whatever I see I swallow immediately.*

Mirrors courtesy of Satan.

"Walk to the wall," Valentina ordered.

TIP: ReflectUrWeight. Instant weight loss visualization app demonstrates what you would look like if you lost (or gained) weight.
WEIGHT LOST: They had to be kidding.

Bulbs mimicking harsh midday light ensured that every bulge became visible through the sheer cloth, advertised every piece of flesh. Shadows drew lines around the apron of fat hanging from Daphne's stomach. Her complexion turned sallow. Her chin sagged. The thin, clinging fabric exaggerated the dimples and cellulite, the map

143

of crevices made by every ounce pushing out her skin.

Valentina plucked small white squares from a blue package and handed a few to each woman. "Clean your faces."

Daphne found herself holding wet makeup removers. She peeked at Alice and Hania. Like hers, their makeup possessed a defining aura. Alice artfully layered shades. Coppery foundation glazed her skin to a perfect finish, highlighting the slight hazel glint in her irises. Hania's deeply brown eyes had been drawn into Cleopatra wings.

Daphne had packed enough makeup for a full squadron of cosmetic lovers, including tricks of her stage trade for fun. Lipstick, mascara, and all their cousins were her security blankets.

Valentina crossed her arms over her chest. "Naked faces, ladies."

Seven women considered the mirror, lit harsh enough to perform an operation. Only Seung had arrived barefaced. Daphne held the damp tissue to her face, unwilling to see herself drained of color under these lights.

Coleen walked up behind her. "Particularly you, Ms. Makeup Artist."

Alice snuck a look at Daphne in the mirror, lifting her chin just enough to send a message of solidarity and an expression that said *Interesting job!*

"This helps us?" Daphne asked. "Seems like an exercise in humiliation."

Before Coleen lifted her notebook and yelled *"Shot!"* Jeremiah walked over, followed by the flannel-shirted cameraman. "You hide, but I see you. You hide in your black smock and your black leggings. You paint yourself into a walking, breathing, Photoshopped copy.

"But at night, when you get into bed with your husband, who's there?" He put a hand under her elbow and raised her arm. "Only by facing ourselves, do we change. Have the guts to see who is there."

Daphne's hand shook as she wiped off streaks of black mixed with beige and rose. Wiping away her mascara revealed colorless lashes she detested. Spots of discolored skin appeared: patches of rosacea; ugly freckles; the childhood scar from when Bianca pushed her, and she fell into the corner of their parents' glass coffee table.

Everything showed.

Jeremiah swept his gaze over them. "You came here for help you couldn't find yourself. See who you truly are."

They stared at themselves and one another in the mirrors. A line of stout women in stretchy jumpsuits of a color that suited nobody. Beautiful Hania's Indian skin appeared jaundiced. Lauretta's golden perfection turned ashy; Alice's glow curdled. Susannah's face resembled skim milk. Seung's now tallow-colored cast clashed with the purple hair. The mottled orange depressed Jennifer's deep brown, in direct opposition to how her bright orange glasses flattered.

Daphne appeared porcine. Her colorless lashes and mottled pink skin resembled a pig's face. Had she any object in her hand, the temptation to pulverize her image might have been impossible to resist.

How did Sam bear waking each morning and seeing her?

"When I call your name, go where I point. Seung, over there." He pointed toward Coleen. "Jennifer, Lauretta, follow her."

He waited a few beats for them to reach Coleen and then turned. "Susannah, Daphne, Alice, Hania, to Valentina."

"What fresh hell . . ." Daphne muttered.

"Shot," Coleen said, pointing at her. "You're skating now."

"Watch yourself," said Valentina when they reached her. "You mess up, and the whole team suffers. Susannah, you are a lucky person. You are only with this group sometimes. You are the one who will switch back and forth."

Valentina opened a door and ushered Daphne and the others into a chilled room.

"This is our medical office. You'll be examined by a doctor in a few minutes and then—"

"Will we have dinner?" Susannah pointed to the clock. "It's past seven. We've been traveling—"

"We eat continental style tonight. I think the doctor will agree there is little chance of anyone starving to death. But if you cannot take it, there you go." She tipped her chin at a mammoth glass bowl filled with M&M's sitting on a low table on the other side of the room. Bowls of celery, carrots, and slices of hard-boiled eggs competed for attention.

"Help yourself. Only one rule. Sit there and face that mirror." She gestured at short stools with tiny backs where they'd be forced to watch themselves squashed into positions that would double their fat rolls. Susannah's thighs and ass would eat those child-sized pieces of wood.

"Here is the story, ladies. You are here to lose weight. I am here to help you, and I will do anything to make you meet your goals. We have two teams. Susannah goes back and forth as told. We built a formula that you don't have to consider. It has been done for you.

"You will see the doctor, and he will tell you every disease facing you if you continue down this road of obesity. And he will suggest you eat twelve hundred calories a day."

Daphne exhaled. Twelve hundred calories. Unquestionably, she'd subsisted on less with one diet or another. The trick here would be adding in hours of exercise. Pounds would disappear. She touched the thick roll at her middle and imagined it gone. Imagined being one with her sisters. Slipping on a simple dress without tugging and adjusting. No more ponchos. No more gymnastics to cover every hated part of her body.

Valentina snapped her fingers. "Do not look so happy. My news will be different. If you want to win and you want to please me, you will never eat that much. Eight hundred calories. Maximum. But I expect less."

They were called into the exam room alphabetically. While waiting, they picked at the eggs and vegetables. First Hania and then Susannah snuck a few lone M&M's. Finally, Daphne's turn for the doctor came.

She walked into a small, blindingly clean room. Glass-fronted hung cabinets showed stacks of medical supplies, paper gowns, and table liners. A deep-blue leather-topped stool offered the sole spot of color.

"Dr. William Ash. Pleased to meet you . . ."—he glanced at the paper on the counter—". . . Daphne."

Central casting couldn't have provided a man less likely to induce comfort in overweight women. Even Daphne's slinky sisters would feel squeamish undressing in front of Dr. Ash, who'd fit better on a soap opera than in a hospital, with his thick, prematurely white hair, square-shouldered stance, and even features.

"Here." He handed Daphne a paper gown. "Everything must be taken off. Opening in the back."

"Am I allowed privacy?" she asked.

"My write-up, my conclusions, will be based on what I see. That report is, of course, under patient confidentiality. Trust me. This is part of the plan for your recovery."

Trust me. Words she never trusted.

He sat on the stool, pen and notebook in hand, and gave no further guidance. Daphne pulled off the orange horror. The fabric spread like a mangy tabby cat when she threw it on the floor, not wanting to cross the room in front of the man and hang it on the hook. Let him write up that. She slipped on the just-inadequate gown and faced him.

"Sit, please."

She perched at the end of the cold table, paper rustling under her bare behind. As Ash peered into her ears and throat, sweet-winey fumes rose from him. Daphne had spent enough hours close to people's faces to immediately recognize the smell. His clammy hands disgusted her when he took her wrist to check her pulse.

He placed the cold stethoscope on her bare back. "You know what sensible weight loss is? Getting it the heck off your body as fast as possible, before you choke. That's what makes sense."

He held up a fist, opened it a small bit and then closed it shut. "See? Your heart, encased in fat, trying to beat."

It sounded like bullshit, but Daphne sat rigid and silent. Naked except for the paper drape. Concentrating on the blindingly white medical jacket covering his light blue shirt and rep tie.

"Lie down, please."

The doctor's hands on her breasts felt less like an exam and more as though her breasts were oranges being squeezed for juice. When he stuck the speculum in for a Pap smear—a test that made no sense, but she kept her mouth shut—he used none of the chatter doctors typically employ to break the extreme discomfort of the moment. Dr. Ash stood between her dimpled thighs as though she were a piece of pork on display.

The oddest part of the horrid minutes Daphne spent with Ash was that he never weighed her, though he acknowledged the shiny scale. "No need to step on that today. We'll let you be surprised."

"I hate burpees," Alice announced two days later. "Of all the exercises, I hate burpees the most."

Daphne was prone on the floor as she listened to Alice's declaration. The three of them—Daphne, Alice, and Hania—lay in a row, face up, too close, resembling tired, panting sardines.

None of them wanted to waste a moment of precious rest time.

"I wish I still thought of Burpees as seeds." Hania groaned. "My mother devours the catalogs all winter. Now it will always seem like she's reading about torture."

"We grew up calling them squat thrusts. Either name, they're wretched, but rope climbing is my horror." Daphne thought for a moment, weighing the horrors of the various exercises. "My sister will probably need to operate on the scars I'll have from sliding down."

"Burns from the ropes might be the worst," Alice said, "but this one is torture, *plus* confusing. I never get the order right. Stand. Squat. Hands on the floor. Flip to push-up position. Do a push-up. Magically bring legs forward, back to squatting position. Jump up. Repeat. Too many damn steps. And why that stupid name?"

"Some guy named Burpee invented the exercise," Hania said.

"How do you even know that?" Daphne asked.

"I collect weird facts."

"Weird hobby." Alice groaned. "My back is killing me."

"Burpees. Rope climbing. All of it makes me feel as though I've gone back in time to seventh-grade gym class. The worst humiliation and—" Daphne stopped.

"My mother got a note from our doctor saying

I couldn't do gym." Hania snorted. "So they put me in a modern-dance class, and I had to wear a leotard. I went from wearing an awful pair of shorts and a box of a tee shirt to having skintight material showing every lump on my body."

"What kind of note kept you from gym but made you do dance class?" Alice asked.

"Something about sinuses and pressure from certain exercises. My uncle wrote the note."

Alice turned to face Daphne. "What happened to you in gym?"

Daphne kept quiet. She hadn't remembered the incident for years, and now that she had, she wanted to jam the memories back into whichever closet of traumas she'd locked them.

"Sometimes saying aloud the stuff that makes you crazy helps the pain go away, right?" Sympathy suffused soft-hearted Hania's words.

"So like a spoonful of sugar making the medicine go down?" Daphne asked.

"That's not an apt analogy, is it?" Alice lifted her leg a few inches. "But I could use the sugar."

"I've never talked about this to anyone." Daphne gathered her courage. If she couldn't tell the story here, where shame had become their daily companion, then where could she? "When it happened, my parents were sending me to an all-girls private school. One where phys ed was a big deal. They chose the place because sports was the holy grail. If I'd known they made exercise the centerpiece here, believe me, I'd never have come."

"I doubt any of us would have come if we had a clue to what goes on here," Alice said.

Hania swiveled into crisscross position. "What happened?"

"Lots. The top two horrors? Swimming—*competitive* swimming, no less—was a big deal. And to make it fair"—here Daphne made air quotes—"they made us wear official school swimsuits with sizes marked by color."

Alice gasped. "That's cruel!"

"Yup. My mother loved the color coding. When I complained, she said, 'Maybe this will finally make you lose weight.'"

"Did it?" Hania asked.

"Are you kidding? On days that we had swimming, I ate twice as much. Especially the day I moved from red to purple. Blue was small, green was average, red was large. And purple? Purple meant you were a whale, and only I got that honor. There I was, in a sea of blues and greens, a big, fat, purple Barney the Dinosaur."

"Did the girls make fun of you?" Hania asked.

"Worse. They moved away from me as though I had a disease. I became invisible. And then, to make it truly gruesome, the softball coach started weighing us on the field."

"On the field?" Alice shook her head. "Why? How?"

"Probably to make it worse for us. The coach lived to teach us how to toughen up. She kept a square piece of wood by the bleachers. And a scale in the equipment shed that she dragged out before the games. She'd call us up to the scale in alphabetical order."

"Was your last name Sorkin then?"

"No. Bernays. I took Sam's last name when I got married." She sent Alice an embarrassed grin. "You kept your birth name, right? I was behind the times."

"Or ahead of it," Alice said. "Seems now everyone is taking their husband's name. But I knew my mother would give me quite a hard time if I took Clancy's name."

"But she took your father's name?" Hania asked.

"Yes. She says everybody did it then—which, despite her swearing to it, judging by her friends, wasn't always the case in the seventies. She wanted to become one with my father. I think her feeling was that if she was gonna marry a black man and put them both in line for constant judgment and jeopardy, then she wanted to totally merge with him, name and all. Somehow, when I married Clancy, she believed the opposite. At least for me. Though *I* made the decision to stay Alice Thompson, not her. I couldn't take on one more identity. I'm black. I'm white. I'm Jewish. I'm Southern Baptist. If I became a Rivera, everyone would assume I was Puerto Rican, and then I'd have one more layer to reveal."

"Did Clancy mind?"

"No. But his father minded. Clancy's an only child, and it became my job to preserve his family name. Argh. Old stuff. So, what happened when you got weighed, Daphne?"

Daphne stared at the metal beams running along the gym ceiling. Something lifted as Alice led them past the shibboleths of discussing race and culture. Why did they avoid the topic, as though it were something shameful? Weighing down issues with forbidden hot zones made it impossible to become the truest of friends. Like, how Daphne had never told Ivy the thing that bothered her most in the world, despite working side-by-side for years.

"With the name Bernays, I was usually first or second in line. Anyway, when they weighed me, I learned the art of dissociation. I shut down my ears. There were people already in the stands. My teammates. And on the worst day, my parents, who'd come to watch a game, were there.

"The coach would announce everyone's weight twice. Like this: 'A hundred sixty-eight. *Bernays.* One hundred and sixty-eight.' I was fourteen. Most of the girls weighed between a hundred four and one twenty-four. I wanted to die. I swear, the coach screamed the number loud enough for everyone in Massachusetts to hear.

She emblazoned *168* in skywriting. When I got home, my mother began insanely lecturing me about losing weight—mainly, I think, because she'd been so embarrassed. I went to my room, got under the covers, and wouldn't come out of my room until they agreed to let me switch to public school. For a week, I just kept repeating, 'I'm never going back.' My sisters snuck food to me."

"How horrible." Hania appeared teary at Daphne's story.

"I held out, and I won. I started going to public school after Christmas vacation."

"I guess my mother told the truth," Alice said. " 'What doesn't kill us, makes us stronger.' "

"Maybe we'll leave here being able to lift the world off our shoulders." Daphne poked at her emotional self, trying to figure out if telling the story helped or made her sore, but at the moment, she simply felt numb.

CHAPTER 13

DAPHNE

By day six of what would be four weeks in the mansion, Daphne, Hania, and Alice resembled prisoners looking to break rules, hating and continually watching their guards.

Above all other humiliations stood the daily afternoon weigh-ins.

Stripped to her underwear, barefaced, and sweaty from exercise, Daphne tried to balance having dropped ten pounds against the horror of standing almost naked, with the *Waisted* camera whirring, while being stared at by Jeremiah, Mike the cameraman, Dr. Ash, and the trainers. And seen, though never peered at, by the other six women.

Sam would have been horrified by everything here, with the two-pound-a-day weight loss topping his list. *It's just water,* she told him in her mind. *Don't worry.*

More like "Don't ask, don't tell" would be how she shared information with him. Even with his asking, most of it she'd never tell.

Eating under Valentina's nonstop watch wearied them—especially at breakfast, a meal that managed to be awful and too small simultaneously. Daphne found herself wasting hours staring at and thinking about Valentina.

She pushed the last bits of mealy egg yolk on her fork. "Have you noticed that Valentina paces in a square?"

"Congratulations," Alice said. "You're partaking in the tradition of all enslaved people: studying the masters and thus knowing them far better than the dominators know the subjugated. We win in the end."

Valentina whipped her head around from where she drank coffee. With milk. Not black like theirs. "Win? Are you talking about winning? You lard butts want to win, you stop stuffing your mouths. You eat like animals."

"Perhaps she thinks we're going to slip carvings of our flesh into our bowls." Daphne spoke low, as by now she was convinced that Valentina had the hearing range of a greater wax moth.

Years ago, when Audrey had chosen the five senses as her sixth-grade class project, she subjected the entire family to rambling discourses, complete with visual aids, about the extraordinary hearing power of the greater wax moth. After days of staring, Daphne saw the resemblance between the bulging, shiny eyes that overpowered Valentina and that creature.

"At this point, I'm ready to go full *Alive*," Alice said.

"What's that?" Hania cut her egg into microscopic pieces. Each used different methods for pretending their poorly prepared, tasteless meals were larger. They all wrestled one egg for breakfast, brought to the table still resting in the old Teflon pans in which they were fried, offering them poison along with utter dullness. No salt. No pepper. Not one sprig of an herb.

When asked why the lack of flavor, wondering why they weren't learning how to prepare spicy, exciting meals on a dime of calories, Valentina threw the party line: "Crutches. All you want are crutches."

By now, they realized the cook, who was also the housekeeper, didn't give a damn how their food tasted.

"*Alive* is a story—decades old, but true—of plane crash survivors in the Andes Mountains," Daphne explained. "The passengers who lived survived by eating the flesh of the dead."

A week ago, Hania would have groaned in disgust. Now she looked as though she understood cannibalism.

Meals were served in the barest-of-bones former servants' area. The other group ate in a basement kitchen. She learned this while whispering to Seung during a rare break after a run, both sprawled on their backs in the cold, leafy grass.

The rough-splintered table was either raw

wood or the finish had been worn away during the last century. The jagged edges of the brown earthenware dishes appeared gnawed. Alice suspected rats. Daphne guessed Valentina—that she stayed skinny by eating shards of old pottery. Hania thought they'd filed the plates. Perhaps ugly plates discouraged eating.

> **TIP:** Control your appetite by using red crockery. Researchers theorize that red is associated with "danger and prohibition."
> —*Researchers from the University of Parma, published in the journal* Appetite
> **DOLLARS SPENT ON RED DISHES AND KITCHEN GOODS:** Endless.
> **WEIGHT LOST:** Zero.

Daphne dipped an iceberg lettuce leaf into mustard and crunched, hoping against hope that she'd learn to appreciate this horrid stuff. Ivy's information about this place had been so far off that she feared she'd come to the wrong place or that the entire project was a scam. After exposing her desperate need to lose weight and uncover who the hell she was supposed to be in this world, Ivy did what Ivy always did. She researched and soon arrived at Alchemy waving a brochure. "I found your place."

The paper on which it was printed, thick and a bit rough but still rich and heavy, imparted a sense of organic money. Good works. Caring. Down comforters with heavy cotton sheets.

The pamphlet made it seem like she'd be going to a Whole Foods version of a Weight Watchers resort-spa, if such a place existed.

Valentina crept up from behind, so quiet that only a wax moth would hear her approaching, and flicked the plate with a square pink nail. "You eat every drop, do you? Perhaps you want more? Toasted muffins to go with the egg? Eh, *chazzer*? Oink, oink! Is that what you do all day? Go snuffle around like pigs?"

Silent connection fizzed between Daphne and Alice.

The days never changed. They woke at seven, ate breakfast at eight, and hit the gym by eight thirty. Lifting kettlebells, running, swimming laps, cycling—all of it went on until they dropped or vomited or both. After lunch, where they fell on every shred of carrot and slice of turkey breast, they returned to the fetid gym air. Daphne could say it was the worst part of her day, but, in fact, it made up the entire day, as they did little else until after sundown. They exercised more than nine hours daily with brief breaks for food and short rest periods during which most of them slept on their sweat-slickened mats.

Nightly, following a seven o'clock dinner, they slogged back to their rooms and crawled into bed. After burrowing under the covers, they took turns telling stories of their real lives, as they recalled the world they'd left behind, and avoided reliving the day, other than assuring themselves no pain, no gain.

"They must know what they're doing," they repeated nightly. The payback had to be worth these awful tests of will.

Without fail, Hania would fall asleep first. Afterward, as though they'd tucked in their child, Alice and Daphne whispered truths to each other. The way Alice described her mother, Daphne imagined the woman as an odd opposite of her own. The woman, Bebe, encouraged Alice in all she did, battled for women's rights, was unapologetic in her undyed gray hair and unmade-up self. What sounded like heaven to Daphne brought confusion to Alice, whose self-worth remained high only when she lived according to the standards of moral perfection that her mother honored, and heeded no white beauty standard—as defined by Bebe.

Daphne tried to understand Alice's discomfort—so different from her own life. Where Daphne never pleased her mother and fed on the slightest positive-appearing nod as maternal affirmation, Alice choked on mother love. If everything you did was considered perfect, and the only way you could upset your mother was by trying to fit in with the norms, what was the logical solution?

They'd barely muster up enough energy to speak for fifteen minutes before falling asleep—often midsentence. And then it all began again.

Like now. Another day, another inedible and meager breakfast.

"Come." Valentina's harsh order brought Daphne back to reality. "Pick up your dishes and wash them. Enough eating."

Once the last clean dish rested on the thin white towel, they walked down the hall toward their workouts.

After washing up and being herded into the gym, Daphne thought of the daily choices and prayed to be chosen for laps in the pool, where at least she became invisible and remained cool.

"Dragon walk!" Valentina shouted. Daphne dragged herself to the right side of the gym, where Jennifer and Susannah stood with Coleen.

"Here." Coleen threw a pair of leather gloves to each of them. "Hurry."

Mike aimed his camera as they tugged on the stiff fabric. Working out with him filming made it far more difficult; the glass eye turned Daphne's movement to sludge. Mike wasn't a hunk, but worse; he resembled someone who could be Daphne's cousin from her father's side. Open-faced and warm-looking, with a wrestler's build. He seemed too familiar, making it difficult for her to dismiss him as background.

"Take positions." Coleen swirled her finger in the air.

Jennifer dropped down first, grunting as she fell to her hands and toes. Daphne carefully lowered herself next. Caution meant everything with this exercise, which Jeremiah had extra-poisoned by having them do it on a stretch of sand-gritted cement.

Finally, Susannah worked her way down. Balancing on hands and feet was especially difficult for her, being so bottom heavy.

Jeremiah ambled over, motioning Mike to follow. "Get this one. This is the top challenge. Heck, even military men have a hard time doing this more than a short time. Let's go, ladies. Let's walk like reptiles. Assume push-up positions. Do everything like me, in sync. Move one arm and opposite leg forward. Bend the knee to touch the elbow. Same movement for the other side. We'll count one repetition per step."

He dropped down and made the exercise—which they barely managed for two minutes—appear easy. They dragged themselves onward.

"Keep your backs straight!" Coleen shouted.

Daphne's forearms burned. Pain increased in her hands with each step. After ten reps, breathlessness threatened to bring her down. The gritty floor waited to rip her knees apart just as it did a day ago. Dragon-walk agony once again tormented her.

"Face forward." Jeremiah squatted over her, pushing her shoulders into position. "Elbow completely to knee. Move."

Susannah flopped down. Even knowing that shards of concrete pressed into her, Daphne envied the momentary break dropping brought.

"Up. Up now!" Coleen plucked at Susannah's sweaty jumpsuit.

Jennifer turned her head and caught Daphne's eye for a moment. *Fuck her,* Jennifer mouthed. *Fuck her twice,* Daphne responded.

They continued for twenty minutes—which in dragon-walk time equaled an hour of straight-out running—and were then sent to the following station. Cycling. Her thighs burned each time she pedaled down, but as in the kingdom of the blind, cycling compared to dragon walking was like ambling versus sprints.

For hours, they continued. Lauretta vomited while walking on a sharply inclined speedy treadmill. Valentina allowed her a moment's recuperation and a trip to the bathroom before handing her rags and a bucket to clean it.

Seung lay motionless next to a pair of twenty-pound barbells. Daphne noticed everyone sneaking worried glances. How long would she have to lie there before someone checked her pulse? Finally, she groaned and rolled over.

Daphne struggled, her arms shaking as she worked on the bicep curl machine.

"Control the weight!" Jeremiah yelled from yards away. Like Big Brother, he was everywhere.

Coleen blew a shrill whistle. "Cool down. Five minutes. Then line up."

The trainer stood before the giant scale, along with Dr. Ash. He held a gleaming black clipboard and silver pen, and his face looked all pinked up—maybe from whiskey or perhaps a recent facial.

They straggled to the scale and formed the line they always made. "Suits off, ladies," said Valentina.

Daphne wished she wore glasses so she could remove them and follow this next bit blindly, groping her way toward the weigh-in, letting everyone blur before her. Instead, she pulled her hair as fully in front of her eyes as possible. The daily weigh-ins were the nadir or highlight of their days, depending on how many pounds they were down.

Each of them had a different way of undressing. Hania shimmied the jumpsuit down quickly, getting over the pain fast. Alice stared straight ahead with her cold "Who cares? Eff you," expression, yanked off the muddy-orange fabric, and left it in a heap at her feet.

Daphne's disrobing felt like déjà vu, shocking her back in time to the horrors of high school locker rooms. Wiggle out one arm and then the other. Bend over while pulling off the damn thing, as though somehow she could hide her body by coiling it into a snake.

"Today we do things differently. More thoroughly." Coleen drew an imaginary circle. "Everything comes off before climbing up. Everything."

The heat from holding back screams flamed on Daphne's cheeks.

"We use this method to provide complete assurance that we award for the absolute most weight lost," Valentina said. "Otherwise how do we know which team is leading in weight loss?"

Bullshit.

Daphne looked around for confirmation that the others shared her disbelief. Did these people think someone might have sneaked in gossamer-thin panties and a bra whose weight would not show up, while some wore lead-lace-edged underwear?

Seung shuffled to the scale, hunching with an air of defeat.

"Move along," Coleen said. "We're all waiting."

The young woman inched off her green bra one strap at a time. Her hair hung lank across her shoulders as though it just didn't care anymore. Then, hooking her fingers into purple lace panties, she pulled them down in one defiant tug.

"Step on and turn, please." Ash held his hand out, gesturing to the scale.

The number *193* flashed on the screen. Beneath, it read *201,* Seung's beginning weight.

"Just eight pounds altogether," Jeremiah announced. "How does that make you feel?"

Seung shrugged as she stood there, her short muscled arms stretched down to cover as much of her stomach as she could manage.

"Are you proud of that?"

Seung moved her chin in a vague circle, swinging her hair, as though hoping if she showed the right attitude, Jeremiah would move on. But he wouldn't. He liked transforming them into squirming bugs, pinned in the spotlight.

"Yes?" she asked and answered simultaneously.

"Doctor?" Jeremiah asked.

"Eight pounds." Dr. Ash cocked his head. "One ninety-three. At five foot four, she is moderately obese. She entered severely obese. Her target weight, to be normal, is between one hundred ten and one forty-four. To be merely overweight, the target is a hundred forty-five to one seventy-five. What number do you want to see, Seung?"

"One twenty?" she asked and answered again.

"One hundred and twenty?" Ash repeated.

"One *ten,*" Jeremiah interjected. "You aim for the best when you're here. Understood?" He swiveled his head. "Understood? Let me hear you!"

They shouted back as instructed, chanting "the best" in unison.

Jeremiah nodded.

Seung pulled on her underwear. Daphne envied her.

Twenty pounds a week? Daphne tried to imagine Seung dropping eighty-three pounds, losing almost half of herself in the remaining weeks. The plan sounded insane. A punishment. Impossible.

Still, the thought that they could drop the worst of themselves in one punishing month drew them like proverbial moths. Why not stew in the revulsion, pounding away the prison of their bodies? Jeremiah called out the truth about the women when calling them prisoners of their own creations.

They needed—wanted—to believe that the goal lived in the realm of possibility and that these people possessed genius, despite the *Waisted* approach going against every so-called sensible diet on earth.

Daphne's misshapen thighs resembled bloated Parker House rolls. Doughy and white. The brown freckles spotting her skin might well have been overbaked dimples of cellulite flesh. Her thighs held years of English muffins, craters filled with melted butter; her stomach layered with crispy chocolate cookies, pot roast, and noodles; her arms plumped up with bowls of whipped mousse, light as air until it hit her body where it transmogrified into sleeves tightened by her expansion.

Daphne watched and waited. At yesterday's weigh-in, the scale registered 173 pounds. Ten pounds lost in five days. Despite hating this procedure, that morning her first emotion had been excitement at seeing what today brought; now, with forced nudity, she approached the scale as though facing the crucifix.

Daphne averted her eyes, hoping to offer some privacy. But even half blind, a sense of fleshy rolls, the other women's thatches of pubic hair barely visible through their overhanging stomachs, swam through her half-closed lids.

Fat women looked more naked than normal-weighted women.

Clothes made the woman. Naked made the shame.

Daphne silently recited a virtual rosary, ticking off things she'd never have to face again if she went through with this: from her mother's shame, to dreading Sam's touch—concentrating on avoiding his hand on her stomach, her thighs, as they made love; guiding him to her breasts and then to finishing the act so she could return to the state of being bodyless.

Her daughter's sadness. Her son's jolly avoidance.

The scale trilled up, hummed up and down, as

though Lauretta had broken the code when she stepped on and showed her weight moving in a week from 175 to 160. What scale wouldn't have sung with such a miraculous one-week, fifteen-pound loss? The programmed music resonated as the inner workings of the machine moved from the upper height of moderately obese to the lower end, closing in on being merely overweight.

Lauretta appeared wreathed in holiness, surrounded by angelic spirals of curls, ready to ascend to the heavens of acceptability, even as she shook and twitched, like all of them, from hunger and exhaustion.

Perhaps each of them prayed for the others to have lost less than she did. Or maybe only Daphne contained such smallness, such schadenfreude.

Not for her team, though, or at least not as much. The team concept had been left vague, with Susannah sent back and forth to balance events. Daily, small punishments boiled up. Treats were given to the winning team—winning a series of athletic competitions, from the five-mile hike (won by Coleen's team), to a swimathon (also won by Coleen's team), and on and on. They finally broke the Coleen winning streak in the tug of war, and then only because Susannah, assigned to Valentina's team, anchored the contest with the competitive ferocity of a starving Olympian trying to win her family's freedom. Grim-faced

Jennifer's gutting her way through any challenge offered might have beaten Susannah but for the grounding provided by Susannah's low and wide center of gravity.

When they learned that Susannah worked as a nursery school teacher, Daphne imagined toddlers climbing up onto her giant lap as though scaling the Matterhorn. Jennifer as a professor fit perfectly once you saw her control any room she entered.

Coleen's women led in treats that on the outside would have been laughable but here were akin to golden tickets. Oversized zero calorie Popsicles with flavors such as watermelon and coffee. The women's personalities played out as they either crunched the delicacies in moments or licked them for what seemed like hours. Lauretta was the queen of slowly mouthing the frozen sticks, drawing them in and out of her lips as though giving a frozen blow job, while they all licked along with her, coveting the chemical ice.

Next, Hania stepped up to the plate and stripped from her lacy underthings with such panache that one would think her a supermodel offering the world her beauty. Even Jeremiah appeared chastened by her haughty display.

Hania was the one-eyed queen in their kingdom of the blind. Her magnificence elevated everyone. Even without rimming her eyes in black and gilt, her deep sable irises against her gold skin reminded Daphne of the treasures in her family's Illuminate jewelry stores.

And, of course, Hania had entered *Waisted* the thinnest. Being the only one who began as overweight rather than obese, even if it was the highest end of overweight, made her the upper crust. Daphne, like all the women, studied the charts posted everywhere as though reading tarot cards. Hania had to travel through only one category to reach the promised land of normalcy.

The young woman carried herself as though she were the queen bee of the *Waisted* cast. Daphne and Alice treated her like their deluded daughter, a lesbian couple who kept their surprising sorority girl in check. Hania complained about everything—including not being able to wear her bright-yellow gold bangles and diamond studs—but the girl accepted anything to stay on the top of the heap.

Hania stepped up, presenting her nakedness as though offering something grand. With youth and luck, her fat was distributed throughout her body so that she appeared more adorably padded and plump than disturbingly lumpy like the rest of them.

Numbers blinked. Everyone waited as the pet of the group, their great hope, registered her success or failure. Digits flew up and down, flashing red until it settled into a fiery *163*. Down from 170. A mere 7 pounds.

Jeremiah sighed. He tried to hide it, but Hania was his favorite.

"Not a great showing, Hania."

Hania pulled her clothes on as though standing alone in the room. Tears trickled down her golden cheeks. "But I have less to lose," she said when she got back in line. "I can't lose as much as them. Right?"

"You have less to lose? You think you will lose slower? You eat less, little girl." Valentina tapped Hania's chest. "Adjust."

"Daphne!" Jeremiah called. "Your turn."

Her legs were stone. She should have been lying on a shrink's couch. Walking into a psych ward. Why had she left a loving man to face this psychopath?

The scale loomed.

Daphne glimpsed the exit sign. Would they stop her if she walked out?

CHAPTER 14

ALICE

Daphne looked like someone who'd been punched in the gut. Alice understood. Her turn came next.

She prayed for Daphne's collapse. Nothing life threatening, just awful enough to create chaos and save both Daphne and Alice from the horror of disrobing. Alice could only imagine her mother seeing this bullshit. Bebe would drag her out of there with the sudden strength of Wonder Woman.

If Bebe saw this, if Alice sent thought waves to her mother, Mom would have her father and Macon on the highway in ten minutes—driving under the speed limit, of course. No cops were trusted, but damn, expressly here, where, as her mother would say, "I do believe Vermont is the whitest state in the union."

Or was it Maine? For a moment, lost in light-headed hunger, Alice confused truth and fantasy. She turned, almost as though to see if her family were entering, but only Daphne, lips pressed together, remained in her field of vision. Poor Daph looked at the scale and Jeremiah as though she were considering a million-mile march. They locked eyes. Such an unlikely friend, Daphne. Not because she was chalk-white in that red-headed manner, or that she came from one of the wealthy towns bordering Boston, or that she spent her life transforming people. Those certainly added up to points of interest. But no, that wasn't the source of the unlikeliness.

Alice's initial reading of Daphne had taken place as they stood in the great hall, still in street clothes: hair styled, jewelry on, makeup masking the true women. She might have dismissed those markers, but Daphne's clothes, nondescript to invisibility—as though she shopped for indistinctness—told such an odd story. Her outfit made a racket of cognitive dissonance with the woman she presented above the neck: hair styled to fall in elegant waves, face buffed and lacquered to geisha-like stiffness, emerald studs gleaming from her earlobes, all topped and garnished with a thin river of gold chain—dotted with green, crystalline, and red stones—wrapping her neck.

Emeralds, diamonds, and rubies decorated Daphne—they shined too purely to be glass or crystal. The woman arrived in Vermont wrapped in treasure yet clothed in sackcloth. At that moment, Daphne had struck her as too complicated. Alice had no spare strength to investigate the duality of personality traits the woman exhibited, but within a day, she saw how Daphne wore her makeup and jewelry as a suit of armor meant to distract eyes from her body. They quickly became close, in that way you do in the first week of college or summer camp, when, alone and friendless, you pick the girl most likely to be simpatico.

Now, clothed in the same horrid material, with Daphne emphasized as a wide brick, and Alice revealed as overlapping circles, their constant exposure meant to break them down, they connected. Alice and Daphne tried to determine the purpose of the humiliation heaped on them. During their nightly talks, they were determined to solve the mystery, preferring to be a pair of TV Olivias—Pope from *Scandal* and Benson from *Law & Order*—more than being fat women trying to make themselves lovable to husbands and mothers.

She didn't know whether to grab her frozen friend's hand and make a break for freedom or push her forward.

"Daphne," Jeremiah said again. "We're waiting."

Her friend took one heavy step and then another, walking as though weights attached by chains dragged behind her.

Alice shivered.

Dear God, they might as well be putting them on a slave auction block, with Jeremiah standing there like a giant white master.

Who was crazier, him or them?

Daphne had rescued her when she needed the bathroom. Alice stepped forward and grabbed Daphne's hand. "Let's get this over. Together."

Daphne clutched her hand. When they reached the base of the scale, Alice squeezed Daphne's hand twice.

Jeremiah cocked his head and smiled as though seeing the funniest and stupidest women in the world.

Screw him.

"We're not taking off one more thing." Alice planted her legs apart and matched her crossed arms to his. "Forget it."

Mystery solved. A shot meant a brutal run.

By the seventh mile of their ten-mile race to nowhere, Alice fell to her knees. Daphne kept chugging, as Alice bent over, stitches knifing through her sides. When Daphne saw, she backed up, stood beside her, and waited, lightly touching Alice's shoulder. Enough to comfort without adding pressure.

"Don't wait for her." Valentina jogged in place. "You run. I stay with her."

Alice couldn't see Daphne's expression, but she imagined that stubborn, tight-lipped face.

"News flash," Daphne said. "This isn't the army, and you're not my sergeant."

But if that were true, what kept them running? What led them to obey these people? Each day,

Alice became more frightened by the crap she took in her pursuit of this overwhelming desire to be thin. Before taking off on this hideous run, they'd been in a wood-paneled room with Jeremiah and a giant screen. He'd pressed a few buttons, and up came images of Alice and Daphne side by side: photos from their applications. Full length. Standing. Hands on hips, as per the written instructions.

"Ready, ladies? Watch the magic."

He moved his finger on the trackpad, and presto! Metamorphosis. Alice became thin—elegantly thin—pulled in as though by enchanted stitches, while Daphne dropped the block of fat encasing her and came out transformed as a hard-muscled athlete.

They stared, mouths open, at the transformation.

Alice wanted to reach out and touch the screen, trace the lines of her body, dress the image in silk and tissue-thin cashmere. Take her curls, coil them on top of her head, and then let them fall.

The image kept her from walking out of the mansion, stomping the many miles to the main road, sticking out her thumb, and hitching home. Or hunting through the massive house until she found where they'd hidden her phone.

Overwhelming nausea hit as Alice knelt on the cold ground. She retched up the small amount of food inside her stomach, bits of carrots floating in a gallon of water.

• • •

"Ten miles." Daphne sounded dazed.

"Doesn't seem possible." Alice lay flat, arms at her sides, hanging over the twin bed. "I never was much of an athlete."

"I joined crew in high school." Daphne, across in her own bed, massaged her calves. "For one term."

"Did you like it?"

"Hated it. But my arms got muscular. That I liked."

"Maybe that encapsulates our problem," Alice said. "We forgot how to do the hard things. The things we hate."

Hania piped up from the chair where she sat reading *Shape* magazine. "Every time I want to escape, I think that even if this is the worst ever, at least they're giving me a shortcut."

"Aren't you afraid it will all disappear when we're back home?" Daphne asked.

Alice imagined herself back in Mission Hill, where she wouldn't be served prison portions in chipped bowls. Was she learning discipline or just taking a punishing cheat?

She tried to lift her legs to leverage herself up, but her limbs protested loud enough to make the move impossible. "I'm more frightened of how far I'll let them push us."

Hania held up the magazine and turned it so that the page of models faced them. "This is who

Jeremiah wants us to be like. He's doing it for us, right?"

"I don't know," Daphne said. "What if we become vaguely similar to those models for one day—the day we leave—and then the moment we get home move back up the ladder? Is it still worth it?"

"Stop!" Hania threw the magazine on the floor. "That's the negative self-talk Jeremiah warns us about. 'Think fat, be fat.' 'Eat fat, be fat.'"

"How much did we not control ourselves that this is what we turned into? Or how much do we despise ourselves? I thought it was just my husband." Alice needed to release the words before they ate her insides. "He drove me here. I convinced myself of that. Because I got fat. Because I'm not beautiful any—"

"You are so damn—"

Alice cut off Daphne. "Not to him. I should marry *you*. Look, I hate him for it. And yet I came here to get thin for him. How screwed up is that? But before this, I was bingeing and throwing up, sometimes twice a week. I have a little girl. What kind of example was I showing her?"

"Why do you keep at it?" Daphne rolled onto her side, slowly. "Try so hard to be smaller?"

Alice turned to face this new friend, ready to tell her something she'd never confessed to anyone.

"I wish I knew. I tell myself I just want to be beautiful; become who I was when I met Clancy. A rail. But when I met Clancy, misery was the center of my world. Being thin? That came from depression. I was heartbroken. Breakup skinny."

"God. Breakups make you so skinny." Hania gazed up as though praying for a Dear Jane letter to float down from heaven.

"It was the first time that stress made me *not* eat," Alice said.

"Small stress means eating, in my opinion. Major stress equals weight loss. Until it doesn't," Daphne said. "Shit. Anything can make me fat. Were you sometimes skinny before the breakup?"

"I was never what anyone could call skinny, except for that one crazy time—just various degrees of what the Irish call a hearty broth of a girl." Alice took a deep breath and went on. "And my mother, all she said was, 'It doesn't matter. You're a strong black woman. Brilliant. Beautiful. You don't need to live up to the white expectations of the world.' "

Hania nodded. "My grandmother. Different words—we're Indian—but same idea. My grandmother lives with us, and I'm like the punching bag between her and my mother, who wants me to be American skinny. My mother pats my stomach and shakes her head, while

Nani tells her to stop and sneaks me chocolate."

"My mother thinks she's black. She's white and Jewish. Likely she'll be sainted someday for all her do-gooding."

"I never thought of my mother as anywhere near sainthood." Daphne stretched her arms up and then out. "More like the devil in my life."

"She's your mother!"

Alice laughed at Hania's youthful shock.

"My mother has been the single biggest reason for *this*." Daphne gestured at her body. "I'd hide food and then gobble it so fast that I learned the art of chewing an entire bagel in one minute. When I was in high school, she put a scale in the entry to the kitchen. She took it away only when company came."

"How horrible!" Hania's face puckered as though tears were imminent.

"It is awful. And you, girl, are as sweet as sugar candy. If I could rise, I'd give you a hug," Daphne said. "But I didn't mean to get the floor." She turned the conversation back to Alice. "So, all that eating. And purging. If Clancy didn't drive it, what did?"

Alice struggled to a sitting position. She wanted to dip her hands into a bowl of popcorn. Dry would be fine. Buttered would be heaven. "I grew up with the same magazines and movies as the rest of the world, so there's that."

Hania and Daphne nodded.

"I wonder if there's a girl in America who doesn't grow up wanting to be skinny?" Alice mused. "Thinner is always better."

"What a depressing thought." Daphne untwirled a ringlet and let it bounce back. "Millions of girls all over hating themselves."

"Maybe that's how the supposed 'Black girls don't care' baloney got started. Everyone wanted there to be someone standing up against the bullshit," Hania said.

"Yeah. We had a shot, but then Oprah had to go on and ruin that with her diet, diet, diet." Alice sighed, thinking about how she begged her mother for *Oprah* magazine. She wanted food advice, and it was a magazine her mother couldn't refuse her. "Think about it. Richest woman in the world—I think—and all she wants is to eat her mac and cheese in peace."

"Mac and cheese." A dreamy look came over Hania.

"I can't figure it out. Why, besides Clancy, did I want to be skinny so damn badly that I ended up here?"

"Did you love it when you were thin?" Daphne asked.

Alice rocked as she clasped her knees. "I loved being loved for it. And to be sickeningly honest, I adored the envious looks I got from other women. Seeing men practically drooling? Disgusting. But it made me feel powerful.

Which, Jesus, is creepy. But, yeah, I loved it. I feel like the guy from that movie *Brokeback Mountain*. Skinny, 'I wish I knew how to quit you.'"

CHAPTER 15

ALICE

Valentina paced.

Alice ignored her, as did Daphne and Hania, all of them concentrating on their plates as though something fantastic lay before them.

"Your weigh-in yesterday, it shamed me," Valentina said.

Alice tried to tune her out as she scraped every piece of egg from the rough plate.

"We will never win with this showing," Valentina continued.

"Win? Win what? Just what is our prize?" Alice, still bleary and exhausted, even two days after the run, had woken so sore that she had to physically lift her legs off the bed. The previous day, forced to exercise through her post run pain, she had been unable to do anything but concentrate on forcing her limbs to move.

Making sense of Valentina's tirades ranked low on Alice's list. Eating took all her concentration. She simply wanted to get the slop down—though the meal was a pinch improved. Yesterday the bits of sewage-like food so nauseated her, eating took a self-lecture on staying strong. For breakfast, lunch, and dinner, as the entire community's punishment for Alice's and Daphne's rebellion, a stew of shaved tofu, celery, broccoli, and tomato simmered in weak chicken broth had been the only offering.

But Jeremiah dropped the nudity rule for the weigh-ins.

The strange victory was noted in his sideways comment: "You can thank your friends Alice and Daphne—some of you will be pushed only so far. Grist for the mill, eh? The question? Will such supposed courage help or hurt you all?"

At yesterday's weigh-in, after the run and the sewage meals, Alice had been down another four pounds, and Daphne three. Hania pouted over her two-pound loss, but they all stared when facing the mirror. Daphne touched the area where a waist might have appeared, Hania turned sideways and sucked in her stomach, and Alice angled her body to catch her carved collarbones.

"What will you win?" Valentina plunked herself down opposite Alice at the rough table, reaching out to touch Alice's bowl. "This. This is a win. Everything you eat, it is a win or lose. Every pair of pants you button or don't. You win the weigh-ins, you win life."

"We win us?" Hania asked. "You mean that we walk out feeling better when this is over?"

Alice shivered at Hania's seeming blind acceptance of the proverbial end justifying the means.

"You leave not only beautiful new women; you march away the best."

"So how did we lose yesterday?" Daphne asked. "In the competition. We worked our hardest."

"Did you?" Valentina stood and rolled up the sleeves of her pink sweatshirt. She pressed her palms on the table until every tendon showed through her chalky flesh, her position emphasizing her tightness, from her snap-hard calves to the ponytail drawing her eyebrows toward her squared hairline. "Best is very top best. Best is surpassing those around you. They lost more than you. Winning means challenging yourself so hard that you guarantee your personal best is better than their personal best. Reaching the top is not getting the most-improved award, it's getting the gold."

Alice tried to resist Valentina's siren song—*win, win, win*—as though rainbows and daffodils waited at the finish line. Winning meant money for either Valentina or Coleen. That was it. The rumor mill had it that whoever brought her team in with the biggest losses received 50K.

Still. Alice's previous win meant stuffing wads of saltines into her mouth, topping off her gluttony before she stuck her finger down her throat. Victory had been a more soothing purge after she binged, using the soft white flour to eat up the acid in her vomit.

Improved retching had become her goal.

"Here. This is something I have for you. A wonderful surprise." Valentina reached into her sweatshirt pouch and pulled out a plastic baggie of capsules. "Take these. I am giving you one a meal from now on."

"What are they?" Daphne tipped her head with suspicion.

"Vitamins." Valentina took out three pills. "A mix made by Dr. Ash. Soon he will be selling these. You are very lucky to be getting these first."

"What's in these lucky pills?" Alice asked, imagining her mother having a chemical assay done before she even touched them with a fingertip.

Valentina drew out a small piece of paper and read a list of ingredients. "Green tea extract, elephant yam, caffeine, and conjugated linoleic acid, which is only just a superhealthy trans fat. All these elements are very good for you. Very healthy."

Alice concentrated on the words, trying to remember the long shelf of vitamins her mother kept lined up in her kitchen, determined to keep her and Dad alive forever. She brought bags from Whole Foods to Alice's and Macon's apartments, diagnosing their problems through her online research.

"Is this actually speed?" Daphne's bluntness

was a blessing. "Amphetamine? Fen-phen? Ephedra? Not that I ever researched those drugs." She cut her eyes to show she meant just the opposite.

"No, no. Nothing illegal." Valentina placed a hand on her heart. "My God, I swear. I want winning, not jail. We work you hard, but we're not crazy. Hey. You're very lucky women. My special relationship with Dr. Ash made him pick me."

"I don't want any illegal *or* legal drugs," Alice said. "Making my daughter motherless isn't on my list." Just mentioning Libby cut deep. Her mother and father—and Clancy—cared for the girl with nothing but tender love, and Alice left taped stories and songs for them to play every night, but a month was a lifetime for a kid.

"We do not want to hurt you." Valentina softened her voice. "The mix will make you strong, build your muscles. When you leave, we may give you each some, even though we have to keep them secret before Dr. Ash gets them to market."

She placed one pill in front of every bowl and whispered, "Take one. You will be amazed. I have tried them. You will have energy. Your mood will soar. You will be like superwomen."

Valentina seldom dispensed smiles, but when she did, the women acted as though pure love enveloped them. Alice recognized the theory

190

of relativity in action. Give someone nothing but chilly dismissiveness for six days, and on the seventh, a smile will come across like an ascension to heaven.

But it worked.

"Do you think they're giving us speed?" Alice held on to the lip of the swimming pool, having just finished twenty laps with ease. "I feel *far* too good."

Daphne pulled off her bright-yellow swimming cap and let her hair tumble out, water darkening the ends from strawberry to auburn. Alice wondered what it would be like to let your hair mop up the water without worrying about chlorine levels, without first applying coconut oil and shea butter, though now, with chemical energy flashing and zinging, dunking her head, running in circles, whipping her hair every which way, and then letting it dry however the hell it wanted seemed within the realm of her new possibility.

Invincibility poured out. "I don't think Valentina fed us vitamins. Not unless *vitamin* is a new word for illegal-drug-to-make-you-insanely-happy. Is your head exploding?"

"You know what I feel at this moment?" Daphne stretched her arms up as though winning a race. "For the first time in ages, I don't care about anything but the next minute. And best of all? I'm not hungry. I'll beg, borrow, or steal to have this shit for the rest of my life."

A week later at the weigh-in, Alice's mood soared. Compared with the women in the other group, who trudged up to the scale, the three of them danced up in their underwear, uncaring about the revelations of midriffs and thighs, grinning as the scales registered the continuing downward trend.

The jumpsuits that had formerly covered them like sausage casings now hung like loose pantyhose. The numbers marking their weight flashed like Las Vegas nightclub signs. Living on an egg a day, along with spinach, dry-grilled broccoli, cucumbers, broth, celery, bits of tofu with mustard, and little else while exercising nine hours a day worked. They shrank. Exhaustion disappeared.

Hania bowed like a beauty queen before stepping onto the scale. The numbers trilled up and down until settling on 141. Beautiful Hania, the poster girl of *Waisted*, everybody's favorite, twirled in an imaginary princess dress.

"Congratulations, Hania," Jeremiah said. "Per the U.S. Army, at your age, you are now seven pounds from the weight they would allow someone your height."

Valentina grinned as though her daughter had been accepted to Harvard. Coleen threw suspicious glances. The trainers' competition had become vicious. News traveled quickly among prisoners. When Alice and Jennifer snuck off to the bathroom together, secrets came out. Jennifer revealed that Coleen suspected Valentina of cheating.

With $50,000 on the line, she bet that Valentina hadn't received those pills from Dr. Ash. The man didn't appear bright enough to invent a piece of toast.

"Your turn, Daphne." Jeremiah gestured for her to come forward.

How different from fourteen days ago, when Alice had to rescue Daphne. Now her friend turned, threw her a big grin, wiggled out of her now-floppy jumpsuit, and marched right toward the scale. When 167 flashed on the screen, Daphne raised her arms, *Rocky* style.

"Not yet ready for the army, but you're on your way, kiddo." Jeremiah nodded in approval.

Coleen and her team glared.

Yes, this week had been better. Valentina stopped treating them as primordial ooze. Jeremiah nodded. Dr. Ash drugged them.

Alice stepped forward, aware of the muscles in her legs carrying her. Her waist felt whittled to a size Clancy's hands could span. As she walked, it seemed within her reach to leap to the sky, weightless and magical.

At bedtime, home truths wiggled in, but if

euphoria ebbed away during the night, it reawoke soon after getting her breakfast pill, when her spirit again moved from lead to aerated. Alice was familiar with how drug addicts moved through stages. She worried that Valentina was pushing meth down their throats.

But when she stepped on the scale and saw 184, a whole 19 pounds below her beginning weight, she was ready to fly down to the nearest army recruiting office and enlist. They'd take her in 4 pounds.

She could run fifteen miles, swim the English Channel, and blast Harper to hell. She had become capable of anything.

At dinner, their clocks ran down. Alice sipped her unsalted, unspiced, and unflavored broth, forcing down the liquid. If she ate only these foods forever, bingeing would never tempt her again. Perhaps this was their lesson: eat only food that tasted horrid. Imagine a life where food didn't matter.

Alice twitched at her hamster-run thoughts. Addictive pills induced shock or withdrawal.

Hunger gnawed without appetite.

"What if we need this vitamin when we're home?" Daphne stirred her broth into tiny torrents. "Where do we get it?"

Valentina shook her head. "You ask me every day that same question."

"And yet you never answer."

"When the time comes, then I will tell you."

"When is that time?" Daphne asked. "What do you mean by 'the time'? The last day? The bus ride home? When we pack?"

"Stop!" Valentina reached into the pocket of her shorts. "Here. Today's pill, plus an extra for each of you. Now we can do more exercise tonight, and you have one in your bank." Valentina's lip turned up as though she were smiling.

Alice knew Daphne and Hania shared her feelings: *I don't want to exercise anymore today. I want to sleep. But I want the pill. And when I get the pill, I will happily swim twenty laps, run five miles, and do a hundred sit-ups.*

The three of them received the pills Valentina offered as though accepting superpowers, knowing that when the chemicals kicked in, they'd be able to run to the moon and back. Alice's hand shook as she reached for water to swallow the capsule.

She shouldn't take any more pills tonight. Only an idiot would consider that. *Think of what your mother, father, and Clancy would say.*

She gripped the cheap water glass and stared at the pill. Defined muscles had begun forming in her forearm. Each day, she cared less if she ever tasted sugar again.

Alice swallowed.

Swimming laps for an hour shriveled their skin—fingertips turned into tiny, wrinkled prunes. After that, they performed a water ballet for their own amusement, sidestroking in circles and diving for invisible fish. But still, despite burning off another ten *Waisted* meals, when they returned to their bedroom, Alice had too much energy to consider taking the sleeping pills.

She washed her face in the bathroom. As she patted her skin dry, just as Daphne had insisted—pat, don't rub—she noticed two things: her face had thinned out considerably. She didn't know what cosmetics would do to this newly hollowed face. What could she look like?

She opened the door and yelled over the music to which Hania shook her hips. "Make us up, Daph! I want to see what I might look like in full face."

Though forbidden from wearing makeup, they'd been allowed to keep their cosmetics in their rooms. In Daphne's case, that meant a treasure chest of everything from contouring creams, to eyeliners worthy of the singer Adele, to lipsticks ranging from faint nudes to screaming reds. Like women in purdah, in the beginning, until the novelty wore off, they'd spent hours decorating themselves when alone in their rooms.

Hania struck a model's pose. "Do something very different!"

"Like what?" Daphne dragged out her tools and potions, setting up a makeup counter in the bathroom. One woman would sit on the side of the tub while the other raised her face to Daphne's ministrations, a closed toilet seat serving as the throne. Then they'd switch.

"We can each choose who we want to be," Hania said.

"Sure." Alice lifted her hair higher, wondering who she wanted to be. "You first."

"Make me look like Angelina Jolie in *Maleficient*," Hania said.

Daphne considered her supplies and then closed her eyes. "Okay." She blinked her eyes. "Got it. Without Google, all I have is my memory."

"No worries," Alice said. "It all washes away. Hania won't sue you."

"What are you thinking of?" Daphne began daubing heavy white base on Hania, mimicking the masklike appearance needed for the dramatic role.

Alice stood and peered at herself. Makeup had always been a question of fitting in for her. Other than combining colors for bold lips, she stayed inside the lines, played with her supposed beauty. Growing up with Bebe meant no dressing tables filled with mystery where Alice could play. Bebe's idea of making up included brushing on one coat of mascara and spreading a thin layer of tinted moisturizer.

Combining Bebe with anything appearance-related meant watching for hidden mines. Bebe believed makeup to be political, and hairstyling terrified her. Her mother treated Alice's hair as a challenge to be addressed with caution, using brittle cheer as her cover while dreading doing something wrong. She tried hard, though—even paying black hairdressers to tutor her in the best ways to care for Alice's fragile curls.

Most of the time, this tentativeness led to Alice assuring Bebe what a great job she did mothering Alice in the girly department—until Alice hit a rebellious streak and made her hair as white-girl as possible, knowing that her mother treasured Alice being natural.

In the end, Alice feared declaring her soul by wearing it on the outside, not trusting anyone's judgment or taste. She wasn't even sure what her soul might look like—did it have a color?

When Alice saw Daphne struggle with her curls, using a pick like Alice's, it surprised her. While it would never be a political issue for Daphne—who'd never be fired for letting her hair frizz out—Alice realized that few women besides Hania, blessed with silk and satin, were satisfied with whatever God gave them.

Hell, even Hania, who, watching Alice twisting exercise-friendly braids, declared that her sheet of hair was boring and complained it would just slip out of French braids.

Alice took out the clip holding her hair. She bent at the waist and ran her fingers through the curls, shaking them out, lifting from the roots until she'd made a nimbus around her head. "Make me Rihanna. Or Tracee Ellis Ross. Lisa Bonet. Hell, make me Meghan Markle. Turn me into a princess."

Daphne leaned over Alice's shoulder. "I'll make you a princess like you've never seen. Can I do Cleopatra eyes?"

"Anything you want."

"I'd kill for your cheekbones." Daphne leaned toward the mirror. "Look at me. I got my period today. My face is a moon."

"First days are the worst," Alice said.

"Headaches. Swollen. I always want *chikki* chocolate-covered peanuts. Every second." Hania moaned.

"What's *chikki*?" Alice asked.

"The Indian version of peanut brittle. My grandmother always gave it to me when I had my period, so now I'm completely Pavlovian in wanting it at that time of the month."

"That's so sweet, going for grandma food. For me, it's Nestlé Crunch," Daphne said. "I never want anything elegant or Whole-Foodish during my period. Just crappy candy from CVS."

"M&M's. Always. A giant-sized bag that my hand can get lost in," Alice said. "Why do you

199

think we want our childhood sweets most of all at that time?"

Hania answered from Daphne's other side. "Because life sucks during our period. Thus, we want the simplest soothing pleasures."

"I wear my biggest earrings at that time. I swear they hide my puffy face," Daphne said.

"I miss wearing my jewelry." Longing wrapped Hania's words. "I feel naked."

Daphne's hands went to her earlobes. "I know what you mean. Even when I'm just lying around on a Sunday morning, I feel better if I at least have a pair of studs. In my ears, I mean."

They laughed as though her joke had been far funnier than it was. The women were as desperate for fun as they were for food and rest.

"I wonder if women should be divided into earring types. Studs. Hoops. Hanging." Alice raised her face as Daphne smoothed on primer. "You're the jewelry store person, Daphne. What say you?"

"You bet there are types, plus a million levels within each one. You should hear my sister talk about it. Marissa thinks women—and men—use jewelry as a shortcut to tell the world who they are. And aren't. How else could you advertise your values, your worth, your religion, your culture? You name it.

"But there's also face shape. My sisters, and sister-in-law, they have delicate faces with small features. Studs look fantastic on them. On me? I feel like they're lost and make me look fatter. That's why I only wear them when I'm lounging around."

"I change it up depending on where I'm going. Jesus, I'm a goddamn jewelry chameleon," Alice said. "Does that make me a phony? Lost?"

Daphne stayed quiet for a moment. Alice realized that talking about culture and race, delicate under any circumstance, became exaggerated tenfold when you had three women of such diverse backgrounds living in the same room, but she wanted to dive into her curiosity about what the other two would say.

"I think we all do it in some way," Daphne said. "Or at least I do. When I'm with my extended family, I pile on too much bling. To keep them from looking at me. I'd rather have them think I'm fashion stupid than notice that I can't wear spaghetti straps. As though it works. Hah. I guess it's my protective gear."

"When I go to work, I don't wear bright saturated gold," piped up Hania. "You know the kind I mean?" When they murmured agreement, she went on. "Work is such a boys' club. If I could, I'd just shine my stuff in their faces—but I have neither the guts nor enough of a foothold as a coder. I want to fade a bit. So, I have these small, dull gold hoops I wear only to work."

"Do you keep your bracelets on?" Alice asked.

"No. They'd bang on the computer. I can't. But the minute I get home, I put them on. I feel naked without my bracelets."

"Sometimes I use jewelry as a weapon," Alice said. "To intimidate. I know that being tall can make folks uncomfortable. When I wear my truly big jewelry—what Clancy calls my Queen of the Nile pieces—then I know I tower more than just physically."

"Do you use it to intimidate white folk?" Daphne sounded hesitant. "Not that I'd blame you. God, you must have to take five steps for every move I make."

Alice waited a few beats before answering, surprised by Daphne's words, and unsure if she should be offended or impressed by the chutzpah. "Yeah. Sure, I do. My father taught me to take every legal advantage I could—though I don't think he meant jewelry."

"Men are clueless about how talismanic jewelry is," Daphne said. "How much more it means than decoration."

"Maybe that's why Jeremiah won't let us wear it here. He's even trying to take away our luck." Alice stretched her arms and examined her hands. "I haven't been without my rings in a long time. Even before marriage, I had *the ring*. I wore my great-grandma's art deco ring from the day my father gave it to me. I keep trying to twirl it, but it's not there."

"Perhaps we can use it as a small bonus, even though Jeremiah means it to break us down," Hania said. "Maybe we can figure out our naked worth."

"I don't even want to think who I'd be without makeup and jewels," Daphne said.

"Why should we stop?" Hania asked. "Let the men decorate themselves more and give us something pretty to look at. Let them be the ones lining their eyes and wrapping themselves in gold. We don't need to mimic them."

"Right you are." Alice closed her eyes so Daphne could dust on glittery gold eye shadow. "When's the last time we pillaged a town? Nope. That's them. I think it's time to examine all the values we're twisted up with. They should be copying us. We're not the ones starting the wars."

CHAPTER 16

DAPHNE

They'd now been at the mansion for twenty-two days. Speed jitters had taken over Daphne's body. From waking up, to the hour when they swallowed their sleeping pills, she felt compelled to move. She jiggled and fidgeted, sometimes with knowledge, sometimes realizing it midtwitch. Even now, as she waited to climb the steps to the scale, she shifted from foot to foot in a pill-induced dance, burning calorie upon calorie.

Weigh-ins had become a treat to Daphne. The numbers on the scale tumbled; her spirits soared. Unfortunately, as much as her mood lifted to near euphoria when seeing her falling weight, panicked agitation came over her without provocation. Only bruising exercise relieved the sudden onslaughts of anxiety.

"Come, come, come!" Jeremiah called. His jolly welcoming tone led Daphne to boogaloo up to the scale in imitation of a go-go girl from the sixties.

She skipped up the steps to the scale and smiled in expectation of another happy number.

Yesterday, she hit 143.4, for a total weight loss of 39.6 pounds. Frankenstein's large base had become a platform of joy.

The white metal was icy under her bare feet. She crossed her fingers and prayed to lose over 4 pounds, a not-unheard-of one-day loss in the mansion. And then, to bring karma on her side, she included Alice in her words to God.

After dinner, stuck in their group bedroom, Daphne drummed her fingers against her chair as she did leg lifts from her sitting position. Her mouth was dry, her armpits were wet with sweat—which seemed an unlikely combination. Slaking her thirst seemed impossible for the past week. "What happens when we don't have pills anymore?" she asked.

"We fatten up like Thanksgiving turkeys," Alice said. "Or we find inner strength."

"Don't you think this—the pills—are just a boost, and that they just got us on the right track?" Hania parroted Valentina, nervousness coating every word.

"I doubt it," Alice said. "Daphne lost three pounds today, you lost two, and I was down four. I weighed a hundred and sixty-two pounds, meaning I lost forty-three pounds in a bit over three weeks. Honestly? It's pretty insane."

"It's not insane. It's pills." Daphne nibbled at her thumbnail, the only one with any real estate left. A dark mood descended. "It's probably us that's crazy."

"How soon until we take our sleeping pills?" Hania circled her arms forward three times, back three times.

"No pills for at least an hour." Alice rose from the chair and began bending from her waist and touching her toes. "Right, Daph?"

Being a doctor's wife, close as they had to expertise, Daphne had been appointed the medic in charge of their small group. She checked the clock. Eight thirty. Once Valentina started feeding them nightly sleeping pills, her medical responsibilities doubled. They were supposed to sleep for eight hours, which meant taking the sleeping pill at nine thirty.

"An hour sounds about right." Daphne began bending in time with Hania.

"One pill makes us skinny, one pill makes us sleep." Daphne swayed as she sang to the tune of an old Jefferson Airplane song her father used to sing. "Let's put on music. Dance till we drop."

Only CDs and an old boom box provided entertainment. Since beginning the pills, each night they danced off their jitters, putting the system on Mix and moving to whatever played. They stood, silent, waiting, until "Single Ladies" poured out.

They talked as they moved, none of them giving a damn how they looked shaking to Beyoncé in their yellow jumpsuits.

"I'm betting Susannah will be the first to gain weight back," Alice said. "All she talks about is what she'll eat first when we're released."

" 'Released.' " Hania's jumping jacks made her words skip like an old record. "You make it sound like leaving prison."

"Isn't it?" Alice dropped to the floor and began a series of leg lifts.

"You always think it will be one of the white women." Daphne jumped from foot to foot, ready for their nightly debate.

"Face it, white women aren't used to deprivation as much as black women." Alice swirled in a fast circle. "And there are only two white women here—you and Susannah—so stop crying about race. At least I'm not picking *you*."

"Pick whoever you want," Daphne said.

"Could we leave if we wanted?" Hania asked.

Daphne and Alice stopped midshake and stared.

"Of course," Daphne said. "What would stop us?" She turned to Alice, who by dint of working in a more socially righteous field than Daphne or Hania had been crowned the group lawyer. "Right?"

"I suppose." Alice sank to the floor, legs crossed, as Beyoncé continued singing. "Why not?"

"How would we leave?" Hania sat beside Alice. "They locked away our wallets. For 'safekeeping.' And took our phones."

"We ask for them," Alice said.

"And our clothes? And a ride?" Hania twisted side to side.

"Do you want to leave?" Daphne asked.

"I want to know I can, damn it!" Alice said. "Don't you?"

"My husband would come if I asked. I guarantee." Daphne pressed her hands to her waist, calming herself by running her hands down her sides.

"But how can you ask if they won't let us call?" Hania continued. "I don't want to go. I want to lose as much as I can. But what if they won't let us go? What does that mean?"

"You sound paranoid, Hania," Alice said. "That's the pills talking. We all know Valentina isn't giving us vitamins. I took a million courses in substance abuse for my job. We're showing so many signs."

"Like what?" Daphne studied Alice, who looked up as though retrieving information.

After a few moments, Alice nodded. "Speed brings on hyperactivity, insomnia, anorexia, and tremors. High doses or chronic use have been associated with paranoia and aggressiveness. And . . . death."

> **TIP:** There are more than a dozen prescription medications and hundreds of over-the-counter drugs and herbal supplements for weight loss. They work in

several ways: by suppressing your appetite, increasing your metabolism, or keeping your body from absorbing the fat you eat. Here's your guide to some popular choices and what you need to know to play it safe.

—Dr. Oz website

ADVICE: Useless.
WEIGHT LOSS: Down one size and then up two.

"We're definitely on speed." Daphne couldn't lie one more minute. Not with her heart racing. Blood thudded through her arteries. "I've been in denial. My mother's doctor put me on something like this when I was seventeen. And I'm feeling the same shitty, jittery, fucked-up way."

"Should we stop?" Hania asked.

Daphne chewed her lip. Part of her feared for their lives; the other part wanted to keep swallowing this shit until every bit of fat fell off. "Stopping suddenly might hurt us. And I don't imagine the dosage is very high—if it is speed."

"Didn't you just say we were definitely taking speed?" Alice asked.

"Hey, what do I know? I'm a makeup artist, not a chemist." Daphne smiled to allay their fears. Balancing losing weight against an unfounded worry, she'd choose the side of trust. After all, these were award-winning filmmakers.

"I don't want to die from being fed uppers and downers." Alice nodded at the dish of sleeping pills waiting for them.

"We may be in danger. Or we're all being paranoid. Or not." Daphne shook her head, unable to stay with one opinion. "Maybe Hania woke us up."

"And there's something I didn't tell you." Hania pressed her lips together until they disappeared.

"What?" Alice reached for Hania's hand. "What aren't you telling us?"

Hania touched her chest. "It feels fast."

"You mean your heart? What do you mean by fast?" Alice led Hania to the closest bed—Daphne's—and urged her to sit. Daphne sat on Hania's other side.

"Does it feel as though it's racing?" Daphne touched the spot where Hania's heart resided, as though a mother's hand were a stethoscope. Then she placed her index and middle fingers on Hania's wrist and looked at her watch.

The three women remained silent until Daphne looked up. "You're twenty-eight, right?"

Hania nodded. Daphne subtracted 28 from 220. With that formula, one she'd learned from Sam, Hania's maximum heart rate during exercise should be 192. Daphne had clocked her pulse at over 220.

"Your heart rate is high." Daphne sent a look to

Alice. "You're a healthy person. My guess is this is the pills combined with exercise."

"You need to reach your husband," Alice said to Daphne. "I'd call someone in my family, but I don't think we need lawyers, retired history teachers, or social workers."

Daphne thought of her options. "Sam will become crazy inside if we call him, but he'll handle it like a scientist."

Hania held up her hands. "I can't do it. My parents would charter a helicopter."

Sam might answer simply and directly. Or he might drive right up. Probably the latter.

Daphne tried to concentrate, think clearly, but pills and lack of food fuzzed her thoughts. The aphorism "Speed kills" floated into her thoughts.

Alice stood. "We've gone crazy staying here. Have we lost our minds?"

"But we've lost weight, right? So maybe they're on to something." Hania considered the mirror, turning from front to back. "I don't ever remember looking anywhere close to this."

Daphne felt the crash coming: that feeling when the pills wore off, leaving behind nausea and a depressed exhaustion. "We bought their bullshit, but, really, how long do you think this kind of weight loss lasts? How long before one of us collapses?" *Or dies.*

"We'll be fine for another week, right?" Hania sounded unsure.

Daphne shook her head, trying to clear the chattering speed. "No. Not with your pulse like that. How do we know if we're okay if we don't know what the hell we're taking? Things might work out. And maybe not. I don't want to wait until one of us drops dead."

"I could die?" Hania brought her legs to her chest and cradled them with her arms.

"I'll take your pulse after you've rested for a bit. I'm sure you're fine." Daphne's words of reassurance were based on air and hope.

"We've ridden on fumes for weeks," Alice said. "Vitamins. Christ. Not facing that they were feeding us some sort of amphetamine makes all three of us either certifiable or so deep in denial we'll need to be dug out of our fog."

"Somewhere in this mansion, there must be a ton of computers," Daphne said. "We should be able to access at least one. Then I can contact Sam."

"Do you think Jeremiah knows? About the drugs? Or is it just Valentina scrambling for money?" Hania asked.

Alice scrunched her face. "Wow. Who to trust more, Jeremiah or Valentina? Talk about rock versus hard place."

Daphne kept thinking about the pills. And Sam, who, if he thought there was an ounce of danger, would drive up and force her to leave. Pros and cons leapt in circles. She thought of her kids, and

Alice's daughter, and came down on the side of contact and safety. Maybe Sam would calm her.

"Should we go on a computer hunt? Now?" Hania sounded strangely excited. She worked in IT. Only extreme workouts and exhaustion had kept her from relentlessly complaining about being separated from her electronic equipment.

"We should try asking Jeremiah." Alice laced her fingers and brought them to her lips.

Daphne laughed. "I can see you weren't the sneaky one in your house."

"My mother believed in open access. We could barely hide our thoughts."

"If we ask for anything, we give them too much information. Too much power," Daphne said. "I don't have a clue what their end game is, but I sure as hell don't trust them. When in doubt, lie. We start by not taking those sleeping pills tonight—ensuring we're alert enough to search— and then pray we're surrounded by deep sleepers. We'll try to find a phone, but if we locate only a computer, then it's all up to you to connect us, Hania."

"Count on me. It would kill my parents if anything happened to me. I'm not using hyperbole. Do you have any idea what it means being an only child in an Indian family?"

"We need to do this fast," Alice said. "God knows what we're taking, and God knows what they're planning."

Daphne nodded in agreement. Like Dorothy, the Tin Man, the Lion, the Scarecrow, and Toto rising from the poppy fields in *The Wizard of Oz*, they awoke.

CHAPTER 17

DAPHNE

The next day, only half their brains were engaged as they ran, swam, and dragon walked. They forced themselves to eat everything available, despite Valentina's angry words and grim glances. They needed to store energy. As they roamed the mansion, moving from gym to dining room to pool to bedrooms, they memorized details and searched out likely places for electronic treasure.

Like spies on alert, they were more than the sum of their seeming parts.

Back in their room for the night, they played gin rummy past midnight until they thought it safe to leave the room, flipping the cards as quietly as possible.

Hania, their sneaky little sister, turned out to have begged an extra vitamin from Valentina for an "emergency," playing on being the pretty, favorite one, who, being the thinnest, had to work hardest to lose pounds. They split the pill among themselves, giving Hania, whose pulse had remained normal, only a sliver—enough to ensure she stayed awake. Daphne vowed to watch

Hania as carefully as she would her daughter.

When it was past midnight, the three women prepared. They removed their socks and then pulled their hair into buns, aware that even the sound of swishing hair might draw attention. They used the thickest of Daphne's face oils on the hinges of the door.

Dim sconces provided murky light in the halls of the house's sleeping quarters. They walked carefully, terrified of bumping into something. If discovered, they planned to declare this a search for food.

They crept down the hall, grateful for the carpeting when sneaking past bedrooms of the other *Waisted* members, even more as they approached the staff area.

Alice, the tallest, led, followed by Hania, with Daphne last. Alice's pulse pounded through her ears as the drug thrummed through her system. She held up her long arm and waved a halt signal and then pantomimed climbing steps, indicating the end of the hall.

Daphne closed her eyes, picturing the next convergence, where the hall turned left and led to the gym and, beyond that, to the dining areas, while straight ahead a narrow staircase led up and down. Uncarpeted. Squeaky. Down led to the main floor. Up went to the third level. The offices.

The only time they'd come up here was on

their way to the pool, situated at the other end of the mansion, overlooking the garden, or, as it was now, a hard, frost-covered expanse of brown lawn. Snow came early and often in the Northeast Kingdom.

Alice held up one finger and then indicated walking upstairs by using two fingers. *One at a time, yes.* Daphne nodded her understanding and watched as Alice climbed slowly. Daphne, meanwhile, stuck to the middle, where a small strip of rubberized treads muffled sound.

The ancient stairs creaked. Not every tread, but enough for Daphne to feel sick as she waited for Alice to reach the top.

Next, Hania showed her youth as she stretched to take two steps at a time, not even needing the banister for balance. Watching, Daphne pressed the heel of her hand into the center of her chest, as though her actions kept Hania going, readying her own ascension.

Grit ground into her soles as she began her journey upward. Grit was good. Grit prevented slipping. Despite thinning out, her thighs still brushed together. In the postmidnight quiet, the whooshing sounded like cannonballs hurtling through the air. She moved her legs apart, climbing the stairs bowlegged. After three weeks of constant exercise, flexibility came easily.

Counting helped. Downstairs they could pretend to be stealing food. For the main floor, they might claim that waves of homesickness sent them searching for a phone. But here?

Again, Daphne wondered why she was so nervous, as though they had planned a jailbreak. Being brainwashed into this state of fear and compliance, as though they were acolytes of kidnappers, made no sense. Free will had led and kept them here, after all.

Well, except for the shots and ten-mile runs. And if they had been truly free, their phones would have been in their hands.

If they didn't find a way to email, Daphne swore that tomorrow she'd demand her phone, and damn whatever bullshit she signed.

With that pep talk, she took the final two steps confidently—until an exposed nail ripped her heel, and pain stabbed through her foot.

"*Aeeii*," she whispered as she pitched forward. She knelt on the top of the stairs, rocking in agony.

Hania pulled at her arm. "Stop. Suck it up."

Daphne pressed against the pain, grateful for her thick calluses. Alice indicated going to the right.

They walked softly down the barely lit hallway. The hall here was wider than the ones below. Chairs placed at odd moments offered weary corridor travelers a place to rest. Eeriness reigned at every turn.

The office marked with Ash's name came first.

Alice touched the doorknob. She shook her head from side to side, indicating that it was locked, and they continued until reaching Valentina's. This was the one they prayed would be easy to enter, hoping for information about the pills, something—a bottle with a name would be nice. A phone. There must be outside lines, yes?

Valentina's door wouldn't budge; nor Coleen's.

Finally, they approached Jeremiah's office. Daphne reached out. The bas-relief of the antique brass doorknob pressed into her flesh. She turned it slowly, pushing past the first stoppage, but nothing gave. Impatiently, she turned it the other way.

She raised her hands in a silent gesture of frustration.

Sam's help floated away like a ghostly apparition.

Hania tiptoed down the hall, ignoring Alice's head shakes and Daphne's frantic motion to return.

Daphne underestimated Hania's breadth of capability. The young woman walked as though she knew where she was heading. When Hania reached the third door, she placed her hand against the wood as though taking its temperature. She twisted the knob. When it opened, she turned, put up two hands and waved at her and Alice to come, calling them silently with her wide grin.

Wires, computer screens, and unfamiliar electronic equipment crowded every surface in the office. Daphne wouldn't call the space dirty, but it sure was extraordinarily messy. Either the office of someone too busy to keep up or too scattered to care.

Judging by the unlocked door, *scattered* seemed fitting.

"Where are we?" Daphne asked.

"The filmmaker's den," Hania said. "Mike brought me here once."

"Mike?" Alice asked.

"The guy who's always shooting us."

"The videographer," Alice said. "Why would he bring you here?"

Hania raised her eyebrows. "Not what you think. We just talked."

"I wasn't thinking anything, actually." Alice looked over the table of electronic equipment. "Are we under surveillance?"

"No," Hania said.

"How are you so sure?" Alice looked all around the room.

"Because when Mike and I were talking about all the damn filming, I asked him. He laughed—saying they were already drowning in footage, and that, anyway, the top guys from Acrobat fancied themselves true auteurs and consider Mike their arms. Apparently that, they insisted, was the difference between filming a reality show and a documentary."

"Did Mike mention that they came into the world of making docs after doing reality shows?" Alice asked. "Perhaps I should—"

"We can discuss this later. Now, search for a phone," Daphne whispered. She turned, looking for a landline. "Or computer access."

Hania pointed to an enormous desktop machine, the kind few owned anymore. "I'll start there." She sat in front of the screen and bent the tower to its right, pushing buttons and bringing the monster to life.

Daphne and Alice prowled the room, following wires, hunting for phones and laptops. The room was small, perhaps ten by twelve, and so cluttered they were forced to move slowly. After a perimeter search, Daphne found two ancient laptops: one sleek, newish Mac; and a wrinkled, though sealed, bag of Reese's Pieces candy, which she held up and shook like a trophy.

"Our reward for success," Daphne whispered. She brought the machines to Alice. "Try these while I keep looking. I'm awful with computers."

She got down on her knees and crawled along the floor, chasing wires until she came to a phone base. Somewhere in the chaos might be an actual landline. After dividing the room into quadrants, she ran her hands in sweeping motions over the oak parquet flooring, the complicated patterns of the past at odds with the tangle of electronics everywhere.

Dust rose. Daphne raised her arm to stifle a sneeze. Gray particles covered her. Dim light—they only allowed themselves one small lamp—hampered her efforts. Her wound from the nail slowed her.

Alice muttered in the corner as she tried out the devices. "Passwords on these. And, of course, the Wi-Fi has a password."

"Keep trying," Hania said. "Maybe he left something connected. Or has a ridiculous password."

Alice closed the ancient laptop and picked up the Mac. "At least this one I'm familiar with."

"I can try the ones you can't figure out," Hania said. "I'm bi-computer."

"Bang!" Daphne held up a phone pulled from the back of a table. She pressed the talk button, praying for the stutter of a dial tone, her stomach sinking as the sound of nothingness greeted her. "*Damn.* No charge."

Alice looked up from the computer. "Can you put it on the base?"

"If I find the base in this mess. And then what? We wait three hours until it charges?"

"Is that how long it takes?" Alice asked.

"No idea." Daphne banged the phone against her thigh. She should have spent less time on cosmetics and more on technical learning. "Ask Hania."

"Landlines aren't my specialty. But since we don't see a base anywhere, it's probably a piece of junk that migrated here ages ago. Anything from you, Alice?"

Alice stared at the screen, peering closer, turning her head from side to side in disbelief.

"Jesus."

"Jesus, what?" Daphne asked.

"Dear Jesus, these pictures."

"Pictures?"

"No. Really. These are stills. From what he's shooting." She held up the small laptop and turned it. "Like this."

Hania swiveled in her chair. Daphne went up on her knees and leaned forward. A frighteningly crisp image of a naked Susannah took up the screen. Though the perspective hid her face, they recognized the insane disconnect between her massive hips and thighs and her far smaller waist. The angle ensured the viewer would be both mesmerized and disturbed.

" 'Jesus' is right. What else is there?" Daphne asked.

Alice clicked a key, and Hania appeared, grimacing, bent over mid-crunch, triple chins emerging along with rolls of fat pressing through the stretched jumpsuit. *Click.* Lauretta standing on the scale naked, an apron of flesh hanging over her thighs. *Click.* Another one of Lauretta, this time from behind, back padding pointing down to her bare bottom filling the screen, dimpled and saggy.

"Stop!" Daphne demanded, not able to face her own image. "What the hell is this?"

"We knew they were filming," Alice said. "But not like this."

"What else do they have?" Hania clutched her throat.

Alice held up one finger and bent over the computer. "I'm looking for the video. It must be somewhere. Hania, how about that desktop? I bet he's using the most powerful machine—that one—for the footage. Look for Sony Vegas Pro, Media Composer. Anything like that."

The bag of Reese's Pieces screamed out to Daphne. Monkeys jumped around her brain, brandishing the hard-shelled candies. *Melt in your mouth!* Just one would release a storm of want.

> **TIP:** You often think about the next piece of candy before finishing the one you have. To slow down and enjoy each piece of candy as you are eating it, eat with your nondominant hand. (If you are left-handed, eat with your right.) This will help prevent you from mindlessly popping candy into your mouth. Research indicates that this simple swap can cut down on how much you eat by approximately 30 percent.

—Dr. Susan Albers, author of the national bestseller Eat.Q.

ADVICE: Probably true.
WEIGHT LOST: Never took advice.

Daphne's craziness led her to believe the candy would all be taken away unless she ate it immediately. She and Sam should move far away from her mother's claws. She should stop gussying up women and begin a life of goodness. Teach Audrey and Gabe about a world away from sparkling jewels and layers of camouflage. Join the Peace Corps.

"Here," Hania said, "I found something. But I don't know this program."

Alice put down the laptop and went to the desk. She bent over Hania's shoulder. "Magix. Sometimes Clancy uses it. I played with it making movies of Libby."

Hania rose and gave the seat to Alice. Daphne stuffed the bag of Reese's down her shirt, came up from the floor, and stood behind Alice with Hania.

After a few clicks, they saw what looked like, even to Daphne's unschooled eyes, a rough cut of a movie. "This is saved to the disk. We don't need Wi-Fi," Alice clicked a few keys.

The screen filled with unedited footage and sound, opening with the day of their arrival, still in street clothes.

Tension thickened as a gasping Alice came

on-screen, straining to gallop around the room with Coleen on her back. Daphne tugged at her hair, trying not to throw up as she watched.

Narration began with Jeremiah's voice: "This is the beginning of our experiment. What would these women do to lose weight? Would they degrade themselves? We knew the answer immediately. The next question was this: How far would they go?"

The shot dissolved to a new setting, as though Mike were experimenting with ideas and cuts. Alice saw Clancy perform the magic enough times to know how making a film resembled working a jigsaw puzzle.

The shot began as a close-up on Seung and her purple hair, moving downward, revealing her removing her clothes until she stood bent over and nude.

Jeremiah's voice-over continued: "We thought for sure we'd get a 'No way!' when we insisted on complete disrobing for the weigh-in, but the more we pushed, the more these women acquiesced, until occasionally one or two protested enough to provide a stopping place. Sometimes, after hours, we'd laugh; sometimes we'd almost cry at the misery they would undergo to meet the American ideal."

Images of thin, beautiful women, interspersed with the *Waisted* women undressing, shame and discomfort showing in their bent bodies, arms covering stomachs, breasts, and privates, flashed on the screen, rolling out with a quality that terrified Daphne.

The slick footage scared Daphne. She possessed no inside knowledge of the documentary field, but could imagine this getting nationwide coverage. Worldwide.

Her stomach fired with bubbles of rage.

The film switched to a scene with Lauretta and Susannah eating. Lauretta, her dark hair wet with sweat, minced an egg into the tiniest flakes and placed them one bit at a time on her tongue. Susannah pushed the whole egg into her mouth, seeming to swallow it whole.

"Might as well get the misery over," Susannah said.

An image of Lauretta wetting her finger and placing another bit of egg in her mouth dissolved, replaced with stills of children from all countries and cultures, bellies distended from hunger as the narrator spoke.

"As children and adults throughout the world famish, these women volunteered for forcible starvation. They are willing to wear the ill-fitting, bizarre clothes . . ."

Daphne appeared, her stomach pressing out against the garish jumpsuit, running next to Alice. With sweat-slicked hair, without makeup or jewelry, she was reduced to nothing but a hideous fat woman stumbling along.

"They spend hours on end exercising in a manner impossible to replicate when they are released—and yet they continue to believe."

The ill-intentioned camera lingered on Jennifer riding a stationary bicycle, her thick thighs engulfing the machine as though she were smothering it to death.

"None of them is giving a thought to those who spend those same hours just to bring water and food to their families . . ."

Video of women and children carrying buckets and balancing baskets on their heads replaced Jennifer. Dust kicked up with every stolid step.

"What if this energy went toward water parity instead of vanity?" the narration continued. "The following week, we began our second experiment: How far would our trainers Coleen and Valentina go to win? Prize money was shifted, to see the difference in how their clients were treated. After being warned against speaking to each other, ever, about the competition, we promised Coleen five thousand dollars if she won the contest for aggregate pounds lost by a team. This was on top of her fifty-thousand-dollar salary for the month. Valentina was working toward a sixty-thousand-dollar bonus, which would augment her twelve-thousand-dollar paycheck for the month of work."

The camera lingered on Valentina's bony hand placing a pill in each of their hands.

Our house doctor approached Valentina with so-called vitamins—which were, in fact, dextroamphetamine, the generic form of Dexedrine. The willingness she showed in taking the doctor's advice without question was in direct conflict with Coleen's request for a list of the ingredients in the pills.

The doctor never complied with Coleen's request, and she never brought it up again, while Valentina pushed her three to take the unknown vitamins. They, in turn, once feeling the euphoria, took them, even begging for more.

Hania appeared with Valentina, wheedling pills with flattery, offering the trainer a golden bangle for two dozen.

"Eff these men," Alice said. "Clancy was right. Acrobat is filled with pigs."

"They'll show this film over my dead body," Daphne said. "We need to do something. Now."

The camera panned on Hania, collapsed in a chair, removing her gold bangles, and then flashed her naked on the scale.

"Oh, we will," Alice said. "We will."

CHAPTER 18

ALICE

Alice flew back to their room powered by wrath, her mental knives sharpened with each step she took. Never again would she allow herself to be anyone's joke or object lesson.

Years working at the Cobb, forced to fill out long-range and short-range goals for the board of directors, including action steps, hadn't been for nothing. Even as she walked, she began planning their revenge and getaway.

Mission: Take back their personal agency by ruining Acrobat's film.

Goal: Find the film and escape. Publicize this bullshit.

Actions Steps: Strategize fast.

"We need to sleep, but we can't take a pill," Alice said. "We'll need it for tomorrow, for the plan I'm forming. And we'll have to beg a few more from Valentina. What do you think, Daph?"

"That should do it. I'm more concerned with titrating our speed for tomorrow—making sure we can stay awake."

"I have plenty," Hania said.

They turned to her. Alice glared. "We thought you only had the one extra."

"What? Valentina wanted me to lose more weight. I also got extra sleeping pills. I've been hoarding them for when I'm home."

"That's dangerous, Hania," Alice said. "And stupid. Especially now. But thank God. Now give them all to me."

When the alarm rang at seven o'clock, Alice rolled over, saw her family photo, and vowed that Libby would be in her arms by tomorrow.

Adrenaline overtook her exhaustion. Well, adrenaline followed by pills. The day was a blur of exercise, weigh-ins, and thinking through the plan until Alice became certain of every detail.

She wanted to attack Jeremiah, but she did the opposite. Each of them had her prey, and hers was the big man. This much she knew: most men wanted admiration. Susceptibility to vanity often became their Achilles' heel. Therefore, Jeremiah could be weaponized by using the ongoing feud between Acrobat and Prior Productions.

Every afternoon, Jeremiah took a slow stroll through the weight section of the cavernous gym, fancying himself a paragon when it came to lifting. Alice made sure Valentina assigned her to that area.

As he moved toward her, she called his name.

231

"Am I doing this as well as I can?" she asked as he stood over her. She put down the kettlebell. "Release is getting close, and I'm scared."

"What are you nervous about?" Jeremiah asked. "Keeping the weight off?"

"Of course. That and much more." She swept her hands toward him. "I mean, look at you. And then me."

Jeremiah puffed up, crossing his arms in a manner that emphasized his every muscle.

"Face it. You're a damn Adonis. I don't care what I say anymore. We leave in a week, and I need every bit of help." She moved closer and whispered, ready to feed him catnip. "You know who my husband is, right?"

Jeremiah nodded, his curiosity apparent.

"My husband may have the reputation of an avenging angel, but trust me, my marriage is nowhere near heaven. I came because of Clancy."

"What? Are you undercover?" His laugh sounded nervous.

"God, no! I thought he might lock me up when I told him that I was coming here. But it's his fault. Because he can't stand touching me anymore." Who cared what she said, how much she exaggerated. "He hates Acrobat. When you guys won at the Mobius Awards, he had a fit. He thought he deserved the top prize."

"You should have left the asshole." Jeremiah leaned in. He looked her up and down as though he hadn't seen her nude and humiliated, as though she were his slave, one whom he just might take to bed for the night.

Alice dug deep. "When I leave, it will be with the rocking bod you guys give me. I am so grateful." She went closer. "You. You're the true expert here. I don't just want to be thin; I want to be cut. I really need your help."

By eight o'clock that evening, they were back in their rooms, ready to debrief and prepare for their postmidnight assault. "What happened with you, Hania?" Alice asked.

After swinging her hair out of her eyes, their golden girl ran her hand over her jaw, simulating pain.

"No!" Daphne said. "You didn't."

"I did my job."

Alice closed her eyes and tried not to imagine Libby at twenty-eight years old. "Your job didn't include fellatio."

"Don't be so shocked. We came close to, um, intimacy, before. Yes, I lied to you. Anyway, my job was to get information. I got that and more." She reached behind her and held up a key on a small chain, the sort with a pop-in connector. "Say hello to the master."

"Seriously?" Alice thought of Hania's pretense at innocence and smiled. Women had a way of hiding their lights—and intents—under a bushel.

Men were usually easier to read. Too many of them forgot to peer down from their positions of power, even if that power was only over a fat girl at a fat-farm mansion.

"Yup. Love me or hate me for it, I cooked up a mash of tears and sex. Irresistible to men who've been locked up surrounded by almost naked women, albeit fat ones, and had only their own hands. And now, through my sleight of hand, we have the master key."

Wearing a huge smile, Daphne rose slowly. Alice didn't know what to expect from her coconspirator's expression. Had she taken her assignment to the extreme and killed Valentina and Coleen? Daphne rummaged through her top drawer until she gave an evil smile.

"I think now is the time to celebrate." She held a ragged bag of Reese's Pieces above her head. "For us." She tore open the worn sack, spilling the candy onto the small side table, and began dividing the pieces into three piles.

Alice's mouth watered. Even during her mother's most strident health food binges, Bebe had still made desserts with fruit and honey. And, of course, it didn't take much for Alice to cajole Zeke into frequent ice cream trips. Now, deprived of all sugar for so long, her hand twitched toward the treat.

Hania picked up an orange piece and moaned in pleasure as she ate it.

Alice pushed half of her pile toward each of them. "You have it."

"I did wrong, huh? I just thought this might be our version of a shot of courage. Since we have no liquor." Daphne sounded hurt by Alice's words.

Alice worked against sounding superior. "I know how I become after being sugar deprived. One taste and I go sugar mad. I can't afford it with what's facing me."

"I *earned* it," Hania said. "Want to hear how I did it? I followed the girl script and made sure Mike found me crying in the corner of his usual path back to his office, postlunch."

"In the chair down the hall from him?"

"Yup." Hania made air quotes. "On my way to the lawn for a time-out."

"Come on, ladies," Alice said. "Hurry. We have lots to do."

Hania spoke fast and staccato. "He knelt before me—he's such a softie—rubbed my knee and—"

" 'Cause a knee rub is the perfect way to comfort any—"

Alice slapped the arm of the chair. "Daphne! We don't have time."

Daphne held up her hands and rose. "Sorry! Must be my sugar rush talking."

"Anyhow, he asked me what was wrong." Hania grabbed back the spotlight. "And I gave him the scared-to-be-out-in-the-cold-cold-world speech. Blah, blah, blah. How much he'd come to mean to me."

"So he took you to his office?" Alice asked as Daphne brought out supplies.

"Yup. I began sobbing. He looked around. I think he was afraid to lose the time with me. 'Cause as he patted my knee, he kept staring here." She pointed to her buoyant breasts. "He tried to hide it. He's not a pig."

"Finish up, Hania. Bottom line?" Acid churned in Alice's stomach.

"He comforted. Then I offered thanks." Hania shrugged. "Hey, I'm a grown woman. He's a man. After, he wanted my number."

"Tell me you didn't give it to him!"

"Do you think I'm stupid?" Hania pouted for a moment. "I told him about my superstrict parents who don't like non-Indian men. I asked for *his* number." She smiled as though waiting for a pat on the shoulder.

Alice longed for the authority she held at the Cobb. Being the boss was far more her preference than working by committee.

"And then . . ." Daphne urged.

"And then I got him to put on music while I gave him a short neck massage. Did I ever tell you guys I put myself through college working as a masseuse?"

Daphne and Alice both nodded vigorously. "Many times."

Alice wondered if they owned any untold stories by this point. The three of them had been one another's entertainment, support, friends, and in loco parentis for more than three weeks.

"So, as I dug into his neck, I reached behind for his jeans. When Mike got undressed, the key ring looked like it weighed a ton; I asked him how he carried them around all day. He laughed—truthfully, he thinks this gig is either a weird lark or a sick joke—and said he needed them because in the next few days he'd need to access some out-of-the-way places."

"Like where?" Alice asked.

Hania shrugged. "No idea. But places where the master didn't work. The master he keeps on a separate chain attached to the whole ring. Or did, I should say." She held up a key that had been part of a quick-release key chain.

"And when he misses it?" Alice asked.

"He's a careless dude. He'll chalk it up to it falling off, and tomorrow he'll search for it. He's too intimidated by Jeremiah to tell him unless he has to."

Alice considered how much to trust Hania's take. On the one hand, she resembled what her grandmother would call a flibbertigibbet, a word that never failed to crack her up when she went down South for visits. On the other hand, this supposed fluff of a young woman had returned with the goods.

"Daph?"

"Project Sleepyhead is done."

"How did you do it?" Hania asked.

"Easy-peasy. I crushed the sleeping pills into a fine powder. Mixed it with water until I had a proper roux, and poured it into that cucumber water everyone guzzles day and night. Jeremiah drinks more than anyone."

"What if it tastes weird? Bitter?" Hania asked.

"I tasted some." Daphne held up a hand. "Don't worry! Not to drink. I dipped in a fingertip. The cucumber's own bitterness covered it up. Everyone is going be sleepy very early."

"Okay. The preliminaries are in place. Now we move to part one." Alice grabbed her watch. "I'm setting this for midnight. Do anything you can to sleep. Use mind over matter. Count sheep or Reese's Pieces, whatever relaxes you. Because before two o'clock, we'd better be in a goddamn ambulance."

CHAPTER 19

ALICE

At the stroke of midnight, Alice, Hania, and Daphne—a jumpsuited trio of Cinderellas—began their journey home.

First they repeated their silent trip toward Mike's office. Alice took no comfort in the sleeping pills Daphne had stirred into the cucumber water, considering it merely extra insurance. The corridors remained quiet, but no more than the previous night. No snores rang out. Alice put her fingers to her lips every few minutes as a reminder to be alert. No tripping on nails as they crept along on naked soles. Not on her watch.

The master key, tucked into her bra on the underside of her breast (where it would be least likely to show), bit into her flesh.

Hania turned the knob to Mike's office. She shook her head at Alice, who dug out the key, and with a prayer, handed over the warm metal.

Once in the office, they worked fast, sweeping through the room using Alice's established order. Daphne, the least technical, searched for every possible device and lined them up for Alice. Hania settled in front of the desktop.

Alice took each laptop and transferred all files related to *Waisted* to thumb drives swiped from Mike. Hania had been right. Boxes of them were strewn around the office. She would have trashed the files on the computers after copying them, but she feared giving away their theft too soon.

They finished fast and made it back to their room without a sound coming from anywhere. As soon as they closed the door behind them, they divided the flash drives, hiding them in every fold on their bodies, for once grateful for their fleshy bits and pieces.

At one in the morning, with the goods hidden, Alice nodded at Daphne and then sat on the closed toilet seat. Daphne laid out her tools and took her cosmetics kit from a bathroom drawer.

Alice sat, impatient, as Daphne worked her stagecraft magic.

"Stay still, or I'll have to do this all over again." Daphne brushed around Alice's eyes with feathery strokes.

"You're not making the Mona Lisa." Alice's heart hammered so furisously that she worried that an actual medical emergency was imminent. There had to be a limit to the number of speed pills of unknown origin a person could take before suffering a stroke or heart attack. Especially when eating became such an afterthought that one lived below subsistence levels.

Daphne spread cool liquid the consistency of foundation over Alice's entire face.

"Are you making me up for prom or disaster?"

"I need a base," Daphne said. "Bare skin isn't the best surface for holding what I'm putting on you. Grip is the key."

"Speaking of skin." Alice tried to frown without moving her face and settled for pointing a finger at herself. "I don't suppose you have a foundation that actually matches me, do you?"

"Oh, be quiet," Hania said. "You should see what she mixed."

Alice cut her eyes to the right, trying to see what Hania meant.

"Stay still!" Daphne warned. "Sorry if I didn't bring shades of makeup for an entire rainbow of women, but I've worked on more than one person of color, for God's sake. And by the way? We're not making you up for the Oscars, Halle Berry. I'm mixing in eye shadow to deepen the foundation. If you want the blow by blow, I'll give it to you. But don't move."

Daphne's cool fingers soothed Alice as she swept some concoction over her face. "Now I'll put red on your lower lid."

"Weird," Hania said. "Will it really look like a black eye?"

"I don't have my professional blood-and-gore

kit, but believe me, I can fake it with anything. You're going to tear up a bit now. I'm going to add some red to your waterline."

"With what?" Alice drew back.

"A thin brush and red lipstick. Don't worry. I sanitized it." She gripped Alice's chin and tilted it. "After I learned how to fake it in drama club, I used this when I wanted to stay home from school."

"Wish I knew you back then," Hania said.

"I'm going to outline where the bruise will be."

Brushstrokes tickled the skin around Alice's eyes.

"Filling it in with red now. Making it splotchy. Adding some purple to the inner lid. And a small amount along your upper lid." Daphne spoke deliberately as she narrated her work. "I'm putting the purple heavier under the brow bone, where blood collects most. Where that weight supposedly impacted you, it would swell and not color as much, so I leave that area lighter. And yes, I adjusted for your coloring. You're not very dark, but you're not pale. When I'm done with the purple, I'll add more red, because this is a fresh bruise. When it's fresh, it's redder."

"Something feels scratchy. What is it?" asked Alice. Staying still was no easy task with the effects of the pills running through her.

"A sponge. I'm blending in different directions.

To make it irregular, the way a bruise forms. Now I'm using a brush again, putting yellow at the bone and covering it with shadow. I make a line with black eyeliner at the corner of your eye, up against the nose, and smudge into the purple. Now, I use creamy eye shadow that I mixed up from different colors and stipple, stipple, stipple."

Daphne backed away from her work, tipping Alice's head this way and that. "I need to do a bit more to make it look like broken blood vessels and make it appear fresher, like a new bruise. A nasty one."

She worked in quiet for a few moments. "Okay. Time to build you a hematoma."

Two in the morning.

Go time.

Alice took deep, cleansing breaths, calling up memories of acting in camp plays.

Daphne held up a bundle of supposed bloody towels. "Done. This is what I'll press against your head. You gotta clutch these to you. If anyone tries to take over for me, you go crazy. Hold on to Hania with the other hand. Dig in to her arms and scream if they try to separate us."

"One more check," Alice said. "Everyone has their thumb drives, yes?"

They nodded.

"Okay. Let's do this." Alice, never someone to initiate physical contact outside her family,

243

surprised herself by giving each woman a hug. "Here's to us."

The three walked to the edge of the bedroom and quietly tipped over a dresser. After, they pushed aside the small scatter rug as though someone had slipped on it.

Hania dragged over a chair and stood on it. Daphne handed her the fifteen-pound weight that Alice had sweet-talked from Jeremiah. Alice and Daphne moved to the other corner of the room.

"Be careful!" Alice said.

"Don't worry, old ladies. Light as the food we eat." Hania held the iron kettlebell high above her head and threw it to the floor. The weight crashed into the dresser loud enough to wake the entire mansion.

"Move." Daphne guided Alice to the spot they planned for her during rehearsal.

Alice rag-dolled her body, and Daphne moved her into position. Hania knelt like a penitent and pressed the bloody towel into the side of Alice's face.

Here goes.

CHAPTER 20

DAPHNE

Daphne jumped at Alice's full-throated scream.

Despite expecting the sound, a surge of panic rose through her as she raced toward Coleen's and Valentina's rooms, first stopping at the bedrooms of the other *Waisted* members, pounding on their doors.

"Help!" Daphne sounded breathless and scared. "Help us!"

Jennifer and Seung stumbled from their respective doors.

"What? What's wrong?" Seung asked.

"Alice." Daphne panted, her hand flat against her chest. "It's Alice. She's injured. Bad. We need help. An ambulance. Wake everyone."

With those words, Daphne continued toward the staff rooms. Waking the participants first, she hoped, would increase confusion and concern, adding to the difficulty Valentina and Coleen would have sorting out the situation.

"Help! Help!" She hammered at Coleen's door, wanting her to be the initial staff person on the scene. Inciting fear in Coleen would be easier

than fooling Valentina, who knew them far better and trusted them far less.

Coleen opened the door just as Daphne lifted her fist to pummel it once more.

"What?!"

Coleen's soft pink sweats, combined with her sleep-plumped face, offered a more sympathetic appearance than her usual mien.

"Alice." Daphne leaned over for a moment, a hand on each thigh, and gasped—true bullshit, as their recent exercise program had so strengthened her. While she was down there, she panted out a slow sentence, as though barely able to speak from fear and being out of breath. "Alice. Weight fell. In room. Unconscious. *Ambulance!*"

Coleen ran back into her room and came back with a phone clutched in her hand. "I'm going. Get the others." She barreled off toward Alice.

Daphne nodded, running to Valentina's room until Coleen turned the corner. She counted to ten when she reached Valentina's and then banged on her door, repeated her story, and went to wake the remaining staff—conveniently forgetting the doctor of the house, hoping the pill-drugged cucumber water combined with Dr. Ash's usual generous helping of alcohol would slow him down.

After finishing her rounds, Daphne sprinted back to the bedroom, just behind Jeremiah, the last to arrive.

"No!" Alice screeched. *"No, no, no!"* She clutched Hania so close they became an inseparable entity.

Daphne rushed over. "You're awake. Thank God. I'm here. You're fine. *Shh, shh,"* she crooned like a grandmother.

"I can't see!" Alice screamed. "Don't leave me." She jerked Daphne down.

"I'll take over," Daphne said to Hania.

"No!!!" Alice grabbed Daphne's hand and pulled her close, as planned, ensuring she was surrounded by Hania holding the bloodied cloth to her head and Daphne gripping her hand.

"She vomited," Hania said to the room in general. "And blacked out. When she came to, she vomited again. I tried to wipe it away, but if I did, stopping the pressure became impossible, and the bleeding got worse."

Daphne inspected Alice, as though checking for danger signs. "She lost control."

Jeremiah pushed through everyone to be in front. "What happened? Where's Ash?"

Daphne ignored the second question. "She got a weight from somewhere and went insane on doing reps. Don't know how she fell, but we heard a crash and her scream."

"What the fuck?! Where the hell is Ash?" he repeated.

"I knocked!" Daphne said. "She needs a

hospital. Now. We can't move her without an EMT. If she has a brain injury—"

"I called," Coleen said. "They'll be here soon. Very soon."

Alice moaned and then appeared to lose consciousness.

"Is she dying?" A tear dripped down Hania's cheek, impressing Daphne no end.

"Wake up," Daphne said. "Stay with us!"

"She's not going to die," Jeremiah sounded less sure than his words.

"I worked in a hospital for years," Lauretta said. "Plenty of people die from brain hemorrhages. She could be internally bleeding out."

Valentina walked toward the three women on the floor. "Let me see what's going on."

"No!" Lauretta stepped in front of the trainer. "You can't disturb her."

"Are you a nurse? A doctor?" Valentina again tried coming closer.

Susannah and Jennifer blocked her, making a fence of their bodies. "Whoa," Jennifer said. "This isn't a game. Don't touch her."

Jeremiah moved forward, stopping when the four women surged toward him.

"So are you?" Valentina asked Lauretta, even as she stepped back. "A medical person?"

"I work in administration. I saw more records of how people died than you ever want to see."

The sounds of an ambulance broke the country silence.

"Where's the weight?" Jeremiah asked.

"Who cares?" Susannah asked.

"I think you better leave the scene as it is," Lauretta said.

"Are you also the queen of crime scenes?" Valentina again tried to sidle closer to Daphne and the others. "Did you file police reports? Solve murders?"

Daphne could scarcely breathe between the sour smell of Alice's vomit—what *had* she managed to bring up?—and fear.

Valentina pushed past the women and wedged in closer. She attempted to kneel, covering her mouth against the stench.

"Get away," Jennifer said. "I'm warning you."

Susannah stepped up next to her. "Or we'll pull you away."

Now the ambulance screamed outside.

"Coleen. Go let them in." Jeremiah ran his hand over his head as though clearing cob-webs. Sleeping-pill cobwebs. "Valentina. Move away."

Two male EMTs carrying a stretcher came in moments before the doctor.

"What's going on?" Ash asked.

Nobody answered.

The men, badges sewn on their uniforms, knelt beside Alice, Daphne, and Hania.

Alice moaned and pulled Daphne closer. *"I can't see. I can't see."*

Ash, ridiculous looking in pressed blue pajamas with white piping, tried to fit himself into the picture.

"Don't leave. I'll die. I know it," Alice whispered.

"Take us like this," Hania begged. "She'll get hysterical if I lift my hand."

Daphne gripped the older EMT's forearm. Success felt so close. His grizzled beard scratched when she placed her lips near his ear and murmured, "We're in great danger. Take us together, or we'll die. They're trying to kill us."

He looked up and gazed over the room, taking in the five women in identical pajamas; the three of them in their jumpsuits; the colossal Jeremiah, standing with folded arms; Ash; and the two whippet-thin trainers.

"No worries," Jeremiah said. "We can treat her here. We have a doctor on staff."

Ash nodded, looking sleepy and dazed, and tried to reach Alice. Jennifer moved in front of him and blocked him from getting closer.

Daphne whispered once more, her lips pressed close. "They've been feeding us pills. Forcing us to exercise around the clock."

"We can treat her with our doctor," Valentina said—so calmly it made Daphne shiver. "Anyway, I think she is high. Probably drunk, yes? Peeing on herself like that."

The bearded EMT squared his shoulders and half rose. The deep timbre of his voice quieted the room. "Everyone but these two women, step back."

"Now, wait a moment." Ash slurred as he spoke. "I'm the ranking medical personnel."

The older EMT barked, "You heard him. Back up, or the police will be here faster than you can produce your medical diploma." His thinning hair, sloped shoulders, and potbelly belied the force with which he spoke.

Jeremiah attempted to regain his authority by repeating the threat in his own words. "Back up. Everyone. Give them room to work. Alice is in danger."

Daphne continued pressing the cloth covering Alice's head until the vehicle reached the driveway. Only then did she let the older EMT pull it away. Hania was in the front with the driver. Daphne had forced her way to be allowed to ride with Alice through sheer will, digging her fingers into the EMT's arm as she hissed, *"Life or death, I swear to God."*

By now, sweat and pressure had smeared the cosmetic bruises into a swirl of ugly colors, no more able to fool a child, much less an EMT. Alice opened her eyes and smiled at Daphne.

"All right, ladies. What the hell is going

on?" the EMT asked as they drove away in the screaming ambulance.

"You have no idea of the overwhelming danger we faced."

"Of what?"

"Being exercised to death, fed illegal substances, and enduring great humiliation," Daphne recited.

"Who forced you to take pills?" He reached for a blood pressure cuff. "Why were you there? Did they hold you illegally?"

"Fine lines run between illegal, coerced, fooled, and brainwashed."

The man held the cuff limp in his hand. "Hey, I'm familiar with car wrecks and drunks. Gunshot wounds. This is out of my league. I'm happy to transport you to the hospital, but maybe it's the police station you need?"

Alice rose to a sitting position on the stretcher. "What I need is a shower. Can you help me with that?"

The man looked confused. Daphne stepped in before the EMT's bewilderment gave way to anger and he called the police. Going home was all she wanted. Nothing could stand in the way of calling her husband.

"Let me explain," she said in the husky voice she affected when a man required handling. "They described it as a weight loss retreat. You know. With proper nutrition and classes. Healthy exercise."

"A place to reflect on our decisions," Alice added.

"Somewhere for us to regain our bodies and hearts." Daphne realized that in trying to fool this man, they were nevertheless finally speaking certain truths about their situation out loud.

"Instead, they abused us. Harshly." Alice began pretty-crying. Mild tears only enhanced the carved beauty of her thinned face, noticeable despite the palette of colors running down.

"How?"

Control-of-the-narrative time. "It's painful to talk about." Daphne read the man's badge. "You rescued us, Bill. They fed us dex-a-something pills."

Bill nodded. Encouraged, Daphne went on. "They increased the dosage daily. Working us ten hours a day. Held us as virtual prisoners. Sure, we could have walked out. But we had no coats. Or boots. Or any way to contact our loved ones. They stole our phones. Everything."

Alice pulled the blankets that Bill had provided closer around her shoulders. "They have our IDs. They played psych games. They fed us speed by day, chased by sleeping meds at night. Without prescriptions."

"We didn't visit that doctor or ask for them. God knows what they forced on us." Daphne placed a hand on her chest, an anxiety attack growing now that the initial drama had passed. "We're under the influence of drugs now. We do need medical attention."

They arrived at the hospital shockingly fast, given how far they'd believed themselves to be from civilization. When they begged to be put in the same room, Bill helped it happen and, more important, kept the emergency room triage nurse from locking them in the psych ward.

The first thing they did was remove their hideous jumpsuits in exchange for scrubs (given to them by Bill, now their accomplice and buddy). Alice washed up as best she could by using the stack of washcloths. When the others started to throw their jumpsuits in the trash, Alice reminded them that they'd need evidence—though she rinsed hers with the bar soap.

Next, Daphne borrowed Bill's phone, craving Sam's voice.

> **TIP:** Breathe away cravings.
> This may seem obvious. After all, you must breathe no matter what, right? But few of us breathe deeply or consciously. Think about it: When was the last time you took a long, slow, deep breath, and leisurely let it out again? Deep breaths of that kind take you out of your immersion in momentary stress, oxygenate your

brain and tissues, and help to reduce stress hormones.

—Huffington Post

WEIGHT LOST THEN: None.
CRAVING SAM NOW: Overwhelming.

"Daph! Ohmigod. I can't believe it's you. They're finally letting you call out. Jesus, what's going on there? I miss you so much, sweetheart. How—"

She interrupted, trying to talk through her tears. "How soon can you drive up? We're at a hospital. We're fine," she hastened to add. "It's four hours away from Boston."

"Tell me which hospital. I'm leaving now."

Hearing his voice, this person who loved her, this man whose words she too often pushed away, this man she took for granted—today, this same man broke her apart with love and longing. She swore to keep him first in her heart from this day forward.

CHAPTER 21

DAPHNE

"I just can't stop staring at you, darling!" Sunny tipped her head and shook it as she smiled. "Lovely, lovely, lovely. I could say it a million times."

Sunny stared at her with so much unreserved admiration that goose bumps rose on Daphne's skin. Here she was, just as she'd always dreamed—her mother smiling at her with love and approval—yet all she experienced was an urge to escape.

"Doesn't she look wonderful, Gordon?" Sunny ran a hand down Daphne's arm with the air of ownership usually reserved for her sisters.

Her father winked at her. "Daphne's always been beautiful inside and out."

Her head might explode from this outpouring of *extraordinary wonderful Daphne!* "Thanks. How about this dinner, huh? Great job, Bianca."

"I miss Thanksgiving at our house." Audrey's pout transformed her into a six-year-old. "I like Mom's stuffing better. What is this? It tastes like robots microwaved bread."

"Don't be rude. Aunt Bianca went to plenty of

trouble to take over this year." Sam's supposed admonishment sounded mild. His relief in having her home shone so hot that all else receded, fortifying Daphne more than her usual comfort level allowed.

"No worries. The robots at Whole Foods cooked it all. Not me." Bianca joined in the Daphne examination team—her medical gaze apparently evaluating everything she saw. "Do you want a bit of tightening for Chanukah? Slackness is the downside of losing a ton of weight too fast."

Daphne longed for a plateful of stuffing. *Her* stuffing. That's what she wanted. Audrey was speaking the truth: Whole Foods, organic or not, tasted institutional, salty, and oily. Yet there was something to be said for its bad taste. Not eating became easier when faced with oversalted, mass-produced food. As did the well-hidden pills she had stolen before escaping from *Waisted*.

After hearing Hania's story of cadging extra pills from Valentina, Daphne had gone one step better. During gym time, the day of the planned escape, she had faked cramps and, needing protection—thankfully, one thing Valentina didn't care to check—doubled back to their room, retrieved Hania's stolen key, entered Valentina's room, found the pill storage, and grabbed a handful that she stuffed into a plastic baggie hidden in her bra. Twenty pills in all.

Daphne's fear of coming home had been as

deep as her want, even as she ran into Sam's arms. Unlimited food terrified her. She hadn't been able to face down even one bag of stale Reese's Pieces.

The past three weeks she hit her cache one tiny sliver of a pill at a time, but no matter how small the crumbly pieces she sliced off, the pile dwindled. Eleven tablets. Her only life source left.

She chewed her bottom lip—a habit brought on by the pills—hoping Sam would never connect this new quirk with pill popping.

Daphne replied to Bianca's offer of cosmetic help with the sort of phony, sweet smile the Bernays sisters reserved for one another. "Ah, so sweet of you. This must be the part of the meal where we have the traditional Thanksgiving offer of free cosmetic surgery." She wondered what it would take to convince Bianca to prescribe her Dexedrine instead.

"I'm offering tweaks, not the full monty. Actual surgery is too expensive for a giveaway. Anesthesia. Surgical nurses. It adds up, you know." Bianca turned to her husband, an orthopedic surgeon. "Perhaps you can do some trading? Your spine-fixing skills for plastic surgery. Family favors. Might be a good idea for holiday presents, eh?"

Sunny spread a microthin layer of cranberry relish on a slice of white meat. "I know you're joking, but wow, what a gift."

"Grandma, that's nuts!" Audrey speared another slice of turkey. Dark meat. Which she never ate, per her grandmother's warnings that it contained more calories per ounce than white meat. "You're talking about surgery. You think my father would trade his skill for a tummy tuck?"

"Your father works in research, dear. I don't think it's comparable. But darling, you know we're joking, right?"

Sunny's disposition so matched her name of late that it frightened Daphne. That her mother was *this* invested in how many pounds her daughter carried and what size she wore should have come as no surprise, but still, the bold joy Sunny displayed hit Daphne somewhere between sickening and terrifying.

But how to fight? Reprimand her mother for being too kind?

And in truth? When she had zipped up the black sheath she was wearing this afternoon, she had shivered with delight. It was a dream dress in a fantasy size. Who cared if the designer used vanity sizing? The tag read 12.

Stepping on the scale that morning, after hovering between 140 and 142 since returning from Vermont, she saw that she had broken into the one thirties: 139, the ruler of her world delivered. She had nearly fallen to her knees and kissed the metal.

Still, her supply of pills diminished each day.

"Aren't you going to eat anything but turkey, Mom?" Gabe dug a fork into the steaming pile of mashed potatoes. Daphne imagined the buttery smoothness gliding over her tongue.

Perhaps she could contact Valentina. Blackmail her. "I'm fine, honey." She cut a tiny portion and chewed. "Yummy."

"Eating is less fun with you starving." Audrey scooped another helping of the maligned stuffing. Sunny gaped.

"I'm hardly starving, baby! I'm still a house compared with your aunts. An entire housing development compared with you."

True or false? Any sense of the reality of her appearance had disappeared along with the lost weight. She caught a glance in the mirror and barely knew who she saw. Making herself up each morning, when she no longer forced herself to wear ten pounds of eye makeup to distract from her body, led to a new fear: Was she fooling herself? Maybe she still needed every ounce of those cosmetics to be palatable to the eye.

She tried to believe. Where Daphne had once rimmed her eyes in black and purple, topped with an unmovable veneer of rich topaz shadow, followed by applying three coats of mascara, she now drew a thin black line and scarcely brushed her lashes with one quick layer.

If she broke into her sister's closet upstairs and tried on one of Bianca's dresses, how far would it gape in the back? Three inches? Twelve?

She didn't recognize her arms. Skin hung in an empty sack. She worked out every morning and night, but still the flesh wobbled. Sam reassured her it would tighten a bit with time. When she considered surgery aloud, Sam shouted, showing anger for the first time since her return.

"I'm happy to have you home," he'd said. "*You*. But this woman who's broken into our home? Her I am not so thrilled with."

Nor was Daphne. Her temper had shortened, as had her attention. Ivy rolled her eyes at Daphne's fullness of self-love when she caught her peeking in the mirror one time too many.

Daphne gulped more ice water. Her mouth dried out constantly.

To satisfy Gabe and Audrey, she grabbed a roll from the basket. Brioche, baked and sent over by Marisa and Lili, who were spending the holiday with Lili's family.

To satisfy Sam, she buttered it and took a bite.

To satisfy her mother, she winked and set the rest aside.

"Just enough to enjoy, yes?" Daphne pushed the bread plate farther away. "And you think I never listened."

"Honestly? I thought you never heard a word I said. So I repeated myself too often."

"We all thought you never listened, Mom." Audrey grabbed the roll left on Daphne's plate

261

and put it on her own. "Here, let me help you out."

"Why are you being so rude to your mother?" Sunny sounded genuinely confused. And her mother defending her? Every family convention seemed shredded to confetti.

After managing to escape from the lunatics running the mansion, why couldn't Daphne hold it together for one Thanksgiving dinner? She missed Marisa and Lili, who recently brought the conversation back to themselves no matter the occasion, thrilled as they were with their new lives as the glam cover girls of LGBT Boston.

She smiled, remembering their serious eyes as they related the honor. At first, being woozy from her trip back from Vermont, she thought they were being sarcastic. Who in their right minds would imagine her modest sister and earnest sister-in-law describing how proud they were of having their hotness honored on the cover of *Vetoed* magazine?

Again. Confetti. Since coming home, only her father had provided real and practical help. Gordon called his lawyer the moment he saw that Daphne was safe. Within a day, Daphne, Alice, and Hania had their wallets, phones, and all other possessions in their hands. That same day, per the lawyer, Jeremiah shut down the program, and all the women returned home.

"Mom, I appreciate Audrey's honesty and help. This is a difficult time. Managing new habits is hard until they sink in. I'm just laying down the tracks."

"Can we talk about something other than Mom's body and Mom's eating habits?" Gabe asked. "In case anyone cares, I'm thinking of premed."

Daphne lifted her glass of water. "To dreams coming true."

"My dream or Dad's?" Gabe raised his eyebrows as they clinked glasses.

"The choice must always be yours," Sam said. "No decisions need to be made today. I want you to make sure the person being pleased is you."

"Sometimes goals are closer than you think." Daphne touched the wide red belt around her waist.

A red belt.

A black sheath.

Wearing a dress without covering it with a matching piece from the Tentmaker.

Daphne still seethed each time she remembered the punishing treatment meted out at the mansion. The idea of that movie being seen by people she knew, people she didn't know, made her nauseous. But, nevertheless, secrets had been revealed. Staying thin required five things. That was all.

1. Desire.

Check.

2. The money to afford decent food.

Check.

3. Time to cook.

If she had time to cook fattening food, cooking thin and healthy meals was possible.

4. Willpower.

Daphne had discovered a well of that. Oh, sure, the pills helped. But she'd figure out how to do without them soon. The pills were only stepping-stones to new habits.

5. Replacements for what food gave you.

This dress taught her something she had never believed before: thinness could be savored with more satisfaction than brownies.

Sunny again beamed across the table. How soft her mother's face became when bathed with admiration and love.

A delicious frisson shuddered through Daphne as the green satin nightgown slithered over her hips.

Tonight, seductress would be her role. Sam had urged her into romance so many times. But this bedtime, he'd be the one pursued.

She smiled at herself in the mirror. This full-length mirror, an art deco antique, a wedding present from Sam's wildest aunt, this glass she'd avoided for too many years, finally pleased her.

She'd bought the gown online at Bergdorf's, her imagination transported by the photo of it. She dared order a medium, trying it on with trepidation when it arrived.

That it fit, how it fit, electrified her. Seafoam fabric matched her eyes. A lacy sweetheart bodice held up her breasts to show a V of generous cleavage. Three-quarter sleeves bypassed her upper arms, the body of the gown flowed out and over her hips. Cut on some miracle bias, the satin turned her into a 1930s film goddess.

Daphne fanned out her mane of red curls. Admired her pale skin and eyes bare of anything but the lightest dusting of gold shadow, the slightest rimming of bronze.

Staring at this new woman became her foreplay.

Sam opened the master bath and grinned. "You're spectacular." He swept her into his arms and ran both hands down her back until they rested below her waist. Then he bent her back and gave her a Hollywood kiss.

When they came up for air, she twirled for him. "You like?"

His smile lowered. "Always and never anything but."

"Oh, Sam. I can't deny it. I love seeing myself this way."

"Anytime you feel happy, you sparkle." He brought her into his arms and grazed her shoulder with his lips.

"But I do look wonderful, right? Better?" She pulled away from his embrace.

"I told you how beautiful you look."

"But I want more. I want you to think I look remarkably better. Miraculously improved. That it was all worth it."

"You did this for you, not me. I was never unhappy with anything but your sadness." He pressed his lips together—Sam's sign for holding back.

"What?" she asked. "What are you not saying?"

"I don't want you to be disappointed. And rest everything on this." He gestured over her body. "You know how . . . *severely* they treated you. This might be hard to keep up. Let it settle to normalcy. And yes, you are lovely. But honey, you're always lovely to me."

He tried pulling her back to him, but she resisted, sour resentment rising. "Do you have to ruin this? Do you have to be the scientist every minute?"

Sam shrugged. "I have to be truthful. Watching out for you includes honesty."

"I did this for you!" Daphne heard herself lie, and, nonsensically, it made her angry at her husband. Why couldn't he have just said she looked beautiful?

"For me? No. Not me. I wish you had done it for you, but all the work was for your mother."

Daphne tried to pull herself back, to rescue the night. She struck another seductive pose. "Did I put on this nightgown for Sunny?"

He placed a tentative hand on her back. "You look like a princess."

"I want to know that you can see me. The new me. And that you appreciate her."

"Honey. Of course, I appreciate her. You. But I can't deny my wife of twenty years. I love and value her just as much. And I don't want you to be devastated if you can't keep this up."

She let him lead her to the bed without another word, vowing never to revert to her old self again.

TIP: There's nothing wrong with dropping pounds quickly—as long as you're doing it smartly. Losing weight more quickly may give you more motivation to keep going, though it doesn't really matter how many pounds you lose a week. The only thing that matters is the method you're using to experience weight loss and how well you follow your maintenance plan.

—*Jillian Michaels*

TAKEAWAY: Fuck you, Sam.

CHAPTER 22

ALICE

S o, how's he doing?" Bebe combined cooked
cauliflower, pepper, salt, and hand-grated
parmesan with the masher she'd been using since
anyone could remember, while Alice folded cloth
napkins into perfect rectangles. "This is almost
calorie free, you know, by the way. Chewing
burns more calories than you get. So, can I put in
a little butter?"

"Mom, you know I don't live inside your brain,
right? Who is *he?* And you can put in anything
you like. I won't blow up like a float from the
parade. I can manage what I put in my mouth just
fine."

"*He* is your husband." She lowered her voice
and tipped her head to the right, indicating the
crowd of men around the television—the testos-
terone of football and beer broken only by the
sounds of Libby urging her stuffed dog to jump
over Uncle Macon's feet.

Twenty-five people would crowd around the
table that Thanksgiving, accommodated by
adding a folding table to the dining room table.

Her mother gathered up the family-less orphans from her work, widowed neighbors, and at least one of her father's former students.

"Don't jump down my throat. I know how much this weight loss thing means to you. I'm trying to be respectful."

"Watching my health isn't a 'thing.' It's not a religion, Mom. Demeaning words don't help, but respect isn't required. Nor is preparing special meals. I can titrate my own calories. And *he's* fine."

"Titrate, eh?" Her mother laughed. "Better living through chemistry."

Alice stepped back and held her arms out straight. Her mother's red apron, astoundingly, wrapped around Alice's waist and tied in the back with room to spare. "But really, do you see how I changed?"

"I'm not blind."

"Sometimes you are. When it comes to me." Alice chopped a green pepper into thin, even slices. "Sometimes the needs of mine that you'll attend to are limited to the ones with which you agree."

"Your fight isn't with me, hon. We took care of Libby. We kept an eye out for Clancy." Her mother got the tight expression that came before a tart tone. "So I'd say that I took care of some needs with which I didn't agree."

With this, her mother raised her eyebrows.

Alice raised hers back higher and with more emphasis.

"Let's forget all that." Bebe scraped the cauliflower mix into a bowl and topped it with wheat germ. The unappealing dish was for her? She wanted the massive bowl of corn bread dressing that steamed on the counter—a recipe from Zeke's relatives down South. Bebe mixed crumbled corn bread with broken bits of buttermilk biscuits. The scent of butter, onions, celery, and the secret ingredients not yet revealed to Alice added up to heaven. Right this moment, Alice wanted to scarf an overflowing spoonful before Bebe placed it on the table. Which would probably make her mother happy. But Alice resisted.

"So?" Again, her mother lifted her eyebrows. "Clancy?"

Smart talk and jokey comebacks rose, but instead, Alice spoke the truth. "Clancy thinks I look great."

"So that's what's important. Right?"

"I guess." Alice popped a slice of pepper in her mouth. The watery crunch provided some relief from the need to grab one of the biscuits warming on a covered hot tray. "Are you asking like you agree, or are you asking like I'm being a jerk?"

"Isn't he the reason you went, to begin with?"

"I guess." She grabbed a second slice of pepper.

"Baby." Her mother took Alice's hand that held

the knife, removed it with a motherly gangster grip, and forced her face-to-face. "Stop with the 'I guess.' Clancy was the reason you went, right? Didn't you tell us he didn't like the supposed weight gain? Which we, of course, thought was insane. And mean. But Daddy and I would never interfere in your marriage."

"Maybe you should have." Eff it. One biscuit wouldn't mess her up. Did she have to maintain her newly hatched 90–10 plan every minute? Nine or ninety green peppers—how many did she need to eat to resist one biscuit?

Alice simultaneously sliced angels on the head of a pin and tormented her mother. Very holiday-like.

"How 'should' we interfere?" Her mother looked so serious. As though Alice expected her to run into the living room and smarten Clancy up this minute.

If asked, she would.

"I'm being horrid," Alice said. "This is on me. I knew who he was when I married him."

"Who is he?"

"Someone for whom the form is the function."

"So your only function is your appearance?"

"He'd never describe it with those words. I meant Clancy sees the world through his aesthetics. He measures everything—even me and Libby—by how much we please the eye."

"Sounds damn cold, hon."

"He obviously cares about much more. You know that, Mom. But have you met your son-in-law? He can be kind of a cyborg." Alice wanted to say that Clancy could be kind of a dick—but if he was a dick, who was the fool? Who had married that dick?

"Here, try this. Auntie Mimi sent it." Bebe, reverting to knee-jerk mothering upon seeing Alice's sad face, reached for a large flower-covered tin, one that Auntie Mimi, still in Brooklyn, and Bebe, from Boston, had used for years to send surprise treats back and forth. With the tin, her mother became more the quintessential Jewish mother and less the hybrid of faux black and hip that Bebe reached for and longed to be. "I'll break off a little piece if you want. Bring a smile to your face."

The chocolate chip cookies would tip over her mother's groaning board—one of the few times of the year Bebe eschewed health. The turkey and dressing would be surrounded by sweet potato pie, and macaroni and cheese, broccoli and rice casserole, corn bread, and all the surprises guests brought. But even with all that, chocolate chip cookies called Alice like Circe's feast.

If chocolate chip cookies were Alice's weakness, Aunt Mimi's version of them was her kryptonite. Elephant ears, she called them. Magic batter made them spread thin and crispy. Each bite brought a snap of buttery goodness, broken up with bittersweet chips of chocolate. Aunt Mimi, so kitchen proud, not only baked from scratch everything she served but also shunned store-bought chips. Broken pieces of the finest darkest chocolate her aunt could find studded every batch.

Alice could practically taste the cookie. Her mouth watered.

Ninety–ten.

Her new mantra. Eat abstemiously 90 percent of the time and cram anything she wanted into her mouth 10 percent.

Easy. Until.

Her tiny mother wore an inviting smile as she held out temptation.

That cookie. How many calories per bite? Just a nibble would be okay.

This is what Alice hated: the constant chattering in her head, weighing every option.

Yes to this. No to that.

"Just take it, sweetheart. Treat yourself." Her mother wiggled the cookie and grinned. "You know you want it."

"Damn it, of course I want it!" Alice batted away the cookie so hard that it fell to the floor and broke into pieces. "I wanted every cookie you ever offered. Even the stupid ones sweetened with applesauce."

A slight quiver appeared in the corner of her mother's lips, which enraged Alice more than any of Bebe's other habits. Strong and steady as she presented herself, everyone in the family lived more in fear of Bebe's softhearted tears than her occasional tirades. God save the child who made Zeke's wife weep.

However, Daddy was in the other room watching football.

"Mom, I'm sorry. I'm sorry. Don't cry. You know I never want to make you sad." A desire to hug and smack her mother at the same time overpowered Alice. "But I can't live my life to make you happy or fit into this insane script you wrote of the strong black feminist woman you want me—expect me—to be every minute."

"I never wanted to fit you into a mold, baby." Her mother blinked away any tears that threatened. "But I understood how hard it would be to have a white mother and a black father. We did everything to put the cards in your and Macon's favor. Living here. Mission Hill might be the most mixed neighborhood in Boston!"

"I know, Mom. But you and Daddy chose it because you love it here. It wasn't some sacrifice."

Bebe shot her a hurt look that begged for appreciation and understanding. "Of course we love it here. But we also did it for you, even though part of us would have enjoyed a greener space. We wanted to give you plays, concerts, sports, the Unitarian church—everything Daddy and I did was in service of making you and your brother strong black citizens."

"But you forgot a few things," Alice said. "Macon and I are different from you and Daddy. We're not black or white."

"Of course. But I wanted—"

"You wanted too many things for me and yet not enough. You wanted me to always be strong. You were allowed the privilege of crying more than me. What did that tell me? Black women crying were weak? You had the privilege of crying. You had the privilege of saying fat was fine for me. Why didn't you tell me I could be anything *including* thin? Why was that reserved for the white girls?"

Years of swallowed words emerged. Alice pressed on through her mother's obvious pain.

"I know you wanted the best for me. I never doubted that for one instant. Nor your love. Nor your commitment to making this world a better place for Macon and for me. You love us so deeply you want to hammer our experiences into your own. You thought your caring inoculated us against the world."

Now they both cried. Alice backed up against the kitchen door so nobody could disturb them. "I love you, Mom. So much it hurts to speak even one word that pains you. And I don't think any mother loved her children more than you love me and Macon.

"I know you want to be with me every step of the way. But that's impossible. You can't be black. Daddy can't be white. Neither of you can be mixed race. Macon and I will always be different than both of you."

"Did we make a mistake? Getting married? Having you? Our family has been the total joy of our lives."

"There's no mistake, Mom. For God's sake, the entire world would be better off being like us. You know I know that, right? But sometimes you got to lighten up. The sum of my existence can't be understood by your reading Toni Morrison or racializing every second of my existence."

Once home, once Libby was tucked in with stories and kisses, once she removed her makeup, brushed her teeth, and massaged oils and creams into her skin, Alice faced Clancy.

Since coming home, they made love often enough to sate her, to chase back the deprivation that had turned Alice into a raging machine of want and scorekeeping. Desire and admiration had returned to Clancy's eyes.

The power dynamic shifted. Need for Clancy's appreciation receded from being in the forefront of Alice's life. Righting herself became center-most, along with figuring out where to put what she'd learned at the mansion—and where to put her wrath. She needed revenge against Jeremiah and everyone else associated with Acrobat Films.

A November chill permeated the apartment. Even the hand lotion she applied felt cold. Hip concrete, wood, and steel didn't warm up well. She longed for the lush comfort of wall-to-wall carpeting.

Her husband believed he wrote the sole book on artistic taste and sensibility. Minimalism, Clancy's god, marked the apartment everywhere but Libby's room. No way was her daughter living in a monk's cell. Clancy filled their home with furniture so sleek that slipping off the edge was a constant danger.

Even here, in their bedroom, a supposed place of comfort and joy, she was surrounded by wood that resembled glass. Their bed rested on an aluminum platform that reflected any defect in the room.

Clancy held up a hand in warning when he saw her applying lotion. "Don't get grease on the sheets." His black robe fell in perfect folds.

"This isn't grease. It is, in fact, extremely expensive skin cream." She pumped another dollop from the white bottle and spread the almond-scented lotion over her arms, rubbing it in with slow, sweeping motions.

"Expensive or not, we don't want to stain the sheets."

"Sheets wash very nicely."

"Not if it's an oily spot."

"Have I been inadvertently messing up the sheets and not noticing? Perhaps my time away gave you a welcome vacation from chaos and oily puddles." Alice pressed down for more lotion and began on her legs.

"What are you going on about?" Clancy lifted the down coverlet and climbed into bed. "I sense a subtext."

Ah, her husband the genius. She flexed her toes toward her and carefully massaged each one.

"Don't disappear again," he said. "Here. Let me."

He reached over and took her arm, and then used his considerable strength to push against every tight spot in her forearm. "Lay back. I'll help you relax."

Touch was her weakness. He knew.

She slid down and rolled onto her stomach. Clancy pulled her nightgown straps from her shoulders and down until her back was bare. He straddled her and pressed his strong thumbs into every indentation of her spine.

First, he unlocked her stiff muscles and then began caressing her with hands well-educated in the book of Alice.

Alice divided in two. The Alice rising to meet him, feeling the love and sensuality of this man with whom she'd made a child, a home; a man who cared about righting wrongs in the world. A man of principal, a quality she found sexy—

even more so after the debacle of the musician boyfriend.

Her other half, the fat girl, the Alice that Clancy had rejected, watched from above. When Alice's passion peaked, she laughed at her other half. The eyes-wide-open wife whispered to the panting woman.

Bought off easy, eh? What about Harper? How much time did he spend with her while you were away?

CHAPTER 23

ALICE

Alice shook and then straightened the post-lovemaking rumpled blanket and then climbed back into bed. "What are we going to do about *Waisted*?"

"Dear Lord, aren't you sleepy?" He ran his thumb over Alice's palm.

She rose to a sitting position, took back her hand, and resisted turning on the bedside lamp. "You asked me to hold off doing anything until you thought about it. Right? So? Have you thought?" Bebe's Jewish inflection seeped into Alice's voice. "I'm seeing Daphne and Hania in a few days."

Alice laced her fingers so tight they began to ache. Releasing perseverating thoughts about the mansion was impossible. She'd go a few hours managing to forget—lost in work, in caring for Libby, and just now, making love, but then memories followed by rage crashed back.

She missed talking to Daphne late into the night, spinning out their lives for each other, whispering so as not to wake Hania, their mansion daughter.

Maybe if she were with Daphne now, she could

wash away her anger with words. Or with a plan. Like the one they'd set up for their escape. How had they woven that strategy so quickly? The strength of their bond—a trust like that forged by soldiers in war—must have allowed the rapid-fire moves.

The attraction and strength of friends was as mysterious as any love—maybe a superior attraction. Love without sex kept you happy and even. Love with lust bounced with untrustworthy pheromones.

Clancy sighed and placed an arm behind his head. "What are you thinking?"

"For one thing, we need to see if we can put a stop order on the film being distributed. Even made."

"You want to be an agent of censorship?"

"We talked about this." Alice pulled the blanket tighter over her lap.

"You were so over-the-top upset; I needed to keep you calm."

"So you pretended to care? They used us. Lied to us. You said they went against every tenet of documentary filmmaking. You swore their ethics were off-the-chart awful."

"Ethics and legality may not be the same, Al."

She climbed out of bed and grabbed her robe. The spotlight-red, bright-as-fuck fabric jumped out in the cool grayness of the bedroom.

"This is about me. Imagine a camera trained

on you in your worst moments, from the worst angles. Appearing hideous. Acting hideous—"

"You signed a release. We're lucky they haven't come after you yet."

"Lucky? No. They're frightened. Look how fast they returned our phones and—"

"But—"

"But nothing. This is me. Your wife. You want me shown to the world like that?"

"Like what? You won't let me see any of it."

She crumpled onto the upright chair in the corner. Show Clancy? Her carrying Coleen on her back, like a horse being ridden by a jockey?

Her naked and being weighed as though she were a slave?

Jesus. What if they did some arty shit interspersing pictures of a slave on a block, her mouth held wide open to inspect her teeth, and then back to Alice?

How could she allow him to see her running, fleshy, bouncing, sweat dripping, and then collapsing as Valentina called her a pig? A slob? A bowl of suet?

Let him look? See the secret shots from their bedroom, stuffed into jumpsuits and whining about what food they missed the most?

Let him look? The day they drove her to exercise so long and hard that she wet herself?

Her father. Her mother. Her brother. Her coworkers. Let them see?

Alice pushed away the images. "I didn't sign up for all that mess."

"When you read all the fine print, you'll be mighty surprised what you signed up for."

Alice blinked against threatening tears. "Be my husband. Okay? The one who loves me. Can you forget everything else for a moment?"

Clancy appeared stricken. He shook his head as though clearing away something and then knelt before the chair where she sat. He took her hands. "Honestly? Speaking as your husband? The one who does love you. Very much. If you want to stop them, you better move fast. No doubt, they are very suspicious. They know you pulled a fast one. If you want to strike before the film is out there, you need to hurry. I'll bet they're fast-tracking it right now."

Alice met Hania and Daphne at Stellina's restaurant. Easy parking and being as equidistant as possible in the triangle formed by their workplaces in Mission Hill, Newbury Street, and Kendall Square, had been the goal, but she'd let herself forget the astonishing food. Temptation permeated the air. Inhaling exquisite scents of tomato and garlic equaled culinary martyrdom. She should at least have ordered soup.

French onion soup. With melted Gruyère. Toasted croutons ready to be unearthed like treasure. Instead, three bowls of dry salad testified to three women cowed by food.

"I just keep getting angrier," Alice said. "I can't sleep. My chest burns with hate. We need to do something soon. To stop them. To punish them. I've been considering an idea. It's a bit edgy. Hell, maybe even illegal. Or libelous."

"What does Clancy think?" Daphne asked.

"He thinks we better act soon. That they'll be rushing to get it out."

Hania lifted a tomato and frowned. "I never want to put another vegetable in my mouth. And yes, I know that a tomato is a fruit. Anyway, I agree with you, Alice. Do you think we could pull off your criminal idea?"

"And is the effort worth it?" Daphne asked. "Are we screwed by our own weight loss? Maybe having lost so much weight, we have no reason to complain?"

Alice nodded. "I've found myself thinking about that constantly: the damage done to us versus how many pounds we lost. Were the humiliations and outright traumas—being fed speed without our consent—mitigated by having left the mansion thinner by so many pounds? I mean, that's what we went there for, right?"

"We went there to heal, not to be abused and lied to," Daphne said.

"Right. And yet, I needed to parse it out. See what part of my need to confront them was based on a righteous need for confrontation, what part was for public education, and what represented pure revenge." Alice pulled out three sheets of paper. "Here. I wrote up my thoughts on it."

Hania smiled. "Boston Latin School trained you well."

Alice scanned her almost memorized words while the others read.

ACROBAT FILMMAKERS PROJECT: REALITY VS. FICTION
from Alice Thompson

1. **Information Provided to Participants Before They Came**

   a/ The documentary *Waisted* would examine if a woman could lose weight not for "society" but for health and for her own personal aesthetic, without losing her dignity and without suffering if she were in a supportive healing environment.

   b/ An atmosphere of respect, health, and mindfulness would be provided. Their words.

   c/ Medical needs would always come first. Their words.

2. **The Actual Premises/Suppositions Enacted at the Waisted Mansion**

   a/ Food was severely controlled. Caloric intakes were below any recommended

285

standards or practices for weight loss.

b/ Exercise was forced, constant, and used as punishment.

c/ Medical oversight was close to nil.

d/ Women were consistently forced to confront themselves in the worst of circumstances.

e/ Weight loss resulted from the unavailability of food, overexercise by coercion, and the use of humiliation tactics.

3. **Suppositions/Theories of Alice Thompson**

a/ The weight loss from *Waisted* was unsustainable.

b/ The imposed "control through unavailability" method was experimental bullshit. The women hadn't learned control—they'd *been* controlled. They'd been used to see how far they would allow Jeremiah, Coleen, and Valentina to bully them.

c/ The women were terrorized into thinness. This was an unsustainable methodology, unless one wanted to build the equivalent of weight loss concentration camps.

d/ They'd been fooled into joining *Waisted*. Nothing in the brochures mentioned the harsh tactics. Quite the opposite. Acrobat presented the mansion as though they were entering a healing retreat.

e/ Acrobat wanted to prove that women

would accept humiliation and shame in pursuit of weight loss. Up to their breaking point, it worked. But what did that mean? That the abuse heaped upon women for centuries had led to women accepting abuse? Thus, was Acrobat a dog chasing its own tail? More important, the actual takeaway was that Alice, Daphne, and Hania ultimately did not accept the terms Acrobat put forward.

f/ There was no truth given to the participants in *Waisted*, only lies of omission—if not commission—by a filmmaker and a director willing to thread them through the needle of their belief system to prove their thesis: *women would do anything to fit society's norm.*

4. What I Think Acrobat Wants to Present in Its Documentary

a/ Women would rely on others to provide control, but could not or would not find their own discipline.

b/ Change sustained from women giving up their agency would be only temporary. Without outside chains, the women would all revert to type. *Waisted* meant to prove the second supposition with the filmed six-month reunion, which they'd relentlessly referenced while at the mansion (and made the women sign on to before they went to Vermont).

c/ Women would go to outrageous lengths to fit into societal norms—even at the cost of their health, emotional well-being, and pride.

5. Takeaway/Plan

a/ The thesis we can present: that the film-makers at Acrobat were cruel and ambitious enough to persecute women into thinness via a twenty-first-century version of foot binding while chasing their prize: fame and fortune. Acrobat chased Oscar gold and was willing to shape, rather than film, reality, to meet its goals.

The waiter walked past with a pastry-filled tray. Alice pulled her salad close and hunted for a stray piece of cheese as she pushed aside the hard-boiled eggs, which, since the mansion, sickened her. Finding one lonely sliver of mozzarella, she savored the creamy bit while formulating her thoughts.

"I have to say this: Clancy thinks we might be better off using a lawyer," Alice said.

Daphne held up the paper and shook it. "And lose this? Is he crazy?" Daphne put up her hands, palms out. "Sorry! I know he's your husband—"

"No worries. I am neither apologizing for nor

acceding to my husband. I think Clancy and I are playing out all sorts of marriage issues. And in the end, his opposite message was whatever you're going to do, do it now. Even as he counseled legal recourse."

"What kind of legal recourse did he mean?" Hania asked.

"Finding a lawyer to see if we can cease and desist Marcus Rhyner, the head of Acrobat, who's producing the film, and Jeremiah, who, as it turns out, is the director, not just the headmaster and bodybuilder of *Waisted*."

"You don't agree?" Daphne poured first a dollop and then a larger serving of dressing on her salad from the pitcher of garlicky oil.

"I don't know if I don't agree, or if I hate them so much I can't imagine keeping a legal lid on my rage. Somehow Jeremiah and Marcus—who I do know, and he's an ass—have become every awful man ever trying to push us into fuck-me heels and a size-two dress."

Hania stuck out her feet, clad in bright red stilettos. "Am I being a traitor?"

Hania looked like ten million slender bucks. Not just unfat, as Alice would describe Daphne and herself now, but genuinely lean and sexy, wearing a sleek jersey dress that clung to her curves.

"Honey, if you're happy, and the shoes make you feel good, go for it," Daphne said.

"You can carry off anything," Alice said. "But those things will ruin your feet."

"You sound like my mother!" Hania stabbed a piece of lettuce and stuck it in her mouth with no apparent delight. "So how do we turn the tables on Acrobat?"

"I have some thoughts, but I don't know how to make them happen." Alice forced a slice of undressed cucumber into her mouth.

"The three of us figured out how to escape a virtual prison. We can do anything." Hania smirked. "Not to mention, I have a surprise. A secret weapon."

Underestimating Hania always proved wrong. Those gold bangles and needle-thin heels were accessories to, not distractions from, a sharp mind. "What is it?"

"You say your idea first."

"Both of you! You're making me crazy. Talk," Daphne said. "Alice, you started this. Go."

Alice nodded and pointed her fork at the paper. "Right. My idea. Here goes: we make a film about their film. Fast. And we release ours first."

"And we use the footage?" Hania asked.

"We use it to our advantage; to tell *our* story."

"Do any of us have a clue how to make a documentary?" Daphne switched the salt and pepper shakers and folded and unfolded her napkin. "A video? A movie? I don't even know what to call it, damn it."

"We can learn, right? I'm not talking about making a major motion picture. There are a million ways to get a video out these days, right?" Alice looked at Hania.

"There are. And, as I said, we have help."

"Say it. What kind of help?" Alice pushed away the greens. Salad had never been something she enjoyed. Mashing cold, raw vegetables in her mouth depressed her. At the very least, it was the opposite of soothing. Why did the world praise women for making the opposite of soothing their goal?

Hania spread fingers topped with glossy red polish on the table. "Mike's been calling me since he left the mansion."

Alice leaned forward.

"Mike?" Daphne slapped a theatrical hand to her forehead.

"Actually, more than just calling." Hania lifted her shoulders in a too-cute gesture. "I guess our time together haunted him. He got my number from the Acrobat files. We've been hanging out."

"And he didn't realize that your *time together* was you using him to pull off a robbery?" Alice shook her head, trying to understand and fit in this new puzzle piece.

"Oh, he figured it out. He thought it was endearing. And brave. As though we were a new kind of *Charlie's Angels*."

"*Charlie's Angels*, the chubby edition." Alice laughed, thinking about this poor schmuck falling in love with the girl who'd made a fool of him. "He really has it bad for you."

"And all that while seeing you at the fat mansion." Daphne touched her midsection, poking as though testing for the truth of doneness. "Sam seems less than thrilled about the new me. I don't understand."

"How about asking him?" Hania opened her eyes wide. "And yes, Mike's extremely interested in me. Hard as that is to believe."

"Not hard at all." Thin, fat, or in between, Hania's exquisiteness drew both men and women. Marcus and Acrobat Films forgot to account for a *Waisted* employee falling for a cast member.

When dry-mouth fear had startled Alice awake at three that morning, thinking of what she planned to propose at lunch, she'd ridden waves of bad memories. Deprivation might be forgotten, but the humiliation—she'd be fighting those feelings until death. Ferreting out why she'd allowed herself to be twisted into a pretzel of willingness, even as she was treated as worthless, that was the work facing her.

"What did they believe the movie was about?" Alice asked. "Did Mike tell you? What was their message? Their point?"

"Hold up a minute. Let's see the dessert menu," Daphne said. "Ninety-to-ten, right?"

Alice had introduced them to her new philosophy of eating, but Daphne seemed to lack the ability for that math. On the other hand, who was Alice to be the hammer of righteousness?

They ended up sharing one large ginger cookie, which equaled three pathetic pops of a sugary bite each.

"So: Mike." Hania drew a heart on the table, indenting the linen. The Valentine stayed for a moment. "Mike says he liked me from the start. And hated what Jeremiah and the others did to us."

"You're seeing him? In person?" The lingering flavor of ginger blessedly rode over kale's bitter aftertaste.

"And he really, really knows that you used him?" Daphne asked.

"Along with endearing, Mike thinks I was spunky."

"Spunky. This guy cracks me up," Alice said. "I can't believe you waited this long to tell us."

"I thought it was a dish best served in person." Hania spun her bangles. "He hated this film. He's worked for Acrobat for quite a few films. He knew they were sleazy, but none of their work made him this upset before."

"How about the first *Waisted*?" Alice asked. Despite Clancy's urging, she still hadn't seen the documentary.

"Not that bad, Mike said. Not like this. That one

was all about the ways we're pressured. It was about the industry—investigating tactics used in places like Weight Watchers. They examined the business of fat, as they called it.

"When they got deep into the planning of the part two film, Mike thinks they fell over the edge. Originally they planned to take it from the point of view of the women ensnared by the business of weight loss, from Jenny Craig to *The Biggest Loser*. But besides not being able to get access to the television shows—which are vaults of secrecy—Jeremiah and Marcus wanted to worm into darker places. They decided to start from scratch for his quest."

"His quest?"

"His quest," Hania repeated. "Finding out which way women would go, faced with both reward—in this case weight loss—versus public shame. According to Mike, the Acrobat team got the idea from *Pounded*, but wanted to see what the results would be with no veneer of help and sympathy. Would the hunger to be thin overtake the desire for dignity?"

"Damn them." Alice tapped her breastbone dead center, which supposedly relieved anxiety. "They used us and are counting on using us repeatedly. Damn them. Here's *my* quest—or hopefully, ours. Make them answer and pay for what they did to us."

Daphne pushed up her sweater sleeves. "Let's

make sure this never happens to any other women. Yes. Damn them. Never again. Cowboys, that's what they think they are, right? Uncovering the Wild West of women and fat. In truth, they're just misogynists."

Alice nodded. "Let the world look and decide. What's the line between documenting and creating? Reality shows are bad enough—I mean, we all know they're more scripted than not. But with crap like *Waisted*? They put the word *documentary* on the footage and make it gospel. Were they all counting on us staying quiet afterward? They probably thought we'd be too embarrassed to stand up and be seen."

"Exactly," Hania said. "Mike said the same thing. And if not, and we spoke up in any way, Jeremiah figures we gave him more press. Win-win for him."

"Mike said that?" Daphne asked.

"Yes. It made him sick."

"Let's control the narrative," Alice said. "We come out first, hard and fast. Let's start with finding everyone else—the other women—and having a meeting."

"We can't ask Mike to do it, though," Hania said. "Too much at risk while he's still working for them. How about Clancy?"

"No way. I can't get him involved. We'll find a way."

"Do we have time?" Daphne seemed doubtful.

"We need to always have time for another battle in the war on women. With how much I hate those fuckers, if need be, I'll invent hours," Hania said. "We all will."

CHAPTER 24

DAPHNE

Daphne raced from the restaurant to her sister's office in Wellesley. Lenny Kravitz blasted through the car stereo as she swung off the Mass Pike and headed toward Route 16. After parking, she reapplied her lipstick, took a deep breath, and walked into the brick building.

"Is Bianca in?"

The receptionist, a woman of indeterminate age who'd been Botoxed into submission, half smiled at Daphne. "Do you have an appointment?"

"I'm her sister."

"Is she expecting you?"

"No. But just let her know I'm here. I'll wait."

Daphne had finished *Vogue*, *InStyle*, and *Vanity Fair* by the time the receptionist nodded her through the doors. Bianca's outer offices and hallway, gleaming blond wood with imitation Kandinsky art, contrasted with the office where she spoke with patients. In the inner sanctum, ivory-pink walls and deep-rose tufted furniture whispered promises of clear, wrinkle-free complexions.

"What brings you here? Is everything okay?"

"If you thought something was wrong, why did you leave me reading an entire library of magazines?"

"If something horrible happened, I figured you'd call. So. Is anything awful going on?"

"It depends on what you mean by awful."

Her sister nodded, quiet, waiting for Daphne to continue, as though Bianca were a shrink and not a dermatologist. Daphne searched for ways to form what needed to be said, staring at her sister. As the middle girl, Bianca had stood out from the beginning, including choosing science over art, and silence over the stream of words used by the rest of the family.

"I need your help." Daphne tried to formulate her request in a manner that didn't sound frantic. Like an addict.

"Reconsidering the tightening? Do you want a referral?" Bianca reached for her phone.

Daphne put a hand on her sister's arm. "The pills they gave us? The ones I told you about? I brought some home with me."

"How? Why?"

"Some they gave us. Others I stole. Because I didn't think I could keep it up without them."

"And?"

"And I found out that was true when I ran out. My weight is creeping up."

"Did you come here for more pills or advice?"

Such a simple question and so tricky to answer.

"Be truthful," Bianca said. "It's the only way through."

"Through what?"

"Whatever ails you. I'm not being cute. Lying to yourself or me will only prolong the problem. That much I do know." Bianca turned toward the window, studying the view across Route 16. Daphne reached for patience. Analyzing always came first in Bianca's world, and no torrent of words would help Daphne's cause.

Finally, Bianca faced her. "How many pills did you take? Steal?"

"Twenty."

"And you came home, what, four weeks ago?"

"About."

"Twenty pills lasted you four weeks?"

Daphne tried to formulate an answer that would capture how she scraped off bits and pieces with her teeth, occasionally breaking one in quarters with a pill splitter.

When she didn't answer, Bianca spoke. "Daph, at most, that's about five pills a week. Less than one a day. It's not something I would ever recommend, but you don't have an addiction—at least not a physical one. And if you left that place with a habit, then you titrated down by how you doled out those twenty pills."

"I need a few more. Just for a bit."

"Why?"

"To manage my appetite. If I get it in control once more, I know I can handle it."

Her sister walked around the desk and knelt before her. She took her hands and squeezed. "You look great, Daph."

"For how long?"

Back in the car, with a recommendation for a shrink in hand, Daphne drove straight to the nearest CVS on Route 9. The giant one, not the one by her house. After shoving a few bottles of shampoo into her cart for cover, she headed to the aisle filled with weight loss aids. Faced with the overwhelming array, she almost ran out screaming. Which one could best mimic the pills she'd been taking? Zantrex-3 swore it would provide extreme energy, while Zantrex Black promised rapid release. Apple cider vinegar sounded too tame, Alli Orlistat capsules frightened her with memories of anal leakage warnings. Her chest tightened. She grabbed the Zantrex Black. Just for now.

Daphne promised herself she'd stop using them by Valentine's Day.

Cooking no longer brought pleasure. Tonight she broiled salmon, steamed broccoli, and mashed squash, boiling a side of pasta with grated cheese for everyone but her.

Meals tasted flat. No matter how many herbs and spices she added, dullness reigned.

Smears of olive oil carried flavor differently than butter. A simple fact. Olive oil necessitated garlic, which called for onions, which meant mushrooms, and before you knew it, every damn vegetable required a coterie of vegetable friends surrounding it. Olive oil required working harder than she wanted after a long day at work standing on her feet and leaning over clients.

With butter, just a shiny smear plus one twist of salt, and your mouth thanked you. Daphne wanted to say "Fuck you!" every time she lifted the bottle of olive oil. "Fuck you and your supposed healthy ways. Fuck you and your cachet of cool. *Fuck you!* I want butter!"

Cook in defense of calories, and taste became the victim. She missed swirling ingredients that burst wide open by themselves and made mad music together.

Before *Waisted*, she'd spent lazy Sundays slicing ten different vegetables into butter— onions, radishes, zucchini, and beyond—and simmer them down in wine. Add cream, tomato, and parmesan, ladle the three-hour sauce over *conchigliette* pasta, add shrimp or sausage, serve it on a brightly colored platter, and bring smiles to everyone—even Audrey, who complained but must recognize that, like Sam, she had the metabolism of a hummingbird. Audrey and Sam scorched calories by chewing. Gabe's burn ratio was yet to be uncovered, as his addiction to biking kept him trim, but evidence pointed to his being in the Sam camp.

The world treated fat people like out-of-control horrors, when, in fact, those who inherited tendencies toward being heavy exerted ten times as much control as the genetically thin, even if all they wanted was to stay plump instead of fat.

Diet books seldom addressed sensuality, but what did cooking do if not marry flavors through heat? Sexy stuff. Daphne grabbed a pair of chopsticks from the drawer and dared herself to score a slippery udon noodle.

She won.

Or she lost.

Who knew.

But tasting the noodle made her groan.

She carried the platter of fish to the table and placed it next to the vegetable bowls. "Audrey, please bring in the noodles. They're in the covered blue casserole dish."

"Why me?"

Daphne wondered if any question requiring any child to work engendered "Why me?" or if her particularly lax parenting (as her mother always described it) brought on the constant complaints.

TIP: A mother who is obsessing about being thin and dieting and exercising is not going to be a very good mother.

—Jane Fonda

TRUTH: She hadn't been a very good mother. But she could change.

"If not you, who? If not now, when?" Sam intoned.

Audrey groaned. "Not new, Dad."

"Nor is your moaning. Go help your mother. And don't point at your brother. He'll be cleaning with me."

Daphne dished out the salmon, unappetizing crap, smothered in mustard mixed with faux maple syrup. She tried not to think about the chemicals killing her family. Did anyone understand what they used to make maple flavors? Well, probably Sam, but at the moment, she wanted her ignorance.

Sam scooped a massive portion of noodles. "Thanks. Must be hard for you to cook these without eating."

"No reason everyone should walk my road to perdition."

"It's awful, Mom." Audrey's desolate expression killed her. "The math just isn't fair. That you can't burn calories like I do."

Daphne peered at her daughter. "So you know that."

"First," she said, "I'm not a child. Or stupid. Second, Daddy told me. We talked while you were gone, you know."

"About me?"

"Of course about you," Sam said. "If the center of your family leaves, voluntarily, to go to a food prison, you talk."

"It scared us, Mom." Gabe speaking about fear at the dinner table took Daphne by surprise. She must have sunk damn far into her own world not to see the impact of her departure. Gabe came home more often these days. Tufts might be close, but his visits home had stepped up considerably since she returned.

"Why did it scare you?" she asked.

"Because how bad did you feel inside that you had to run away to fix it?" Gabe reached for the pasta, stopped, and took an oversized portion of broccoli.

Daphne held back from pushing noodles at him. "Oh, honey, I wasn't running away from you guys. You know that, right?"

"Not really." Audrey's honesty never failed. "You had to get away from us. And stop cooking. Because you love it so much. Cooking. And us, of course."

"You glow when you're making something for us." Sam reached for a roll. Damned if she was going to stop serving them, even though her hand twitched for the entire meal. "So it made sense for you to take a break from us. Every hour in the kitchen, you faced temptation and frustrating choices."

"Going to *Waisted* didn't exactly solve my

problems, did it?" The words escaped before she considered the impact of admitting to being still unhappy. Or unsatisfied. Un-*something.*

"But you're so much skinnier," Audrey said. "Did that make it worth it?"

"Despite having to escape, that is," Gabe said.

"Being a prisoner of war does make you thinner," Daphne said. "Every time. I don't recommend it."

"Do you think you would have lost weight without *Waisted*?" Audrey appeared apprehensive, but, on further analysis, Daphne also saw relief on her daughter's face. The giant elephant that had roamed their house for too long had come out in the open. Daphne and her obsession with her body.

"I don't know. Any method of weight loss might have worked, simply because I was ready. Yes, being tortured and harassed worked in forcing off pounds, but having it work this way left me messed up."

Fear plastered their faces. Too much truth— Daphne had gone too far. "No! Not in a long-term, send-me-to-be-fixed way. But in a time-to-look-at-myself way."

"You never say stuff like that, Mom." Audrey took her hand.

"I guess that goes on the top of my mistake list."

"Is this why you guys want to make the movie,

Mom?" Gabe asked. "To work out what the hell happened?"

"More like who the hell those horrible people are," Audrey said. "We can help, you know."

"You're helping me now."

"No. We don't mean by 'being supportive.' "

"Being supportive isn't chicken feed." Sam reached for Daphne's hand. "In fact, it indicates just how much you've both grown."

"Jeez. Were we such monsters up until this moment? Not everyone wears the mantle of sainthood, you know." The patronizing way Gabe patted his father's shoulder cracked up Daphne. Sam did carry his saintliness a bit far. It made her and the kids want to tease him until he cracked and became less than reasonable and understanding.

"What we mean is that we can help make the video," Audrey said.

"How?"

"Time to accept that Audrey and I know more about technical things," Gabe said. "We're young. Don't make me spell it out."

"Just how much *do* you know?" Sam asked. "Should we be worried?"

"Ship sailed, Dad. Anyway, you saw our work." Seeing Daphne's puzzled look, Gabe pointed to his ever-present computer on the side table. "Show you later. But you should know that given the proper materials, Audrey and I could have a video up by tomorrow. Might not be great, but it would get the information across."

"How long until you—we—might have a decent-enough one?" Excitement grew as Daphne listened to her son. "And is this a thing you're interested in?"

"Hell, yes. I might end up producing exposés," Gabe said, throwing premed out the window as though switching from building blocks to Legos.

"I'll join. We can be the new Illuminati." Audrey gave an evil grin. "Instead of jewels covering you, we uncover companies that prey on women. They actively lied to get you there. They set you up to be made fools of."

"I guess if we walked right out, they wouldn't have made their point, right? So, were we idiots, or were they guilty of malfeasance? Who was more at fault? We thought we were prisoners, but was that true? Should we have tested them?"

"Stop! Don't forget what you said."

Audrey rose and ran out of the room, returning with her computer. "Repeat what you just said. I think you hit the core. The thesis to make it more than just 'see what they did to us.' This will be you three examining it from a serious point of view. 'Did we victimize ourselves, or did they make us victims?'" She typed as she spoke.

"Or both," Daphne said. "Did they simply want to drive us, test our limits, or was their hypothesis that they could throw any humiliation at us because we wanted so badly to be thin? Are we all that desperate?"

"Enough to take what you had to realize were illegal substances." Audrey kept writing.

Daphne nodded. She thought of the pills she tried to beg from Bianca and the new ones hidden on the bottom of her closet.

"Let's go, champ," Sam said to Gabe. "Time for us to clean up."

"Champ? For real? Sometimes I think you belong in the fifties."

"Perhaps you're right, buddy." Sam winked at Daphne. "Let's go, pal."

"I married a comedian. So, funny guys, I'm going to give you a treat: *I'm* cleaning up tonight. I want to throw out some leftovers that might be from the fifties." Daphne stood.

Gabe leaped up. "Don't have to ask me twice."

"Let's write some video ideas down." Audrey stood and gathered water glasses.

"Guess we raised them better than we thought," Sam said.

"Better than *you* thought. Didn't I always say we had perfect children?"

CHAPTER 25

DAPHNE

Daphne spun Sam from the kitchen toward the living room. "Out. I'd have to do about ten years of dishes to make up for what you've done for me."

"Like letting you go to a prison for fat women? I suppose I deserve some gratitude for that."

"Don't be sarcastic about my terrific husband." She squeezed him hard around the waist, pressed her cheek to his back, and then pushed him away. "Go catch up with your work so we can both go to bed early."

Daphne began cleaning, grateful for the mess. She required action to keep from eating: hands washing dishes, scraping debris into the trash, loading the dishwasher—anything that kept her from the choice between stuffing the onion rolls down the drain or into her mouth.

"Mom!" Audrey yelled from the dining room.

She opened the door and peeked out. "What?" Audrey and Gabe sat side by side at the table with open computers.

"We're putting together ideas. Searching for similar videos. Making lists. We have a bunch of stuff we want you to see. Are you finished in there?"

"Just about," Daphne said. "Give me five minutes. Keep going."

Daphne closed the door, walked back to the counter, grabbed a knife, and stabbed the butter sitting in her pretty cornflower dish. She tore the roll in half and spread a thin sheen, just enough to moisten the bread. Then Daphne turned her back toward the door and bent over the dishwasher, loading plates as she chewed, afraid of being caught.

By whom?

Who gave a damn except her?

She crammed the bread in and choked it down.

Sam's wineglass was to her left. She picked up the Zinfandel and poured, followed by a trip to the cabinet, where she opened a pack of Wheat Thins—equal to caloric heroin for Daphne. Continually, she bought a box "for company," but then continually ate every one and then hid the empty cardboard in the bottom of the recycle bin.

Who did she think acted as the trash police? Daphne lived as though her mother still lurked around every corner, but self-awareness didn't stop her insanity.

Honesty—with her children, with Sam—should have brought relief, broken open her dam of self-loathing, and led her to the path of sanity. Instead, as though there would never be another crumb of deliciousness left in the world, Daphne jammed crackers in her mouth until choking became a possibility. The crunch, the sweet malty flavor, fed her addiction for the savory. Like nicotine for her mouth, she pushed them in. One single cracker provided the hit, so why keep packing them in? The idea of swallowing one at a time made sense. But she didn't.

> **TIP:** Eating bite-sized portions, and concentrating on flavor for several seconds will help you feel gratified, and you'll eat less.
> —*Weight Watchers meetings,*
> *postpartum with Audrey*
> **WEIGHT LOST:** 11 pounds.
> **TIME KEPT OFF:** 5 weeks.

She spat the half-chewed Wheat Thins into the trash and emptied the remaining crackers over it. Then, knowing how likely it was she might reach in and grab one right back, she poured her wine on top and covered the purple mess with rubbish from dinner.

"I'll be right there!" Daphne said, zipping past the kids. She ran into her bedroom, raced to the closet, grabbed the diet pills, and swallowed one dry.

Immediately, she calmed down. She brushed her teeth. After, she outlined her lips in a dusty rose, blotted, nodded in the mirror, and went to the children.

"Here you go." Gabe pointed to the computer screen. "We started making the movie."

"Impossible. Hania has all the material." Daphne ran her tongue over her teeth, feeling for debris she'd missed with her toothbrush. The minty taste and lipstick would keep her from the kitchen. She prayed.

"We mocked up ideas to give you a sense of how much could be done in a supershort time." Audrey pointed along with Gabe. "With what we found online."

"How do you know how to do this?" Daphne, like all parents, she supposed, was consistently amazed that her children sopped up tools for living and art that came from sources outside the house.

"Mom, it's not that difficult. Just Google 'How to make a movie,' and, whomp, you're on your way," Gabe said.

"Is that what you did?"

"Long ago." Her son tapped a few keys, and YouTube appeared. "This is my channel."

He clicked a video titled *My Double Aunts' Wedding*. "I made that for Aunt Marissa and Aunt Lili."

"Why haven't I seen it before?"

"I kept it a secret. To give them as my wedding present."

312

"We both made it," Audrey said. "We sent it to them and to everyone in the family while you were at that place."

Daphne stared at her sister and Lili in the still shot, exchanging rings, wreathed in smiles. At that moment, instead of enjoying the sight of her ridiculously happy sister and new sister-in-law, Daphne had been worrying about her upper arms, blocking joy with her jealousy of any woman who didn't need to wear a jacket over her dress.

The screen turned golden. "Marissa & Lili's Wedding" appeared in a modern font.

"One of Lili's sisters played the piano for the soundtrack. We didn't want to give a present with stolen music," Gabe said. "We know how strict you and Dad are about those things."

The DeCordova Museum materialized, bathed in soft yellowed light.

"You're looking at an establishing shot. To anchor the viewer."

Daphne smiled at the seriousness of Gabe's tone.

A montage of both families swept by. A series of shots. Her mother and father smiling, with Gordon's arm draped casually around Sunny's shoulders. Pride on his face. Lili's sisters tossing rose petals.

Gabe and Rosie laughing, heads thrown back, pleasure on their faces—perhaps at the sheer wonder of themselves, young and vital and beautiful.

"I took that." Audrey grinned when she appeared on-screen. "You were right. That dress rocked."

Bianca hugging Lili's mother. The camera panning in on Bianca's hands, sunscreen-pale as always, on Audrey's glittered shoulders.

Shots of shined-up shoes made statements of joy. Her son possessed artistry.

Daphne pressed her nails into her palm. Waiting.

Her mother, head thrown back, laughing at something said by Lili's brother.

Finally, the camera landed on her and Sam.

Daphne turning to smile at them, the camera catching magically flattering angles. Sam gazing at her. Her joy regarding her children showed.

How lovely she looked with her hair cascading. Oddly, the mauve suit contrasted well with her hair. Perhaps she'd been unkind to the saleswoman at Saks.

The video continued for twelve minutes, a memory of a wedding that held special significance for having two dazzling brides—one white, one black—the family pictures notable for the changes from the early depictions to last toasts. In the beginning, there was Lili's family on one side, Marissa's on the other. Like an image from *West Side Story*. By the end, they made a mosaic.

They included no shots of her that were less than as flattering as possible.

She thought of how much work her son and daughter must have put into that and then thought with shame about how little she appreciated her life.

CHAPTER 26

ALICE

Alice parked on Daphne's street. Houses from the sublime to the ordinary lined the Chestnut Hill neighborhood—what you paid for the same residence inside the city limits of Boston doubled here, where location provided entry to top-rated schools.

Gray clapboard shingles and a wraparound porch made up the public face of Daphne's house. Remnants of gone-by flower gardens sprawled everywhere.

Alice entered a hallway jumble of coats, boots, and abandoned backpacks—the overflow of life that only the casual or secure allowed to be on view. Family photos and framed children's pictures hung in the entrance. In the dining room, intricate white sculptures lined white shelves.

The kitchen, visible through an open door, revealed white wood cabinets against blue tiles, a crisper room than Alice had envisioned for where Daphne cooked.

Coffee cups and platters of crudités sat untouched on the dining room table. The display turned her stomach. Since *Waisted*, Alice's aversion to raw vegetables marched up the ladder of antipathy to the rung of abhorrence. She begged her mother for soup recipes.

"I was going to put out sliced hard-boiled eggs, but . . ." Daphne laughed as she entered the room with a plate stacked with what looked to be crackers. Alice prayed yes and no, striating her wishes in a crazy quilt of hope.

"What are those?" Hania appeared caught in the same conundrum as Alice.

"Baked gouda crisps. Not low-fat. Or low-cal. But low-carb. And tasty without the impossible-to-stop-eating-ness of crackers."

"Hard to make?" Hania asked.

Alice reached for one. "How many calories?"

"Not that I'd bake them," Hania said. "Cooking only makes me eat more. But my mother would make them for me." She grabbed three, her fingernails a ghastly and yet engaging emerald.

"I might try making them. If they're like ten calories each." Alice figured one would be safe if followed by three broccoli florets.

"They're from Whole Foods. Not good enough to want a ton, not bad enough to feel like a punishment." Daphne grabbed a handful.

"Apt description of how effing wretched our aspirations have become." Alice considered the display.

"Meet my kids," Daphne said, cocking her head toward her children.

"Yikes. Sorry for swearing." More relativity struck Alice: having a five-year-old, Daphne's children might as well be full-fledged adults. Embarrassed by her language and candor, she switched topics. "How in the world did you two make a draft of the movie so fast?"

In different ways, Audrey and Gabe both resembled Daphne. Audrey had the same flawless skin and overly broad shoulders, and tilted her head wearing the same curious expression. Gabe's eyes were Daphne's bluish-green, though his dark lashes matched his father's almost black hair—as did his serious mien.

"We're on school break and figured this as our Chanukah gift." Gabe glanced at Daphne. "Apologies that you're missing having your present be a surprise, Mom."

"What a present." Hania hugged them both.

"You better wait until you see it before thanking us." Gabe tipped his head, seeming a bit self-conscious. Perhaps it was the roomful of women or Hania's beauty. He adjusted his glasses, pushing them higher up on his nose with the air of someone who did this hourly, and then turned to his sister. "Let's set up. You guys can come in when you're ready."

When they left, Alice nodded in approval. "Great kids. And a fantastic house. If I didn't know better, I'd say you have it all. Wait a minute—I met your husband. You do have it all." She smiled as though kidding.

"I know," Daphne said. "Recently all I've been doing is working at kick-starting myself into gratitude and studying why I act like such a whiny victim."

Hania reached over and took Daphne's hand. "Look at your kids. You must be a wonderful mom."

"I don't want pity. I'm trying to figure out what the hell is wrong with me." Daphne picked up the trays.

"Sorry," Alice said. "Sometimes jealousy flies out from my mouth."

"Each of us has something the other wants. That's always the way. I'll take your mother, for instance."

"She's not for sale. But my mother would love to meet you." That was true. Bebe loved nothing more than meeting anyone in Alice's life.

In the family room, a three-sided arrangement of overstuffed couches faced a giant television screen. With the curtains pulled shut, dimness prevailed. Soft blue fabric and shades of ivory provided calm. Bookcases invited browsing by appearing jumbled and well used. Family photos were interspersed among the volumes, along with a collection of antique pens and ink bottles.

"Put your feet up." Daphne pointed to a large

coffee table showing scuff marks. "This is a room designed for comfort."

"Which, believe me, is the opposite of the living room," Audrey said.

"Sorry, but your dad and I like having one room where we can bring guests without blindfolding them."

"No worries," Alice said. "No masks needed in there or here."

Pride and money were stealth in Daphne's home, but they showed nevertheless. Jealousy threatened to steal Alice's appreciation. Whereas Alice's house demanded attention and straight spines, Daphne's embraced her.

Gabe cleared his throat, perhaps anxious to show their work. "We used everything we got from Hania."

"Wait till Mike sees it." Her broad smile showed how completely calm she was. Not a trace of nervousness.

Hania had been the keeper of the stolen material—a cache she increased with data from Mike.

"He knew why you wanted it, right?" Alice worried about liability. And how soon Clancy would kill her.

Hania shrugged. "I told him we wanted to see everything. But either way, I don't care. I might like him, but I love you guys." Hania propped up her feet, showing off high-heeled boots.

"And he's on our side. Otherwise, I'd dump him."

Alice wondered what that level of ease could be like, until remembering where she met Hania, for goodness' sake. Ghosts inside clawed them all—they merely wrapped them in different cloth.

"Sam doesn't think Acrobat will go after us. He thinks they'll simply pray that it will sink as a project made by crazy, angry women." Daphne stuffed a pillow behind her. "How about Clancy?"

"He doesn't know." Alice stretched out her long legs, admiring her strong thighs wrapped in a pair of damn jeans. The view calmed her. "About the video."

"What will happen when he finds out?" Hania asked.

"I guess he'll find a way to punish me."

"Punish you? How?" Daphne looked so unfamiliar with the concept that Alice wanted to call a divorce lawyer, now, before Clancy saw the video. She wanted to be as surprised by cruelty as Daphne.

"Ready?" Gabe tapped a few keys on the computer. A foggy image floated on the screen, clearing as a voice-over began.

"These seven women never knew how far they'd go, how damaged they'd been by family, by friends, by magazines, television, and every other form of media. Not until they came up against a film crew in a mansion in the Northeast Kingdom of Vermont."

The image sharpened until Alice saw that it was an image . . . of her from behind . . . with Coleen riding her back. The racialized misogyny hit like a gunshot.

"This picture was taken the first day, when they met the crew—who'd lied to get these women to the mansion and then tortured them to get their message on camera."

The shots went into a montage of views from the gym, where the women struggled with a variety of old equipment.

"This is all stolen video footage, taken by the three women who escaped the *Waisted* mansion, fearful for their lives. Their trainer almost forcibly fed them pills, a few of which they smuggled out for a chemical assay. They turned out to be Dexedrine. Amphetamines."

The narration stopped. Muddy original taped sounds began with Jeremiah's voice.

"Face it, ladies: you look like shit. And you're here for that very reason. No amount of will-power has worked for you, right? Seeing how disgusting you are hasn't had an impact."

Jeremiah approached Susannah, grabbed one of her hips, and waggled the fat back and forth.

"How do you get through even one day carrying that around?"

The camera zoomed in on Susannah's stricken face, eyes blinking as though willing away tears.

"She gave us permission to include this footage," Hania reassured and reminded them.

They'd worked overtime during the past two weeks, dividing tasks and feeding information straight to Gabe and Audrey. Daphne and Alice contacted the *Waisted* cast, swore them to secrecy about their plans, and then shared everything. Hania acted as the go-between with Mike and Gabe and helped with technical jobs. Alice wrote narrative voice-overs. Hania and Audrey interviewed the women.

"Who's narrating now?" One of the voices tickled her memory, but Alice couldn't pin it down.

Gabe paused the video. "My aunt Marissa and aunt Lili. They sound solemn, right?"

That was the familiarity. Alice had met Marissa at the hospital. She had driven up with Sam.

Alice studied Susannah's image. "Did anyone say no to showing their faces?"

"Everyone said yes," Daphne said.

"Everyone?"

"Yes, everyone. Listen to what they say," Daphne said.

"We fit an unbelievable amount into twenty-seven minutes," Gabe said.

"Twenty-seven minutes?" Alice repeated.

Hit hard and fast. Clancy always said longer

didn't mean better. *Sometimes you don't need a feature film, just a video punch.*

"We should trim it."

"We should get it out right away. It's not like we expect to win prizes," Hania said. "No offense, Gabe, Audrey. So far this is incredible. But we need it out before Acrobat gets organized. Mike thinks that any day they're gonna go lawsuit. Not because they're genuinely considering a battle, but because they want to tie our hands."

"If you want, we can have this ready to release tomorrow," Gabe said.

"We can do it tonight if we keep going." Audrey reached over to the laptop.

The three women stiffened as the video continued, seeming as nervous about how fat they appeared as they were at the prospect of being sued. Alice imagined Clancy's reaction to having his coterie of filmmakers watching twenty-seven minutes of them embarrassing Acrobat and, he believed, Prior Productions. And him.

"Why didn't you leave immediately?"

This voice was new. Alice thought it must be Lili, who sounded like silk and iron. Seung answered.

"The first thing they did, after that horrible first humiliation in the grand entrance, was remove everything we had. They took our clothes and then gave us these hideous clinging jumpsuits designed to make us feel foolish and ugly."

The shot went to all seven women lined up in the gym before a pound was lost, flab and fat stretching the semi-sheer fabric to its limit across hips in some, stomachs in others.

Her own image sickened Alice. She tried to pull up love for fat Alice, with her vast rolls of belly fat. The chins. The woman Clancy had pulled away from in bed, but now desired as he had during their initial heat.

What did it mean that Alice had wanted her husband with such a burning intensity before and now scarcely cared about the bedroom? Why was life seven thousand layers of fog and conundrums to figure out before clarity came? Each time Libby said how beautiful Alice looked— "like a queen!"—she died a little inside, wondering what she had taught her little girl in the past months.

"Then it got cruel," Seung continued. "They broke us down."

The movie shifted back to the gym. The screen showed the women being forced to strip and then stepping up to be weighed. Video magic had been applied to display the horror while masking identities.

A disembodied and obviously disguised voice spoke as the camera lingered on the disguised women's most sensitive spots. Susannah's massive thighs. Jennifer's pendulous stomach.

"The naked weigh-in showed us how far they'd

let us pile up the humiliation," the robotic voice intoned.

"Surprise! That's an altered Mike." Hania swept out her arms in a gesture of "Ta-da!"

"Isn't he scared they'll fire him?" Alice asked.

"He's so done with them that he doesn't care. And he says they're not gonna advertise any of this. Not with the tactics they used."

"Things were set up for no other reason than to see what these women would do in their lust to meet the wants of the world."

"Wow. I can't believe we have this," Alice said.

Hania kicked off her shoes and pulled her knees up to her chin.

Mike's narration continued: "Every night Jeremiah would have a beer and shake his head. 'These stupid women,' he'd say. 'Is there nothing they won't do to lose weight? I'm afraid to know how far we can push them. What the hell won't they do?' "

"What did you think? You were working there," Marissa's voice asked, though Alice figured it had been Hania asking the questions. The magic of cutting rooms.

"I thought I'd never get clean again. Jeremiah always thought he was the cleverest guy in the room."

Scenes of the women eating flashed. Now thinner, haggard. Shredding lettuce to tiny bits. Drinking water with shaky hands as Valentina handed out pills. Coleen stood over her group with a stopwatch, not letting them eat more than five minutes.

At one point Coleen poured hot sauce over every morsel of breakfast.

"What would have happened if one of the women said, 'I want to leave'?" Lili asked.

"That did happen. With Lauretta. The softest-spoken of all, but she came crying to him. First, she tried Coleen, who laughed at her. And then Jeremiah did his thing."

Lauretta appeared in front of a gym mirror, being forced to stare at herself in a bra and underwear. Nobody but Jeremiah, Lauretta, and, presumably, Mike, were in the room.

"Do you see this, Lauretta?"

The giant man held out one of her arms. He grabbed hold of her underarm skin and flapped it. "You look like an ancient crone."

Next, Jeremiah took hold of a hunk of her still-swollen stomach. "Is this blob what you want to take home?" he sneered. "This piece of failure hanging for the world to see? You think you can hide it? How? With a gigantic, cutesy sweater? A huge sweatshirt you have to buy God knows where?"

Then he stood behind her and lifted her chin. "Such a pretty face, right? Who the hell do you think is going to date your face? Were you happy back there in the world? Were you?"

Lauretta sobbed, flinching, trying to get away from Jeremiah's meaty paws.

"You'll never be happy while you're a fat pig. Not one day. The only thing people see is an ugly, overweight woman."

He released her and drew back.

"We're your only hope. But if you wanna go, *go*."

CHAPTER 27

ALICE

Alice let her coat swing unbuttoned. A December thaw had crept in that morning.

"Miss Alice!" Keely, apparently having escaped the after-school program, grabbed Alice as she locked her office. "Are you leaving? Are you going home? Are you getting your little girl? Will you bring her in to play and—"

"Whoa!" Alice stopped Keely before the breathless little girl collapsed. She took her hand and led her to the chair by the check-in desk in the hall.

"Okay, here are my answers: Yes, I'm leaving for the night to go home. My little girl is with my mother." Alice lifted Keely onto her lap. "She's been here before, but not lately. Should I make sure to bring her in one afternoon when you're here?"

Keely released another torrent. "Yes. Bring her! She can be like my little sister. 'Cause she's younger, right? Do people like you better skinny?"

Alice didn't know where to start. Keely reminded her of the puppy in *The Poky Little*

Puppy, all plump and adorable. Did this eight-year-old girl already consider herself less than, and had Alice made it much worse?

"I think people like me the same." She hugged the girl. "Nobody likes me better or less."

Which was a lie.

"Everybody thinks you look so good. All the teachers. You know. But why did you have to go away for so long? Didn't your little girl miss you?" Keely gave her a sideways glance, changing from poky little puppy to nosy neighbor, arms akimbo and all. The little girl was the first person to outright demand answers about the absurdity of Alice's running to the mansion.

"She did miss me, honey. Yes, she did. And I missed her. *So* much. And you know what I learned?"

Keely stared with wide-open eyes, her puff of a ponytail bouncing as she wiggled. "That being fat is just as good as being skinny?"

Everything inside Alice shrank at the question. *No, Keely. Being fat sucks. People treat you like shit.* Because of *Vogue*? Husbands? Culture? Heck, Alice should write a thesis on the intersectionality of misogyny, fat shaming, faux health concerns. And cultural differences through the ages.

But what should she tell this amazing little girl?

"Keely, baby. You can be fat and be the best

person in the world. You can be skinny and be the meanest rat around. You can be skinny and sweet as sugar. You can be fat and be rotten to the core. You don't always get to choose skinny or fat—and most of us are somewhere in the middle. But you can always choose what kind of person you'll be. Concentrate on that."

"Being good?"

"Not just being good, but being smart and strong and finding your special talents."

She ran a finger down Keely's silky cheek. "Okay, cookie. I have to pick up Libby."

"So, are you going to be fat again, Miss Alice? Everyone says you will. That it's just gonna come right back on."

Alice pressed her lips against words she shouldn't say. Answering Keely as though the child meant to hurt her wouldn't do. "You know what, baby? That's always the million-dollar question. 'Cause don't we all love to eat? And aren't we all being told to be skinny? So, am I gonna be fat again?" Alice shrugged her shoulders. "I hope not. But more, I hope it's not the most important thing about me."

With Libby tucked in, the dishes washed, the living room straightened, and the mail sorted, Alice couldn't avoid talking to Clancy one more minute. She poured eight ounces (measured) of white wine (120 calories) into a crystal glass.

The austere wineglass stuck out its tongue at her. When they registered for wedding gifts, she wanted heavier, more ornate stemware. She still remembered the dramatically etched Waterford Dungarvan, how she enjoyed running her fingers over the sharp delineations of the design, but Clancy would have none of it.

She carried the glass to the living room, where he sat with a pile of paperwork. So very handsome, her husband.

Sometimes when she saw him with Libby, she worried whether his love for his daughter was built purely on the protection of fatherhood or if it included too many whiffs of narcissism. Beautiful Libby resembled Clancy. Alice feared he loved their daughter as an extension of himself.

What would he do when Libby hit the inevitable awkward stage; when she cried about her thighs, as Alice had to her mother? As much as Alice resented her mother's brushing off Alice's complaints about her every-single-thing-wrong, she now appreciated that two people in this world—Bebe and Zeke—always thought her perfect precisely as God had formed her.

The idea of a plump Libby having to face a rigid Clancy hurt her heart.

"Can I get you one?" Alice held up her glass and prayed that he'd say yes to an alcohol blur.

Clancy looked up. His eyebrows were drawn

together. "I never drink when I work. You know that."

"I was hoping we might talk for a bit."

"Can it hold? These contracts are going out in two days." He reached for his mug, filled with his nightly decaffeinated green tea.

"Can you put it aside for a moment?" Alice sat beside him and touched his shoulder. "I need to share something."

Share sounded better than *tell*. As though they were in partnership fighting Acrobat.

Clancy lowered the sheaf of papers to his lap, keeping them in his hands, ready to lift them back up to his face the moment Alice finished. But, she noted, his face softened as he studied her, perhaps appreciating the effort made for him, for this discussion.

Soft ivory cashmere fell off her right shoulder. A delicate gold chain with a religious medal from her mother-in-law hung from her neck. It was Priscilla, the patron saint of marriages.

Alice had invoked Daphne's artistry when making up her face that evening, using virginal tones, letting all drama weigh in on her eyes, pouring out love and, most important, trust.

Please believe in me, Clancy.

"Please believe in me, Clancy." The words escaped, as though her prayers and wishes had taken on their own volition.

Her husband appeared startled. He placed a

hand on her cheek and caressed her. "Of course I believe in you, *mi amor*."

"I have to tell you about a . . . a project I worked on." Dressing this up was difficult.

"What kind of project?" He leaned back, professorial, ready to give advice. "Something going on at the Cobb?"

Dive in.

Rip off the bandage.

"It's about *Waisted*."

He laid the papers on the table, pushing them into a neat pile, sitting back with the blank expression she recognized as pre-anger.

"What about it?" He rested his right ankle on his left leg.

"Well, we—"

"Who is 'we'?"

"Me, Hania, Daphne, and her children." She didn't include Mike.

"Her children?"

"They're in high school and college." The last thing Alice wanted was to blurt out an incoherent version of their plan. "But that's not the point."

"What is the point?" Clancy shifted. He reached for her wineglass, drinking half of it. "Clearly, you find it important. And something about which you are quite nervous."

When Clancy fell into his boarding school Anglophile speech patterns, he showed himself to be on the highest alert.

"We made a video. About the horrors of what we went through. Revealing their methods: the humiliation, the lies, the hatred. How they laughed at us behind our backs. How their point was to see how much they could break us before we broke and how much—"

"You made a movie?"

"A video. A thirty-minute short. Just for YouTube."

"You made a *video?*" His voice rose. "And put it on *YouTube?*"

"Nobody will—"

He stood and poured a full glass of wine. "Now you've made things very difficult," he said.

"This isn't about you. The movie is about me. My humiliation. I—"

"You chose to go there of your own free will. You signed that contract."

Alice stood and went face-to-face with him. "Just who are you standing up for? Marcus? Acrobat? How about that they made a fool of all those women and me?"

"Jesus Christ, Alice. Why did you not come to me? How could you put out a film about important people in my field and not check with me? How do you think this will look?"

She stared down at her shaking hands. "My name isn't on the credits." She took a deep breath followed by one more. "I made that decision.

Because I was aware you might otherwise be damaged."

"Are you in it?"

"Everyone is in it."

"You got permission from everyone?"

"Yes."

"*Mirabile dictu*! You've learned something." He pressed his fingers to his temples. "You're in it. People will see you. They'll recognize you as my wife."

"You are completely missing the point."

"I guess I am. When you chose to go away and lose weight, you knew everything would be filmed. And you didn't ask for my input. Notice that I am not using the word *permission.* Take note. Aren't you the one always talking about communicating? Well, darling, you didn't communicate about going there. And you didn't tell me about this so-called video."

"Well, you sure let me know how much you hated me fat. Free will? Decisions? Or was it because you shamed me until I had to do something drastic?"

"Don't blame your awful decisions on me."

"I didn't tell you about the video because I wanted you to have deniability. At least, I thought that was my motive. But maybe it was more. Maybe I was scared that you'd never defend me."

Clancy appeared stricken. For a moment, Alice

saw behind his blank eyes to sadness. Then the curtain came back down. "When did you ever put me before anything?" he asked.

"What are you talking about?"

"I've always loved you, Alice, no matter what you may think. I fell for you so hard. You stunned me with the gifts you possessed. You were magnificent—"

"Were, were, were—"

"Stop. Let this be about something other than how I disappointed you. For one moment." Clancy appeared teary. "Yes. You dazzled me when we met. When the beginning scintillation wore off, I fell in love with you. You and your entire damn family. They were so incredibly warm, I thought. But your parents, your brother, they never accepted me. I knew what they thought. *Uptight Clancy.* Your mother acted as though you married a piece of wood. They embraced me only when I became Libby's father."

"What are you saying? That my family didn't treat you right, so you decided I was too fat? That you flirted with Harper because my mother wasn't warm enough toward you?"

"I'm saying that . . ." Clancy fell against the couch cushions. He held out his hands in confusion and gestured around the room. "Look at this place. You hate it. I know. You act as though I rammed it down your throat, but you never said a word while we shopped and planned. After it seeped out and out, until making a beautiful home for our family became perceived as an attack on you. Or so I thought."

Alice opened her mouth to argue and then shut it. Though her house gleamed, resembling a spread from *Architectural Digest*, Macon mocked it, and her parents tolerated it with a smile. The only room where Alice felt comfort was Libby's room.

"I don't want to fight," Clancy said. "Look. You're putting me in a hell of a spot with the video. But just like everything with us, you're fire and I'm ice. You're always ready to react and burn your way right through a problem. I need to consider every move and know the end game. I like steel beams. You like cushions."

"You don't really even like who I am, do you?" Alice asked.

"I love you more than anything in the world. Do I *like* you? Do you *like* me? What do you think? If you hadn't become pregnant, would we have gotten married? You knew where I came from. Nobody teased me with love when I was a kid. My parents didn't make it clear morning, noon, and night that everything about me was a gift from the gods. I was expected to serve God. Not the other way around. Do I like you? Hell, Alice, I'd like to *be* you."

Alice's chest hurt, seeing how far apart they

remained, how locked she and Clancy were into their personal pain and fear.

Alice realized that Clancy, too, was lost. And that each was waiting for the other to change. Both wanted to be loved unconditionally. But neither wanted the other just the way they were, and this just about broke Alice in two.

CHAPTER 28

DAPHNE

Daphne watched her reflection as Ivy held up a dark-navy dress, and then a lighter shade, cornflower blue, wondering if they would reach the same conclusions. Unlike her stupidity before her sister's wedding, Daphne knew enough to have Ivy help dress her for the upcoming press conference.

"Who thought that a week before Christmas the world would give a damn about a hoax involving seven fat women holed up in a mansion?" Daphne asked.

"Who wouldn't find that interesting?" Ivy said. "A more pertinent question: Who knew there would be seven women crazy enough to end up at a place like that in the first place?" Ivy substituted deep-purple fabric for the shades of blue cloth.

"I like that better," Daphne said. "Why do you sound so angry every time I talk about the video?"

"Angry? Who's styling you for the press?" Ivy's answer could be related to either of Daphne's statements. Ivy walked to a rack of clothes, flipping through dresses, blouses, and skirts. One caught her attention, she frowned, and then released the item.

"You're judging me, sure as the scale I now climb on nearly daily," Daphne said.

Ivy held up a black sheath, considered it, and jammed it back.

"What's wrong with that one?" Daphne asked.

"Unsuitable neckline. You are not a princess neck person."

"What am I, then?"

Ivy stood in front of her, hands firmly on hips, and cocked her head. "We've been best friends for how long? And yet I know more about your most flattering neckline than the depths of your despair." She spoke with her trademark flippancy, but Daphne caught sadness underneath.

"It's not you, it's me," Daphne said.

"What, are we breaking up?"

"Never." Daphne twirled the chair around to face Ivy. The pill she'd allowed herself earlier now brought forth dry-mouthed speed talking. "I tried to hide from myself, not just from you. Despair? Yes, I admit I'm in the midst of it. But why does that make you angry? If I seem obsessed, blame my constant battle to look like more than the sum—the pieces—of my body parts. That's what I feel like. My neck? A bit less thick now, but still too short. My stomach? Don't get me started. The only improvement that I am certain of is that I can wriggle into Spanx without cutting off all my circulation. My upper arms still wave bye and hi, but they're—"

"They're nothing but fine," Ivy said. "They can hold up your hands and lift weights. So what if they wobble a bit? Who gives a damn except you?"

"I'm not allowed to care about my arms?" Resentment rose as she held back the words she wanted to say. "Or, again, be more than 'fine'?"

"You might find it refreshing to concentrate on something besides your arms. And your stomach. And your chin. And—"

Daphne ripped away the swath of material draping her and pushed out of the chair. "What the hell? Am I not allowed to enjoy something I wanted for so long?" She held out her arms. "Just what you wanted. I'm not draped in black *schmattas*. See this? A sweater that doesn't end below my knees. Pants without an elastic waist. I'm wearing jeans! That thrills me. So, what's your problem?"

"My problem? *Your* problem. You look terrific. But you were terrific before. Your obstacle was in your head."

"My head? May I remind you that you found *Waisted* and encouraged me to go?"

"I encouraged you to find a way to make your pain go away. I thought this would help. I was wrong. You're like a junkie who quit but who

342

sees syringes filled with heroin dance around screeching 'Shoot me up! Shoot me up!' You keep staring at your arms, hoping just not having tracks will make it all better."

Ivy took her by the shoulders and turned her to the mirror. "This is you. Are you going to win a modeling contract with *Vogue*? No. But is that what you want? *Look at yourself, for goodness' sake.*"

Daphne stared and tried to piece together who was in front of her. "Every time I eat anything that isn't a carrot or the equivalent, I get emotional hives. Yes. I hold my breath until I weigh myself. The number that appears rules my entire day. All day I wonder, *Am I fat? Am I normal?* If you drew an outline of me, would it show a normal-sized person?"

Tears rolled down her cheeks. "Thanks. Now I'll have to redo my damn makeup."

Ivy plucked tissues from a red holder and dabbed. "Oh, honey. I didn't want to make you cry. Once again, my timing sucked. Just thank God you don't date me. Imagine the horror. I only wanted to break that shell of terror, not traumatize you."

She wiped one last tear. "Good as new. This stuff stays like iron, right? Waterproof, I assume. What brand?"

Daphne shrugged, even knowing it made her appear more teenage than Audrey.

"All I wanted to say was stop being ruled by the scale. Start living a larger life," Ivy said.

"How about a better axiom?"

"Nitpicky, aren't you?" Ivy grabbed a sweater from the rack and held it up below Daphne's neck. "This one. Come on. We're gonna make you a tough girl."

She flipped through the rack, stopping to pick out a pink camisole.

"Pink for tough?" Daphne tried to imagine what look Ivy aimed at achieving.

"Almost purple. Which you liked. Now, wait for it." She peered at her. "Stand up."

Daphne stood and spun around.

"I like the black cords. But you need the right boots. Eight, right?" Without waiting for confirmation—Ivy sized up a person's dimensions in less than a minute—she took off her broken-in Frye motorcycle boots and handed them to Daphne.

"But those are yours!"

"And now they belong to you. These boots have hard-hitting magic." She put a finger to her lips, squinted, and then chose a different sweater from a short pile. "Here. Get behind the curtain. When you come out, I expect a Valkyrie to emerge."

Daphne drew the curtain closed and pulled on the soft tank. Hanro cotton, smooth as silk, but without the shivery silk sensation that became unsettling in winter. The sweater color was an unusual choice to wear with pink. Deep russet, with flecks of gold and amber mixed in with the dark orange-red.

She slipped into Ivy's still warm boots and stood before the mirror. Unbelieving. For years, Daphne chose her clothes using two parameters: that they (1) be roomy, yet (2) come in the smallest possible size.

Now she saw someone completely different. The crossover top defined her body modestly but not with shame. The soft pink peeking out lifted the spirit of the deep-colored sweater that slouched at the perfect point above her hips.

Wearing the black corduroys and boots, she appeared defiant.

She left the mirrored alcove and twirled. "I'm a new woman. You made me who I always wanted to be."

"Not true." Ivy took Daphne's arm and slipped on a copper bangle. "I only brought out who you could always be. Whatever you weighed."

Daphne ignored Ivy's words. She stared, seeing this woman she might like.

> **TIP:** Girls of all kinds can be beautiful—from the thin, plus-sized, short, very tall, ebony- to porcelain-skinned; the quirky, clumsy, shy, outgoing and all in between. It's not easy, though, because many people still put beauty into a confining,

narrow box. Think outside of the box . . .
Pledge that you will look in the mirror
and find the unique beauty in you.

—*Tyra Banks*

TRUTH: What she said.

Alice must have written quite a press release. A throng mobbed Alchemy's waiting room. The sizable space, airy and filled with light, became hot and crowded. Cameras flashed as reporters and photographers jostled for the best angle.

"Okay, folks!" Gabe almost shouted. "We'll take questions now. Back up so we can get into position."

"How long do you think they'll grill us?" Hania posed the question to Alice, their chosen coordinator.

"I told Gabe to chase them out in forty-five minutes or less."

Daphne doubted he'd stick to that vow. Her son fancied himself a newly hatched muckraking filmmaker.

"One more shot!" a photographer from *People* yelled. "Get closer, ladies!"

People.

They formed a ragged group, each trying to stand behind the other. Alice, being the tallest, won the prize and had her hips and thighs blocked partially by the others. Daphne remembered the lessons she learned from years of making actors shine. She stood straight. Lifted her neck high into the air, brought her head well above her shoulders, and stuck her chin out, but not up.

In person, the pose looked ridiculous. In pictures, double chins disappeared.

"Get to the mikes, ladies," Gabe instructed.

Daphne tried not to smile as though her son were a precocious ten-year-old. The first question shot out.

"Harry Oaks, *Boston Globe*. When did you realize that the entire program was a sham?"

Alice took it. "The initial shock of our treatment overwhelmed any thoughts of malfeasance." She tugged at the cherry-red cardigan she wore over a fitted black dress. The stack-heeled boots seemed to bring Alice to six feet. "When they started feeding us drugs, we understood the danger of our situation."

"Was your plan to escape the first thing you thought about when, as you said, it became weird?" The reporter from Channel 7 didn't offer her name. "Or was your goal to see what was going on and steal the footage?"

Daphne leaned toward the mike. "At first, our only thought was to find a computer or phone. They took all our electronics the first day. I planned to contact my husband about the pills they gave us. To see if they were safe. He's a doctor," she added. "When we saw the footage, it changed everything."

"Gretchen Henderson, *Boston Herald*. Why didn't you confront them instead of running away?"

Daphne contemplated how to put across the sheer terror under which they lived. How rapidly humiliation, shame, and having one's rights and individuality removed led to powerlessness.

"I'll answer that," Hania said. "They made scared fools of us. They played on every one of our fears, and drummed into us, morning, noon, and night, that we were pathetic. That we had nobody to blame for our bodies but ourselves. That we'd never truly be loved. They worked to convince us that they were our only hope."

"So they frightened you?" the *Herald* reporter followed up.

"That's too simplistic an analysis," Alice said. "They didn't frighten us because they were strong, and we were weak. They worked it hard. They set out to humiliate us, overwork us, and embarrass us—and make us into creatures. Perhaps using techniques from prisoner of war manuals. Their goal was most decidedly not to help us become thinner or healthier—their purported mission. Or to explore what it means to be overweight for a woman in America. Their objective for this project? Documenting how far women would go to lose weight. How demeaned we'd become before we said stop—or if we ever did."

"But didn't you, in fact, lose weight?" The reporter appeared to have last eaten at Halloween. "So, in fact, didn't they do what they said?"

Gabe stepped up to the mike, waving back the women. He took a brochure from his back pocket and unfolded it. "This is the literature that Acrobat sent to every woman applying to participate in its weight loss program and documentary:

> "You, like too many women across America, judge your worth by your dress size, by the numbers you see on the scale, and by the jeans into which you can fit. When was the last time that you based your value on your humanity? Your talents? Your ability to soothe a child's tears, write a book, or compose a song?
>
> "When did you last bake a cake for your family without fear or go out for dinner and not worry about every calorie you ingested?
>
> "*Waisted* is looking at the 'why' in that equation. Can a woman lose weight—for her health, for the fashion statement she chooses to make, without, in fact, losing her dignity and her commitment to herself?
>
> "Our backers, so committed to this

project, will match your monthly salary so that no woman is turned away because she can't afford to miss a paycheck.

"Those joining us in the green hills of Vermont will be afforded the unique opportunity to spend an entire month exploring ways to bring themselves into balance.

"Respect. Health. Mindfulness. We believe by bringing these values to the forefront, women will have the opportunity to choose exactly who they want to be for just the right reason."

Gabe nodded at the reporter. "Does that sound like these women were prepared for what would face them? Does it sound like they expected to face ridicule?"

Hania stepped forward. "If you watch the video, you'll hear those same words. They are also on our website: www.waistedthevideo.com."

Alice and Daphne joined her, and the three held hands. Alice bent her head to the microphone. "Thanks for—"

"Just one more question. Jules Godfrey, *Boston Globe*. I'm directing this to you, Ms. Thompson."

Alice crossed her arms over her chest. Jules Godfrey reviewed films. "Yes?"

"Your husband. Clancy Rivera?" He waited for Alice to acknowledge that this was indeed her husband. She remained quiet, waiting for the question.

"Mr. Rivera, like Mr. Rhyner at Acrobat Films, is a documentary filmmaker. His company, Prior Productions, is well known. How does your husband feel about you attacking Mr. Rhyner—someone in the same field as himself—and his project?"

CHAPTER 29

ALICE

Clancy interrogated Alice for weeks following the press conference, throwing around words such as *loyalty* and *rationality.* Just when she thought he'd calmed down, another explosion came, like this morning when getting Libby to preschool peacefully was all she wanted.

"Do you realize how this reflects on me?" Clancy paced the kitchen as Alice whisked eggs in a copper bowl.

"What's 'reflect'?" Libby asked. "Like in a mirror?"

"Yes, very much like that. For instance, *reflect* means to see one's image in something else. Like Daddy thinks that what I'm doing makes him—"

Alice stopped. How bad had her marriage become that she was sending messages through Libby? "Makes him think about his work," she finished.

Clancy jumped in. "What Mommy means is that I am thinking about her *and* my job," he said. "How they are colliding. Sometimes people have to be careful when things collide."

"Careful about what?" Libby wrinkled her nose,

wrestling with Alice's and Clancy's multiple messages. "Collides how?"

Alice waited for his answer as she stirred the pancake batter. Good angel syrup and bad angel syrup waited on the counter. The chemically sweetened nonsugar Mrs. Butterworth's smirked at her, all holier than thou, while the sugar-packed Vermont Maid winked with a come-hither smile.

"Daddy means that he and I have different times our work needs to be done, and our schedules don't always match."

"What does that mean?" Libby's exasperated tone might have been lifted straight from Alice's voice box. "I don't understand. Why do your works need to match?"

Sometimes small-crafted avoidances ended up strangling one's intentions, so, in the interest of the greater good—Alice convinced herself—one reached deep for a big fat lie. "To be sure that you and *your* schedule are number one. Who picks you up and drops you off?"

"Do you want blueberry or banana pancakes?" Clancy shared Bebe's tendency to ensure something healthy went into every dish served. Once Alice resented the habit, but now she imagined the fruit pushing out the flour and sugar. Go, produce!

Libby, sensing her parents' desire to nudge her off the topic, pushed her advantage. "No fruit. Chocolate chips! Like Uncle Macon uses."

Clancy's brain clicked—thoughts showing on his face—weighing Libby's future obesity against a fast way out of his stupidity in communicating with Alice through Libby. "I have an idea," he said. "I'll make a raisin-and-nut face on the first pancake."

"Grandma and Zayde say raisins are fruit with the freshness taken out and the sugar left in."

Her family was insane. Libby's fate glowed from the future: circus-lady fat or nail thin. Alice grabbed a step stool and reached to the very top shelf of the cabinet, where she hid everything tasty—from herself—and brought down a dull-brown tin decorated with wreaths.

"Chocolate chips." She pried open the lid and poured a ridiculous amount into the entire bowl of batter. Clancy would hate them, and Alice found such cloying sweetness sickening, but they'd manage to choke down the pancakes. Sometimes the idea of sweet meant more than the reality.

Clancy's expression told her everything she needed to know. The moment he returned to the car after dropping off Libby, tamped-down rage from breakfast bubbled from his eyes, the set of his mouth, and, somehow, even the way he jammed the keys into the ignition.

"You need to kill that article in *People*. You can't talk to them."

"Don't you mean, 'Thank goodness you're shining the light on Acrobat's evil empire?' What happened to your rants against them? You're the one who said that they turned documentary filmmaking into crass 'gotcha' movies. Have you changed your mind?"

There's something you should know. About the People *interview.* That's what she should have said.

Steam puffed from Clancy's mouth. His clouds of breath in the January temperature looked like fury drawn in cartoon shape. "Stop insulting me. How do you think it looks that my wife, my damn wife, is the one who uncovers Marcus's ugliness? Making it seem like either I sent you to do it, or that I twiddled my thumbs while you walked into the belly of the beast."

She threw back her head against the headrest, disassociating as she waited for her husband to leave the car and head to the train station.

The Cobb's main floor was quiet and empty except for a senior exercise program. The Tuesday Ladies in Their Eighties bumped their hips to an old Chaka Khan song, with one particularly perky woman shaking extra hard, winking at the two old men sitting in the stands. Did it never end?

She slipped into her office and pulled up the email she'd sent to the *People* reporter in response to her questions. The past two weeks, she'd used magical thinking and counted on the unlikeliness that the magazine would use all the information sent by her, Hania, and Daphne. This morning, she faced the truth. Squeezing her eyes shut against the oncoming train wreck was hardly a plan to save her marriage.

Now, rereading what she had written, the anger in the response blazed from the computer.

> Dear Karen,
> Here are the answers to your (so thoughtful) questions.

She squirmed reading how she sucked up to the reporter. Did everyone get so googly-eyed at the idea of appearing in *People*? Perhaps even murderers stood straighter at the thought. Probably particularly murderers.

She scrolled through her blah-blah-blah about self-image, and so forth. At least she hadn't written about her marriage. Some wisdom or vanity kept her from telling the entire world that her husband slept with her less, so she ran away to a weight loss farm.

> In answer to your question "What next?" and how the experience impacted my future, here you go:
> My husband's next film follows Brazilian

street children. He's doing a spectacular job. I'm in awe of the footage I've seen.

So far, no problem.

However . . .

And here it came.

However, I was disappointed by one massive gap in his research.

She had to say *massive,* right? Why not just leave *gap* be?

Sex slavery. While there is an incredible dive into the economic conditions that lead to the problem of homelessness, poverty, violence, substance abuse— even the soul-sucking definition of the nomenclature "street children"—Prior Productions is brilliant here—I felt as though I stared down a maw of missing information when I looked at the early footage.

And yes, in answer to your unasked question, I did address this with him. He broke my heart with his answer: "That is a different movie, Alice." As though one could ever separate sexual assault, misogyny, and domestic violence from the root causes of why children end up living on the street.

This led me

Oh, there she went, diving straight into self-righteousness. Thanks, Mom.

This led to my own work in the Cobb Community Center. What was I missing? How did the growing war on women impact the girls in my care?

Thus was born my next project: helping young girls, from the earliest of ages, learn to define themselves in the face of misogyny and with empowerment.

Three things became apparent upon reading this. 1. She liked the program she proposed. 2. If *People* published her words, her marriage was over. 3. She'd been cruel to Clancy.

Everything she'd written would drive Clancy to the edge.

But why fight for a marriage where her ideas—even ideas that walked out of his work—enraged her husband?

Bullshit. What kind of woman berated her husband through a national magazine?

But where was his marital loyalty when he denied the trauma of *Waisted*?

The strands one needed to separate when contemplating the end of a marriage resembled untangling fine gold chains. One moment you had your hand flattening out and holding down a dozen reasons why you should leave:

How being appreciated or condemned
    made or broke your day.
The secret eating you did to stay married.
The bingeing.
The fear that both will return.
The idea of living your entire life
    clutching your reality close enough to
    hide.
Raising a daughter in an atmosphere
    where beauty is translated as love.
Having joy squeezed from your life.
Being trapped in cold steel.
Feeling you had to earn every hug.
Envying your parents' relationship.
Turning your passion from your husband
    to your work and daughter.
Weighing every decision in life against
    Clancy's lips pursing or smiling.

And then, like last Sunday, all reasons to leave disappeared. Sometimes all it took to slap her to the other side was an ice-skating session on the Frog Pond. Seven of them rode the train to Boston Common, holding hands, laughing, and ignoring the usual double takes, stares, and concerted efforts folks made to seem extra-approving that accompanied their public outings as a mixed family: her and Clancy; her parents; Macon and his girlfriend, whose red curls rivaled Daphne's; and Libby, a blend of every corner of the world.

When they rented skates, Clancy took charge, writing sizes on his ever-present reporter's pad, paying the most serious of attention to outfitting the family. As Macon and Red skated away with Libby between them, Clancy, the best skater in the group, reached his hand out for Bebe's.

Bebe, known for her clumsiness as well as her stubbornness, frightened them whenever she stood on ladders, held tools in her hands, and, most certainly when she walked, much less skated, near icy areas. Still, she insisted that her childhood skating in Manhattan's Wollman Rink prepared her for moves worthy of Nancy Kwan.

Knowing Bebe's treacherous tendencies to charge ahead, Clancy always chose her as his skating partner. He locked her in a tight hold, and then spun her out and back. In a miracle of Clancy's physical and creative strength, Bebe appeared to be floating on air as though she was once again the girl from Brooklyn fighting against her limits. Whether she believed that her talents added in any way to their smooth trips around the frozen Frog Pond, Alice didn't know, but the pairing worked.

Love for Clancy rushed back. Anger had driven joyful memories underground and brushed away present goodness when it appeared. At that moment, reasons to stay overcame thoughts of separation. She questioned her reality and wondered if she trusted any decisions. She had been the one to stick her finger down her throat. Weakness and gluttony had been her choice, right?

Clancy, staying up all night, rocking Libby, and then driving them from New Hampshire and back at two in the morning, when only the rhythm of wheels on the road soothed their infant daughter's colic.

Clancy proposing at midnight in the Top of the Hub restaurant, when February 13 turned to February 14, holding out a diamond ring sparkling just like the sky surrounding them.

Lying in bed with infant Libby, her fingers twined in Clancy, each soft breath of their baby a miracle.

She dug deeper, craving the exquisiteness of their love back in her heart:

The two of them in bed, side by side, imagining the color of the two of them spun in the baby curled inside Alice.

Their early wild lovemaking, drunk on each other.

The commitment Clancy and his parents had in believing that family mosaics could save the world.

Alice didn't want to stop loving Clancy. Her desperation not to make a mistake—not to *be* a mistake—for her family not to shatter at Libby's feet, overwhelmed her.

Her fingers hovered over the keyboard. She wished it were possible to tug the email back from the ether in which she sent it two days ago. Perhaps she should pray *People* would cut her words down to one or two bland sentences. Damn praying. She must call the reporter.

Exhaustion overwhelmed her. Tears ran down her face as if her taps had been opened.

She didn't want to be alone.

She didn't want to be a single mother.

She didn't want to be with this Clancy.

CHAPTER 30

DAPHNE

Daphne snuck up on the scale as if approaching it slowly would trick the machine.

"Weigh yourself every day." Alice offered the advice as though it were a secret formula designed to fool the gods of flesh, acting like she was the only person in the entire world who ever thought of using a scale.

Daphne kept it up for a bit. Listened to Alice—and Ivy—who also swore by this supposed foolproof method.

"Choose what you consider a danger weight! If you hit that number, cut back!"

Daphne quickly slipped off the daily weigh-in wagon. She'd trusted too many cures and sure things over the years designed for the same goal: Don't eat. Don't enjoy.

Like the smuggest of men, the scale mocked her. Scales seemed so damn masculine, particularly the machines in doctors' offices, standing above her with their air of superiority, their broad shoulders meant to keep her in place, the metal scornful as she stepped on, smirking when the numbers settled.

None, of course, worse than the giant monster in the mansion.

Daphne had avoided weighing in during the weeks of December's holiday overeating, beginning with the indulgence of Chanukah brisket cooked for hours, sealed in apricot leather, smothered with her secret gravy, falling into succulent strings of soft, moist meat, and ending with Christmas dinner at Marissa and Lili's, complete with roast beef, buttermilk biscuits, and pecan pie.

The mirror revealed her round, puffy face. Her hair massed in wild curls. Botticelli, Sam often said. If only. She wondered how many ounces her hair weighed. Perhaps she should shear it off before stepping on the scale.

She tapped the cold white metal. Double zeros appeared. The ideal weight.

Truly lovely women pared themselves to nothing.

Daphne stepped on, holding her breath, but then worried the held breath might register, so she exhaled. She closed her eyes and made a wish: she promised God she would do nothing but good deeds for the rest of January. All she asked in exchange was a weight gain totaling no more than two pounds. Two pounds would bring ecstasy. Five, and she'd spiral down into hell.

She didn't record her weight. Unlike Alice, who wrote each day's number in a journal, straight as soldiers, no doubt, she had no desire to document these numbers. Anyway, Daphne didn't need reminders: each time she stepped on the scale, the verdict tattooed itself permanently in her brain.

The number appeared.

Eight pounds? She'd gained eight pounds?

Just where had the fuckers landed?

That morning, she'd woken content, pressed to Sam, back-to-back, sharing their sleepy warmth. The sun showed through the windows and danced on their bright-yellow winter comforter. The alarm went off. He smiled and kissed her shoulder.

She'd ground coffee beans, the rich scent building anticipation for the daily pleasure brought on by that first cup. Audrey wandered in, poured a glass of cranberry juice, mumbled "Morning," and blew her a kiss. The newspapers had been placed on the doorstep just right. Happiness reigned.

Until she stepped onto a metal contraption.

Moments ago, pixie dust surrounded her. Now Daphne loathed herself.

A long-dormant desire for a new diet book hit. Before work, Daphne planned to stop at Newtonville Books.

Her first client arrived twenty minutes early. Knowing the likelihood that the nervous young girls Bianca sent might bolt, the receptionist had brought her into the private waiting room usually reserved for celebrities.

Pro bono clients tended to go into a toxic stage of shock when confronted with their faces in the harsh lighting. These girls knew what they looked like; they needed no "before." They avoided their reflections whenever possible. Whether acne, scarring, hyperpigmentation, or facial hemangiomas troubled them, shame accompanied the skin disorders. People regularly came up to these girls with ill-considered ideas and remedies to cure the problems. Baking soda! Get a tan! Spread toothpaste on your zits! Everyone considered herself or himself an expert.

> **TIP:** People who are overweight don't want unsolicited advice. Guess what. We know we're fat. We live in homes with mirrors.
> —*TV personality Al Roker*
> **TRUTH:** What he said.

An uncle once came up to Daphne at a funeral to talk about how fat her aunt had become—her aunt lying in the casket. He'd shaken his head. "What a shame. Natalie was such a beautiful girl. You better watch yourself. You don't want to end up like her."

Thanks for the new goal, Uncle Chickie: dieting for a thin, desirable corpse.

"Scary doing this, huh?"

The girl nodded. She clutched a worn backpack.

"Do you mind?" Daphne asked, gesturing toward the bag. "Can I put it safely over there?" She indicated a low table to the side.

Constance loosened her hands so that Daphne could take it. "Wow, what is this?" One side of the fabric showed a painted collage of landmarks: the NYC skyline, the Eiffel Tower, the Painted Desert, the Sphinx and more, one melting into another, making a swirl of the world's jewels.

"I painted it." Constance's words were barely audible.

"It's phenomenal. How did you choose which places to paint?"

She shrugged, but a small smile appeared. "Those are places I want to visit."

"And you shall. A talented girl like you." Daphne placed a hand on Constance's shoulder, to encourage, comfort; to help her adjust to being touched.

Waist-length, tangled ropes of dyed black hair almost covered the girl's face. "The first thing I'm going to do," Daphne explained, "is put on this cape. You ready?"

The girl shrugged her assent.

Daphne shook out the silky silver material,

lifted the girl's hair, and snapped the back closure.

"Now I'm going to pull your hair back with a headband. Do you mind?"

Constance's shaking hands gripped the cape fabric tight enough to crease it, even though Daphne had explicitly chosen the material for wrinkling resistance. She stiffened as though awaiting a painful surgical procedure to be performed without any anesthesia.

Daphne concentrated on which color headband would be the least problematic against the girl's massive skin eruptions, racing through a montage of imagined snapshots, until choosing the translucent plastic. She slipped it on and fluffed out the girl's hair, so safety cloaked her.

"See these products?" Daphne pointed to the tray on her rolling table, covered with items from CVS. Using hard-to-get or expensive cosmetics guaranteed failure. Whether in a shelter or a motel, with the teen's mother searching for safe housing while also working double shifts as a hotel maid, as Bianca had told her, replacing lost or stolen cosmetics was close to impossible. Expecting Constance to buy a brand that Sephora or a department store carried would be like asking her to replenish a skin care line from the moon.

"I'm going to give you a set of all the ones I choose for you. With written instructions, because, really, who in this world remembers everything they hear the first time? Not me. If you lose anything, come by, and I'll give you replacements."

Constance gave the barest and quickest of smiles. "Thanks."

"These are your helpers, to use while Bianca heals your skin. Soon you'll hardly need these." She tipped Constance's chin, touching her face, feeling the girl flinch. "We're going to make you so pretty. Playing up all your very best features. Your skin will fade into the background. We'll see those gorgeous big brown eyes. And the shape of your face! Did you know you're a perfect heart?"

"A heart?" Constance met her eyes for the first time.

"Yup. Imagine what you might have had if not for winning the facial shape lottery: a square. A circle. A trapezoid!"

Constance actually laughed; Daphne's spirits lifted. "Okay. I'm teasing with that one. There's a pear. Oval. Diamond. Rectangle. Inverted triangle—be glad you don't have that one!"

"What do you have? You're so pretty."

"Oh, no, hon. I'm what's known in the trade as 'makeup pretty.' Not much naked-faced, but able to paint myself pretty. My face is round, bordering on oblong. No prize from the genetic factory. While you, though you lost the skin trophy, have what we call perfect bone structure.

Count yourself lucky. Skin, you can fix. Bones are forever."

Daphne never minced words about the skin conditions of her clients, but she gave back in triplicate by hammering away at their best attributes. Teenage girls without homes focused only on their faults, so Daphne changed the story line.

"Ugly and beautiful are only a few millimeters apart." Daphne ran her finger gently along the outline of Constance's face. "A heart pleases most. Science has proven that people react the most positively when faced with the very dimensions that you have. The sharp jawline. The perfectly aligned, large eyes. Fringed, I might say, with outstanding lashes. One coat of mascara will always be enough for you, young lady. Any more, and that lily will be way overgilded."

Constance sat higher and straighter. "How long do you think it will be before the medicine your sister is giving me works?"

Daphne stepped back and evaluated the girl. Constance's case appeared to have never been treated in any way other than harsh washing, as though she'd hoped to scrub away the problem. A homeless kid without health insurance didn't have a chance against cystic acne.

Some would question why Bianca and Daphne worked on this, securing a home for families surely being the more important problem. Folks didn't understand that the sisters could give gobs of money for safe permanent housing—which, in fact, they did—but no agency would spend a dime on improving skin for these kids. Something that drastically improved their lives.

And few women understood as well as the Bernays sisters the value placed on beauty.

"You have to ask her, but I believe you'll have a new face in about five to six months."

The girl appeared stricken, though Daphne was confident that Bianca had already shared this time line with Constance. Blocking out the unwelcome happened all the time. "That's forever!"

"I know it feels that way, but the time goes fast, because your skin improves a bit more every single day. Every morning, your complexion will become smoother. But today, right this minute, you are special: you're strong and beautiful and oh-so-talented. Plus, while you're waiting for your skin to become what you want to see, I'm going to give you everything you need to paint yourself pretty if you feel like it. Just like me. Then you can concentrate on more important things."

CHAPTER 31

ALICE

By lunchtime, writing and revising emails to her *People* connection had driven Alice mad. When in doubt, *Call Sharon Jane* had been her maxim since high school. So, she called.

Following the three-minute conversation, she hung up the phone and escaped her office.

Twenty minutes later, Alice parked across from the red doors of the Menino YMCA in Hyde Park. Despite the Cobb being replete with elliptical machines and exercise classes, Alice never used the facilities. Sweating where she worked was impossible. Staff interrupted to remind her of supplies needed. Patrons settled on the treadmill next to her so they could fill her ear with complaints about locker room messes. Workouts became more teeth grinding than endorphin-inducing. Not that Alice previously spent much time working out anywhere, but since returning from the mansion, she often joined Sharon Jane at the Y, where they swam, rode stationary bikes, and, their favorite, sweated in Zumba, the class where she was headed today.

Sharon Jane waited for Alice upstairs. Her friend was a carved-down version of Susannah, her thick legs encased in yellow leggings, and her surprisingly thinner top half covered in a worn purple Prince tee shirt. S.J. chatted with an older white woman, the owner of the local coffee shop, outside the Y's exercise rooms. The waiting area was filled with the diverse population that made Hyde Park a virtual United Nations. The class attracted a mixed crowd—in age, race, and culture. Of the regulars who fancied themselves co-instructors, there was a teenager with Down syndrome, a seventyish woman with the body of an Olympian, and a pair of sisters who glared at anyone who talked during class.

The actual teacher, a doctor with a passion for leading Zumba, brought so much joy to her work, Alice considered asking her where she practiced medicine.

The class was a montage of body types attracted to the mix of music—from Afro house to Brazilian samba, with klezmer providing an occasional aural change.

Susan Jane patted her companion's age-spotted arm and then walked up to Alice. "Her son is in the hospital. She called his problem wasting disease. I think she means AIDS. Poor thing."

Alice nodded in sympathy as she tugged Susan Jane toward a more private area. Sharing S.J. with others, no matter the tragedy, wasn't why

Alice had played hooky from work. Sadness always managed to find her friend. Since high school, Alice competed for attention from S.J. with Latin School's neediest, pleading their cases to Sharon Jane, the Oprah of the classroom.

"How are you?" Alice asked.

"Do you actually care at this moment?" S.J. tugged the bottom of her tee shirt to cover her hips. "Weren't you the one begging for my attention an hour ago?"

"Allow me two minutes to pretend I'm not the most self-centered person on earth. How's your husband, mother, kids, and work life?"

Sharon Jane held up her left hand and wiggled one finger at a time. "Working himself to death, monitoring everyone in the retirement village, still the laziest tweens on earth, and filled with coughs, cramps, and drug problems. You?"

"I think I ruined my marriage with an email." Alice shared everything from her anger at Clancy's reactions to their anti-*Waisted* video, to answers she'd previously given *People*, the thought of which now roiled in her gut like a greasy burger.

"Guess you forgot the wait-ten-minutes-before-pressing-Send rule."

"You do that with every email? Even you're not that damn wise."

"I do it with delicate work emails," Sharon Jane said. "Or when I'm angry. Most of all, I do it when I might be—I don't know—maybe ruining my marriage."

"Christ. You think this might be that bad?" Alice had just spent the entire drive over trying to convince herself of the opposite.

"What do you think?" Sharon Jane tilted her head in lawyerly fashion.

The words Alice wrote to the reporter appeared as though on a teleprompter. *"However, I was disappointed by one massive gap in his research. Sex slavery . . . I felt as though I stared down a maw of missing information when I looked at the early footage."*

"Sometimes we do something because we're too scared to go after it directly," Sharon Jane said. "Other times we're just damn stupid. Or entranced by ourselves. Which way were you going? Come on. Class is starting."

They joined the race for the back of the room. Alice considered the question as she moved to the fast music. As the woman in front of her struggled to move her behind in a twerking motion, Alice thought of honesty. Zeke prized that trait, raised his girl and boy to live a truthful life. But her father also talked about compassion, often repeating the words of the nineteenth-century writer, feminist, and abolitionist Alice Cary. How her parents loved finding namesake role models.

" 'There's nothing so kingly as kindness, and

nothing so royal as truth,' " he'd recite. Then he'd switch to Zeke philosophy. "But sometimes truthfulness and kindness fight. Truth must hew to the golden rule: doing unto others as you would have them do unto you. So, use truth as education, illustration, and edification. But don't use precision or facts as punishment or to bully someone."

Alice spent years considering that wisdom. Now, with the question dangling in her own life, she wondered, Was she educating or punishing?

"Step right. Step left. Reach for the sky and pull the ropes!" The teacher raised her arms higher than Alice thought human physiology would allow.

Sharon Jane appeared ecstatic as she pumped her arms. S.J.'s husband spent ten hours a day, minimum, away from their house, leaving his wife to manage three daughters between the ages of nine and twelve, all while working and ferrying her mother to chemotherapy appointments, and yet S.J. usually appeared happy. Certainly cheerier than Alice.

Alice leaped from her right foot to the left, until realizing she'd lost the beat of the music.

"Be your own best friend," Zeke counseled Alice during her roughest years in New York—advice she ignored, choosing instead to make reckless decisions as she traveled around the boroughs.

Now twirling in time to a Kenyan rhythm, she opened her heart to the spirit of being two people: herself and her personal best friend.

Nothing came.

Alice imagined Libby. Her baby all grown up, twisted into ropes of confusion, allotting her energy to molding her man into the right person and then postponing decisions until reaching a peak perfection relationship.

What would she tell her child?

"Stop waiting for him to give you permission to save your own life. Concentrate on what *you* want to do, instead of what you don't want *him* to do." That's what Alice would say.

Back at the Cobb, Alice rushed into her office and locked the door. The first thing she did was think of how her mother would handle this dreaded chore. Finally, she took a calming breath and dialed the *People* reporter.

"Hello, Karen?" Alice spoke in the briskest of tones. "Quick question. I just got off the phone with my lawyer, and he says I need to change a few things in the interview I sent. I'll be emailing an updated version in a few minutes. Uh-huh. Uh-huh. Yes. Great."

Peace arrived for the first time in days. Turned out the word *lawyer* worked well, and the article had been only a "maybe" for this week, vying for space with the solving of a decades-old kidnapping in Oklahoma. Perhaps it would run in next week's issue. Or not. Send new answers to the interview, the reporter instructed. No problem.

Apparently Alice wasn't the center of everyone's world.

After reading through her messages, she triaged her work life, home life, and future. She stood and stretched. Then she picked up the phone.

"Clancy? Can we call a truce? Just long enough to actually talk to each other. Without either of us being hateful."

He answered in seconds. "Call your parents and see if they'll watch Libby tonight. I'll make the dinner reservation."

Without their daughter in tow, Bella Luna restaurant, where they usually ate as a family, became more romantic. The same place Alice adored for the casual plates—hand painted by multitudes of Boston children—tonight she appreciated for the oversized, sparkling stars hanging in the dim light.

More, she cherished that Clancy had brought her here—a place filled with color and energy. She knew that if her husband had focused on his taste, they'd have been dining on white linens.

By their second glass of wine, barely sopped up by their matching Silver Moon salads with grilled chicken, the two of them slipped into the digging-at-wounds portion of the evening.

"How would you describe me to a stranger?" Alice asked.

"How? I'm not sure I know who you are anymore." Clancy broke a roll in half and spread the butter thick. "Capturing your essence right now? That's too hard."

"Who did you think I was up until now?" Alice worked at neutrality.

"I thought you were meant to be a happy woman," he said.

"You met me at the worst possible time in my life. Happy is what you considered my descriptor?"

He fumbled with his silverware. "Your unhappiness seemed a product of that guy, Patrick, not your life or your past. I saw that you had wonderful parents, you were well educated, beautiful, and brainy. Yes, when we met, you were anxious, angry, a bit lost—as well you should have been after what he put you through, but also energetic and curious. Devoted to your new job. Your basic nature seemed optimistic and hopeful."

"We went through big changes so quickly," Alice said. "We barely knew each other when we got married. I know we've had this conversation many times, but we have yet to figure out the meaning."

"I don't know how to analyze it," Clancy replied. "I thought I knew who you were, and now I must readjust my outlook. Not entirely. But some."

"Who was the woman you thought you knew?"

Clancy held up the bottle of wine. "Another?"

For a second, Alice counted the calories—and then pushed away the numbers. "Yes, please."

He poured them each a half glass. "I thought you were on my team. I hope that's still true."

"What did being on your team mean?"

"That we believed in the same things."

"Like what?"

"Fighting for the underdog," he said. "Making a better world for our daughter. Taking care of family."

"How about, I don't know, being soul mates?"

"I feel like we're family. Is that what being a soul mate means? I'm always proud to be seen with you. Lord knows that you lighten me up."

"And Lord knows you need that." Alice tried to imagine Clancy with someone even more serious than her. "Perhaps I needed your grounding."

"We were attracted to each other. That was always magnificent."

"Until it wasn't."

"You never stopped enticing me. I know you think you did, but I just wanted you to care about yourself more. Honestly, of course, I wanted you to look . . . healthier. But look!" Clancy waved his hand in a semicircle around her. "You changed that. For you as well as me, I hope."

"But how I did it was insane. What about that? What about punishing those evil people? Isn't that part of fighting for the underdog?"

Clancy straightened in his chair. "I never asked you to take that crazy step. If you'd asked me, I'd have done anything to keep you from going."

"But you didn't like who I was here."

"So you ran away and trusted those *frauds?* How did *I* become your enemy?" He paused. "We're going in circles again. What do you want me to say?"

"I want you to explain," she asked. "Do you know what you did to me?"

Clancy breathed a bit of fire and seemed to count to ten.

"Okay," Alice said. "Let me say that another way. Do you know how you shattered my view of myself?" She tried to wipe away the escaping tears without him noticing.

"I never wanted to make you sad," Clancy said. "I am so sorry for that. There I was, thinking I was being honest. Helping you."

"Editing me like one of your films? Though honestly, I had become pretty big."

"And I became a snotty oaf." He raised his glass. "Using truth as my excuse."

She clinked. "Arrogant."

He clinked back. "Self-important."

"Mighty self-important," she agreed. "But still

mighty. Perhaps I should have respected more how I crashed into your realm."

"Perhaps. But certainly, I knew better than to waltz in carrying dresses for you to wear." He laughed. "I didn't tell you this, but Zeke gave me quite a lecture after you left. The Tadashi dress had its very own chapter in the book of Zeke."

"I didn't tell my parents about that!"

Clancy and Alice looked at each other, laughed, and at the same moment said, "Libby."

They reached for each other's hands across the table. Alice felt a moment of hope so tentative that she didn't dare rest a bit of expectation on it.

Alice rearranged the trays on her coffee table once more, this time putting the cascading slices of banana bread her mother provided— whole grain, of course—to the left of the pot of cinnamon tea. Members of the now-forming Cobb's Smart Is Beautiful Committee would arrive in twenty minutes. Alice had spent three weeks readying for this meeting.

"Why?" Clancy walked in from putting Libby to sleep.

"Why what?" Alice fanned the napkins into a different arrangement.

"Why are you switching the bread and tea?"

"It just didn't seem right the other way."

"Doesn't look too good this way, either." Clancy took the tray to the kitchen. She followed, annoyed but curious.

Clancy squatted in front of the fridge, staring, steady as always, and then rose, balancing on nothing but his rising legs, holding a dish of clementine oranges.

"Watch and learn." Clancy winked and arranged the fruit in a bowl made of red lacquered spokes that twisted open to create a circle from a bundle of the wood.

Alice shook off her initial annoyance and then nodded, trying not to laugh as he fussed over the placement of each orange. Step one in looking at life from new angles, rendering unto Caesar that which was Caesar's. She and Clancy might have different tastes, but his artistic sense surpassed hers. She could give in to that actuality.

For so long, Alice resented the hard edges of their home, so that time and again she dismissed the talents Clancy applied to their lives. After years of comparing her parents' cozy surroundings with her inlaws' perfectly polished home, Alice finally recognized another truth: their home looked lovelier than that of either set of parents. He took Libby to every art museum in Massachusetts—pointing out painting techniques that even Alice had never heard of before—as well as to classical concerts that put Alice to sleep.

A family had room for more than one outlook.

Clancy put the white mugs back in the cabinet and laid out glossy black ones. "These."

Alice saluted, picked them up by the handles, and brought them to the coffee table. Then she stepped back and nodded. "What can I say? When you're right, you're right."

He touched her waist with a tentative hand. When she leaned into him, he kissed the curve of her neck. "Good luck."

Alice placed agendas on the table, excited and nervous about tonight's discussion. Much of her energy had been poured into this project, even as she and Clancy walked their tentative path. They tried to live their marriage instead of putting it on trial daily. Alice started plunking marbles into a glass jar at work. Purple for days with Clancy that were awful, pale yellow for neutral, and orange—bright as Jennifer's glasses—for happy. She planned to give it four months and see which color dominated.

An idea she stole from some long-ago novel, a plan vetted by Sharon Jane.

The women arrived within five minutes of the invited time. Once the small talk ended, and noticeable inroads had been made into the snacks, Alice marked the official part of the meeting by leaning forward, crossing her legs, and clasping her hands. She smiled so hard that

Harper's dimples might be rivaled. The woman herself had been filed as a memory of Alice gone amuck. "Time to work."

She gave each woman a one-sheet rundown of the project to be discussed.

"Good job. I always tell my students, if you can't describe it on one page, you're building something too twisted." Jennifer F., known in the world outside *Waisted* as Jennifer Fitzgerald, taught business dynamics, among other courses, in her role as a professor at the Boston University Questrom School of Business.

Daphne and Alice pulled out eyeglasses— Marissa, Daphne's sister, already wore a snazzy purple pair, and Jennifer, of course, still looked at the world through her bright-orange frames.

Papers rustled as they lifted Alice's synopsis of the program she planned to bring to the Cobb. Susan Jane winked at Alice from across the coffee table.

SMART IS BEAUTIFUL CLUB

What: Girls (6–9, 10–14, and 16–18) will spend two hours a week in their Smart Is Beautiful Club, exploring arts, literature, and sports in an atmosphere merging the pursuit of excellence with exciting activities. College seniors representing the cultures of Greater Boston will lead the clubs alongside (and supervised by) staff.

At the Smart Is Beautiful Club . . .
- We will think differently about beauty and explore all the forms it can take.
- We will teach that wisdom is stunning.
- We will help our girls (and boys) believe that the kind of beauty to which so many young women aspire is only skin deep, and know that if young women believed this, they would be profoundly happier with their lives.
- Lipstick fades and nail polish chips, but the nourishment gained by literature, art, and science lasts forever. The best way we can prepare girls for fulfilling lives is by giving them the power to know and understand that *Smart Is Beautiful*.

Through Smart Is Beautiful, we will share our history of:
- How we learned the hard way. We had mothers and bosses and boyfriends who paid attention to our facade while overlooking our talents and capabilities.
- Why we bought endless tubes of lipstick and mascara, only to learn that real happiness eluded us until we believed

that we "could." *Could* create. *Could* innovate. *Could* use our brains and make something. Until we *did* achieve.
- How we learned to understand that beauty without brains is an empty promise.

Activities will include:
- Meeting with successful female designers, writers, actors, comedians, entrepreneurs, educators, and more in hands-on workshops.
- Book clubs led by local female authors.
- Clinics led by local female athletes.
- Visits by female politicians.
- Ongoing support groups, think tanks, and mentorship programs, culminating in a quarterly presentation decided upon by the group.

"Is the intent clear?" Before they could share ideas, thoughts, and, no doubt, speak over one another, she handed them a second sheet. "Here are the more granular details and plans."

"I already love everything about it," Daphne said.

"Genius." Marissa shook the papers. "I can see it."

"What if we bring in local groups like WriteBoston and City Year?" Sharon Jane ran her finger up and down the page as though seeking tactile inspiration.

"We need more political fervor, feminism, and racial awareness," Jennifer said.

"One step at a time," Alice said. "I just wrote this up a few days ago."

"Jennifer's right," Marissa said. "If we don't ground the program in current realities, we're only offering another version of arts and sports, right?"

"Of course Alice is putting that in." Daphne grabbed the end slice of the banana bread. "Give her a chance to—"

Sharon Jane interrupted. "But if it doesn't infuse the program from the get-go . . ."

Nothing made Alice happier than the sound of intelligent women getting all up in one another's faces with smart. She loved it.

Perhaps she was Bebe's daughter after all.

CHAPTER 32

DAPHNE

Cymbals clashed as Stravinsky coursed through the room. Daphne chopped the onions rough and hard, throwing the coarse pieces into a sizzling pan, followed by smashed garlic, mushroom, carrots, and celery. Most of her meals began with this combination—although too often of late, that combo seemed to be Daphne's entire meal.

Tonight she was cooking a feast, something she'd planned upon returning from Alice's the previous night. The invitation she sent to her family resembled a summons more than a kindness.

As the vegetables married, she added sliced chicken breasts, poaching them until tender, and at the right moment poured in high-quality marsala—stopping midway to pour some in her wineglass. As the mix bubbled, she spooned out about a half cup of the liquid to make a roux with flour, and magic chemistry turned it silken. Cooking was ephemeral, disappearing into memory. Not unlike the enchantment she created with makeup.

389

But oh, the pleasure.

Most people didn't understand cosmetology, viewing it as nothing but artifice, whereas she considered it an art, like music that wafted away even as it played or films that wove dreams for two hours, transporting you for that time. Geniuses flourished in her field—Pat McGrath, the late Kevyn Aucoin—as in any business.

Constance had received the purest of conjuring in the chair. With creams and potions, Daphne showed a troubled seventeen-year-old what it felt like to be enchanted by herself, even if only for a moment. Daphne taught her the art of illusion and gave her the tools so she could love herself.

Her last words to Constance held wisdom that Daphne must finally apply to herself:

"Work with what you have and then add a bit to that. But never create from hatred. Self-loathing is the surest way to misery."

The surest way to misery.

Daphne had worked on changing herself using the point of view of self-hatred for far too long.

Daphne carried in platters and baskets of food, chosen and arranged to please all senses. Taste, smell, sight, and even touch. Break apart the crusty rolls, and you revealed a puff of steam ready to melt butter. Irresistible.

"What's this?" Sunny reared back as though Daphne carried a hydrogen bomb.

Lili took the handle of the wine cradle and filled Sunny's glass. "Looks like Daphne is gifting us with presents for the palate."

Her sister-in-law dimpled in her butter-wouldn't-melt-in-her-mouth way. Lili intimidated Sunny. She held moral authority over Sunny simply by being black. Or maybe it was because her mother bowed down to the most exceptional beauty in the room every time. Whatever the reason, Daphne's gratitude grew with each month of her sister's marriage.

Sunny's daughters all managed to pick partners who provided a screen against their mother. Lili did it with her surety and dimples. Bianca's husband, Michael, intense as a surgeon, sardonic everywhere outside the operating room, did it with his humor. Sam did it with goodness.

Her sisters wondered if Sam's virtuousness went over the top. "Can there be enough zest without a touch of bad boy?" Bianca had mused aloud one night after too many sisterly martinis.

"Sam overflows with great qualities, and he's never my sad song." That had been her answer.

When you accumulated enough wisdom, you learned the right lesson about love. Bad boys remained, in fact, bad. Bad for your heart, bad for your children, bad for the world.

She forgot to learn not to put her mother's judgment and opinions before Sam's. Before everyone else in her life. Before her own.

Daphne had rented rooms in her head to her mother for far too long.

"This, Mom," she answered Sunny, "is a beautiful dinner I cooked for our family."

"Is there an occasion I missed?" Sunny tipped her head, lifted her eyebrows, and glanced with intent at Daphne's midsection.

Daphne weighed responses and then laughed at the choices that came to her.

"What's so funny?" Her mother frowned. "Are you laughing at me?"

"I'm laughing at both of us." She raised her wineglass and stood. "A toast. Many toasts. First, to Audrey and Gabe for their patience in taking second place to my obsessions: thinking about weight, worrying about weight, taking off weight, and—"

"For which we toast you," her mother said. "And—"

"Hold that thought, Mom. I want to toast Sam. Love of my life. You've had more patience with my insanity than could be expected from any man. I am endlessly grateful. I will take you for granted no more."

She leaned down, kissed him softly, smiled, and rubbed his shoulder.

"Yes. We all know your husband is a saint," Bianca said.

Daphne stuck out her tongue at her sister's droll words and then lifted her glass. "Bianca? I toast your generous heart. Even when you try to hide it, we all know you use it every day. To my sister, Marissa, I toast your ability to be true to yourself, and to constantly and consistently show kindness in a hostile world."

"We're hungry, Mom. Almost done?" Gabe's discomfort with deeply felt emotions was no doubt her fault, but she saved that *mea culpa* for another day.

"Soon. To those married to my sisters, I toast how very much you have nudged my family to being that much closer to some semblance of normality."

Everyone smiled.

"And to Dad. You took your father's business and grew it far beyond his dreams—thus making enough of a fortune to pay for our lifetime of therapist bills. Just teasing, Dad. Well, not completely. I toast you for providing ballast. For your sense of humor. And most of all, for sneaking me out to get ice cream when I needed it so badly."

Her mother looked first at Daphne and then at Daphne's father with a baffled expression.

"Lighten up, Mom. That was a million years ago," Marissa said.

Her mother reached out for her wineglass, now looking worried. For just a moment, Daphne wanted to let loose with sarcasm and say, "Oh, and thanks for all the diet tips, Mom!" But it was way past time to let go of childish things and move from being a daughter to being a mother, a wife, and, most of all, to becoming an adult of her own making.

"Mom. I toast you for being a tiger mother. You never took your eyes off us. No matter how hard we begged." Even Sunny joined the laughter on that one.

"I remember what you always said to us when we complained. *Would you rather have a mother who doesn't care?* Well, of course not. I'm happy that you cared. You made sure we had good grades. That we worked every summer, so we understood the value of earning our keep. I'm touched that you loved us so much you wanted to make us over in your image."

Daphne walked over to her mother and took her hand. Her father rose so that Daphne could take his seat. "But no more. You want to be skinny? Great. Be as thin as you like. But I'm never apologizing for eating again. From this day forward, your job is to take your eyes off my body."

She leaned forward and hugged Sunny, tight enough, she hoped, to take the sting out of her words, but not so much that they didn't land. "Here's my goal: I refuse to hate myself anymore. Whatever I weigh, I will embrace myself. If I must buy a dress at the tentmaker's, because of the oh-so-broad Namath back nature gave me, and if the size of that dress is XXL, it will be made of the softest silk, and I'll wear it with joy and pride."

Daphne gleamed with night cream when she walked into the bedroom. She held the cold white scale. "Here. Take this to work. Throw it in the trash. Lock it in the safe deposit box. Just make sure I can't find the thing."

"First your mother and now this? What happened today?"

"Maybe life clicked into place at long last. Perhaps it came from giving advice to a kid; advice that I should have given myself a long time ago. I don't know where the light shone from, but at least it came. No more instruments of agony in my life. No more making my weight, my body, or my face my defining trait."

Task-oriented Sam took the scale and left the bedroom.

Imagining and playing out losing weight had become the song she woke to, played all day, and to which she fell asleep. She'd chosen not to marry sad songs, so why was she living a life of whiny ballads?

Sam clapped his hands as though dusting them off when he returned, signaling a finished job. "Safely tucked away. I guarantee you'll never stumble over it."

"And if I search for it?"

"You will have embarked on a lost battle. Will Audrey be upset? Without having a scale, I mean. Do she and Gabe have one in their bathroom?"

Being a man must be lovely, never having to know the existence and location of every item in the house. "They did, but our daughter doesn't believe in scales anymore."

"I thought for certain your mother had infected her."

"Oh, she did. Haven't you noticed the tape measures and caliper? Audrey now subscribes to the school of measurement and body fat versus muscle. Muscle weighs more than fat, she tells me. Far too often."

Sam fell on the bed and pulled Daphne down with him. "Is that an improvement?"

"I suppose exercise is better than full-on anorexia." Daphne tossed the useless throw pillows on the floor. The ones she picked up again each morning, only to repeat the loop each night.

Not once did she lie on those ridiculous pillows. They existed to clutter and crowd her life. She vowed that tomorrow morning, they would be gone.

"My mothering hasn't been golden in this arena. Passing on weight phobia—just what I wanted to avoid and precisely what I managed to do."

Sam became the analyst he was. "Do you think

your benighted trip to Vermont made it worse or better for Audrey?"

"I'm sure I made it worse by going. She witnessed her mother run away and devote a month of her life to getting smaller. I showed her that there was no other way to deal with my insanity except by leaving you guys."

Sam tipped his head. "She knew you were running from your mother. And the kitchen."

"Does that make it better or worse?"

"Did you choose your mother issues over us? I suppose you did. Yes, you chose yourself over us. But we were fine. You needed to do something rash. You ended up in crisis, but perhaps that trauma broke the barrier. You didn't come back the truest new you, but you came back on a path of exploration. And you invited Audrey and Gabe on the journey. And me. For the first time, you didn't shut us out of the most overarching issue coloring your entire life."

"What path did I come back on?"

"A route where you crashed out of what you saw as 'bad you' in an awful and abusive way. The way those people treated you was so horrific, they voiced things worse than you ever said to yourself. It put you in shock. But—big but—you loved the way you looked. On a third hand, you had no handle on what to do with a change brought on in that manner."

"And of course, despite being wounded by

what they did, for the first time, I nearly liked my body. Which felt like a miracle amid madness."

"Like cancer," he said.

"What?"

"People, during cancer, often lose a lot of weight. If they began fat, at some point they usually think, *Wow, I look great.* But the reason they became thinner is not only beastly, it's unsustainable. The situation becomes cognitive dissonance at its loudest."

Sam had wrapped up Daphne's conundrum into a perfect sound bite. "I don't know how to proceed," she said. "I do love the feeling of verging on small. Should I be like my mother and make thin my goddess?"

"Your mother doesn't have to fight for her beliefs, hon. She has the metabolism of a hummingbird," he explained. "The way she acts toward you? Sunny is like a natural runner pushing her crutch-using daughter to keep up with her on the track."

"That's kind of harsh. I have a crippled metabolism?"

"No. But you don't have hers. Sometimes genes are genes. You can modify your activity for workarounds, but none of us is blessed with the right gene for every pursuit."

"Sunny always had unsustainable dreams for me."

"For the most part, yes. You can choose where

you want to be, but maintain it only when it's within reasonable ranges. *Waisted* had impossible methods to maintain, even taking away the fact that for them it was an intellectualized form of proving how much women hate themselves."

Daphne crisscrossed her legs on top of the quilt. "But you know what? It taught me how vulnerable I am to the worst in myself. And far too vulnerable to my mother. Sunny's voice accompanies me everywhere."

"The words you said tonight were a good beginning. Where will you go from here?"

Daphne reached over to the stack of books on her nightstand and grabbed two volumes. "*Flavour: Eat What You Love*, by Ruby Tandoh," Sam read the title from the first one and then groaned. His face fell. "No! Another diet book, Daph?"

"No. A not-diet book."

"How is that different?" Poor Sam had seen her through so many fads and beliefs that *this was it*.

"She's a food writer with a cooking show in Britain who struggled with eating disorders as a teen. Now, the only rule she tries to follow is this: eat what you love. Those words petrify me. Eat what I *love?* I might as well consider running through the streets in a bikini. I need to find out what that means. Do you understand?"

Sam took her hand. "Sort of. But not really."

"Here are my thoughts broken down to the simplest chunks: I have no idea how to eat what I love. I thought I did. I could list beloved foods forever. But I don't eat them. I cram them. I sneak them. I jut out my chin and swallow them whole. But I never appreciate them.

"Every bite I take is accompanied by internal chatter: *You're a pig. Apply that to your big fat stomach. Why can't you ever control yourself?* No food is purely enjoyable. Not an apple. Not a bowl of cereal. All I think about is how many carbs. How many grams of sugar. How much fat and how many calories."

"My poor baby. Why don't you—"

She stopped him with a palm held out. "Don't fix me. Or give me a lecture. Please. Just listen. Never in my entire life could I imagine eating without screaming at myself. That's why I worked so hard at not telling Audrey she was beautiful or thin or anything but smart and healthy. I was afraid to give her the voices."

"And now?"

"First, I'm banning diet books. And diets." Daphne held the second book aloft. "This one is to inspire me."

The title and author's name, *Embrace: My Story from Body Loather to Body Lover* by Taryn Brumfitt, was on a black background. The only other visual was a nude woman, in a position that revealed her curves and smile. "I want to learn to love my body—or at least to see if liking is possible."

Sam pulled her in for a hug. "You will. Feel like and love. And then there will be two of us."

Daphne brushed away a tear. "I have three other goals. One, I will enjoy eating, and I will no longer let it be the soundtrack of my life. I don't know if I can achieve that, but tonight I took the first step. Two, I want to move my studio off Newbury Street and relocate someplace that's easier for everyday women and kids like Constance to come. I don't want to turn my back on my life's work, but I want to use my skills in new ways.

"We don't need the money. I proved I can conquer Hollywood. And the wealthiest of Boston. This one is a present for me—so I can concentrate on people like Constance. People like me, but who don't have our advantages."

She thought of telling him that, in truth, there were four goals: the fourth being to throw out the stash of pills hidden in her closet. Daphne thought of those as her soldiers, lined up for battle when she got out of control. With reinforcements always waiting on the shelves of CVS.

She planned to rid herself, physically and psychically, of that insurance policy.

"What about Ivy?" Sam asked. "If you move the business."

"Ivy's half of Alchemy thrives all on its own.

401

We can manage just fine. She can be Alchemy Uptown. She'll be happy to see the last of my pro bono work draining money from the business."

"And number three?"

TIP: Darling girl, don't waste a single day of your life being at war with your body, just embrace it.

—Taryn Brumfitt

TRUTH: Daphne had finally found the right tip.

Daphne sat up and crossed her legs. She leaned over and picked up her phone, fiddling until she found the right music. "I don't just want to be grateful for a lack of sad songs. From this day forward, I'm looking for joy."

CHAPTER 33

ALICE

D oes the banner look straight?" Alice asked.
Keely cocked her head to one side and pursed her lips, tipping first to the left and then the right. Libby imitated the older girl, adding in a Grandpa Zeke mannerism by cupping her chin with her thumb and forefinger.

"Perfect," Keely said finally.

"Perfect!" Libby echoed.

Alice had begun bringing her daughter to the community center when Libby started kindergarten last month. Keely and Libby, both in the afterschool program, had become inseparable. Alice used her rank often, unfair as it was, to bring the girls to her office, using several reasons—most of which translated to *My daughter, my prerogative.*

When claiming boss privilege induced guilt, she excused herself via motherhood trumping job. Six months ago, right around the time Alice and Clancy began working on their marriage in a down-to-the-guts way, Libby exhibited new neediness, as though she sensed her family was in danger. Immediately, Alice promised herself two things: she'd always be there for her daughter, and she'd give her only the truth.

She promptly broke both vows, but at least she tried. Bebe stepped in when Alice faltered, Alice stepped up for Clancy if his brittle side took over, and Zeke covered for everyone.

" 'Smart Is Beautiful,' " Libby read. "How long till the fair? Will there be clowns?"

"We're not talking about that kind of fair," Alice said for the hundredth time. Libby acted as though by asking often enough, the upcoming celebration of talent and brains would morph into Ferris wheels and cotton candy.

"This is a time to think about all the good things girls can do even if they're not pretty." Keely's patronizing cadence grated, reminding Alice of her own voice.

"Not exactly, hon. Happiness should never rest on being pretty or not."

Keely appeared unconvinced.

"No fun?" Libby's lower lip curled under. "No candy?"

Again, Alice gave a silent *Sorry* to her own mother as she remembered rolling her eyes whenever Bebe pushed biographies of mixed-race achievers.

"We'll have a fantastic time. Learning is cool."

Both girls threw you-gotta-be-kidding looks. She missed Keely's accepting everything Alice said as gospel. Now, as Keely pretended to be as much Alice's daughter as Libby was, the girl idolized Alice less.

"Is this like how grown-ups say something is fun, but they really mean it will be good for you?" Keely asked.

"Possibly. But listen to what we'll have: artists drawing comics of you—both by hand and by computer. You'll see yourselves as cartoons. We're having jump-rope contests. Funny tests to find out your talents. And cooking classes."

"But no ice cream." Libby let loose a theatrical sigh that she must have learned either from their Brooklyn relatives or down South visiting Zeke's family.

"Come to my office, girls." Alice once more inspected the three-foot-high banner, the music, art, computer, and book stations and floating balloons.

If it killed her, these little girls wouldn't hum songs that attempted rhyming *bitch* and *tit*. Alice couldn't protect Libby and Keely from everything, but she planned to devote her fight to keep them from thinking they started out worth less than one other person on earth.

"Each of you can have one lollipop." Alice unlocked her office. She held out the glass jar filled with cherry pops, the one flavor she hated. That way, she ate only three or four throughout the day.

Her life had become a series of trades and

shaving. Her food intake resembled the budget techniques she used to cut the Cobb's expenses when deficits threatened. At those times, she examined columns of numbers, trimmed here, flaked off a bit there, and eventually reached her bottom-line goal. Replicating the technique for calorie consumption worked. Plus, Alice's gene for competition had been activated in the good-eating arena.

On the not-proud-mother side, presenting her way of eating as a health choice and flavor preference in front of Libby ensured that much of each evening she felt like a liar and a phony. Being Mommy Truthful was no snap.

"I thought this day was about being gorgeous and skinny." Keely grabbed a sweet. "You know. Being smart to be beautiful."

Alice wouldn't jump down the kid's throat; no, she would not. Lord only knew what topics Libby and Keely covered. Perhaps wordplay required an older sophistication. "No, hon. We talked about this. Being smart is beautiful."

"Being pretty is being beautiful." Libby took a lollipop.

"What do you think being pretty means?"

"You know! Like having nice hair." She shook her curls till they flew. "And smooth skin. And ruby red lips, like Snow White. And being skinny. Like why you went away."

Her daughter, noticing her stricken face,

ameliorated her words. "But you looked nice before you went away! Even Uncle Macon says so."

Damn you, Macon.

Alice should have been stuffing her face right now to show them fat was just fine. The hell with *smart is beautiful.* Who wasn't judged by her face and butt?

"Listen up. I like being strong. So I exercise. I like being muscular and lean because I can run faster and bend easier. Ski. And ice-skate. That's why I lost—" She stopped and tried to think of a better word to describe her journey.

"You got skinnier to be strong?" Libby seemed less than convinced.

Parsing life had become motherhood. "Yes. Losing weight was the route to feeling better. For me."

"But, come on, Miss Alice. We want to be smart. Sure. But isn't it good to look cute?" Keely ran her tongue around the edge of her lollipop. "My sisters are happier doing themselves up for a date than doing homework."

Libby looked from Keely to Alice. "Do you think studying is more fun, Mama?"

"*Fun* could be the wrong word, girls. Amused, satisfied, and rewarding are different ways to be happy in this world. Nobody should try for all one way."

Screw it. What would Alice's mother say? She

might find faults in Bebe, but being dishonest was never on the list. Alice trusted her. Whatever came out of Bebe's mouth was what her mother believed to be the solemn truth. It might not be *the* truth, but it was her mother's certainty.

Marbles in a glass container glinted in the corner. Pale yellow for neutral. Bright orange for happy. Purple for misery. For the first six months, each time a yellow marble interrupted the purple jar, she felt gratitude.

It began with the smaller gestures. Clancy helped Alice pick out a soft cobalt-and-yellow couch. He solicited her feminist perspective on his films. She asked what he thought of each iteration of Smart Is Beautiful as she shaped the program. They adopted a kitten, litter box and all, thrilling Libby. Alice made her parents call before coming over.

Baby steps.

"Fun can be a bunch of things," Alice said. "Getting a new doll makes you happy, right? Eating a hot fudge sundae is incredible. Watching cartoons on Saturday morning feels terrific."

"All those things are good, Mama. But you only let me do some of it. How about fun all the time? That would be smarter." Libby nodded at the wisdom she spoke.

"But we need other things. If you never fed Skitty because you were too busy looking at cartoons, what would happen?"

"She'd starve. But feeding her only takes a minute."

"True, but life is filled with Skitty feeding. Taking care of those we love. As we grow up, we find out that there's quick fun, like watching cartoons, and must-do work, like cleaning your room. Work we share, to make it fair, is another kind."

"Why can't nobody clean?" Libby asked.

" 'Cause everybody would be smelly and sick and disgusting," Keely said.

"Right. And there's work you do for yourself." Alice grabbed a cherry pop.

"Like washing up and stuff like that?" Keely crossed her legs on the chair, moving into her listening-hard position.

"Sure. Scrubbing and brushing your teeth is a great example of work we have to do for ourselves." Alice opened her eyes wide. "Unless you girls are planning to have no teeth by the time you're fifteen years old."

"And pimples!" Libby added.

"And dusty, crusty elbows!" Keely and Libby giggled.

"Life is all about balance. Just like a clean face feels better than a muddy one, working to meet your goals can be the most rewarding thing in the world. I went to college so I could get a job like running the Cobb. Every day, I get to come here and make sure tons of kids like you guys are cared for, and seniors get to teach people to knit, and we have sports to keep everyone healthy and strong. My work makes me happy in a way that eating a hot fudge sundae never will."

"Is that why you went away to that place, Mama? To help you get happy in a different way?"

"I went away because I felt confused."

"About being fat?" Keely asked.

Alice took a moment, daring herself not to jump to the most facile answer. "That was part of it. I didn't like that it made people think I looked less attractive."

"Like Daddy?" Libby's voice shook.

"Sort of."

"Daddy likes people to be skinny."

Alice didn't want to throw Clancy under the bus or trash him, but she couldn't lie. "Daddy likes to be thin and thinness is a quality he likes. Just like Uncle Macon loves when his girlfriends have curly hair. Grandma always adored tall men. But those are preferences. Uncle Macon has had straight-haired girlfriends. Grandma had short boyfriends. Daddy loves me no matter what size I am. Funny, generous, kind—love is made up of tons of ingredients. Nobody should choose just one thing. Or expect anyone to hold every quality they like."

"Grandma likes tall men, but she's so tiny!" Libby pursed her lips, becoming a Clancy replica.

"Does Grandma like black men? Is that why she married Zayde?"

"Grandma married Grandpa because she fell in love with him, not because he was tall or black. Grandpa and Grandma acted very smart in their choices. They married the goodness each of them had on the inside."

"But isn't that why Daddy married you?" Libby asked. "Or was it because you were skinny, like in the pictures. Did you have to go to Vermont because you wanted to get like that again for him? To make him happy?"

Telling truths pained her more than making up stories.

"I thought I went to make him happy. But I was wrong." Alice came around her desk and scooped up Libby. "Finally, I found the real reason."

"What?" Libby asked.

"I wanted to be strong in every way. Strong in my body, strong in my mind, and strong in my heart. And smart about you, baby girl."

CHAPTER 34

ALICE

A heady mix of pink and blue streaks in the sky, margaritas, and chlorine dizzied Alice. Late September weather in Provincetown ranged from fifty to ninety degrees. Tonight, as the sun set on the third day of their *Waisted* reunion, temperatures in the eighties warmed the seven women lounging in the pool. Everything from the tequila, to the sultry breeze, to the ocean water lapping only a few yards away brought a heady buzz to Alice's mood.

Cape light sparkled on her new silver bracelet. She and Daphne had stopped in every store on Commercial Street until they found matching bangles, feeling as young and goofy as Keely and Libby when they slipped them on. They walked out twinned, "Smart Is Beautiful" engraved on the metal.

At least fifty emails had zipped among these so-called women of privation—named thus by *People* magazine—based on the shot of the mansion provided by Hania, via Mike, which showed the sign dangling at the entrance.

Welcome to Privation

"Who could have imagined us here, swimming in Provincetown, when we first met?" Susannah stretched out her legs and kicked.

"I barely imagined us getting out alive after that first hour," Seung said.

"I'm waiting for them to pop up and throw us on a scale." Hania sank a bit lower in the water, grinning as she pretended to hide.

Alice stayed quiet, immersed in the joy of being together with these women, free and lovely, fighters all.

"I'm looking around in case they come up from behind and grab my monster hips." Susannah shifted her hands on the concrete lip of the pool.

"Childbirthing hips." Jennifer reached behind her for a towel to wipe her fuschia sunglasses. "They're damn useful. Once women start pushing a baby out, they all wish they had them."

Susannah twisted her face into a wry expression as she slapped her sides. "What a waste for me. A shame I never had kids."

"But if you do, you're ready." Lauretta dunked under and came back with water streaming down her Madonna-like face. "My mother would kill me for doing that. *Cloro, mi hija*! The woman is obsessed with my hair. Chlorine is a tool of the devil."

The women, some with arms resting on the

edge of the pool, others submerged up to their necks, appeared at ease to Alice. Some of them had gained weight since leaving the house of horrors, like Susannah and Daphne, but were still thinner than the day they'd arrived at the mansion, if not tremendously so. Seung, like her, had lost additional pounds, while Jennifer seemed about the same as she'd been upon leaving.

Lauretta and Hania arrived at the reunion having gained all the weight they'd lost and maybe more.

Alice tried to figure out if their individual net outcomes matched what she knew of them. Lauretta and Hania remained perfectionists with glossy manicures and seemingly waterproof makeup—until Lauretta did something like dunk herself in chlorine, and Hania came to breakfast wearing a ragged college tee shirt of Mike's and messed up Alice's theory. She'd tried to formulate an analysis based on how uber-control meant their letting go all squeezed into one outlet: eating.

Hania and Lauretta struggled to make their parents happy by pretending they lived by their rules. That constituted the most potent clue. When you tried to please everyone, or pretended you followed directions that you secretly ignored, or you tried controlling every single nuance in your life, then the world became a vise where only food snuck past rules.

Food held the position of being the very last friend in your life.

Or maybe they just loved food.

They all looked like they were just the women they should be.

"I miss M&M's. And Reese's Pieces." Alice didn't know from where that came. She lifted her toes out of the water, admiring the perfect coral polish.

"Don't you ever let yourself have them? Just a few?" Susannah asked. "My problem is every time I let myself have one, soon I'm eating the bag. Giant-sized of course."

"Hell, I can even gorge on Tic Tacs, but M&M's are my special weakness. I can allow splurges on other things. But never M&M's. Or bagels." Alice concentrated for a moment. "And—oh God!—my aunt's chocolate chip elephant ears. With any of those, even as I'm chewing, I'm holding the next bite ready to go in."

"Calories on deck. All the time." Seung opened her mouth and mimed throwing in food. "Landing strip. And go."

Seung's bright smile advertised her skills. Three of the women now went to her dental practice in Kenmore Square.

"What is that about? The way we'll hold a handful of popcorn up even as we're still chewing." Alice tilted her head and stared at purple streaks in the sky. "Are we so afraid of privation that we need to have it ready for the first moment of an empty mouth?"

Susannah scooped small eddies in the water with her hands. "I'm terrified of food and petrified I won't have food."

"Fear makes it worse. At least for me," Daphne said. "I learned that at the mansion. The place turned out to be the very worst form of my mother. I spent my whole life hiding, sneaking food from the kitchen, petrified my mother might catch me eating. Naturally, every moment alone, I ate. The mansion became my mother on steroids."

"Did that help at all?" Jennifer asked. "Making you confront your monster?"

"It made me crazy. I came home and thought about food, 24/7. Privation? Their motto? Also, my mother's slogan. I guess it worked in one way: if there is no food to eat, you lose weight."

Seung snorted. "Prime example of what leads to people wiring their mouths shut."

"Exactly. All the outside stuff in the world won't provide magic. No one's giving us lifelong monitors. Do we even want one? Because of them, because of my mother, because of battling this shit my entire life, I ended up having no damn idea what I wanted or didn't want. I just stuffed in everything." Daphne twirled her new bracelet.

"And now?" Lauretta asked. "Speaking as

416

someone with a mother who weighs and measures her with every glance, I feel what you're saying."

"My work is learning how to eat. Really," Daphne said. "I have to figure out how I want to approach food—not how my mother doesn't want me to eat. I declared Independence Day."

Alice laughed. "Don't let my mother catch you talking like that, Daph. Not unless you want a lecture about what freedom actually means."

"When I work on my body, my mother says, 'Stop that business, girl! Are you trying to look white?'" Jennifer said.

"Me too," Alice said. "My mother almost says the same thing—except she *is* white. My life has been a course in cognitive dissonance."

"My father, he walks through the supermarket pointing out all the thin Asian women," Seung said. "'Look, look,' he says. 'Do you see any fat Asian women? Look, look. What's wrong with you?'"

"We're too old for this," Daphne said. "Carrying these voices. The strangest outcome of this entire thing was my mother's reaction to my declaration of independence from her. Not immediately, but after a few weeks she came over and apologized. In a way that made it possible to accept. 'We always want to protect our children from pain,' she said."

"And you believed her?" Lauretta shook her head as though it were difficult to imagine.

"She thought wearing anything larger than a size six guaranteed an awful life. I think, finally, she understood how it backfired and had the opposite effect from what she wanted. We're different people. The terrors she tried to guard me against were her terrors. She passed them on to me, but I couldn't change my body to please either of us, so the anxiety made me think about nothing but food. And, like I said, she apologized." Daphne laughed. "Kind of."

"Are you satisfied with what she said?" Alice asked.

"I suppose. Though, in truth, I know the problem that Sunny will never admit is that along with wanting me not to be hurt, I embarrassed her. Being with me was like wearing a pilled sweater." Daphne shrugged. "Nothing I can do will change that."

Alice floated, weightless. A pool was the perfect place to talk about fat.

Her blessings came into focus. Neither Zeke nor Bebe cared how much she weighed. Clancy did, but he kept it under wraps for now. She didn't have a clue about her husband's reaction if she traveled up the size chart again. But the world? She knew the voices of the world around her.

Alice knew that as much as the heartbreak of romance with Patrick made her skinny, the everyday unhappiness she'd pushed away with Clancy had made her fat.

Daphne gathered her wet curls and twirled them into a momentary bun. "My mother has as much power as I allow her. That's what I'm trying to teach myself. Same as the damn Photoshopped magazine pictures, same as the people we faced down at *Waisted*. We just give them an immoderate amount of space in our head."

"True," Alice said. "But don't they make a hell of a chorus?"

"I should move out from my parents' house," Lauretta said. "Between my father locking down the bread, and my mother sneaking me rice pudding, my favorite, I'm fighting their war in my body."

"For me," chimed in Susannah, "my boyfriend is the weapon. His pet name for me? WL. Wide load." The laugh she attempted came out strangled. "But, hey, would anyone believe a freak like me could even have a boyfriend?"

"Stop that shit. You're not a freak," Hania said. "You're terrific. The only thing I'd change about you is to tell you to start using brown eyeliner. The black is too stark against your face. But honestly, you rock. Mike says you remind him of an Amazonian woman, all grounded and threatening. Own it. And get rid of the loser."

Susannah stretched across Lauretta and grabbed

Hania's hand. "You tell Mike to treat you right, honey."

"You know what I think?" Alice asked. "Being alone and lonely is better than lonesome with a guy who doesn't want you just the way you are."

"But you're still with Clancy," Hania said.

"I am. But not as who I was before: Angry. Stuffing my face and throwing up. I like the way I am now, but that can't be the reason Clancy's with me. My body is mine." She rolled her eyes. "Sounds like bullshit, right? But for now, it's my story. He's loosening up. We're shaking off the chains. Getting rid of what we don't need and doesn't work." And daily her marble jar became sunnier.

"Good for you, working so hard," Jennifer said. "Good for Libby."

The others nodded in quiet agreement.

Thoughts of being alone with Libby had terrified Alice. Imagining the sad eyes. Passing her back and forth between two homes. But staying just to ward off her daughter's unhappiness would never work.

Alice would die for Libby, but living for her might kill her. In some ways, the best time of being a mother was during pregnancy. Keeping your child safe and secure, tucked inside, made mothering a snap compared to after delivering them. Once born, life became their needs against yours.

As for her marriage, for now, she and Clancy walked the line.

Hell, the man had gone shopping for area rugs last week. Area rugs! That might not sound like much to others, but for Clancy it was the equivalent of dancing in the streets. Plus, the more they laughed, and the further they let each other talk, the more they shined in the bedroom.

She couldn't deny that *that* helped.

More than that, Clancy finally cracked open his perfect cover. Vulnerability, the worst emotion he could feel, and the idea of losing Alice and Libby had forced him open, even if just a step at a time. All that need for perfection, in body, mind, and surroundings, didn't pop out of the atmosphere. His parents had built him to be a superman. Coming to the realization that he lived in a mortal man's body pained him. Giving up his steel shell was difficult, just as letting go of food as protection had unsheathed every one of Alice's nerves.

Being fat had provided protection, muffled her mistakes. Every bite of a Milky Way soothed and loved her, but blind eating had indeed served to take away her sight. With purging, she'd found a way to empty the pain. Alice needed to own that—recognize the help being fat had pro-vided—before she could give it up. Giving up the protective extra layers of fat had to be her choice alone.

Being female, a mixed woman, in this country, meant that every day you had it harder than guys, than white people. Fat, you were judged. Work at not being fat, you might be mocked. But being fat, you could leave many of the playing fields.

If Alice stared into a mirror of the world, she wanted to use wisdom, not reactivity, when she saw her worth reflected. How Libby valued herself would rest on Alice's strength.

No more falling in and out of happiness based on the approval of any man with whom she happened to lock eyes.

Alice wanted a life that brought pride to her mother and father. For herself, she planned to live righteously, without denial, and with forgiveness. She yearned to bring out the best in Clancy and have him do the same for her—they'd love each other for who they were, not who they might be.

Most important, Alice would live a purposeful life and leave her slice of the world better than she'd found it. If she could manage that, and then pass on to Libby the values her parents entrusted to her and Macon—well, if that happened, as her mother's people said, *dayenu*.

It was enough.

ACKNOWLEDGMENTS

Writing *Waisted* allowed me to face many obsessions: my fixation on the number on my scale reigning supreme; how women are judged, above all else, by appearance over the quality of their character; and how wretchedly we divide ourselves by race, culture, and religion.

With *Waisted* I posed the questions to which I always wanted the answers: *How far would you go to lose weight?* As a young woman, my friends and I asked one another how many years of our lives we'd give up to lose X, Y, or Z pounds. A question we'd answer so seriously that I now wonder if we thought some angel of the scale might appear to grant our wishes.

Waisted gave me the opportunity to step into the shoes of women who differed from me, in skin color and heritage, but who shared so many of the same fears and hopes for ourselves and for our families.

I am grateful to all the people who helped me during this deep dive into places that were sometimes difficult to explore.

Many people supported me while writing *Waisted*, but none more than Stéphanie Abou, the most exceptional agent possible. She has been my wise, warm, and determined agent and friend from the beginning. I can't imagine this journey without her. Thank you Massie & McQuilkin, for being not only a great agency, but an agency with compassion and morals.

Libby McGuire, my publisher, has brought a rush of energy, passion, and excitement to Atria Books, and I am thrilled to be working with her. Rakesh Satyal is an extraordinary editor—he pushed me to higher levels, bringing his skilled and graceful editing hand to every page. Loan Le is a fount of editing strength, warmth, and intelligence. The sales force works hard (and behind the scenes!). A special shout-out to Brandy Bishop, who lifted my spirit and my heart.

Suzanne Donohue and Kimberly Goldstein, thank you for the thousand unthanked things you do for our novels. William Rhino, thank you for your deft hand and attention with an array of artful help. Alysha Bullock and Andrea Gordon's attention to detail—and my lack thereof—saved me time and again. Kitt Reckord-Mabicka, thank you for the grace and goodwill you bring to Atria and all who enter. Lisa Sciambra, Alison Hinchcliffe, Bianca Salvant, and Tasha Hilton: without you we'd be nowhere! Quite literally.

Philip Bashe, you performed miracles with my error-ridden work and, as always, provided wit and wisdom.

Ann-Marie Nieves of Get Red PR—thank you for not only your incredible work ethic, your fabulous energy, and your super results, but for your unflagging upbeat attitude.

Thank you to Andrea Peskind Katz for unwavering support and wisdom, and for forming the incredible Great Thoughts, Great Readers—and for deep-dive early reads! Nancy MacDonald is a friend, a genius, and a rock of stability who improves everything she touches. Carolyn Ring, I know we have the beginning of a fantastic partnership.

I'd be lost without my writing sisters, who provide ballast, friendship, and love. Ginny Deluca, my first reader, my BFF for decades and forever, thank goodness no topics are off limits between us. Melisse Shapiro: who knew such love, friendship, and writerly admiration could bloom from the first time we met! My beloved and forever writing group—Nichole Bernier, Kathy Crowley, Juliette Fay, and Elizabeth (E.B.) Moore are four of the wisest, warmest (and, when needed, strictest) women in the world.

To my cherished and trusted writer friends— Cecile Corona, Ellen Meeropol, Brunonia Barry, Robin Black, Ann Bauer, Julie Wu—you are all way beyond talented and loving.

Heartfelt thanks to the Grub Street Writers' Center of Boston—especially Eve Bridburg and Chris Castellani, for bringing writers together and making dreams come true. Much gratitude to Dori Ostermiller for welcoming me to Writer in Progress. Real-life hugs to everyone in the fabulous online Fiction Writer's Co-op, with a special shout-out to Cathy Buchanan for putting us together and Catherine McKenzie for keeping us that way.

Thank you, Nina Lev, for listening to me agonize and offering "walk" therapy, Kris Alden for telling me which authors I should be reading, and to Stephanie Romanos for being the best road companion possible. Special thanks to a group of writers who energized me when I needed it: Gina Bolvin, Jack Gleason, Katherine Dangler, Liz Kahrs, Evelyn Herwitz, Marianne Lambelet, Marlene Kim, Carol Reichart, Sherrie Ryan, Peter Scanlon, Marshall Stein, and Jackson Tobin.

Deep love and thanks to my family, including sisters of my heart, Peggy Gillespie, Diane Butkus, and Susan Knight. I bask in the love of my cousins Sherri and Steve Danny, sister-in-law Jean Rand, and brother-in-law Bruce Rand.

Thank you to those who own my heart, who offer comfort, joy, and understanding: my children, Becca Wolfson and Sara and Jason Hoots; my granddaughter, Nora Hoots; and my sister and best friend, Jill Meyers. You are all so sweet, loving (and funny!), and always there.

And again, thank you to the love of my life, Jeff Rand, the very best man I know.

ABOUT THE AUTHOR

Randy Susan Meyers's internationally best-selling novels are informed by years spent working with families impacted by violence—and a long journey from idolizing bad boys to loving a good man. Her novels have twice been chosen by the Massachusetts Center for the Book as "Must Read Fiction," who wrote, "The clear and distinctive voice of Randy Susan Meyers will have you enraptured and wanting more." *Waisted* is her fifth novel.

The Widow of Wall Street was called "compelling" by Associated Press. *Library Journal* wrote, "Full of deceit, scandal, and guilt, her novel expertly explores how rising to the top only to hit rock bottom affects a family. The consequences will leave readers reeling."

People magazine chose *Accidents of Marriage* as a "Pick of the Week," writing, "This novel's unsparing look at emotional abuse and its devastating consequences gives it gravity and bite, while a glimpse into a physically damaged mind both surprises and fascinates."

The Boston Globe wrote of *The Comfort of Lies*, "Sharp and biting, and sometimes wickedly funny when the author skewers Boston's class and neighborhood dividing lines, but it has a lot of heart, too." *The Murderer's Daughters*, Meyers's debut, was chosen as a month-long Target Book Club pick for the country, a "One-Book-Read" in Boston, and was called a "knock-out debut" by the *LA Times*.

Meyers teaches writing seminars at Boston's Grub Street Writers' Center and Writers in Progress in Northampton, Massachusetts. Raised in Brooklyn, New York, Randy now lives in Boston with her husband.

Center Point Large Print
600 Brooks Road / PO Box 1
Thorndike, ME 04986-0001 USA

(207) 568-3717

US & Canada:
1 800 929-9108
www.centerpointlargeprint.com